BLOCK PARTY 666

BLOCK PARTY 666

MARK OF THE BEAST

VOLUME ONE

AL-SAADIQ BANKS

Author: Al-Saadiq Banks

Contact Information:
True 2 Life Publications
P. O. Box 8722
Newark NJ 07108

Email: alsaadiqbanks@aol.com
Twitter: @alsaadiq
Instagram: @alsaadiqbanks

www.True2LifeProductions.com

Edited By: Pen 2 Pen
Email: info@pen2penpublishing.com
2261 Talmadge Road Ste. 71
Lovejoy, Ga 30250
For Editing, and Typesetting Services

THIS BOOK IS dedicated to all my readers who have supported me continuously over the years and have helped to keep my name alive. Without you, there is no me, as a writer. True 2 Life Salute!!

1

FLORENCE COLORADO

THE PLACE IS ADX Florence, a Supermax prison also known as the Alcatraz of the Rockies. It is currently home to 490 convicted terrorists, gang leaders and Neo-Nazis. The facility is best known for housing inmates who have been deemed too dangerous, too high-profile or too great a national security risk for even a maximum-security prison. However, the majority of the inmates have been sent here because they have an extensive history of committing violent crimes against Correction Officers and the fellow inmates in other prisons, up to and including murder. These inmates are kept in administrative segregation.

They are confined in a specifically designed single person cell for 23 hours a day. They are removed under restraint, on a 24-hour clock for one hour out of the day. The hour outside of the cell is for showering, exercise, and a phone call. Their diet is restricted as well to ensure that the foods they are served can't be used to harm themselves, or to make unhygienic conditions in their cell. Inmates have labeled the circumstances inhumane, as if some of the crimes they committed in order to get here were not.

Three huge, monstrous-sized Corrections Officers step toward the cell. These officers are not your typical ones. They all are highly trained Navy Seal officers. Their hearts all race for they know the inmate on the other side is highly dangerous. They know removing him from his cell will be an adventure.

Two of the officers take a step back, forcing the biggest one to take the lead. He takes a deep breath of air before sticking the key into the lock. He gives them a head-nod to get prepared. He snatches the door open and as soon as it parts, the first officer is greeted by a splash. Fluid mixed with feces comes at them full force.

With no time to waste, they rush into the cell toward the inmate who stands with his back against the wall, ready to rumble. The frail man stands completely naked with no weapon but his bare hands. The officers surround him as they plan their attack. Before they can fully set up, the inmate lowers his head and, like a bull, he rushes the officer in the middle. The officer grunts as all the wind escapes his body. He stumbles backwards, holding onto the inmate's torso with a tight grip. The other two officers both grasp an ankle. They spread his legs wide as he flops like a fish out of water.

With great struggle the two officers manage to shackle his ankles together. They then quickly shackle his wrists behind his back. He continues to flip and flop while the officers lift him high over their heads. "One," an officer shouts. "Two." Before the count of three they let the inmate go and stand free of him. With his hands cuffed behind his back, he falls like a bird with no wings. A loud thump sounds off as his face crashes onto the floor.

The inmate lays there putting up no fight at all. One officer turns him over and there he lays knocked out cold, unconscious, with his mouth leaking. His teeth look like broken and missing keys on a piano, covered with blood. One officer grabs the inmate by his ankles. He drags the man across the floor like a proud hunter who has conquered his prey.

2

CAMDEN, NEW JERSEY
8:20 A.M.

HEAVY TRAFFIC FILLS the block as the parents of Leap E.C.D.C Elementary School drop off their children. A line of cars are double parked from corner to corner. In the middle of the block sits a tinted-out Dodge Caravan. The van on the outside calls for no attention at all but it's what and who is in the inside that demands attention.

Inside the van sits Skelter, one of THE MOST action packed young women in all the city of Trenton. She's one half of the infamous twin duo, Helter and Skelter. Skelter sits in the backseat in silence as she always does before making any major move. The driver on the other hand won't seem to shut up.

The passenger's seat is empty yet Skelter rides in the back. This is her practice and she never veers away from it. In her life she's seen so many get rocked to sleep while being in that passenger's seat. She's witnessed some be put to sleep and she's put some to sleep while they were in the passenger's seat. Because of that she's vowed to never be a victim of that. It's always by someone you know, so she is die-hard against sitting in anybody's passenger seat.

"Dig, this shit gone be easy as cake," T-Mack says from the driver's seat. "I'm telling you," he says for the twentieth time.

"No, you dig," Skelter interrupts. She lowers the hood from her head so he can see the seriousness in her eyes. "I'm going all off your word on this. I'm gone ask you one more time," she says as she looks over to the driver. "You saying it's twenty of them in there, right? And a couple hundred grand in cash, right? I don't have no time to waste on a dummy mission."

"No, I'm saying at least twenty in there and at least a couple hundred grand in cash. This ain't no long-shot. This came from an inside source that I trust," T-Mack says with certainty.

Skelter pulls her hood over her head and adjusts the edges of her hair, flipping them so they hang out from underneath. Skelter can almost never be caught without a hood on her head. That's her trademark. Without a hood on her head, she feels wide open and transparent. "I don't know your inside source. All I know is you and all I have to go on is your word," she warns.

T-Mack's attention is diverted. "Bingo," he interrupts. "There go our mark," he says as he points to a raggedy Honda Civic that double parks on the opposite side of the street. They both watch quietly as the driver's door opens slowly. Their hearts pump with adrenaline as they set eyes on the short and homely looking Spanish woman who appears to be no older than her late 20's.

Dressed in an oversized t-shirt, leggings and flip-flops, she looks like she just crawled out of bed. The woman drags from the backseat a small child about 5 years of age. Two other small children slide out of the backseat and take off sprinting toward the school. She holds the hand of the smaller child as he tries to chase behind them. The woman's fast paced steps evolve into a trot as the child drags her along.

Once she disappears into the school, the Dodge Caravan makes a U-turn onto the opposite side of the street and parks a few feet ahead of the Civic. In 2 minutes flat, the woman reappears and jogs over to her car. She gets in, swerves around the Dodge van that she pays no notice to and speeds up the block. T-Mack slams the gear into drive and prepares to pull off.

"Nah, not yet," Skelter demands. "Let her hit the corner first." They watch with great anticipation as the car reaches the corner. "Go, now."

3

COLORADO ADX

IN **THE DIMLY** lit room there's an old wooden table, 2 wooden chairs and 4 bare walls with no windows. The inmate sits in a safety restraint chair, which looks like a chair with wheels. His mouth is still bleeding, and his right eye is swollen shut. Being dropped on his face seems to have done more damage than is visible on the count that his face is covered by a restraining mask with a steel cage front.

The mask has been placed on his face to prevent him from biting and even spitting. The inmate's feet are strapped to the bottom of the chair and his wrists are strapped to the arms of the chair. The facemask which covers his face is attached to the headrest of the chair, giving him limited head movement.

One Federal Agent stands over the man while the other two agents pace the room. The agent grabs a chair and slides it in front of him. He takes a seat and *lean*s in close to the man so he's sure to hear him.

"Manson, why do you insist on putting yourself through this torture?" the agent asks. This inmate is Newark's own, Black Charles

Manson. "It could all be so simple for you," the agent says. "You can agree to help us and all this can be over." He places a reassuring hand on Manson's shoulder. "I know your reputation means everything to you, but your reputation will never be tarnished. No one will ever know about this."

The agent grabs an old newspaper from the table and holds the page in front of Manson's good eye, the one which isn't leaking with blood.

"Look closely for the one-thousandth time. The article clearly states that you were murdered by Feds during the raid because you refused to resist. You know why we had the newspapers print it that way? We did that for you so you could cooperate and save yourself while still retaining your dignity. You can go to another state across the country and start a new life for yourself where no one knows you, or you can spend the rest of your life under these conditions. The choice is yours."

The agent drops the newspaper on the table and plants another hand on Manson's shoulder.

"Listen, I don't feel comfortable talking to you with this mask on like you're some wild, uncivilized animal. I'm gonna take this mask off you so we can talk face to face, man to man and look into each other's eyes as we talk about the needs of both of us." The agent gets up and steps behind the man. He slowly unstraps the mask and pulls it off Manson's face. He steps in front of Manson, but out of spit's range.

Manson sits there with a distant look in his eyes. His head bobbles as if he has no control of it. He stares off into space with a starry look in his eyes. It's as if he has no knowledge of where he is or what is going on. His current state is a result of the thorazine that he's been injected with. His violence and lack of respect of authority has given the authorities no alternative but to medicate him with drugs that will suppress his rage and violence.

Manson has been in this prison for over 2 years now, yet he has never been anywhere near population. He's been housed here in lock-up for his entire stay. The reason he's been away from other inmates is to conceal his identity. His family and all his gang banging followers believe him to be dead. All of this was done at the Federal Government's request for their selfish gain.

"Listen, your buddy and former business partner, Eli Dweck, he's waiting on you. Y'all were the perfect team out there. We can set you and Dweck up in another state and with new identities y'all can get on with your organ trafficking business. We could kill two birds with one stone. We can crack down on the doctors who pay for these illegal organs and we can crack down on the gangs all in one shot.

Eli has made several requests for you. He says he only feels comfortable working with you. He agrees that you and him were the perfect team. He's ready to go to work with us so he can work some of his sentence down. We just need you to come onboard.

Only you can infiltrate the Blood organization. You're impressionable and have great leadership skills. You can set up in any city and take control. We will get one of our Federal informants who owe us a favor to step in and vouch for you. You can get those gang members to bring you the bodies for the business and there's no telling what other cans of worms will be opened up in the process."

The agent stares into Manson's dilating pupils. "So, what do you say? I told you my needs, now let me guess what yours are. What else could you want more than freedom? One hand washes the other. What do you say?"

Manson's head bobbles up and down as he stares at the agent. He seems to be snapping into awareness. All the agents stand close with hopes that he's ready to cooperate. "Huh, Manson, what do you say?"

"I say, suck my dick. Guard!" He shouts with bloody spittle spraying from his mouth. "Guard, I'm done here! Guard!"

4

GREENWOOD AVENUE, CAMDEN, NEW JERSEY

SKELTER STEPS AT a turtle's pace as her eyes are glued on the woman who stands at the trunk of the Honda Civic. They tailed her for an hour, hoping that maybe she would lead them to another potential lick but instead all she led them to was a host of errands. She went from Target, Dollar General, and Walmart, not once ever noticing them behind her.

The woman struggles to slam the trunk closed with both arms filled with shopping bags. Jeezy, Skelter's accomplice, dressed in all black, gets out of the older model Jeep Cherokee that's parked across the street. Jeezy has been sitting in the same place since early this morning, just to keep an eye on things. He's sat on high alert all morning trying to catch anything that could be an obstacle and result in danger for the team.

Jeezy scales the walls closely, peeking around, making sure the coast is clear. Out of pure awareness of her surroundings, the woman takes notice of Jeezy and puts some pep in her step. In the second it takes to double-take, Skelter eases up beside her. Skelter latches onto the woman's arm and with their arms linked together, she buries the 9 Millimeter into the woman's love handles.

"Just keep on walking, Mami. Open your mouth and I will blow your lil fat ass in half," she whispers while peeking around.

Jeezy fast trots across the street and follows them up the stairs of the one-family house. Suddenly as they get to the top of the staircase, the door parts, catching them all off guard except for the woman. It's obvious that he was expecting her. What he wasn't expecting is the unwanted company that she has with her.

Jeezy aims his gun at the door and at the sight of it the man behind the door attempts to close it in his face. With a slight back and forth pushing battle, Jeezy manages to force his way in. With one hand he grabs the Spanish man by the throat and with the other hand he places the nose of the .40 caliber against the man's forehead.

Skelter grips the back of the woman's neck, pushing her inside. She slams the door and with no hesitation they force them through the hall and into the house. Skelter flings the woman onto the couch, while the man is clunked with the butt of the gun. He falls to his knees from the impact.

Skelter aims the gun at the woman's head as she looks over at the man. "I ain't come here for no fucking games. Y'all know why we here. Get me to it!"

"I got nothing, I promise," the man cries with fear in his eyes.

"Oh, you gone fuck me around?" Skelter asks with a devilish smile. She snatches the woman by the chin, squeezing her cheeks until her mouth is wide open like a fish on a hook. She slides half of the gun into the woman's mouth. "Lie to me again and watch her brains fly outta the back of her head."

The man stares at his wife with sadness. He hates that he has her in a situation like this. As the tears trickle down her face, his heart melts. "Okay, okay," he says loudly. He shakes his head in despair. "It's in the closet."

Skelter removes the gun from the woman's mouth. "Come on and get up." She drags the woman onto her feet. They force the couple into the room and the man leads them right to the closet.

"Right there," the man says accompanied with a head-nod.

Jeezy places the gun against the back of the man's head. "You get it," Jeezy demands.

The man pulls a duffle-bag from the back of the top shelf. Jeezy snatches the bag from him and hands it to Skelter. Skelter lays the bag onto the bed and unzips it while still holding the woman at gunpoint. She takes a deep breath of anxiety as her eyes soar across the prize. Beige tape covers the kilos snugly. She sifts through the bag, quickly counting a total of 11 of them.

"The shit don't stop right here," Skelter says. "I came for everything."

She watches with satisfaction as the tears run a marathon down the man's face. This will be easier than she thought.

15 MINUTES LATER

The woman sobs silently in fear of an outburst. She's already been warned that if she lets another peep out, off goes her head. Her nor her husband take the threats lightly, but they can't get hold of their emotions. The man is sobbing harder than the woman as he watches his jewelry and cash being stacked into the duffle-bag on top of the kilos.

It's as if he's watching his life flash before his eyes as the 11 kilos and the 72K in cash get zipped up in the bag. For each kilo he owes his connection, $32,000. That plus the cash will put him in the rear almost $425,000. He's sure this movie that he's starring in can only end one way. The fact that they are barefaced he's sure is a sign that they have no plans on leaving them alive. He's in a bad situation either way. It's almost better to be murdered now than to be murdered later by the plug. He's sure they will kill and maybe even torture him for coming up short with their money.

He's hoping this murder would at least be less painful though. He's heard stories of how violent his plug is and how he thrives off pain and torture and he would hate to be on the other end of it. Although he rather be murdered now, his concern is his children. What type of life will they live with both their parents dead?

He watches as the bandits whisper to each other. The look in their eyes can only mean one thing. In his mind the credits are rolling but he has one last shot before him and his wife's screen go black. He must say something to possibly save their lives or forever they will rest in peace.

"Ma'am, please?" the man says as he looks to Skelter with pity in his eyes. "Can I talk to you in the next room?" He can tell by her display of leadership that she's the one that makes the calls and she's the only one that can spare his life. "Please?" he begs.

"Ain't shit to talk to me about unless you got something else for me," she says coldly. The man nods his head up and down with his eyes lowering in submission.

Skelter snatches him from the floor by his collar and pushes him into the next room. She aims the gun at his head. "Talk fast motherfucker."

"I'm in a lose-lose situation," he says. The tears trickle rapidly. "I know you're gonna kill us. If you don't kill us, I will be killed for this loss that I can't pay back. They will believe that I'm in on this robbery. They will never believe me. Please, don't kill us," he begs. "We have three babies together. I have six other children in my country." He can no longer hold back. He cries loud and hard shamelessly. "What if I have something better for you? Something ten times bigger than this?"

"I ain't making no promises but I'm listening," Skelter replies.

"All I ask is if I can get you a bigger job, you can leave me to keep my business and my family in order. I will give you time and place and all the details and it won't be tied to me. That way I can continue to live and provide for my family." Pity covers his face.

"Listen," Skelter snaps. "You better talk and fast!"

The man blurts out. "A big shipment with a hundred kilos is coming."

Skelter's eyes bulge with excitement. "Coming in where? To who, you?"

"My brother in law...my wife's brother," he says while pointing into the other room. "He's my connection. And it's my job to deliver the work to all the other people in our network. If you let me live, I can give you all the details. Time, place, everything."

Skelter snatches the notepad from the nightstand and hands it to the man along with a pen. "Before we get into the details, I'm gone need you to give me a list of everybody in the network and all the information you can think of about them. Let's start with your brother in law, the connection. How can I find him?"

The man knows he's playing a dangerous game with his life but at this point he's trying to save him and his family. "I don't know where he lives," he lies. "But here in Camden, he owns an entire block. Almost every house on the block is his. He has a barber shop, a beauty parlor, a laundromat, a grocery store, a phone store and a liquor store all on the same block," the man informs. "They all have All-Star in the names. All-Star Liquor, All-Star Beauty Parlor," he says.

Skelter nods her head up and down. "Good to know. Write that down," she says as she points to the pad. "Now as far as the details of the drop off, I'm all ears." Skelter listens attentively as the man spills the beans, detail by detail, leaving nothing out in between.

MEANWHILE IN HERMOSILLO, MEXICO
CAFE' DE COLOMBIA-COLOMBIAN COFFEE SUPPLIER

The cargo van backs up close to the dock. A short, scruffy Mexican man jumps out of the van and walks toward the dock. His eyes are glued onto the clipboard that he holds in his hand. He climbs onto the dock where the workers await him. They all have dollies with boxes of coffee piled high onto them.

An elderly, yet energetic and quite dapper Colombian man appears. His presence demands respect as he walks toward the dock. As he reaches the dock area, he extends his hand toward the Mexican. As they shake hands the older gentleman leans forward to the dollie in front of him. He reaches into an opened box and retrieves a can of what appears to be coffee. He unscrews the cap and sifts through the coffee beans and in seconds he pulls a square block, covered in cellophane. The can is a ploy to hide the kilo of cocaine inside.

The Mexican nods in approval and the Colombian tucks the kilo neatly into the can. He meticulously shuffles the coffee beans until they cover the kilo. He screws the cap back onto the box and seals the box with tape.

"Tell Cha-Cha to call me when you reach your destination. It's always good to check in," he says with an arch of his thick and bushy silver eyebrows.

"Yes, Sir," the Mexican replies with great respect.

The Colombian gives the command for the workers to load the van. In less than 15 minutes they have the van loaded with coffee and kilos. The Colombian watches his operation with satisfaction. The Mexican turns back to the dock before getting into the van. He salutes the Colombian before climbing into the van and slamming the door shut.

Once inside the van, he cuts his eye over to the man in the passenger's seat. "Show time." The driver puts his game face on and wastes no more time before pulling off. He knows that in this game timing is everything and one second can cost everybody dearly. He cruises through the parking lot with tunnel vision. The only thing on his mind is making it to the finish line.

5

YELLOWSTONE PARK, WYOMING

A MIXTURE OF spices creates an aromatic fragrance in the air. The pure white Egyptian cotton cloth is soft enough to sleep on, but instead it drapes over a small dining table. The table is bare except for a bottle of red wine in the center and two drinking glasses that sit in front of the occupants of the table. The sound of musician, Paul Hardcastle's, *Lost In Space* plays faintly in the background, creating the perfect ambiance.

The dining area is so intimate it's just barely big enough for the small table. The occupants have a clear view of the kitchen area which is a combination of stainless steel and porcelain. The Master Chef and his assistant work vigorously at the stove. Pots banging and spoons stirring makes music of its own in the background.

This luxurious kitchen and dining area is easily one of the best designed, even amongst the most prestigious 5-Star restaurants, but it's not even in a restaurant. Not even 25 feet away from the kitchen area is a cozy antique decorated living room. And not too far from there, separated by partially opened double doors is a beautifully designed bedroom. Two smaller sized bedrooms are positioned on op-posite ends. A few feet behind the occupants of the table there sits a cockpit. In the cockpit the driver is doing his job of driving. The RV Motorhome floats over the road like a plane does over the clouds.

Tony Austin holds two glasses of wine in one hand, and in the other he holds a bottle of wine with a napkin covering the label. He stares into the eyes of his beautiful girlfriend, Miranda as he passes a glass over to her.

"Wine for breakfast," Tony says with a chuckle. He holds the glass high in the air, signaling for her to do the same. She reaches over and they tap glasses.

"Salud," they say simultaneously.

"It tastes better on an empty stomach anyway," Miranda replies.

Tony takes a huge gulp of the wine and swishes it in his mouth, analyzing the flavor. A look of uncertainty covers his face. He looks to Miranda. "What do you think?"

"Ah, it's okay," she replies. The look on her face shows that she is unimpressed. "We have had better. I guess it's okay as long as the price point is under thirty bucks," she says like the true wine connoisseur that she is.

Tony trusts her taste buds wholeheartedly. He's groomed her well. He has opened her mind and exposed her to a world that she never knew existed. That wasn't too difficult to do based on her last boy-friend. In no way is it hard for Tony to outdo him. He could do that with the bare minimum, yet he still plays his game at the maximum, just outdoing himself every time.

"Under thirty bucks?" He chuckles as he frees the bottle of the napkin.

Miranda reads the label and is surprised. She's familiar with the wine but after hearing so much ranting and raving about it she expect-ed so much more.

"So, what would you say if the price point is over thirty-thou-sand bucks?" He licks his lips, trying to find the appreciation in the wine. The 1951 Penfolds Grange Hermitage is an extremely rare wine. "Only nineteen other bottles left in existence," says Tony.

"I would say, the saying is true... a sucker is born every day," she says with a smile of sarcasm. "I would also say, somebody needs to hurry up and drink those other nineteen bottles up fast and get them all out of existence," she says, as she fights back the laughter.

"So, ungrateful," Tony teases. "I open a bottle of the most expensive wine you've ever had for your birthday and you shit on me and the wine."

"No, I'm not shitting on you. You shitted on yourself," she says before busting out in laughter.

"Yeah, okay, you got me. I admit its bullshit, money down the drain. Damn, thirty-eight racks." He stares at the more than half-filled glass. "Hey, you win some, you lose some."

"But you really lost one," Miranda sings the lyrics of Lauren Hill in a teasing manner. "You just lost one, it's so silly how come?" She rubs it in with a huge smile on her face.

Tony wears a huge smile as well. More than anything Tony appreciates the fact that he can laugh and have fun with Miranda. With him being a man of such high caliber, the women he's run into after his divorce were all either boring brainiacs or bourgeois morons. All in all, very few of the women in his past could understand or relate to him. Miranda on the other hand can. She is laid back like he likes them but knows how to stand up and put her foot down when she needs to.

When he got her she was what he calls a reformed hood chick, still a little rough around the edges. Catching her fresh out of prison worked to his advantage. Her head was in a great space. She was open minded, and ready to learn new things. She saw what was on the other side and refused to ever go back there. She was thirsty for knowledge and ready to exert all she learned and use it to achieve a better quality of life for herself.

The whole time she was incarcerated she promised herself if she ever obtained her freedom, she wouldn't take a second for granted and she would make her new chance at life all worth it. And that she has done. Her modeling agency is doing well over high six figures a year, with just four years in business. She predicts next year she will climb into the seven-figure bracket. She had no doubt in her mind that she would become successful at whatever she set her mind to do. What she didn't know was the fact that she would have help building that success.

Tony has been more than the launching pad to her success. He's also been her cheerleader and her cornerman who keeps her in the fight even when she wants to throw in the towel. He's given her financial support, but really, it's the emotional support that he gives her that means more than anything to her. She feels like having him by her side there's no mountain she can't climb.

She loves Tony more than any man she's ever had. She only had two relationships before Tony and one doesn't count because they were junior high school lovers. Sha-Rock is the only relationship she counts. Every day she thanks God that her relationship with Sha-Rock didn't ruin her entire life. It may have set her back a decade, but Tony has managed to get her caught up and ahead of the game in less than half the time of the set back.

At times Miranda, feels she doesn't deserve Tony. Words can't describe how grateful she is to have him. She also feels like she's in debt to him for all he's done for her. She knows she can never repay him, financially but what she does have to give him is her heart and her loyalty. For nothing in this world will she ruin what they have.

"I get you a bottle of forty-thousand-dollar Pinot Noir and you're not even the least bit appreciative," he says with a smirk of sarcasm.

"No, that wine wasn't for me. It was for you and your and selfish pleasure. And I am appreciative, just not impressed with it," she says before taking a small sip from her glass.

Miranda is correct. The wine wasn't for her at all. Her birthday gift from him was more meaningful than any bottle of wine could ever be. Tony offered to take her to any island in any country of her choice. That's typical from him so she decided she wanted something a little different this time around.

What she wanted was more special, simple and more intimate; something neither of them have ever done. She knows Tony has traveled the world by plane so what she wanted was a simple road trip. She wanted to rent a Motorhome and travel across country in it.

That was way too simple and average for Tony, so he wanted to do something extra and he did. He not only accommodated her with the road trip, he purchased the $400,000 motorhome for her and hired a driver and a Master Chef to cook for them while on the trip.

The chef and his helper stand at the table ready to serve breakfast. They lay the silver dishes in front of Tony and Miranda. "This morning I have prepared something a little different and I hope you enjoy it," the Chef says in a heavy French accent.

"Escoffier, I'm sure we will – just as every other dish you prepared along this trip," says Tony.

"I thank you, kind Sir. I would like to say I feel guilty that I enjoyed this trip so much when I was supposed to be working. It's been quite a pleasure. I hate that the trip is soon coming to an end."

"Don't worry, Escoffier," Miranda interrupts. "There will be plenty more. Right, babe?"

Tony sighs before looking away. "Yeah, yeah, sure, just no more Wyoming trips," he says mockingly. "I'm a waterfront property, sand in the backyard, sky-rise building type of guy. Y'all can have the forest, wildlife, trees and bugs. Another one of those trips, y'all must be going without me," he says with not a trace of a smile.

Miranda becomes agitated. "I've traveled to places with you I had no interest in going. I've eaten food I had no desire to taste and done anything you've asked of me and never complained. One thing I asked of you and you've complained the entire trip. Can it never be about you?"

The mood changes quickly. Tony is stuck in amazement at her words. The look in her eyes shows him how serious she is about what she just said. "Baby, please. It was just a joke. You know for you I would move to Wyoming and live with you happily ever after."

She cracks a smile and melts like putty in his hands. "Awl," she sighs. "How sweet."

"Yeah, you could live in the woods and I would build me a high rise, skyscraper building, not too far away for me to live in. You could come visit me anytime," he says with humor that she can't appreciate.

They enjoy their breakfast while staring out the window into the tranquil forest. They've gotten used to the bears and wildlife walking around them. Tony doesn't find anything about this trip the least bit romantic but what he has learned from his previous marriage is, sometimes it's not about him, just as Miranda stated. And sometimes for man to find peace within his woman, he must be her peace.

Miranda eats in silence, not once looking up at Tony. Her energy can be read from across the table. She's highly pissed off with him and he knows it. Years ago, his cockiness would make him take Miranda to war and give her attitude for attitude but today he realizes there's no room for ego in a relationship. He stands up and leans forward close to her. He kisses her on the forehead. "Happy birthday my Cuban Link."

6

CAMDEN/3 P.M.

SKELTER RIDES IN the passenger's seat of the tinted-out Honda Civic. She holds her gun on her lap but aimed at the driver. The man is a nervous wreck, barely able to drive. He tries to keep his eyes on the road, but he can't help but to keep peeking over at Skelter.

Skelter left Jeezy back at the apartment watching over the woman. It's time to pick up the children from school and Skelter wasn't sure if they should let the woman or the man do the pickup. She decided it's better to let him do it because in his right mind he knows if he tips anyone off his wife is a dead woman. The woman on the other hand may react emotionally and cause big problems.

As they bend the corner onto the crowded block, Skelter lifts the gun and plants it against his side.

"Now listen to this carefully," Skelter says. "You are going to get out of the car so your kids can see you. You are not to step past the curb. And any way that I feel like you are giving any type of signal I'm knocking everybody shit off except yours. I will let you live with the pain of knowing you got everybody killed. That will haunt you every single day, forever. You understand me?"

"Yes, I understand," the man whispers with a heart filled with sorrow.

She nudges him with the gun once again. Right now, she's instilling more fear in him just in case he's thought of doing something erratic. "You understand what? Tell me exactly what you understand so that I'm clear that you understand and that way if you fuck up I know you knew exactly what the repercussions would be."

The man lowers his head submissively. "I understand if I make any stupid move everybody will be murdered except me, and I will have to live with that pain forever." The tears build up in his eyes at the very thought of it.

The man finds an empty parking space and pulls right into it. Before getting out he looks to her for any further instructions. "Go ahead, get out," she commands.

The man gets out and walks slowly around the car toward the sidewalk. His legs are trembling so much from nervousness he can barely keep his balance. He steps onto the sidewalk, right in front of the car so Skelter can see him clearly. She rolls the window down slightly, just enough for him to see the barrel of the gun aimed at him. He quickly locates his children lined up with their classes. He waves his hands high in the air, hoping to get their attention. He looks to Skelter and gives her a nod. "They over there but they don't see me."

Skelter rolls the window down. "Don't worry, they will see you. Even if we have to wait until the whole school let out. Stand right the fuck there." She drops the hood on her head low enough that it doesn't hinder her visibility.

He obeys her command not lifting his feet up once. He stands there waving his hands high like a prisoner of war, hoping to be rescued. Ironically, in his mind he may have thought about it that way, but he knows if he's rescued his wife will end up a casualty of war.

Finally, his youngest child notices him standing here and takes off toward him. The teacher chases behind him before she sees the father waving at her. The older siblings see the smaller one and run behind him. They all attack their father with happiness as he tries to hug them all in one bear hug. His gratefulness to still be alive shows. He realizes if he hadn't made the decision he did 5 hours ago, his children would've never seen him again. That thought alone makes him think he made the right decision.

As they cruise through Camden the children are loud and unruly in the back. They argue, fight and tease each other, paying no attention to their father who is driving under extreme pressure. Skelter sits in the passenger's seat with her arms crossed. The gun is tucked under her left arm with the barrel aimed at him.

Up ahead the golden arches glow dazzlingly. "Pa, can we go to McDonalds?" the younger child begs. "Please?"

"No, baby, not right now."

"Please, Papa, please?" The man hates to tell his children no and it shows. "Please?"

"Go ahead," Skelter intervenes. "Go through the drive-thru," she says as she digs into her pocket. She pulls out a hundred-dollar bill. She hands the bill to him. Get extra everything. We gone be sitting for a while."

MEXICO-UNITED STATES BORDER/BAJA CALIFORNIA

IT'S BEEN A long 5-hour drive on pins and needles. The slightest mistake could have costed them, so they were sure to not make a single one. The two men switched places halfway through the trip just so the driver's eyes would stay fresh and keen. Even in the passenger's seat there was no rest period because it was up to the passenger to pay attention to everything off the road.

In fact, the passenger's position held more responsibility. It was up to the passenger to keep his head on a swivel, look for police in marked cars as well as unmarked cars, watch for police in hidden spots, as well as keep his eyes on the driver to make sure he's on point and not doing anything that could draw the slightest bit of attention to them. They sit here at the border finally and still they can't rest assured. They're under more pressure right now than all the entire 5-hour ride.

The cargo van sits at the border surrounded by armed guards all equipped with assault rifles. The two Mexicans sit nervously in their seats as the sweat rolls down their faces. One guard comes to the driver's side and another to the passenger's side while another guard appears in front of the van. The one in the front snaps a photo of the van's license plates. The driver hands over the paperwork with a false sense of confidence.

The guard opens the door for the driver to get out. The driver leads the guard to the back of the van. He opens the door confidently. Boxes are stacked neatly and tightly across the whole van. Another guard walks over holding a K9 on a leash. He leads the K9 into the van and unleashes him. The dog sniffs around the van, stopping every now and then but picking right up.

The driver looks in every direction but inside the van. He doesn't want to come across as worried. The guard stares back and forth in between the driver and the K9. He hates to have go through every one of these boxes, but he will if he gets the slightest inkling of some funny business. He's already feeling some kind of way about the coffee being transported. Everybody knows coffee prevents the dog from detecting drugs. That alone is grounds enough for the man to declare a thorough search.

After a ten-minute sniff session the dog steps to the ledge of the van. All the other guards watch him closely, hoping for some action. The guard grabs hold of the dog's leash and guides him out of the van. The guard nods at the driver, who quickly shuts the doors.

The guard looks up ahead and he gives the signal that they are good. Defeat covers the guards' faces. The guard shouts to the guards at the gate and they make way for the van to enter. They slide the barricades to the side slowly.

The guard gives a nod to the driver. The driver pulls off nervously. He looks over to his passenger and sighs relief. They cross the finish line with the pride of two runners who have completed the marathon. They smile as they look up to the overhead sign.

"Welcome to California."

8

CAMDEN

THE WOMAN AND her children sit shoulder to shoulder on the couch uncomfortably while T-Mack lays back in the recliner comfortably. He's made himself at home. He watches the television as the children watch him. They have no understanding of who this strange man is nor his reason for being here.

T-Mack feels them all staring at him and can't help but to cut his eye at them. He looks over and they look away. As he looks away, they lock their eyes on him again. He quickly looks back in their direction and they all turn away, still peeking at him side eyed. He's found fun in this little peek-a-boo game and does it ever so often just to break the boredom of being a sitting duck.

The minutes seem to creep by slower and slower. He tries to focus on the come-up on the way and that gives him the ability to withstand the situation. Also, to help him with the boredom he's been medicating himself. Right now, percocet has him woozy and floating. His mouth drops like a junkie as he fights to keep his eyes open. He rocks back and forward with his eyes on the television when he's not in a deep nod.

He pulls his right pants leg up and begins scratching his calf. In seconds, his left pants leg is rolled up and he's scratching his shin. One leg at a time he relieves that intense itching of his legs. The itching episode spreads from his legs to his stomach and to every part of his body. The itching is a result of the *lean* (codeine syrup) that he just guzzled down a little while ago. His eyes roll back in his head pleasurably as he scratches his neck and his back. Ashy scratch marks cover both legs.

With his eyes still rolled back in his head, and him rocking back and forth, he kicks both shoes off. The women and her children watch him in confusion. So caught up in his high he doesn't realize that he's a spectacle right now. He's not only kicked off his shoes, but he's taken his socks off as well. He's bent over scratching in between his toes. If the fungus covered black toenails isn't enough to make them turn away, the sour smell of his feet should be. It's a stomach-turning sight for them to view and smell as he picks and scratches his feet. A smell similar to that of parmesan cheese fills the room quickly.

The woman studies T-Mack and realizes how high he really is. She counts the seconds in between each nod and notices he dozes off for approximately 20 seconds before he snaps back to reality. Curiosity makes her wonder how far she can actually get in 20 seconds. He nods off again and this time she counts 32 seconds. Adrenaline races through her veins.

She slides on the edge of the couch and picks up her smaller child. She plants the child right on her lap, so she has the ability to get up in one motion and take off. She waits for T-Mack to nod again and when he does, she slides her oldest child onto the edge of the couch and onto his feet. The child looks to her in a baffled state as she grabs the other child by his hand and pulls him onto his feet.

They both stand on opposite sides of her with their full attention on her. Her full attention is on T-Mack who is easing into another nod. The woman counts the seconds, which are now up to 36 seconds in a nod. She grabs her smallest child with a reassuring grip and with her elbow on one of the children's back and her hand on the other's back, she waits for him to go back into his nod.

His eyes get heavy, his mouth drops and right before he nods, he adjusts his gun which is in the chair underneath his crotch area. The sight of the gun changes her mind. If she was alone, she's sure she could get away from him. She's afraid that if she makes a move, one or two of her children may get caught up in the mix of it all. That fear makes her sit back in her seat and inconspicuously command her two children to do the same.

They all sit back, hostages in their own home and the children have not a clue of what is taking place. The mother is hurt and distraught that her children are in this mess. This situation here has her reevaluating her life. If she makes it out of this situation, she's sure to make some changes. Even if that change means changing her marital status.

9

HISPANIOLA AUTO TRANSPORT COMPANY/VISALIA, CALIFORNIA

THE SMALL ONE-LEVEL office building maybe minimal in size, but the amount of business provided is evident by the parking lot and the nearby dock area. The parking lot is filled with company vehicles of all sizes, ranging from cargo vans, to box trucks to 18-wheelers. Workers run rampant jumping in and out of the vehicles as their overseers watch and shout out commands. It's obvious the size of their business is not determined by the size of their business.

The back of the building has a dozen dually trucks with carriers hooked to the backs of them. High line automobiles such as Mercedes, Range Rovers and even Bentleys are stacked onto the trucks. Their main source of revenue comes from transporting the vehicles to dealerships all across the country. With the fee of an average of $2,000.00 per car, one dually truck can bring in about fifteen grand for one cross-country run. A load to a destination and the picking up of a load on the way back to California is an estimated $30,000 run.

Two Dominican men work hard, loading their carrier. Their load is of the least prestigious of all the vehicles on the lot. They appear to be junk cars but the value in their load isn't in the cars. With 9 cars, at less than a grand apiece for the job, the value of this load to the company is less than seven grand. What they are about to transport earns the company another one-hundred grand.

In the inside of the building bigger business is taking place. Just short of an hour ago the Mexicans made their drop off and now they are on their way toward the border, going back to Mexico. In the office, they left behind five hundred kilos with El-Jefe. El-Jefe is the owner of the company who happens to be a middle-aged Dominican man.

El-Jefe is not only the owner of this transporting company but also the direct link between the Dominican and Mexican alliance. Many years ago, El-Jefe—just like many other Dominicans—had a direct alliance with the Colombian drug lords, but over the years the Mexicans have been able to slide in and interrupt that alliance. At one time, the Dominicans had a great deal of control over the cocaine trade in the States but now the Mexicans have full control due to their partnership with the Colombians and the fact that many Mexican Cartels have managed to blossom and take over. Because of these factors, Dominicans have dropped down the ladder and now must look to the Mexicans as their plug.

On the desk, kilos are stacked in piles, ten kilos high. El-Jefe quickly stacks 25 kilos into a large army duffel-bag. He packs 4 bags each with 25 kilos. He throws the 4 bags onto the floor with no regard that each bag has a wholesale value of $750,000 apiece.

The man shouts. "*Gigante!*" (Giant) "*Gigante!*"

In seconds, a man the size of a midget rushes into the room. He's signaled by head-nod to get the 4 bags from the floor. "*Rapido, rapido! El tiempo es dinero!*" (Let's go, let's go! Time is money!) The man then picks up a walkie talkie and shouts into it aggressively.

The midget of a man snatches the bags from the floor and rushes out of the room. He struggles with the total of over 110 pounds of cocaine in each hand. He drops the bags onto the wooden dollie and pushes it as fast as his little legs will go. He stands at the dock as the dually truck backs its trailer close to the dock.

El-Jefe stands at the dock, deep in the back, out of sight. He watches his operation closely as the driver and his helper rush out of the truck and snatch the bags from the dollie. They quickly climb onto the trailer and start working under the cars. They plant 10 kilos into all four tires on two of the cars and only in the front two tires of a third car. These cars are only stash cars that belong to the company itself. The cars will be shipped to the location where they will sit idle until they are filled with money and shipped back here.

Once the cocaine is packed securely into the vehicles, the driver and his helper hop into the truck. El-Jefe dials numbers on his phone and he watches the van pull off slowly as he listens to ringing in his ear. The other end is picked up by the third ring. "*Todo bien,*" (All good) El-Jefe whispers sternly. He ends the call with no further words.

The driver of the van pulls off with no further hesitation. East Coast bound they are with over three-million dollars' worth of cocaine. Their pay for this is less than two grand apiece; a dirty job but somebody has to do it.

Camden, New Jersey here they come!

10

FEATHER NEST INN MOTEL - CHERRY HILL NEW JERSEY

SKELTER LAYS BACK on the King-sized bed watching television and stuffing her mouth with food from Camden's landmark fast food restaurant, Donkey Steaks. Every few seconds she peeks over to the other bed where the Dominican man lays uncomfortably. He's barely eating. He doesn't have an appetite due to the circumstances.

He's worried about his wife and children who are being held captive in their own home. Her first thoughts were to tie them up in a basement somewhere, but the man convinced her that he would cooperate with no need for torture. His only concern is the welfare of his family.

"Yo, so let's go over this one more time," she says as she smacks on her food like a cow. "So, 9 tomorrow night they will be there, right?" He nods his head in silence. "And how many of them will it be again?"

"Two, just the driver and the passenger," he replies.

"And there will be no hidden surprises in the back, right?"

"Nah, it's been the same routine for the past five years. It's only those two that come."

"Okay," she says as she nods her head. "You already know how shit gone go if this don't play out as you said it will, right?"

A ping of the phone sounds off, interrupting their moment of silence. The man looks down at his phone which sits on Skelter's lap. A bolt of nervousness rips through his body.

Skelter walks over and holds the phone close enough for him to read the display. He can barely speak for his heart is pounding in his throat. "That's him right here," he says.

Skelter reads the text aloud. "Flight is still on schedule for tomorrow morning. 9 A.M. American Airlines." Skelter looks at the man with suspicion.

"That's code for tomorrow night everything is still on schedule."

Skelter hands him the phone. "Text him back your normal shit. I swear to God on everything I love," she says as she bites onto her bottom lip. "Any funny business and it's gone be a Camden Massacre. We gone make history. Wife, kids, granny, the dog, every damn body! I will track down any and everybody you love and murder them where I find them." She lifts the gun and aims at his head. "Text back."

The man texts back with no delay. After he finishes, he hands the phone back to Skelter. She reads the text aloud. "The car service will be there on time."

Skelter rubs her palms together slowly. She stares in the man's direction but actually she's staring past him. She's staring into the future. She hasn't even landed the score yet but in her mind she's already gone triple platinum. She has so many plans for her city. The 11 kilos and the cash they already scored is tucked away safely. She's waiting to get her hands on this score and it's then that she will flood her city like the famous flood, Hurricane Katrina did New Orleans.

The last time she made some real money was over 2 years ago. Once the Feds blew open the Organ Trafficking situation that was the last time she touched money in huge quantities. Ever since Manson has been gone she's been living like a bottom-feeder, a scavenger just eating whatever crumbs she could get her hands on. She's landed a couple small-time robberies, here and there.

She's even beat a couple small-time dope plugs, but never got anything of real value. If not for her weed plug she would drown. She keeps the bills paid and herself alive by flipping a little weed here and there. All in all, she hasn't been anywhere near a life changing opportunity in years. But this move right here will change the scoreboard in her favor. That is if all goes as planned.

A devilish smirk spreads across her face as she nods her head up and down. "Feel me on this," she says while staring him square in the eyes. "I haven't had no real money in years. You telling me this gives me hope that I'm about to touch some real money. You got me excited like a kid the night before Christmas. If you got me like this for nothing and this shit don't go as planned, I will make your life a living nightmare," she says very convincingly. "I sure hope this goes right for your sake."

11

WYOMING/2:37 A.M.

EAGLE PEAK MOUNTAIN, the highest point in Yellowstone park, escalates over 11,000 feet into the air, and spreads out over 6 miles. The rugged mountains and deep glacier-carved valleys makes for a beautiful sight. Hundreds of thousands of acres of wilderness surround the mountain. The moon peeks from behind the mountain like a silver ghost. The sound of wildlife can be heard in the air, echoing for miles. Grizzly Bears, Black Bears, Moose and even Bison roam throughout the darkness.

On a cliff, about 30 feet in the air, there sits Tony and his lover Miranda. They can barely be seen. The whites of their eyes illuminate brightly. Both stark naked, facing each other, their legs crossed Indian style with their hands palm down resting on their thighs, they find peace and serenity.

"Ohhhm," they chant simultaneously, and their voices echo into the night.

Performing yoga and meditating here in the mountains is an experience they both find equally satisfying. Neither of them has ever felt a connection of this magnitude to the universe. Miranda begged him to give it a try and stubbornly he denied. He couldn't get past the thought of being out here with wildlife roaming. The only reason he agreed was to calm down the rage that he's created within her from his complaining the entire trip. Once he got out here and allowed himself to let go, he's extremely happy that he agreed.

This was the purpose of the whole trip. The road trip was what she wanted for her birthday but meditating on the mountains in the middle of the night was the icing on the cake for her birthday present. This is a dream come true for Miranda. This was at the top of her bucket list.

Together their spirits are one and nothing or no one else count right now. Not even the many packs of wolves that are howling in the distance can disconnect them. They are so caught up in the moment that they don't even hear the howling or any other sounds of the wild animals that are lurking. What they can hear is the rhythm of each other's heartbeats.

Tony opens his eyes for a second just enjoying the beauty of the goddess that sits before him. "Oohhm," she chants, holding her mouth wide open letting the sound roll from her lips. Her beautiful teeth glow in the dark. Her luscious lips curve with the perfect arch. Her silhouette flows beautifully. Her shoulders are chiseled perfectly. Her firm breast sit up, mid-air, pointed like missiles. Her Hershey kiss-sized nipples aim at him with precision. The outline of the muscles in her abdomen expand and reveal themselves more each time she chants. "Ohhmmm," she chants again.

Tony's eyes drop into the darkness in between her legs. Not able to see a glimpse of her box yet his imagination is so sharp right now that he can envision it clearly. "Ohhhm," she chants again. His eyes soar over her long and beautiful legs. Her legs crossed with her feet resting on her thighs comfortably in relaxation plants her weight onto her buttocks. With all her weight on her buttocks, the curves of her hips ooze beautifully and spreads onto the towel that she sits on.

Miranda's spirit elevates to a higher level causing her to roll her head back sexily. The energy shoots through her body like lightning. Her body waves in a snake like motion, flowing with the wave of the energy. Her nipples get more erect. Her abdomen muscles tighten up.

Her legs stiffen as her toes move one by one as if they are playing the piano. "Aaaggghh," she sighs as if she has just orgasmed.

Seeing Miranda like this is driving Tony insane. They have performed yoga together a million times and he's learned that during yoga and meditation Miranda becomes a sexual maniac. She's admitted to Tony more than once that she sometimes imagines herself having butt naked sex in public, in the wild, with spectators watching. This moment is the closest that she has ever gotten to her fantasy, minus the sex.

Tony watches as Miranda squirms and fidgets. The ball of sexual energy that's brewing inside her has her overheated. She rubs her hands over her breast gently. "Aaggghh," she sighs again. Tony is familiar with that sigh. It's the sound she makes as she orgasms.

Tony can barely contain himself. Miranda performs so well alone that he's becoming jealous and wants to join in. He hates the fact that his woman is able to please herself without him. He must outdo her for fear that she may believe she has no need for him.

He watches for as long as he can until he dives at her. With great force, like a caveman or one of the wild animals in the background, he pulls her by her long hair and forces her into a doggy-style position. With his left knee on the ground, his right foot flat on the ground, he has just the right foundation to give Miranda both pain and pleasure at the same time.

He arches his back, as he wraps her long silky hair around his fist. He uses his body like a slingshot, throwing himself deeply into her. With each back breaking stroke, he yanks her hair. She looks up at the silver lining of the moon and chants, "Ohhhm." With each stroke she chants louder, "Ohhmmm!" And louder, "Ohmmmm!"

Miranda gasps for air as Tony palm grips her box. His tight grip evolves into a deep massage of the kitty. His deep strokes and the massage work together rhythmically. He releases his grip, allowing the cat to breathe. He can feel her kitty panting in his hand as he continues to slow, deep stroke her. Her love button stands up erect, demanding his attention. With two fingers, he fiddles her button like the strings of a guitar. "Ohhhhmmmmm!" she chants.

A ball of fire rips from his head to his toes. He can no longer refrain from ramming himself into her. He pounds on her abusively but lovingly. Tough love is what one may call it. He pulls her hair harder and harder as he digs deeper and deeper into her body. The deeper he goes, the louder she chants.

Without realizing it, Tony is howling like the packs of wolves in the distance. She's managed to bring out the wild animal in him and he loves it. Her chanting and his howling echoes loudly for miles and miles, interrupting the serenity of the mountains and they couldn't care less. This moment is worth every mile it took for them to travel here. It's not just the highlight of their entire trip, may even be the highlight of their entire lives.

With a gentle tug of her hair and a tight gripping of her waist, Tony gives her the deepest stroke of them all. Miranda grunts as she absorbs the painful but pleasurable stroke. She looks up to the moon which is now full and chants, "Ohhhhhhmmmmm," Tony stares at the moon as well and sends a chant of his own into the universe.

"Ohhhhm," they shout simultaneously. They carry on like wild animals with no shame. An experience that neither of them will ever forget. "Ohhmmmm."

12

SKELTER IS DRESSED in a black army flight jacket and black Timberland boots. Instead of her having a hood on her head as she usually does, her hair is tucked in a messy bun underneath the black skull cap. She paces around the motel room in deep concentration. In just a few hours it's showtime. Skelter can't believe she's this close to the biggest score she's ever had. The minutes can't fly by fast enough.

She stops short in front of the Dominican man who sits at the foot of the bed. He's sweating bullets from being drilled over and over. He feels like he's in a homicide bureau interrogation room.

"Now, let's get this right," Skelter says as she tilts the skull cap to the left side of her head. She scratches her forehead as she thinks of all the details she needs to be aware of. "So, it's just those two entrances? You sure?"

He looks up at Skelter, then shifts his eyes to Jeezy who sits on the dresser behind her. Jeezy holds a bottle of Sprite in his hand. The purple liquid inside is a dead giveaway that it's more *lean* in the bottle than actual soda. He takes a huge swallow and stands motionless, just allowing the syrup to flow down his throat. His eyes roll into the back of his head with satisfaction. "Aggh." He smacks his lips, greedy for more.

"You're taking too long to answer," Skelter snaps. She grabs the Dominican by his collar and snatches him off the bed. You gone fuck around and put yourself in a bad spot!" Spit jumps out of her mouth with each syllable.

"No, it's only one entrance for the trucks to come in and out but there are two walking entrances."

Heavy coughing interrupts the man. They all look over to the window where T-Mack is standing. He coughs hard, choking on the marijuana blunt that he's puffing on. He walks over to Jeezy. "Let me get a lil swig," he begs as he reaches for the Sprite bottle.

"Oh, hell no!" Skelter shouts. "You got to drive. You ain't hitting that shit. We got work to do!"

"Shit, he got work to do too," T-Mack says while pointing to Jeezy.

"Nigga don't worry about me. I do my best work under the influence," Jeezy says while grinning from ear to ear.

"Can I ask one question, please?" The Dominican man begs. Skelter looks at him awaiting the question. "I'm putting you on a bigger score. Can you please leave me with my work and money just so I can pay my tab and it won't look like I had anything to do with this? If I come short, it will look like I'm in on it."

"You're making a lot of requests," Skelter replies with obvious agitation. "As if sparing the lives of you and your loved ones are not enough. The work or your life? You don't have to answer now. You have a few hours to make your decision. You let me know what means the most to you."

13

TONY STANDS AT the full-sized mirror inside the bathroom. His black cotton suit is tapered to perfection. His broad shoulders and trim waistline makes for the perfect Euro fit. The monotony of the basic black on black is broken up by a pure white v-neck tee shirt. He switches from his left side to his right side, paying attention to the two different shoes he has on his feet. He can't decide whether to go with the subtle black Jimmy Choo leather driving shoe on his right foot, or the loud and attention-grabbing Louboutin spiked sneaker on his left foot.

He looks to the timepiece on his wrist and it quickly helps him to make the decision. Although the Vacheron Constantin 'Overseas Dual Time' values at $60,000, to the average eye it looks no different from a plain old Invicta. Because of that he decides to go with the Louboutin spiked sneaker and take the outfit from boredom and traditional to trendy and popping.

He quickly makes the shoe replacement and steps out of the bathroom and into the bedroom of the RV motorhome. He makes his way over to Miranda who is standing in front of the mirror applying her makeup. He grabs her from behind. They lock eyes through the mirror.

Miranda, standing here so calm and laid back now makes it hard to believe the wild animal she was a few hours ago up on the mountain top. Tony always loved and appreciated her high sex drive but last night was a totally different experience. Last night she was uninhibited and more passionate than ever. Tony is thinking of what he can do to recreate the mountain type effects at home so he can have her like that each and every night.

Staring into her eyes Tony can still see that flame in them. He replays the scenes over. He gets an instant erection and Miranda feels him poking at her back. She shakes her head from side to side with a smirk. Tony assumes she must have been seriously backed up and that is why lately she's been so irritable with a lack of humor. Sex on the mountains changed all of that though. She's been floating like a beautiful butterfly ever since.

He plants a soft kiss on the nape of her neck. "The end to such a lovely ten-day getaway," he says in his most convincing voice. Miranda is not convinced the least bit. She snatches away and rolls her eyes at him through the mirror.

"Seriously," he says convincingly. "I enjoyed you."

The eagerness to get back to work can be seen in his eyes and his body language. While most people complain about working, he is the opposite. He complains about not working. When he's away from it he misses it dearly.

He loosens his grip of her slowly. He grabs his briefcase from the dresser and dashes to the door.

Although she's still slightly agitated with him, she still can't allow him to leave without expressing her love for him. In her life she's learned to never take a second for granted. In that second anything can happen, and you can be stuck holding onto a wish that you would have told them how much you love them. "Love you!" Miranda shouts.

"Love you too!" Tony shouts back as he makes his way to the front of the RV. He stands behind the driver in the cockpit watching the highway in front of them. The driver pulls into the Short Hills Mall parking lot and Tony stands on the stairs, awaiting the door to open.

As he exits the RV, he takes a deep breath of the New Jersey air. He's so happy to be back at home. He found no enjoyment nor appreciation of the trees and the wildlife in Wyoming. He found it to be equally depressing as it is watching Animal Kingdom on television. To him, actually being there is far worse.

Tony stands to the side as the driver walks to the center of the RV. He hits the remote in his hand and the bottom of the RV lifts slowly. A car garage is built inside the bottom of the RV. Tony's car sits on the flatbed, with the huge chrome grill beaming.

In a matter of seconds, the Belladona Purple Rolls Royce Cullinan SUV—$425,000 worth of luxury—is being served on a silver platter. The truck sits on a silver bed which slides from underneath the RV electrically. Once the truck is completely on the ground, Tony doesn't hesitate to hop in. He opens the driver's side door and seats himself, melting into the soft, butterscotch-colored upholstery. He tosses his briefcase onto the passenger's seat.

"Peace My Queen," Tony shouts at the ceiling.

"Peace to you as well, my King," says a soothing voice through the speakers. It's the voice of Tony's Virtual Smart Assistant. "Glad to have you back, King. What can I help you with today?"

This smart assistant is closer to Tony than any human in the world. She knows some of his deepest secrets. The topics he's researched and the conversations that have been held in his vehicles he trusts her with wholeheartedly. He couldn't imagine anyone else knowing as much about him as she does and that is what makes her, his Queen. Who needs Siri when he has his Queen? He's designed her to be the best woman in the world. She does whatever he instructs her to do. She does his research for him and even listens to him vent without saying a word. She may be artificially intelligent but still he finds more appreciation in her than he has in most of the women he's dealt with in life.

"My Queen…open humidor."

"Yes King…humidor opening."

In seconds, the right side of the dashboard slides out slowly. Watching this reminds Tony of the old days when he had electric stash spots equipped in his cars to hide his drugs. Today he looks at the glass covered humidor with the same admiration. Tony flips the lid and grabs hold of his favorite cigar.

He places the cigar underneath his nostrils and takes a whiff. The fragrance of the tobacco and the wrapper is beyond pleasurable to him. Miranda made a bet with him that he couldn't go the whole 10 days with smoking a cigar. He won the bet, but it almost killed him. He couldn't wait for this moment.

"My Queen, close humidor."

"Humidor closing," the voice replies as the dashboard slides and the humidor disappears. "Is there anything else I can help you with?" she asks.

"No, my Queen," he replies as he bites the cap layer off the back of his cigar. "Thank you."

"Can I play something relaxing for you to soothe your mind my, King?"

"Yes, please," Tony replies. "Thank you." Tony spins the cigar around in his mouth, biting on it to soften the tip.

"No need for thanks my King. It's my duty to serve you and make sure you are comfortable and relaxed as a King should be."

A bright smile spreads across his face. He can't help but to think of how spectacular life would be if real life women were like his smart assistant. "My Queen, will you marry me?" Tony asks with a bright smile on his face.

"I would be honored, my King, but what about her? Let's just remain virtual lovers as you refer to us."

Tony laughs hysterically. "You are too smart for your own good, my Queen." Tony lights his cigar with deep concentration.

"Your tunes will begin in a few seconds. I will be leaving you now. Call me if you need me. Enjoy your cigar, My King."

With no further delay, the sound of Zen Meditation music comes through the speakers, immediately making the inside of the car peaceful and serene. At this moment Tony is in a bubble, with the world not even existing around him. He takes a deep pull of his cigar and holds the smoke in for as long as he can. As he slowly exhales, he puts the car in Drive and slowly cruises out of the parking lot. He enjoys the tunes and his cigar as he makes his way back to the money.

14

CAMDEN

THE LOUD SHRIEKING of a small child pierces the airwaves. The whole room is filled with pandemonium. The Dominican woman sits on the couch cradling her child close to her bosom in attempt to quiet him down. It's hard to console the baby when she's crying just as hard. The other two children are sobbing as well.

"Yo, lady, y'all better shut the fuck up," the young thug says as he walks around the living room frantically. The thug, known as Lil Pop, is one of Jeezy's soldiers. He's been brought in to watch over the woman. His aggression is scaring them all up, making them cry harder and louder. The doorbell rings and stirs up more chaos. The young thug stops in his tracks, ears on alert. "Yo," he whispers to the woman. "Who the fuck is that?" The bell rings again and again. He quickly picks up the phone and starts to dial.

MOTEL 6

Skelter and Jeezy stand on opposite sides of the full sized bed. On the bed is enough artillery to stop an entire police force. Handguns equipped with drums filled with 100 rounds, handguns filled with rifle bullets, two assault rifles, Desert Eagle big-body revolvers along with speed-loaders, infrared beams, extra clips and way more than enough ammunition cover the headboard to the foot.

Skelter takes inventory of the weapons while Jeezy cleans his old faithful Dan Wesson Valor .45 caliber with adjustable night sight. This gun has gotten him out of some of the stickiest situations. He's had it for 10 years now, yet she still works as smoothly as she did back then and that's because he takes care of her just like a baby. He gives her the spa treatment every 2 weeks regardless if he's put in work with her or not. He knows her so well, knowing when she's in need of a little tender loving care. He also knows her so well that he can take her apart all the way down to the tiny screws and bolts, and then reassemble her all in under 5 minutes. Jeezy puts the butt of the gun up to his lips and plants a soft kiss on it before staring at the gun in love.

Jeezy notices his phone lighting up, indicating that he has an incoming call. He looks over and realizes who the caller is. He snatches the phone from the bed quickly. "Yurp," he sings into the phone. He hears chaos in the background.

"Yo, I'm two minutes away from doing something crazy over here!" Lil Pop yells hysterically. "I'm about to tweak, On the Set!"

Skelter doesn't like the look on Jeezy's face. "What's up? What's going on?" she asks.

"The bitch bugging," Jeezy says before Skelter snatches the phone from him. She hears the children and the mother crying in the background. She also hears the doorbell ringing. "What the fuck is going on over there?"

"These motherfuckers are going crazy," Lil Pop replies. "And somebody been at that bell for a couple minutes now." Skelter becomes nervous as she hears this. They've come too close to blow it all now. She must think quick. "This bitch falling apart over here. And these damn kids won't shut up. I know how to shut them up though."

"Yo, just chill," Skelter replies. Skelter quickly walks over to the other bed where the Dominican man is sitting a nervous wreck. She sits next to the man with her gun gripped tightly in her hand. "Listen, you better get them to shut the fuck up before they get shut the fuck up. I'm telling you, I ain't fucking around with you."

Skelter speaks into the phone. "Put the bitch on the phone." The sobbing gets louder as the woman puts the phone to her ear. She hands the phone to the man. "Holler at your bitch before I tell my young boy to holler at your bitch," she threatens with stone cold eyes.

"*Dimelo*," the Dominican man speaks into the phone.

Skelter leans her ear close to the phone, listening closely. "And speak English, motherfucker."

The woman is crying loud and hard. "Mami, mami?" The man's heart shatters into pieces as he hears his wife and kids crying in fear and despair. "Calm down, please."

CAMDEN

"*Calmese*"(Calm down?) *Como*(How?) *Los extranos estan en nuestra puta casa con armas que amenazan con matarnos!* (Strangers are in our fucking house threatening to kill us.) *En que nos has metido* (What have you gotten us into?) *Que clase de hombres eres para dejar que esto nos pase* (What type of man are you to let this happen to us?) *Nos dejaste aqui para defendernos contra hombres negros con armas!* (You leave us here to defend for ourselves against black men with guns.)"

Skelter points the gun in between his eyes. "What is she saying? Tell that bitch to talk English."

"Okay, okay," he says in a terrified state. His wife's words have crushed him. His eyes are filled with tears. "Juju, please just calm down. All this will be over in a couple of hours and we will be back together like a family."

"*Una familia* (A family?) *Dejaste a tu familia Como un cobarde* (You left your family like a coward! *Un verdadero hombre nunca dejaria' a su familia por nada!* (A real man would never leave his family for nothing!) *Somos familia! Vivimos juntos y si tenemos que morimos juntos!* (We are family we live together and if we have to we die together!)"

"You better tell her to pipe down, I'm telling you," Skelter whispers to the man. "If she blow this situation for me she will pay. Trust me." The bell can be heard ringing in the background. "Yo, ask her who the fuck is at that bell!"

"Juju, please quiet down. I will fix this and I will be right back with you and my children, one family."

"*No. No voy a estar callado* (I'm not going to be quiet.) *Tendran que matarnos juntos.* (They will just have to kill us together.) *Yo y mis hijos* (Me and my children!) *Ya no los hare' vivir a traves de esta tortura* (I will no longer make my children live through this torture.)" She throws the phone onto the floor with fury.

Skelter realizes that the women's emotions has overpowered her fear. They are way too close to let her ruin it for them. She snatches the phone from the man at the same time Lil Pop grabs the phone. "Yo," they say at the same time.

Lil Pop's heart is relieved as he sees the Comcast Cable guy walking back to his truck. "Yo, it's all good. That was Comcast."

"Cool," Skelter replies. "But it's not all good. The bitch is falling apart. She ain't scared no more. Do whatever it takes to put her back in line."

"Say no more!" Lil Pop replies.

Skelter ends the call. She looks to the man with treacherous eyes.

"No, please, no," the man cries. He stares up at Skelter with puppy dog eyes.

At this moment he's ready to take his chances. If only he could get to one of the guns, he feels he may have a shot. His intentions can be seen from across the room. He's really thinking about it. He wants to rescue his family but he knows if his move isn't successful he will no longer have a family.

He envisions his family being harmed this very moment. All of his logic and common sense is replaced with desperation. He peeks over to the bed full of guns. He peeks back at Skelter whose eyes are locked onto him.

"Go ahead," she says with a smile. "If you feeling froggy, go ahead and leap. Go ahead," she says with a sinister smile as she aims right at his head. "I bet you I will catch you in midair when you leap. Try me."

The man looks away and remains seated like the coward that he is.

15

SHORT HILLS, NEW JERSEY

THE YOUNG AND extremely beautiful secretary stands behind her desk with her full attention on the unruly man who stands before her. The old, and baggy faced Black man is dressed for the winter when it's the dead of summer. His trench coat is covered in years of dirt. Lint balls the size of golf balls cling to the fine hairs of the cashmere overcoat. The man's trousers and oversized sweater looks stuffed as if he has four outfits underneath them. He carries a duffle-bag in his hand big enough to have his whole life in it. The Vietnam War Veteran cap on his head makes the secretary believe that he's obviously an old and crazy, homeless war veteran.

The secretary is afraid yet she stands her ground. "Sir, you can't just walk in here like this with no appointment."

"Well, I have an appointment," he replies in a low and hoarse voice.

"Yes, and that date isn't until next week. Anyway, as I've told you, Mr. Austin isn't here yet."

"I don't have until next week. I need to speak with someone now," the man says hastily. "Where is his office? In the back?" he asks as he starts to proceed around the desk. "I will just wait for him in his office."

"Sir, you can't. Stop or I will be forced to call the police."

"Well, that's just what you will have to do then," the man says before making his move.

Tony steps in the office just as the secretary is picking up the phone. He's in awe of the disturbance. He looks at the man with a cold glare.

The man looks at Tony, unbothered by his presence. "Attorney, Tony Austin, right? I need to speak with you. Your office is this way?" he asks as he leads the way through the corridor.

Tony follows the man, amazed by his demeanor and his approach. Tony winks at the secretary and flashes a cocky smile. The man stops at the door, allowing Tony to take lead. Tony opens the door and steps inside.

The man follows and looks around at the huge, luxurious office with astonishment in his eyes. Tony offers him a seat and he takes it gratefully. Tony sits in his chair across from the man. He leans the chair on its wheels. He rocks back and forth watching the man. Anxiousness is in the man's eyes, but his facial expression is blank. Tony can't help but to notice the stiffness of the man's face but charges it off as him maybe being wounded somehow in the war.

"Tony Austin," the man says in a low hoarse voice. "Graduated from Hampton University, June 6th, 1994. Attended Law School at Duke University. Passed the Bar on September 18th,1998. Sworn in by Beth A. McKnight in Essex County on January 21st, 1999." Tony sits back wondering where all this is going and how does the man know so much about him. His first thought is this man must be a Federal Agent. He remains cool, not giving a sign of discomfort.

The man continues speaking, not once looking Tony in the eyes. Instead his eyes scan the room. "The Davidson case in 2000 was just the beginning for you. The Blackhead, aka The Mayor case in 2003 showed your persistence and ability to make use of all your resources.

"Most people believe the kingpin, drug dealer, The Mayor built your career, but I don't. That was just a piece of the puzzle. Defending him gave you an edge but in my opinion the Bennett case was pivotal in your career. Taught you to view the world differently." He still hasn't looked at Tony.

Tony sits upright with confusion plastered on his face. Hearing all this has him bewildered. He listens closer as the man states more cases and statistics like a crazed sports fanatic who has finally met his favorite player. Hearing his stats read out like this makes him more impressed with himself, if that is even possible.

The man looks at Tony for the first time. "I know you're wondering how I know all of this. Well, I've been following your career for some time now. And I believe with all of my heart that you are the right attorney for the case I have for you. This case I have for you will be the biggest case of your whole career. You will go down in history as the best attorney in the state, better yet the country."

Tony chuckles. "Oh, after this case?" he asks with sarcasm. "Oh, okay."

"This case will make history. This is a different kind of case and I will tell you how, after I introduce myself. It's a tricky case and can cause a lot of problems. It's quite risky but I believe you are all about risks if I know you correctly. But this case is crossing the point of no return. If you accept this case it can be detrimental for the both of us."

Tony listens to the man's every word and by now he's about ready to charge him off as a nut job, a wacko. He's seconds away from hitting the panic button on his phone and have the police escort the man out of the office. But he doesn't because he's curious as to how the man knows so much about him.

"Are you up for the challenge?" the man asks.

"How can I agree to something that I know nothing about?" Tony asks.

Tony watches in amazement as the man grips the skin under his chin and pulls it upward. It looks like something from a horror movie until Tony realizes he was wearing a mask the whole time. Tony is at a loss of words as he looks at the woman who sits before him. The Caucasian woman appears to be in her late 60's. She could be younger but her long silver-grey hair makes her appear older. Her hair is pinned into a tight and neat bun on the top of her head. The blue surgical mask covering her nose and mouth causes Tony more alarm.

Tony gets up from his seat and backs away from the woman. He's mindful not to offend her but whatever she's infected with, he doesn't want it.

"No, worries, I'm not sick. You can't catch anything from me."

She lays her duffle-bag onto the desk and tugs on a wire that is discreetly connected from her nose into the bag. She unzips the bag and adjusts the wire that can now be seen to be connected to an oxygen tank. The woman looks at Tony for seconds before speaking. "I told you all about you. Now let me tell you about me.

"My name, we will just say Jane Doe for now, until I'm reassured that I can trust you. My occupation let's just say I worked with the United States Government for over forty years. Only five of those years I did my job my willingly. The last thirty something years I done by force."

Tony is now eager to hear the woman's story. "Let's cut the charade. What is it that you are here for?"

"I'm here to bring awareness of all of America's dirty secrets," she says with a conniving smile. "Have you ever heard of genocide through vaccination? Just like in the 1930's to the 1970's when syphilis was spread through vaccination when black men were told they were being given free health care? How about the tales of autism being transferred the same way?"

"Oh, a conspiracy theorist," Tony chuckles. "One of those."

"What if I can give you proof to back up all that I say? What if I'm able to provide proof that certain celebrities and public figures have been killed off by the injection of cancer and other diseases? What if I can prove to you that the allergy shots given at the local CVS and Walgreens are infected with some type of disease.

What if I can prove to you that scientists have figured a way to alter the X and Y chromosomes and have found the perfect mix. In their laboratories they have created the chromosome responsible for homosexuality. How, you may ask, is this chromosome transmitted? Through the foods," she says while nodding her head. "Not even the foods we eat are safe. Nor the air we breathe," she says as she points to her tank.

"You prove all of that and then what?" Tony asks.

"And then we have the biggest lawsuit in the world. We expose the government and their corruption and we make history." Tony nods his head up and down. He likes the sound of this. "Now for the dangerous part of this. Anybody gets word of what we are about to do, our lives will be over. There's no doubt in my mind that we will be assassinated, shot down like dogs," she says with a twinkle in her eyes.

"For thirty years I worked for the Government in these same laboratories, creating diseases and spreading them throughout the world to fuel the economy. It's all business. I was afraid to quit or resign for I knew they would kill me. All the information I had stored right here," she says as she taps her temples. "They would never let me leave with such information."

"So, how did you leave?" Tony questions. "You retired?"

"No, I expired," she says with a smile. "She digs into her bag and pulls a leather binder from it. She pulls a document from the binder and holds it in the air. She uses her thumb to purposely cover her name on the document. At the top of the sheet "Death Certificate" is printed boldly.

Tony looks at the woman with a peculiar eye. "That's right, I faked my own death," she says with a smile. "A funeral and even a burial. I may be the only person to ever be present at their own funeral. It was so sad I even cried." She flashes a smile for the first time she's been here and her smile warms up the room. Nothing about her smile says wacko. Her teeth are perfect and pearly white like a person who has never missed a dentist appointment in life.

Tony is totally confused at all that he's digested in these few minutes. He's not sure if he should believe this story or charge the woman off as a coo coo bird. What he does know is if he could crack this case he would be bigger than life. He's been bored lately with his career.

"So, does this sound like something you would be interested in?"

"How do I know that you're not a nut job in here wasting my time?"

"You won't know that until our next meeting and I show you certified documents," she says as she places her Death Certificate into her binder. The woman gathers her belongings before placing the mask over her face. Tony watches in confusion as she transitions before his eyes. Once her disguise is in place, she gets up from the seat.

"Does this sound like a risk that you are willing to take or are you afraid to have your career ended if this doesn't go in our favor? Even though I'm sure I have enough information wherein that could never happen."

"You have been following my career before I even had a career, you say right?"

"That is correct," the woman replies.

"Well, you should know that my whole career has been based on taking chances," Tony says with a cocky smile. "Go out there to my secretary and find out when the next available appointment."

"Oh, no," the woman says. "This is on my terms. Our next appointment will be one week from today. At this same time," she says as she makes her way to the door. "I will call you one hour in advance to give you the details of the meeting place."

The woman exits the room without looking back. Tony walks to the door, where he watches the woman stroll through the hall. He's still in a bit of confusion but he has to admit he's curious. This just may be the adventure that he's in need of to break the boredom and monotony. This could be the case he needs to bring some excitement into his life.

16

TITAN SALVAGE JUNKYARD/CAMDEN, NEW JERSEY

THE CAR CARRIER trailer, hauling 9 cars, backs into the parking space with finesse and superb expertise. The sound of the airbrakes exhale into the air. Both, the driver's door and passenger's door swing open simultaneously. The driver hops off the truck and takes a deep stretch, arms high in the air. As he's stretching he takes a quick glance around the area. He sluggishly makes his way to the back of the trailer.

The passenger seems to be a little more alert. He studies the area closely. The driver's door of the Honda Civic parked two spaces away opens and Skelter's hostage walks in the direction of the tractor. His steps are shaky and hesitant, yet he tries to play it cool and calm. He continuously peeks back and forth across the parking lot. He attempts to keep his eyes from soaring across the lot but his fear controls them.

All three of the men meet at the back of the trailer where they greet each other properly. The driver twists the lock of the carrier as his passenger looks around suspiciously. The hostage cuts his eyes across the parking lot once again. He turns his back just to help him refrain.

From across the parking lot, inside the van, Skelter is positioned in the backseat directly in the middle, eyes locked on the men and the trailer. T-Mack in the driver's seat and Jeezy in the passenger's seat have their eyes glued on the windshield watching the men at work. The cars are backed off the trailer one by one. Adrenaline fills the caravan as they sit in silence, in deep concentration like they are watching a movie. Both Skelter and Jeezy grip their guns tightly just waiting for showtime.

"Yo, I got a feeling that motherfucker gone give us up," T-Mack says.

"That motherfucker ain't stupid," Skelter replies. "He knows if he do, he will never see his wife and kids again." She has her eyes fixed onto their man who seems to be playing it cool and calm. He stands at the back of the trailer, keeping his attention on the man before him.

"I'm telling you that red Camry is the car," Jeezy says. "Who wanna bet?"

"I will take that bet," Skelter says.

"A hundred bucks," Jeezy says as he reaches behind him. Skelter bangs his fist, accepting the bet.

The driver of the car carrier trailer runs to the front and climbs into the truck. Skelter and her guys watch with their undivided attention. The driver backs the truck on an angle, blocking the view of all the vehicles. "Fuck!" The man in the driver's seat yells with frustration. "Now what the fuck we gone do?"

Skelter attempts to look under the trailer, over the trailer and even in between any space she can find but still no luck. "We gone have to make our move."

On the opposite side of the trailer one of the men get underneath the Ford Taurus. He slides around underneath that car before moving on to the next and the next. In seconds he hands a long, duffle-bag to his partner. The oversized military duffle-bag looks big enough to place a small body in it. The partner drops the duffle-bag onto the ground as he looks around suspiciously. The man then gets underneath a Mitsubishi and even faster than the first time he hands another duffle-bag to his partner. In less than four minutes 4 duffle-bags filled with kilos are out of the cars and ready to be taken away from here.

The hostage and the passenger of the Auto Carrier pick up 2 duffle-bags apiece. The passenger of the Auto Carrier leads the way toward the Civic while Skelter's hostage follows behind at least 20 steps. His heart pounds with fear. He realizes the moment that he's been dreading is finally here. He has no idea of how this whole ordeal will play out. He prays that it is simple and easy.

As he struts he tries to prepare for himself for what is about to happen. He knows it's coming soon, just doesn't know exactly when. Just as he gets within arm's reach of the van he hears, "Don't nobody fucking move!" He slowly turns around where he finds Skelter standing in between him and the other man. The assault rifle in her hands looks huge and exaggerated. She grips it tightly, aiming it back and forth at the both of them.

Jeezy appears from the opposite end of the trailer. He grips the collar of the driver's shirt tight enough to strangle him. He holds the Wesson Valor .45 caliber handgun to the man's temple as he shoves the man toward the others.

Jeezy slams the man against the trailer. He quickly pats him down. After a quick but thorough search, he slams the man face first onto the ground. The man lays there spread eagle in fear.

Skelter gives Jeezy a head-nod, signaling for him to check the other man. He quickly checks the man and he immediately locates a little compact 9-millimeter. The sight of the gun sends Jeezy into rage. He backhands the man with the butt of the gun and sends him sailing back a couple feet. He aims both guns at the man's head as he hands the 9-millimeter to Skelter.

Jeezy then looks to their hostage who is standing with the duffle-bags in hand, weighing his arms down. "Drop the bags and lay the fuck down!" He drops the bags and stretches his arms high in the air. Jeezy reaches over and snatches the man by the front collar of his jacket and flings him onto the ground. "Face down!"

With all three of the men laying on their bellies, Skelter looks to her accomplice and gives the signal. He stands over the driver. With the gun aimed at the back of the man's head, he squeezes the trigger. Before his gun sounds off, the sound of rapid fire from a Mac 11 rips loudly echoing throughout the junkyard. The sound of Jeezy's gun is heard faintly in between the consecutive rounds of the Mac 11. Two shots leaves the man on the ground, lifeless.

Both Skelter and Jeezy duck low, trying to figure out where the shots are coming from. The sound of bullets ricocheting distracts them from identifying the direction where the gunfire is coming from. Suddenly they see an older Dominican man standing at the front entrance of the building. He races toward them fearlessly, screaming vulgar language as he fires relentlessly.

Skelter aims the AR-15 at the man and fires at him to back him up. The loud bark of the AR-15 is not enough to stop the old man. He continues at them courageously. They exchange fire before the man ducks behind a parked car. He continues to fire without him being seen. Two more gunmen come running out of the building both waving handguns. Skelter and Jeezy weren't expecting this and it shows. They start to move frantically, looking for an escape.

"Grab the bags!" Jeezy shouts as he lets the .45 bark in the two men's directions. Pure luck is on his side because one man is struck in the shoulder. He spins like a top before stumbling backwards. Two sloppy steps and he's laying flat on his back. The other man stops and ducks low behind an old pickup truck. He spits two shots in their direction before ducking low for safety. The window of the car that Skelter uses for a shield is shattered into pieces. She lifts up with rage and desperation as she sends a round of fire of her own.

In the midst of the heated gun battle, the hostage and the other man get up from the ground and run in opposite directions. The hostage runs around the trailer for safety while the other man isn't as lucky. Just as he takes his third step Jeezy takes a clear shot at him with the .45 caliber. The bullet crashes into his back and lifts him off of his feet. The impact causes him to do a full semi in the air. He lands on the ground lifeless.

Skelter backpedals away, with the assault rifle waving in the air. The duffle-bags hang on her shoulders, holding her down. She can barely take a step. One-hundred pounds and some change of cocaine plus the big and awkward AR.15 is slowing her down dramatically. Just 115 pounds herself, she's carrying her weight. She's feeling a bit relieved once she sees their getaway car a few hundred feet away.

T-Mack, the driver has the passenger's door open wide for her entrance.

"Come on!" Skelter shouts to Jeezy who is backpedaling slowly, keeping his eyes wavering in front of him. He drags 2 duffle-bags with him as well.

Through the darkness the older Dominican man creeps, graceful and light on his feet. His eyes are locked onto Skelter and Jeezy. He refuses to let them get away with this because if they do his life will be ended for sure. He would rather be murdered on this battlefield than to have to face and explain to the boss how he let them get away.

As he creeps around the trailer he sees Skelter and Jeezy a few steps away from their escape. He tiptoes in between two parked cars, keeping his eyes on his enemy. He creeps around a van and, like a jack in the box, he pops up. Jeezy spots the glare from the man's chrome gun. He aims his gun at the man and fires. *Click! Click! Click!* Jeezy looks at his gun in shock. He attempts to fire again. *Click!* Jeezy turns around and makes a run for it.

From where the old man stands he has a clear shot at Jeezy and he takes it. In fact, he takes a series of them. He spits everything he has at him and is surprised to hear a scream so ear piercing that it almost deafens him. Jeezy falls forward. The duffle-bags falls on top of him, with his gun still in his hand.

Skelter is in shock as Jeezy lays on his stomach, stiff as a board. "Come on," she screams with desperation. She looks around in the darkness for the old man that has disappeared. Suddenly gunfire sounds off from the Mac 11. Skelter spits a few rounds into the darkness just so she can back her way to the getaway car.

Police sirens echo throughout the air. Skelter looks around in disarray. She looks up ahead where Jeezy lays, not having made one single move. Her heart sinks.

The sirens are getting closer and closer. She blasts off into the darkness blindly, no target in scope as she dumps the duffle-bags onto the floor. She quickly dives into the seat. Before she can even land, the driver speeds off.

T-Mack zips through the junkyard recklessly at top speed. He bangs a few fenders and knocks off a few mirrors along the way. The sirens are coming from every direction. Flashing lights can be seen flaring from blocks away. This is all playing out right before their eyes like a bad movie that you can already predict the ending.

Skelter sits in the passenger's seat with both hands wrapped around the AR-15, the butt of the gun glued to her chest. She's prepared to go out in a blazing fire if it comes to that. Getting nabbed by the police is not a part of her plan. If by the chance the police are not willing to die out here tonight, they better not attempt to stop her at this point. Death before capture is what she says in her mind over and over, and she means it.

THE DOMINICAN MAN runs hard through the pitch blackness. He feels like the main character of a horror movie. He's out of breath and his legs are fatigued but he refuses to stop running. The escapade that just played out before his eyes plays over and over in his mind as he runs. He wishes he could shake away the scene but he can't and he's sure he will never be able to.

He can't help but to wonder where it all goes from here. How will all of this end? He's sure this is only the beginning. He wonders if the girl and her crew made it away. For his own sake he prays they were all murdered. With all the gunfire he heard ripping in the air, he's sure there were a lot of casualties left in that junkyard. What he's not sure of is if he would have rather be one of the casualties or have to face this music when the Big Boss finds out.

He stops running. He tries to catch his breath as he fast trots along the dark block. He peeks around nervously, hoping and praying. After days of being captured, he's finally free. Well, partly free that is. Several times since making his getaway out of the junkyard he thought of disappearing just so he doesn't have to face the Big Boss.

Right now, he feels he could get so low out of the way that no one would ever find him. He already has his hiding spot and plan in effect. The only problem is his wife and children. With the Big Boss being her brother, he will always know where to find them. And because of that, he's not sure if he should go on with his plan without them.

MEANWHILE
COLORADO ADX

Manson sits in the corner of the tiny cell with his head in between his knees, cradling himself as he rocks back and forth. As usual he's drugged up out of his mind, just as he is every other day, all day long. The authorities believe that Manson is less violent when he's drugged, but even when drugged, he's pretty much violent.

The sound of the feeding hole being opened snaps Manson out of his zone. He quickly stands to his feet and prepares to rumble. He's so used to the guards attacking him that he's always prepared to rumble. He refuses to sleep because they have even attacked him while he's sleep. Because of that he sleeps with one eye open at all times.

He's been labeled violent from day one, only because he refused to comply with the Feds. They promised them they would make his prison stay hell, and they have. The involuntary medication, the beatings and the disconnect from the world is enough to break the average man, but still Manson stands as strong as he can. Even during his weakest days he still manages to give them the fight of their life.

"Calm down, Bryant," the officer says. "Chow."

Manson walks toward the door hesitantly and with suspicion. He's prepared for the gate to open any minute and the war start. He becomes slightly at ease as he spots the face of the officer. He then picks up his pace. The only thing on his mind is the water that sits on the tray. He's close to dying from thirst.

Manson stares into the deep blue eyes of the officer awaiting the signal as he head nods toward the water. The officer gives a slight head-nod, signaling that it's ok. Manson quickly snatches the water from the tray, holds it up to his mouth and gulps it in one swallow. He pants like a thirsty dog as the officer reaches in his pocket and pulls out a bottle of Poland Spring water. He sneakily pours the water into the cup.

Manson snatches the cup and this time he drinks it slowly with appreciation. Manson looks down at the slop on the plate and then looks up to the officer for a signal. Manson learned a long time ago, during his last bid that the food is off limits. The officers have been known to lace his food with medication and even feces. His water has even been urinated in. They may have caught him early off before he realized it but in no way would he fall for those antics this day and time. He's disgusted every time he thinks of what he has eaten and drank. That disgust is part of the rage that fuels him every time he's in battle with them.

The officer shakes his head negatively, giving Manson the signal to not partake in the slop. He has no idea what could be in there but with the officer telling him no, that is all he needs. The officer shakes his arm and three granola bars with no wrapper on them, falls out of his sleeve. He shakes his other sleeve over the tray and a few un-wrapped brownies fall from them.

Manson rakes them all into one pile as he looks at the officer with gratefulness. If not for this officer Manson would have been died from starvation or dehydration. Manson trusts not one other officer in the building but this one. He earned his trust almost a year ago. It's strange that with all the Black officers who work here, the only officer he semi trusts is a blonde hair blue eyed, white man.

At a time when Manson was at his weakest, this officer always came through for him. Manson knows nothing in life is free which makes him believe that the man must have some type of agenda, some ulterior motive. He just has no clue of what it could be. Manson is so grateful and appreciative for all the man has done for him that the man could get Manson to do almost anything for him. That is as long as it stays within the lines of his manhood and his reputation that means everything in the world to him.

The man looks around with caution. "Listen," the officer whispers. Manson stares into his mouth in shock. Speaking is something the officer has never done. Up until now only word that Manson has ever heard him say is 'chow.' Manson steps closer to the gate. "I see how they treat you and I hate it," the man says with sincerity. "It's not just you they do this to. I've been forced to sit back quietly. I've been work-ing here for twenty-five years. I did my time. In a few months I will retire. You fucked up your life and got yourself into this mess but what they are doing here isn't right. As much as I hate it, I have to keep my mouth shut in order to keep my pension in place.

"I can't let you fuck up my situation. Once I retire and my pension is locked and loaded, I promise you I will be sure to shine the light on this shit they've been doing. I have to. The fact that I have stood in silence about this so long tortures my spirit. But trust me, in a few months, I got you."

The officer holds his fist against the gate as he looks to his left. "You trust me," he whispers.

Manson places his fist against the gate where the man's hand is. Their knuckles press against each other. "For sure," Manson replies.

"I promise I got you." The officer removes his fist from the gate and walks away.

Manson watches the man until he bends the corner of the tier. He doesn't trust many, but in a time of such desperation, all he can hope is that the man will do what he says he will do.

SKELTER RIDES IN the back seat staring in a daze as T-Mack speeds through Camden. Adrenaline still races in their veins and they haven't come down off of their high yet. It all still seems quite unreal. The vision of their fallen soldier laying in the middle of the junkyard is fixed in their minds. They haven't quite digested it yet. The only thing on their mind right now is making it to safety. In between their thoughts of making it home, the sound of Jeezy's scream echoes in their mind.

Neither of them is a stranger to death. It's not the first time that they've witnessed murder, whether it be the enemy or one of their own. In fact, they have witnessed so many murders that they have become desensitized. No matter how many murders they've committed or witnessed it's slightly different when it's one of their own because they know how easily it could have been them laying there instead.

Skelter can't help but to think of how Jeezy's trusted bitch failed him. He always told her that his bitch would never fail him because he always took good care of her. Two things Skelter knows about a bitch, it doesn't matter how good you treat them that doesn't mean she will never fail or cross you. She also knows just when you think you have them figured out, they will change up on you. She knows this because she is one.

She can't help but to wonder how all this will play out. She prays that in no way it leads back to them. She's sure right this very moment police are swamping the scene looking for leads of the culprits of the massacre they left behind. She can't put too much thought into it because the show must go on. Right now, she has enough cocaine in her possession to lift up the entire city of Trenton and every surrounding city that their arms can reach.

She feels so close to the finish line that she can taste it. She doesn't want to count her chickens before they hatch because where she comes from anything is possible. All she would need right now is to get pulled over by the police and it will be the perfect story gone bad.

"Yo, slow down," Skelter says. "Let's just ride into the sunset, nice and easy."

T-Mack takes heed and slows down the van. He takes a deep breath just to obtain his composure. He's still on a high from the movie they just made. Thoughts rip through both of their minds of their very next move. This is the biggest heist that they have ever pulled off.

"Today we made history!" Skelter shouts. "In all the war stories ever told in the history of Trenton, no one has never heard one of this magnitude!"

Skelter can't help but to think of how proud Manson would be of her. She can't believe it herself that she was able to pull off a caper like this. She wishes he was here to be able to be a part of this. If he was, she would turn her entire portion over to him and let him run the show from here. She asks herself; how would he handle this situation?

She wonders if he would bust the score down evenly with the accomplice or if he would slump him and keep it all for himself. After all, T-Mack is the one who made it all possible. T-Mack brought the situation to Jeezy, who brought it to her. Her loyalty is to Jeezy but she does feel indebted to T-Mack as well.

She quickly looks over to the driver and the vision of her slumping him plays clearly in her mind. What she doesn't know is he's had those thoughts of slumping her running through his mind a few times already. As many times the greedy and selfish thought of slumping him creeps through her mind, the honorable thing of splitting the score intervenes. Her honor is intact, but she needs to be worried if he's standing on the same honor system.

MINUTES LATER

After debating back and forth a thousand times, the man decided to do what any real man would do in this situation. He decided to go back home to his family. As hard of a decision it was to make, he had no choice. His heart races as he approaches his house. The thoughts of turning around and making a run for it is still near the front of his mind. He has to pep talk himself into doing the right thing because if he does not he will keep walking right on past.

As he tiptoes slowly up the stairs his mind plays a serious trick on him. He quickly envisions his family inside no longer living. As he steps onto the porch he stops short. If that is the case, in no way is he prepared to face that. Also, he will never be able to live it down that he lost his family behind his actions. He becomes nauseated at the thought of what could possibly be behind the door. He becomes weak as his mouth fills with what tastes like saltwater.

He proceeds to the door and before he rings the bell he thinks one last time if this is really what he wants to do. He feels as if he's walking himself into a death sentence. He closes his eyes and presses the bell. In seconds, he hears the living room blinds shuffle. About a foot over the ledge the blinds open. The man sees his younger child and feels some relief. At least he knows his baby is alive. Now he prays that they all are. Both of his other children pop up at the window as well. The sight of them brings tears of happiness. They all leave from the window and in seconds the hallway door can be heard opening. The door is snatched open and there his wife and children stand. The fear and misery is still painted on all of their faces. *"Todos estan bien?"* (Is everybody ok?) He looks in the hallway expecting to see one of Skelter's men.

"El se fue," the woman replies. (He's gone.) *"Salio corriendo de aqui hace unos momentos.* (He ran out of here a few minutes ago.) *Estamos bien.* (We are all fine.)" She can no longer fight back the tears. *"Que hay de ti?"* (How about you?) She looks her husband up and down to make sure he's all in one piece. *"Estas bien?"* (Are you ok?)

He steps inside and pulls the door shut behind him. He falls to his knees with his arms stretched wide open. His kids step inside his embrace and he hugs them tightly. His wife stands over him stroking her fingers through his hair.

"I'm fine now," he says as the tears race down his face. "Right now, I am," he mumbles to himself. "I'm not sure what tomorrow has in store for me."

TRENTON

Skelter speaks after minutes of silence. "We need to ditch this car. I'm getting a funny feeling. Shit feeling type weird."

"What you mean?" T-Mack questions cluelessly.

"I don't know but my gut telling me we need to get out of this car," she says as she's reaching onto the floor at her feet. She retrieves a bag and starts to fumble through it. The first thing she pulls from the bag is Jeezy's phone. She stares at it with sadness.

Manson taught her to never bring your phone to a robbery and he had a rule that every phone and any personal belongings had to be thrown in one bag before making a move. His reason was situations like this wherein someone gets left on the scene and that could possibly result in everybody being caught. It's not until now that Skelter has ever been faced with this situation but she's glad she followed Manson's rule, even without him here.

She shuffles past Jeezy's wallet and grabs hold of her own phone. She quickly scrolls. She finds her desired contact and sends a quick text. "YO I NEED YOU ASAP." she texts in all caps.

Surprisingly, in less than 10 seconds the contact texts her right back. "What's up?" The contacts texts back.

"I need you to pick me up from our old job. I'm running late. Hurry," she texts.

Close to a minute passes and the contact texts back. "K."

Skelter looks to the driver. "Change of plans. I don't think we should go too deep into Trenton in this car. I'm sure this car hot right now. We gone ditch this motherfucker and switch cars," she says as she stares straight ahead.

"You the boss," T-Mack replies. "Just tell me where to go."

"Church," Skelter says.

T-Mack immediately busts a U-turn in the middle of the street and zips through the block. Minutes pass and the closer they get to the destination the faster Skelter's heart races. Her palms are sweating and her mouth is dry. She has her fingers crossed, hoping her contact is there waiting for them. She knows that one-second can cost you your freedom.

As T-Mack turns down Church Street all they can see in front of them is pitch darkness. "How far to go?"

"Pull to the middle of the block. I hope this motherfucker is here. If he ain't we can't wait. We got to keep it pushing. Pull over... right here," she says as she points to the right up ahead.

He parks and Skelter lifts her phone to start texting. "He said he already here." She looks around in the darkness. She quickly tucks the phone into her pocket. "Where this..." she says before she interrupts her sentence and pops up in between the front seats. Her gun aimed at T-Mack's face.

Out of fear he forces his body toward her, arms wide open, in attempt to grab her. *BOC! BOC!* Two shots to the midsection forces his body against the door. She aims the gun at his head and fires two more times. *BOC! BOC!* His upper body folds at the waist and his head bangs onto the middle console. She puts the gun to the back of his head and squeezes. *BOC!* A blood shower splashes in her face. She quickly wipes her eyes before reaching over and hitting the power lock button. She snatches the bags from her lap and forces the door open.

She runs to the driver's side of the Cherokee as the window is sliding downward. She throws the duffle-bags into the window and hands her gun inside as well. She dashes back over to the back of the van. She lifts the hatch and grabs hold of a gas can and a t-shirt.

Another one of Manson's golden rules that he's instilled in her, that she's never had to use until now. His rule was to always have a full tank when on a mission and always keep a spare gas can. The spare gas isn't necessarily for the gas tank. It's there just in case things get sticky and you need to 'deactivate,' as he called it.

She quickly empties the gas container, letting the gas leak all over the trunk space of the van. She tosses the can and the t-shirt inside. She reaches inside her pants pocket and retrieves a book of matches. One match is all she needs to strike before the entire book is on fire.

She flings the burning matchbook into the van and takes off running to the Cherokee. Before they can pull off the sound of an explosion roars loudly. Skelter looks behind where she sees the van going up in flames. "Go, go!"

19

CAMDEN/ONE HOUR LATER

THE PERIMETER OF the junkyard is taped off, one big crime scene. Detectives and local police comb the area searching for leads. News reporters from every local station are present. They've labeled it, 'The Camden Junkyard Massacre.'

Two unknown Dominicans and one unknown black man all lay slain in puddles of blood. Detectives stand over Jeezy's body, staring at him laying there with his gun still in hand. They search through his pockets looking for some trace of who he is, yet they find none. The duffle-bag filled with kilos is confirmation that it's a drug deal gone bad. They know for certain that it had to be a robbery and based on their years of experience they assume Jeezy had to be the robber.

Inside the office, detectives have the owner of the junkyard under heavy scrutiny. He was called in minutes ago and they wasted no time putting the pressure on him. With the car carrier truck barely parked, and all of the cars not even unloaded, they know the drug deal had to be intertwined within the car business. Now they are trying to figure out if he was aware that the business was all mixed together.

"I don't know those men," the man lies with a straight face. "I get shipments of cars from all around the country. My business with that company is legal business."

"But one of the men laying there dead, you do know right? He is one of your employees, correct?"

The man nods his head slowly. "Yes."

"So, do you know him to be involved in any illegal business?"

The man shrugs his shoulders, with his hands high. "I don't know. He's been working here for months and he does his job. That's what I know."

"What is his job though?" the detective asks with sarcasm.

"He's a mechanic."

Another detective walks over and intervenes. "Cameras? You have a surveillance system in place, I'm sure, right?"

The man shakes his head negatively. "No, I don't."

The detective flashes a smirk of sarcasm. "How ironic?"

TRENTON

Skelter walks along the dark and abandoned block, close to the houses, away from the streetlights. Up ahead, she spots an older model, tinted out raggedy Bonneville. She picks up her stride and in no time flat she's standing at the rear passenger's side, tapping on the window. The driver, Lil Pop is startled until he realizes it's Skelter. He leans over and forces the door open.

Skelter drops herself into the back seat, not once looking his way. "Shit got crazy back there," she sighs sadly.

"Yeah?" Lil Pop asks in suspense. He turns to face her.

"Yeah, real crazy," Skelter says. "Jeezy didn't make it out."

"He got caught?"

"Nah he got murdered," Skelter replies with sadness. She can't believe the words she's saying.

The young man's face goes blank. He turns to face forward, lowering is eyes onto his lap. Jeezy is the one that brought this man into their caper. He was only brought in to watch over the woman and the kids. He's saddened at the thought of it. Jeezy is one of the older dudes in the neighborhood that he always idolized. To be called in by Jeezy was an honor to him. All he wanted was to do his job and make Jeezy pleased with him. "Murdered though, damn."

"I know right," Skelter agrees. "I'm fucked up," she says as she cuts her eye over at him, making sure his hands are in clear view. Both hands are planted on his lap, gripping his phone. Skelter takes a quick glance of the area before sitting up and shoving her gun into his face.

His mouth stretches wide open to scream but fear prevents it. *BOC! BOC!* Two slugs spiral through his forehead, dead and center. His body jolts forward and his head bangs onto the steering wheel before ricocheting into the headrest, then banging into the driver's window. His head sinks into the glass, leaving an imprint with shattered glass around it.

Skelter coughs from the thick gunsmoke. She reaches over and grabs his phone from the floor before pushing the door open. She gets out of the car, cool and calm, adjusting her hood securely over her head. She slams the door and takes a few steps before dashing through an alleyway. She climbs a tall fence and hops over a small wooden gate before ending up on the next block where the Jeep Cherokee awaits her.

The two murders of her accomplices she just committed had nothing to do with her being slimy or disloyal. The last thing she needs right now is codefendants. With every accomplice she had in this caper, now dead, she feels somewhat relieved. There's only two people that can tell on her and she plans to fix that real soon.

CAMDEN

One block away from the junkyard there sits a tinted-out Toyota Tacoma pickup truck. Behind the dark windows two Dominican men watch the crime scene from the front seat. They watch every movement that they can see in the darkness. They're still in shock that this has happened. The man in the passenger's seat is the gunman who murdered Jeezy. He sits in the seat, still boiling with rage.

In the backseat, a third man is the surviving deliverer, who was able to get away during the robbery. He's saddened by the fact that his partner wasn't as lucky. They traveled here to New Jersey together but unfortunately, he will be traveling back alone. He counts his blessings that he will be returning home though. That is after The Big Boss has gotten to the bottom of this and figures out who could be behind all of this. Until then no one will be able to leave.

The man in the backseat stares up ahead, caught up in a trance. The flashing lights have him hypnotized. The only thing playing in his mind is the murder of his partner. He can't shake the vision from his mind.

The passenger pulls his phone out and locks in on it. On the screen is the video footage of the entire scene. The surveillance that the man being interrogated claimed he didn't have. He doesn't have it because they managed to get rid of it before the police arrived. The man watches the screen closely, hoping to find some type of clue of who the robbers were. He can't see their faces due to their masks. He can't even see their license plates. The only lead they have is a dead, John Doe.

ROCHESTER, NEW YORK

The black Chrysler Pacifica van speeds down the highway. Black on black, with dark tinted windows and bright halogen lights, the van looks more like a spaceship. Inside the van every seat is filled. Bachata music blares loud enough to burst an eardrum. Although it's upbeat party music, no one is in a party mood. All of the Dominicans have one thing on their mind and that is revenge.

In the passenger's seat is the mastermind behind the cocaine enterprise. He's known as The Big Boss a.k.a. Quabo. Hearing this name one could expect him to be some old and fat, old-school Dominican with a beer belly and a cigar dangling from his mouth. He's nothing of the sort. The Big Boss is a young, slim framed, very Americanized type who is just barely a few days over 28 years old. His thick and bushy triple black Muslim type beard would make one mistake him for an Arab instead of a Dominican. His thick and curly mohawk, tapers off on the side into a super-tight fade.

Quabo is a rather fashionable man, dressed in all designer attire. He looks to be on his way to a party instead of a war. He sits quietly in his seat, eyes locked onto his phone. He's not a man of many words but when he speaks everybody listens. One can be confused by his look and not understand the magnitude of his viciousness. Those who may have gotten him confused are no longer here and alive to set the records straight.

Quabo watches his phone without blinking. On the screen a blue dot travels slowly along. He swipes over and there's another screen with a blue dot. This blue dot is sitting still, no movement. The man notices the streets and intersection points on this particular screen and realizes this dot represents the middle of the junkyard.

He's been told that the robber is laying dead in the middle of the junkyard right next to a bag of kilos. That bag of kilos represents the blue dot. No one but Quabo and the man back in California know about the GPS tracking devices that have been planted in each of the duffle-bags. Quabo swipes to another screen and watches as the dot continues to travel across the screen.

Quabo looks over to the driver. "They've just stopped. They're in Trenton. They won't even be expecting us."

20

THE NEXT MORNING
NEWARK, NEW JERSEY-NORTHERN STATE
PRISON GANG UNIT/F-WING

IT'S FRIDAY AND the gymnasium is filled with men, young, old and every age in between. It's not packed with men on the basketball court; it's packed with Muslims. The Friday Jumu'ah service is held here in the gymnasium every Friday. Every week, inmates young and old, pious and obedient, and even sinners report here on time. The pious and obedient men who come here come to hear the word. Some of these men were tyrants on the street and prison has helped to save their lives. They are grateful for prison because it is where they have found religion. So, every week they are present faithfully, listening to the word that keeps them on the right path.

And then there are those who may not be as devout nor obedient, and the word is not what they are here for. They are here for everything except the word. There are others who are here for safety. They have become Muslim only to be protected by the Muslims and have to come here in order to keep the brotherhood on their side. As much as they may hate coming, they have to if they want the other Muslims to believe that they really are Muslim because they love the religion. They realize by being Muslim they have the entire brotherhood behind them and any attack towards them singularly, all the Muslims will have to come to their aid.

Others who are present may be the fence riders, one foot in, one foot out and their reason for being here is convenience. By being Muslim, they get more freedom and more movement during Fridays and religious holidays. Some of them only come to Jumu'ah just to converse with inmates from the other side of the prison that they can't see any other time, or to collect on gambling debts or even collect on their drug debts. With all the Muslims in the prison from every wing in one spot at the same time, it's the perfect opportunity to connect any dots that need to be connected.

Even though the gym is packed, it's nowhere near as packed as it usually is. For some reason, the presence of brothers seems to have decreased every week for the past three weeks. What should be a room filled with peace, love and brotherhood is really a room full of tension. While some inmates have their undivided attention on the brother in the front of the room giving the Khutbah, others are looking around plotting and scheming.

The slim framed, young man stands at the front of the room, dressed in full Islamic attire. The dark prayer mark on his forehead, the size of a tennis ball is the result of his countless hours of praying and asking for forgiveness. He looks over the room one last time before speaking.

"*Rabbana la tuzigh quloobana ba'da idh hadaytana wa hab lana milladunka rahmah innata antal Wahhab,*" the young man says with beautiful Arabic pronunciation. His recitation is so precise and accurate that just by sound one would believe that he was Arabic and not African American.

"Our Lord! (they say) Let not our hearts deviate now after Thou hast guided us but grant us mercy from Thine own Presence; for Thou art the Grantor of bounties without measure," he says in translation of what he just said in Arabic. "*Wa aqimas salah* (establish prayer)," he says.

The *Adhan* is recited and the brothers all line up behind the young brother. They all bow their heads as he recites Al-Kahf. He recites from memory, word for word. This may be a big deal to most but for him it's quite the ordinary for he is a Hafiz, which means one who has memorized the Quran by heart.

The young brother recites eloquently and consistently for over 15 minutes without taking a breath. His recitation warms some of the brother's hearts and spills tears from their eyes. Other brothers stand restlessly and fidgety, sighing, huffing and puffing with agitation. Their reason for agitation is the longer they stand here in prayer, the less time they will have to handle whatever business they planned to handle.

After 20 more minutes the brother finally concludes and wishes his peace amongst the room. The room transitions quickly from peaceful to energetic. The men make their way around to connect and meet and greet with each other. Huddles form and the eyes of the men change as some of them get to their sinful meetings.

The young brother places the microphone on the stand and as he goes to take his first step four men surround him. They guard his every step as if he's the President. Men line up to speak with the brother. "Brother Imaam," the first man says as he stands before the young brother with a stack of papers in his hand.

Every week it takes him an hour to get out of the room for brothers attack him in seek of his help and counseling. Some have Islamic questions, concerning what's permissible and what is not. Others have marital problems with their spouses or family issues. All in all, whatever they have on their minds, they come to this brother for help.

The young brother quickly replies to the first two men in the line and there stands the third man; an older man in his early 60's. This older brother is the actual Imaam. He's not an inmate. He comes from the outside to make sure the brothers on the inside are getting the word. The Imaam has given the young brother the opportunity to give the sermon a few times.

The look on the older brother's face is sunken. "As salaamu alaikum, brother."

"Walaikum As Salaam!" The young brother quickly returns the greeting with love and pride.

"We need to talk," the older man says. The young brother gives the signal for his men to step to the side and they move away swiftly. "Akhi, I hate to be the bearer of bad news but...." He pauses for seconds. "You do realize how empty Jumu'ah service has gotten the past few weeks since I've been giving you the podium to give the khutbah, right?"

A cheesy smirk plasters across the young brother's face. "I ain't even gone lie Shaykh. I haven't even noticed. I just been up there doing me." The young brother isn't lying. He's been so caught up in his glory that he hasn't even noticed the absence that the Imaam speaks of.

"Well, I was wondering what was going on until today I got pulled to the side by a brother and he explained to me what's been going on." The young brother's face shows impatience as the brother seems to struggle with words. "Here it is," the brother says before sighing. "Apparently some brothers have a problem with praying behind you. And they have gotten together and taken a stand."

"Praying behind me?"

"Yes, they seem to be convinced that you are a gang member and say they will not pray behind you because you are of the *fasiqun* (sinful, rebellious and disobedient)."

The young brother is taken aback and struggles for a reply. "Who are those brothers to judge me? Only Allah can judge. They don't know what's in my heart. Judge me on my Islam. Don't none of these brothers know more Islam than me," he says with his voice raising with rage. "Tell me who these brothers are. Who came to you about me? Backbiting is a sin, right Shaykh?"

"Nah brother, I gave my word to keep the brother anonymous. And it is permissible to speak on a man's reputation and not be considered backbiting, isn't it?" The man's face saddens. "I think we just need for all of this to be cleared up. For the next few weeks I will continue on with giving the khutbah myself."

His face saddens even more. "I don't know if the allegations are true or not but if by chance they are you will have to make a choice. Allah or the Blood gang? Can't be both, Akhi. You have to decide. I ask you to respect my decision on this matter when I ask you to no longer come to the Jumu'ah or any other services until you make that decision. I'm not just pinpointing you. I have a list of names that I will ask to remove themselves from the Ummah(congregation) until they get right with Allah."

"Get right with Allah?" The young brother asks with sarcasm. "Oh, you judging too?" He asks with a smile. "If y'all so sure about all of this, why don't you just give me the name of who told you this? You're going on rumors. You don't even know if it's true or not."

"I don't know if it's true or not. I'm here asking you. Are you a gang member?"

The young brother stares into the man's eyes and as quickly as he thinks of lying, he changes his mind even quicker. This young brother isn't just a member of the Blood Gang Organization, he's top ranking. His name rings from the streets of Newark and in every prison across the nation. He's legendary. On the streets he's known as Smith of the Newark Blood duo, "Smith and Wesson." They were vicious as a duo but ever since the murder of Wesson, Smith has become even more vicious alone.

On the streets Smith had no use for religion whatsoever. He really had no use for religion in jail either, but with him being so knowledgeable about Islam, he found himself helping brothers with recitation. His father Mumit, Rest in Peace, taught him to write in Arabic before he learned to write in English. The Islam his father instilled in him he had no use for, yet it's always been second nature to him. As corrupt as his heart is, his knowledge of the Deen can't be denied.

He's taught brothers to speak and write Arabic. The feeling that he gets when his students who were struggling, no longer struggle gave him a sense of purpose that he's never felt in life. For years he's never stepped foot into the masjid. He would teach his students in his cell or in private. One day, he got the urge to go to Jumu'ah service and ever since that day he hasn't missed one Friday. He became the Imaam's favorite inmate and he was kept close.

He just turned the khutbah over to him and now this. Smith, a.k.a. Mujahid (Warrior), feels like he's being stripped of his purpose in life. He would love to know who has ratted him out so he could bring torment to them.

"So, are you?" the Imaam asks. "Are you a Blood, gangbanger?"

"Aye man, y'all got it all figured out," Smith says sarcastically. "Allahu Al'm (Allah knows best)," he says as he walks away.

His security walks behind, in front, and to the sides of him. This security he has are more his soldiers to him than they are soldiers of Allah. Smith is so much of a feature attraction that these men stay on guard most of the day to stop any unwanted trouble from coming his way.

As they step through the gym, Smith's path is obstructed by a familiar face. Gunsmoke, a member of Smith's sect displays nervousness as he approaches. "Sa'Lakem Shake," he says with a nervous smile. His bottom lip trembles as he reaches to shake Smith's hand.

Smith returns the handshake but watches Gunsmoke closely, wondering what he wants. Smith rarely converses with his underlings. He understands that familiarity breeds contempt which is why he never allows his underlings to get familiar with him. He likes to keep them all walking on eggshells around him.

"What it do?" Smith asks with aggravation plastered on his face.

"I got some information for you, big bruh." Gunsmoke's eyes have a spark in them. He's sure this information will earn him brownie points.

Smith is becoming impatient. "Talk, tell me, then."

"The fuck boy Baby Manson," he says with a smile. "He just landed on C-Wing over there with me."

Smith's eyes light up brighter than Gunsmoke's eyes. In the County Jail he could never get his hands on Baby Manson. They were able to keep the two of them separated. Smith hated when he was shipped here to Northern State because he felt like his chances of getting his hands on Baby Manson were slim to none. But now to hear this news, it's like music to his ears.

"So, you said he over there on C-Wing with you right?" Smith questions.

"Indeed," Gunsmoke replies.

"You've just been given an assignment," Smith says. "Holler at him for me." Smith walks away, leaving Gunsmoke standing there. Smith stops walking and looks back. "I don't want this lingering on either. Shit already been years as it is. I want that done like asap. Like yesterday. Feel me?" Smith asks.

"Say less," Gunsmoke replies in agreement.

Smith and his soldiers exit the gym. Gunsmoke expected to earn points with Smith for the information but he didn't expect to be assigned to make a move on Baby Manson. Now he's involuntarily committed to making the hit. He's thinking maybe he should have kept his mouth shut. He didn't, so now he has a job to do. And if he doesn't do the job, he's sure he will be penalized.

As Gunsmoke walks away, wishing he kept his mouth shut, he damn near trips over the feet of the man that sits on the floor, face buried in the Quran as if he's reading. In fact, he was reading, but that didn't stop him from getting an earful of conversation. And what a valuable earful he has gotten. Now what he does with this valuable information can change the plot of those two men's story.

21

NORTH CAMDEN

QUABO PACES CIRCLES around the small coffee table while his eyes are glued onto his phone. He watches the footage of the junkyard massacre over and over and the more he watches it the more furious he becomes. Silence fills the air. The men sitting here all have their eyes on him, just waiting for his command.

All the men who are present are familiar with each other except for one. The deliverer is the only one who is a stranger. He was told he could not leave until Quabo interviewed him to be sure he wasn't in on the caper. Quabo is almost certain the man knows nothing. He's certain this had to be an inside job, but he has no clue who would put themselves in such a hazardous situation. After watching the footage over and over he thinks he may have it figured out.

Quabo looks to the deliverer who is staring at him anxiously but nervously. "You are free to go. My guy will take you to the airport and I will pay for your ticket home." Quabo stares at the man through cold eyes. "I'm sorry for the loss of your friend. Leave your phone number and I will stay in contact with you, and I will pay to have his body shipped back to California and I will also pay for his funeral. You lost a friend. I lost three million dollars. Trust me when I tell you whoever that is responsible for this will pay dearly."

TRENTON, NEW JERSEY

Skelter paces circles on the porch of the small house waiting for the door to be opened. Her impatience is evident. As soon as the creaking of the door sounds off she switches her direction and makes a strong cut into the door. She bombards her way in, almost knocking the man over.

He doesn't utter the slightest rebuttal. He just closes the door shut and follows her into the house. Skelter forces the door open and walks into the small apartment. For such a lousy neighborhood, the inside of the apartment is immaculate. Her twin sister known as Helter sits on the couch, breastfeeding her small infant. She looks up at Skelter briefly, before rolling her eyes and looking back to her baby girl. Helter doesn't even try to hide the rage and disgust that she feels for her sister right now.

Skelter doesn't show the slightest concern for her sister's attitude. She walks over with googly eyes, stuck on her niece. She strokes her finger through the baby's silky hair. "Hey, niecey poo," she says with a gentleness that not many have ever seen from her. With Helter being her only true loved one, this baby feels more like a daughter than a niece. She's the soft spot in Skelter's cold heart.

Last year, Helter traded in her gangster pass for love. For the first time ever she feels she found true love. The love of her life pulled her away from gangsterism and turned her into a housewife without the ring and a marriage license. Three months ago, she became a mother.

Skelter refers to the child's father as Bruh in Law but she hates the ground that he walks on. In her eyes he's a weak man who is so unlike the men they are used to being with. Although she hates him, one thing that can't be denied is he's a good boyfriend to Helter and a great father to his daughter. And because of that Skelter gives him a pass. She respects him for both of those reasons but still she can't respect him as a man.

"Love you niecey poo," Skelter sings in a soothing voice,

"Bullshit," Helter snaps. She strokes her daughter's cheeks. "Ask her if she loves you why would she call me out to get involved in something that could result in me not being in your life? Huh? Ask her that?" Helter looks up to Skelter with sarcasm spread across her face.

Helter is still angered by the fact that Skelter called her to come and rescue her that night. Skelter hated to call her sister but instinct led her to do so. Also time was not on her side and Helter was closer to her location than anyone else that she could have called. Helter has told Skelter on many occasions that she will no longer partake in anything that could take her away from her daughter. She knows what it feels like to grow up without a mother and she refuses to put her daughter through that. No matter how many times she tells Skelter this, she still can never leave her sister deserted in a time of need. And regardless of what her mouth says, her heart and the love and loyalty she has for her sister causes her to put it all on the line every time she's called upon.

"The fuck out of here with that shit," Skelter says with agitation. "Don't compare my love for her to me needing you to bail me out. If I didn't need you, I wouldn't have called you. All my life, if you ever needed me I was there regardless of what."

Helter looks up with anger. "And I been there every time you needed me too!"

"I didn't say you didn't!" Skelter replies.

"I'm just saying stop being so selfish. You know what I'm trying to do over here. I'm just trying to be here for my baby, that's all."

"Well, be there for the baby then. I'm sorry I needed you that night, but I won't ever call on you for shit again. Know that!" Skelter knows her sister is dead right and it hurts her to even think that she put her sister in a situation that could jeopardize her motherhood but her stubbornness will never allow her to admit it.

Helter can read her twin sister like a book. She stares into her eyes. "And the crazy part is, you know I'm right, just won't admit it. Admit I'm right."

Skelter looks away from her. "Whatever!" She looks to Bruh in Law who stands in the cut watching them both. Watching and listening to them spat is nothing new to him. It's amazing to him how two people who love each other so much can argue all day long about every single thing. Two people that look exactly alike, talk alike and for the most part think alike, but can't agree on anything.

Skelter gives Bruh in Law a head-nod. "Let me holler at you for a minute," she says as she starts walking out of the room. She leads the way as if it's her very own home. He follows behind her like an obedient puppy. He steps in the room where she awaits him. He stares at her closely in fear of her as she pulls the Gucci fanny pack from over her shoulder. He watches closely as she unzips it, wondering what's inside.

"Check this out," she says as she hands him over a block covered in layers of masking tape. He's familiar with what's inside as soon as he sees it. "Open it up and check it out," she commands. "Beautiful, you hear me?"

The man hesitantly does as she instructs. He grabs a pair of scissors from the dresser and carefully cuts open a corner of the tape. As soon as the tape and plastic sealing is slit open the pungent smell of raw cocaine seeps into the air. He pinches away a small rock and rubs it in between his fingertips. The cocaine disappears in seconds, leaving his fingers shiny and oily. He studies the snow white hard exterior and shiny, scaly interior.

"Damn, I haven't seen it like this in years," he says in awe. "Everything out here on these streets now is stepped on crazy. Paying sky high for garbage, but that's all that's out there."

"Not no more," Skelter claims.

He can't pry his eyes away from the cocaine. "Damn, this that back in the day coke."

"That's what everybody saying," Skelter says." She nods her head up and down with cockiness. "And it's a lot more where that came from. I'm coming to you first because you like family. I have to look out for you like family because you look out for my family." He swallows a huge gulp of fear. Not only is he afraid of her, he's also afraid to deal with her. He doesn't trust her the least bit. He knows how slick, vicious and conniving Skelter is and he never wants part of anything that she has going on.

As much as he hates to deal with her, she has piqued his interest. He can't let work of this quality get past him. He wonders where she got this from. He's sure she's robbed somebody for it and he's afraid that if he buys it from her he may get caught up in any revenge that is to come her way. Still he has to ask. "How much a gram?"

"Fuck that gram shit, Bruh in Law! I got enough of these shits to build a small house with brick by brick. No more thinking in grams. Think big you get big."

Bruh in Law is a small-time hustler but he does well for himself. In a hood full of petty hustlers who are barely getting by, it's not hard to shine like a diamond. He's a real low-key man who makes his little money and knows how to save it. Because of that he makes a little look like a lot. He keeps himself laced in designer clothes and always drives up to date cars and that makes people think he's a bigger deal than he really is.

Embarrassment covers his face. "I ain't really in position to buy the whole thing right now though."

Skelter is shocked at his words. "What position you in then?" She's trying to get a gauge on how he's moving. Really, she has other plans for him but now he has her curious.

"I just be grabbing what I need and hitting my fiends that be hitting my phone," he admits with no shame. "I be off my phone."

"Ok, well you can just hit me with the paper now that you be grabbing with and hit me with the rest when you finish."

He feels like he's being boxed in right now. "Nah, I don't really like to rock under the type of pressure of owing people. That ain't really how I move. I buy a hundred grams and it's mine so if it take me three weeks to move it, it's cool because I paid for it with my own money, feel me?"

"Actually...no," she replies. "I can't believe you actually out here thinking on such a small level."

He isn't bothered by the attack at all. He's sure that he could move on a higher level if he chose to do so. He's had plenty of opportunities to have work given to him on consignment and he's denied them all. He likes to stay within his little box, his level of comfort. Part of the reason for that is he knows moving up the ladder can bring him unwanted attention. He knows if he shines too brightly the wolves and vultures will be coming for him. He fears that pressure and believes staying low will keep him underneath the wolves' radar.

"This is just where I like to be. How I like to operate. I ain't really trying to be no kingpin status nigga. I'm just trying to feed my family, your sister and your niece," he says in attempt to tap into her soft spot.

"Well, you can do that with a 9 to 5. Ain't no need in playing around in these streets if that's all you want." He has no defense for her so he just stands in silence. "So, dig what I'm gone do. I know your phone be jumping so I'm gone throw this one at you on consignment. Give me back thirty-four stacks."

His eyes bulge out of his head and he's looking for another excuse but she doesn't give him time to make one. This is six dollars a gram less than he pays with his plug now. That's an extra six hundred dollars off every hundred grams he sells, which equals out to six grand on a kilo. Getting through a few of these can get him ahead of the game.

"I'm sure you got some people you know that be moving shit so what I'm gone do is throw like four more at you to hit them. You can sell it to them at like thirty-eight, thirty-nine a brick and score four or five grand in between."

He quickly calculates in his mind. In this one move she speaks of, he will be ahead close to thirty grand extra. That is on top of his normal movements. All of this is sounding like a promising situation to him but he's not ready to jump out there like that. He isn't ready for all that comes with it. "I don't know nobody that be buying whole joints. I got a couple little fiends that be hitting my phone and that keeps me alive," he says with fear in his eyes. He prays that she accepts this as an answer.

"Think outside the box. Stop thinking small. Think hard, I know you can think of some people you can sell weight to. Get out your comfort zone and get to work. I will be back later on tonight with the other four pieces."

"But," he says as he looks for another excuse.

"No buts. I will be back. By the time I get back I'm sure you will be done thought of some people you can holler at. Later on," she says as she walks away.

He can't believe that he's been forced into a situation like this. If only he could just tell her no but he fears the repercussions of doing so.

Skelter stops at the door. She turns around to face him. "We are on our way to the next level. I'm gone show you how to get some real money. Get ready." She makes her exit.

"But I don't want to go to the next level," he mumbles under his breath. He slaps his palm across his forehead, staring into the sky. "What the fuck did I just get myself into?" He realizes that he just got into bed with Satan.

22

HOURS LATER
9TH STREET/CAMDEN

MERENGUE MUSIC PLAYS loud enough to shatter every window in the small Bodega. The Pork aroma in the air is so pungent that it smells as if a whole farm of pigs are being cooked at once. In the front of the store normal business is taking place. A young girl is behind the counter servicing customers, while a man is at the back, cooking on a grill. Standing at the door like a guard dog is an older man. He has the perfect view to make sure the customers are not stealing from them. His eyes soar up and down the aisles and bounce onto the overhead mirrors that are positioned to get an all-around view of the entire store.

In the back of the store, 20 men are crammed in the tiny space like sardines. Quabo stands in a corner, away from everybody else. His eyes are glued to his phone screen just as it has been for the last couple days. He must have watched the footage of the robbery a thousand times already. He's studied it long and hard as if he's going to be tested on it.

In the center of the room is Quabo's Homeland Security, as he calls it. This man is the reason that no one even thinks of playing with

Quabo. He's an old and militant Dominican who loves war. His specialty is torture which is why he has earned the name *Tortura* which means Torture in Spanish.

Tortura, a short brolic, broad shouldered man speaks in Spanish in a loud and aggressive tone as he unzips the huge duffle bag. Dressed in a cheap grey sweatsuit, no pockets, and a thick and fuzzy skullcap, he looks like a lifer on a prison yard. He passes guns around the room like free cheese. Every man gets a gun. Some get 2 and a few of them get 3.

Tortura's whole army is a bunch of old killers. Most of them Tortura imported straight from the Dominican Republic. None of them speak a word of English. The only English word they can understand is 'Kill.' He promised them a better life here in the States and thanks to Quabo he has kept his word.

Once every gun is passed out he reaches inside the bag and grabs hold of a bulletproof vest. He immediately straps the vest over his tight fitted t-shirt. As he looks around the room at his army his right eye doesn't move. Well, his glass eye that is. Many years ago, he lost his eye in a shootout. A .45 slug to the eyeball shattered his eye socket into pieces. Now the whole side of his face is hard as stone and his mouth is permanently twisted. All in all, he looks like the monster that he really is.

Tortura stuffs a .357 revolver down the back of his waist band. He then sticks a 9-millimeter down the front of his waistband. Finally he bends over and pulls up his pants leg. He grabs a small .22 automatic from the table and places it in the holster that's wrapped around his shin. He looks to Quabo and then his army. "Vamonos! (Let's go!)"

Tortura leads the way out of the back entrance of the store and his army follows behind him. In the alley waiting for them are five tinted out vehicles lined up. Tortura and four of his closest men get into the Chrysler Pacifica. Tortura seats himself in the passenger's seat while the driver sits down and straps his seatbelt on. Two men hop into the back seat and Quabo gets in and sits in the middle row alone.

Tortura immediately starts yelling to Quabo very angrily. "*Te dije que no necesitamos que te vayas! Podemos manejar esto sin ti! Tu' eres el jefe. Por que' te involucrarias en el trabajo sucio? Tu trabajo es hacer dinero! Mi trabajo es deshacerme de cualquiera que se interponga en tu camino para ganar dinero!* (I told you we don't need you to go! We can handle this without you! You're the boss! Why would you involve yourself in dirty work? Your job is to make money! My job is to get rid of anyone who gets in the way of you making money!)"

Quabo ignores the man's speech, not once even thinking of entertaining the thought of staying behind. His eyes are locked onto the blue dot on his phone screen. The blue dot hasn't traveled in a day now which means the duffle-bag has been sitting somewhere. Quabo looks up to the driver. "Kirkbride Street, Trenton New Jersey," he yells to Quabo.

The driver presses the address into the navigation system and he quickly pulls out of the alley. All the vehicles follow each other almost bumper to bumper.

Tortura rubs his hands together like a mad scientist. *"Hora de ir a trabajar!* (Time to go to work!)"

NEWARK

Bergen Street is blanketed by darkness. Abandoned houses and vacant houses that are barely standing occupy the block from Clinton Avenue to Springfield Avenue. Not a person walking and not a car on the block except for the black Mercedes SLS 63 AMG roadster that zips through the darkness like a guided missile, exceeding well over 80 miles an hour. Triple black paint and blackened windows, with a red convertible top, the car looks like the Grim reaper with a red bandana tied around his head.

A strong left, all gas leads the automobile up Rose Street, alongside of Roseville Cemetery. The car is stopped short at the middle of the block. After minutes of sitting idle, the driver's side door ascends into the air, opening like a scissor arm. The driver, Attorney Tony Austin glides out of the driver's seat rather smoothly. The bloody red interior seems to ooze out of the car with him.

Tony looks around into the creepy darkness before dialing numbers on his phone. The old cemetery has been deserted for decades and it shows. The old and rusted gate surrounding the cemetery is barely standing. In some places it's strong and in others, it's laying on the ground as result of cars knocking it over. Fallen trees lay dead on the ground just as the bodies that lay underneath the ground. Garbage bags with God knows what inside lay scattered around. Old sinks, stoves and refrigerators and car parts are lying around, making it look more like a junkyard than a cemetery.

The hairs stand up on the back of Tony's neck as he listens to the phone ring. The receiver picks up before the fourth ring. "Yes?"

"I'm here," Tony says into the phone. "Where are you?"

"I'm here as well. I see you. Turn to your right."

Tony does as instructed and still no sign of who he's looking for. "I still don't see you," he says with agitation.

"Walk straight ahead," the caller commands.

Tony looks around nervously. "Straight ahead, where?"

"In the cemetery," she says. "Come inside."

"Oh, hell no," Tony says with a nervous chuckle. "You come out." Tony is starting to feel foolish about this whole ordeal. He wonders how he even took this nut job serious. "You know what? I'm out. I ain't got time for this," Tony says before hanging up the phone. He turns around, preparing to get into his car. His phone vibrates in his hand as his door is raising open. He drops himself into his seat. The phone vibrates non-stop, agitating Tony more. "What, what?"

"The biggest case of your career and you're going to let fear of a cemetery cause you to blow it? You shouldn't fear the dead. You should fear the living."

"I don't fear anything. I just don't have time for bullshit."

"Come inside then. I told you my situation. I've already taken a major risk by even walking into your office and opening up to you. I feel that warrants you to trust me. I will meet you halfway. Here I come."

Tony's attention is snatched by a bright light in the middle of the pitch-black cemetery. As the light gets closer Tony can make out the face of Jane Doe's disguise. She's carrying a single hanging light. His heart races with a fear he hasn't felt in years. He thinks of the scary movies he's seen. He thinks of the fact that Jane Doe could be some psycho, serial killer.

He's just about ready to pull off until his curiosity keeps him still. What if all she told him is true? This really would be the biggest case he's ever had. All his life he's prided himself on being a risk taker. He can't stop now. Tony mutes the phone. He leans closer to the stereo and whispers. "Peace, my Queen."

"Peace King," the smart assistant's voice whispers back. "How may I serve you tonight?"

"Open Humidor," Tony whispers.

"Humidor opening, King," she says as the dashboard begins to slide outward.

Tony leans over and quickly lifts his cigar humidor. Laying in its own special case is a beautiful chrome snub nose Sig Sauer P226, equipped with infrared beam which is perfect for a night like this. Tony grips the gun and tucks it into his jacket pocket. "Close humidor."

"Humidor closing. My King, may I ask, what are you up to tonight? Is everything ok?"

"Yes, my Queen all is well. Thanks for asking."

"My King, be safe. And be sure to use your head. Think smart," the smart assistant says.

Tony smiles with satisfaction. It amazes him how she converses with him as if she's a caring human. Sometimes he forgets she isn't a human and is a mere system that he's programmed. "I will, my Queen, always."

He quickly peeks to his right where Jane Doe stands looking quite spooky in the darkness. He gets out of the car, slams his door shut and stands for seconds, debating if he should carry on with this. Jane Doe waves him on. Tony takes a deep breath before taking his first step. With each step he grips the gun tighter.

As he steps over the broken gate onto the soil of the cemetery a creepy sensation shoots through his body. He's never had a real fear of cemeteries but then again he's never been walking in one at night either. The leaves crunch loudly under his shoes. An owl whooing causes Tony's ears to twitch with nervousness.

Tony finally reaches Jane Doe who turns around without saying a word. She leads the way as Tony follows many steps behind her. In his pocket, the gun is aimed at her back, just in case. For a second he entertains the thought of how stupid this would sound written up in news articles. He's sure the writers would have a ball writing this article on him. *Attorney Kills Mentally Ill Woman in Cemetery.* People would think he's mentally ill for just being here. What would he tell the people was his reasoning for being in the cemetery at night anyway?

As Tony is walking he stares at the ground where a few tombstones can still be seen underneath fallen branches and debris. The most of them are fully covered by dirt or garbage. One tombstone in particular catches his attention. The headstone reads "Adalard Schmidt, 1798-1881. Tony stares at the headstone in awe.

Jane Doe notices that she no longer hears his footsteps behind her and turns around. "The exact same thing I thought," she says.

Tony watches her closely as she steps closer to him. "A German buried in the middle of Newark. This cemetery seems to be filled with tens of thousands of Germans. I've done research and was amazed that so many from Greece, Ireland and Italy and some of Eastern Europe are buried in here. The black section of this cemetery was way back there in the corner, a little bitty section. It wasn't until the late 60's that Blacks were buried amongst the rest of the people."

Tony listens with close attention and is amazed by the history lesson she's giving him. "Over the years the cemetery has been filled with more blacks than any other race. You'd be amazed at how many War Vets," Jane Doe says as she taps the brim of the Veteran's Hat she's wearing. "That are buried in here. Some are from the War of 1812 through the Vietnam War. Hundreds of them." Tony stares at the hat, wondering if maybe she took the hat from a dead veteran. He becomes even more baffled about this ordeal.

"It's a shame how they've left this place in such a mess. Whole graveyard full with not an empty spot for a single burial. No money left to be made so the family has left the place to rot. A certain amount of money is given a year for the upkeep but they take the money and run and leave the bodies here, not even able to rest in peace," she says as she shakes her head sadly.

"Enough about them already," she says. "They're dead and gone. We need to get on with our business." She turns around and leads the way. Tony follows her hesitantly. "After this case I have for you, when we are laying in our graves, we will be legendary. "Will be legendary?" Tony asks with sarcasm. "Speak for yourself."

"That's no attack against you, Mr. High Power Attorney. I know you've already made your mark. But what I have for you will impact the world."

She makes a right turn up a narrow path. This area must be the darkest area of the entire cemetery because Tony can't even see in front of him. He can see the butt of the chrome handgun peeking out of his pocket though.

Jane Doe stops short in front of a beautifully structured Mausoleum. She looks back at him as she grabs the doorknob. Tony's heart skips a beat as she steps inside. "Come in," she says as she stands at the entrance.

"Oh, hell no," Tony says in a high-pitched voice. "This whole shit is weird but I was giving you a chance but you've gone too far now." Tony turns away.

"Trust me, you are walking away from the game changer," Jane Doe says with great confidence. "All I need is twenty minutes of your time to prove to you." Tony peeks inside and is shocked to see a dimly lit lamp in the corner, with a small coffee table with papers stacked high on it. "Come on in," Jane Doe says very inviting.

Tony is not sure if curiosity or pure stupidity leads him inside but he finds himself stepping inside. Jane Doe closes the door behind him. The screeching of the door ends with a hollow echo once the door slams. Not surprising at all, the smell of death is in the air. Tony looks around in amazement at the setup. The small 400 square Mausoleum is set up like a studio apartment. The small generator in the corner sends electricity through the spot. A comfortable looking cot, a doll house type dresser, a full body mirror and even a small wardrobe, makes it look more like a neat and tidy apartment than a house for the dead.

Jane Doe pulls off her mask. "Have a seat," she says as she extends her hand toward the recliner that sits against the wall. Tony sits down, still in awe. "What the fuck is this?"

Jane Doe smiles and chuckles. "It's my home. It's obvious that I trust you. I have told you my story. I have even brought you to my place of residence." She points up to the wall where two vaults are. Across the first vault is the name Paul Warnes. "My husband," she says as she points to the solid gold name tag. "And of course, that's me in there," she says quite normally. "Well, if I was actually dead that is where I would be," she says with a big smile.

"So, wait, this is where you and your husband will be buried?" Tony asks.

"Oh, no, my husband is already in the vault, dead as a doorknob" she says with a weird sense of humor. "He's been there for almost a decade."

"So, who is laying there in your spot?" Tony asks.

"Ask me no question and I will tell you no lies," she says with a smile. "We will talk about all of this in due time. For now, let's get on with our business."

Tony stares closely at Jane Doe and notices without the surgical mask, oxygen tank and her disguise he can actually see her and she appears to be a normal middle-class, mature woman. She's dressed casual yet still classy. Tony pays attention to the small details and all her pieces are lined up, from her costume jewelry, to her Anne Klein attire. She looks like a beautiful older model from a Better Homes and Gardens magazine.

"Google," she whispers while looking upward at the ceiling. "Turn the air purifier on," she says as points toward the ceiling purely out of habit. As her hand flings into the air Tony's attention is snatched by her wristwatch. The overhead vents open up and the sound of the air being sucked into them can be heard faintly. Seconds later roaring sounds off from in the vents before the air is forced back out of them. "The only air that I trust," she says with a smile.

Tony reciprocates the smile but still can't remove his eyes from her watch. "The Van Cleef and Arpels, 1990 edition," he says with a smile.

"Huh?" she asks without a clue of what he's talking about.

He points at the 18-karat gold watch. The bezel and crown is covered in diamonds but not unnecessarily gaudy. The gold staggered link bracelet tones it down perfectly. "Your timepiece," he says. "Great choice."

Jane Doe smiles bashfully. "This old thing is a gift from my late husband. There's a story behind it," she says with disgust.

"I would love to hear it."

"No, let's just say, he couldn't keep his dick in his pants," she says with no filter at all. "And every time I caught him cheating his answer was buying expensive watches to ease my pain."

"What an expensive price to pay," Tony says, knowing the value of the watch is well over $30,000.

"Yeah but the watches only satisfied him, never eased my pain. I have a collection of over two dozen watches, and that's just the times I caught him cheating. Imagine the times I didn't." She dazes off in memory of her husband. "Great man, but like I said, just couldn't keep his dick in his pants." She shakes the memory away. "I still loved him the same and I miss him dearly. He's been in there for 15 years now."

"Sorry to hear that."

"No need, it's life…it happens."

"But that collection of yours, I would love to see it," he says with enthusiasm.

"A watch connoisseur huh?" she asks as she gets up. "And I bet you thought I didn't know that too, right. I told you, I know every detail about you," she says as she walks away toward the dresser. "I've researched you thoroughly as I told you."

In minutes she returns holding a velvet case. Tony's heart pumps vigorously as she lays it onto the coffee table and flips the lid open. He sits there like a kid in a candy store as his eyes feast on one of the most classical timepiece collections he's ever seen outside of his own. "Wow," he sighs. "Can I?" he asks, while fighting back the urge.

"Sure, it's only watches," she says with no real interest in them.

Tony picks them up one by one and is familiar with every one of them. The value of the watches range from 5 grand to 125 grand. He has her collection worth well over a million dollars.

"Your husband had to be a very classy man." Tony is captivated by the collection. "I would love to hear the story behind this one," he says as he digs underneath and finds one that was buried at the bottom. He holds the two-hundred-thousand dollar, Greubel Forsey with gentleness like he's holding a newborn baby, fresh out of the womb. "This must have been more than cheating," he says with a smile. "Must have been a full-blown affair."

She chuckles at his remark. "Let's just say, he has children in Greece, a second family." Tony lays the watch down gently. Jane Doe slides the case away from him and closes the lid. "Enough of this. Let's get down to business. You're here so I assume you're onboard," she says awaiting his reply.

Tony stares her square in the eyes. After seeing her in this form makes her story a little more believable to him. Her collection of rare watches has definitely sealed the deal for him. Maybe she is the real deal and no nut job, he thinks to himself as he takes a seat in the plush recliner.

"So, let me ask you, what's this all about? You said you faked your own death. You have the death certificate to prove it so I'm sure you have all new paperwork and ID, correct?"

"Correct."

"So, what is this about? You can go on and live the rest of your life with no problems. Your ties with them are over."

"This isn't about me," she claims. "This is about you and your people. This case will make you bigger than life. You are the perfect person to reveal the government and their bullshit. You will be the hero."

"And what's in it for you?"

"It will mean the world to me to see them exposed. All the years of being a part of their bullshit ate me alive. Killing innocent people. I knew so it made me just as filthy as them. This is my way of cleaning my slate. In those laboratories we created death. Diseases that were created by the Government. Sexually transmitted diseases as well as diseases such as Autism. All spread through vaccination."

"But why though?" Tony asks curiously.

"Genocide and population control. Also, medicine is the biggest business in America. A kid is diagnosed with Autism and for the rest of their life they are prescribed medicine. Ever notice that six out of ten kids are diagnosed with ADHD? All bullshit. Just another way to hook them onto drugs and make money off of them. And I'm sure you know where most of these diagnosis are being made? Yep, in the urban areas."

"Wow," Tony mumbles to himself. He's always thought this but to hear that what he thought is really true is mind-blowing to him.

"How about the rapid growth of ADHD?" Jane Doe asks. "How about this? A small child sits in front of the television watching his favorite show. Two minutes of their show, and then it's followed by three minutes of commercial advertisements. This is how it goes every show, every day, all day. Their minds are programmed and trained this way.

So, now they go to school and the teacher wonders why she can only hold their attention for two minutes before they get restless and start jumping off the walls. The child is sent to the doctor for the behavioral issue and the doctor diagnoses the child with ADHD and prescribes medicine. There's no issue at all. His mind was just programmed for a short attention span. It's all part of the big plan to hook the world on medicine."

Tony looks at Jane Doe in awe. His wheels are turning. Jane Doe can sense that his fire has been lit but she feels she it's only fair to warn him once again. The last thing she wants is to drag him into this and he not know what the future may bring.

"As I warned you the other day," she says sternly. "You pull this off and you are the hero. If we don't pull it off, I don't know what my end result will be but your career could be ended. The Federal Government will fuck you around for the rest of your career. That I know. With that in mind, I will totally understand if you reject my offer."

"How can I reject an offer that you have yet made?" Tony asks.

"I think by now; you realize that me and you both speak and understand the same language." She rubs her fingertips together, symbolizing money. "You name your price and whatever it is I will come up with the money," she says with sincerity in her eyes. "Money is nothing to me. My husband made sure that I would be more than taken care of for the rest of my life. Can't take the money with us when we die and, technically I'm dead," she says with a sparkling smile. "So, I don't have much use for it. May as well spend it on the right cause. And I've found that right cause, so name your price."

23

THE TINY ROOM has fresh paint on the walls, yet the oldness of the walls and framing still peeks through. An old and outdated dresser drawer, a futon bed, two air mattresses, a small refrigerator, a tray for food, a microwave, a rolling wardrobe and a loveseat combines the kitchen, the dining room, and the bedroom all in less than one hundred square feet. Three young men all crammed up in one room.

The most luxurious asset in the room is the 72-inch television that is hanging from the wall. Three separate sneaker collections are spread out in three corners of the room. The collection consists of everything from Jordans that value $800 to Yeezys that value $1700, to Christian Louboutin, Gucci and even Hermes. In total, over $100,000 worth of sneakers packed into a room inside of a rooming house that costs $100 a week to rent. In the room is Skelter and three of her soldiers. This may be considered uncomfortable living circumstances to most but to these young men, it's home.

"I can't take that smell," Skelter says with disgust. "I don't know how y'all put up with it."

"What smell?" says the Middle Child, as Skelter refers to him.

"You don't smell coke being cooked up? The smell of it being smoked in a pipe?"

"Nah," they all reply in unison; two by actually speaking and one by shaking his head no.

"Shit, I feel like I'm getting high just being in here. Y'all nose must be fucked up."

These young men have gotten used to the smell. The aroma of burning cocaine is in the air all day and all night because 10 of the 12 rooms inside the rooming house are being rented by crackheads

"Nah, shit, I guess we must have gotten used to it," the man says in his defense. "We like the only motherfuckers in here that don't get high. The rest of these motherfuckers in here are fiends.

What he says is all a matter of opinion; the opinion of the younger generation that is. For some reason him and so many others of the younger generation believe that a fiend is one who is addicted to cocaine or dope only. Shockingly, their addiction to pills and syrup doesn't make them classify themselves as fiends though.

"Stop playing that game for a minute. That's all the fuck y'all think about anyway," Skelter says. She hates that they waste so much time playing video games. Sometimes she forgets that they are still kids in a sense and that is what normal kids do.

The three of them are barely legal. They sit around like most 18 and 19-year olds playing Grand Theft Auto all day. Only difference is, to most young men their age, it's just a game, an escape from reality. For them it's like art imitating life. It's like target practice for them.

On the game, they commit senseless murders, shooting and killing for the fun of it just as they do in real life. They rob and carjack and stack their money doing so. On the game they have millions of game dollars stacked in their accounts but in real life they are penniless. And that's the reason they spend most of their time in video game land, away from their reality.

One of the most serious effects of their game playing is the desensitizing that has resulted from all the years of them shooting and killing executioner style. Death to them in real life means nothing to them just as it does on their video games. This is one of the reasons they are so valuable to Skelter. She's practically raised them. They've been under her wing since they were going through puberty.

Growing up with drug addicted parents, they had no guidance, nor the bare necessities of life. She raised them like they were her own children even though she's not even 10 years older than them. She's the cross between their mother and their big sister. She and everybody else in Trenton refers to them as her Godsons. It's as if they don't even have names. Skelter refers to them as her First Born, her Middle Child and her Baby Boy which is the youngest. The streets of Trenton have given them other names though. Together they are known as The Godsons.

When they were young she was the first one to take them skating and bowling and bought birthday cakes and gifts for them when no one else did. When they were in school she bought school clothes. Most of her life she had not much more than them but still she made sure to give them whatever she can. For that reason they will and have killed for her with no questions asked.

It wasn't her plan to do all she did for them to use them as killers later. It's just the way the ball bounced and them being products of their environment that turned them into the vicious monsters that they are. Even with them being vicious Skelter never uses them the way she really could. Instead she protects them like her very own children.

MEANWHILE

The Chrysler Pacifica bends the corner onto the quiet block. An old work van turns right behind it, and an old Chevy Suburban right behind that. Quabo looks up ahead and spots a Cherokee and an Explorer turning the corner at the opposite end of the block. All of the vehicles cruise the block slowly, coming toward each other.

Quabo studies his phone, eyes locked onto the blue dot on the screen. As he looks at the red dot representing the vehicle he's in and sees the distance between the red and blue dot getting closer and closer, he becomes more and more anxious. He can't believe he's actually this close.

"Pull over right…here," Quabo says. "Park." The blue dot and the red dot are so close they are almost connected. As the driver is parking Quabo looks up at the raggedy looking row home. He wonders who and what can be behind that door.

The men all start adjusting their weapons and preparing to go inside and reclaim the treasure as well as make the culprits pay for their actions. As Quabo looks around at his army he has full confidence that they are prepared for whatever is behind that door.

"Let's go!" Quabo commands.

Tortura is the first to get out and everybody else follows. In seconds all of the men are following Tortura to the house that sits right where the blue dot is. As Quabo is walking toward the house, he notices three of his men, that were dropped off around the corner. They walked in from the back block, jumping over a couple of fences but now they are already on point in the backyard. They stand there, fully prepared just in case the culprits try to make an escape out of the back door.

• • •

The young men gather around Skelter as she digs into her bag. Like children who are about to get a surprise gift, they watch her with suspense in their eyes. Skelter digs into her bag and pulls one kilo and sets it onto the table. Their eyes widen with amazement. She pulls a pocket-knife from her pocket and slits the tape that's covering the kilo. As she unravels the tape, the bright and beautiful snow-white cocaine peeks from within the plastic.

"Shit been tight for us the past few years but through it all y'all remained loyal. I'm sure y'all had plenty of opportunities to ride with the other side and leave me abandoned," she says, never once looking up at them. Once the kilo is fully exposed and laying there naked on the plastic, Skelter digs into her bag again. She retrieves a handheld digital scale and lays it on the table. She breaks the kilo in what she estimates to be a third and lays the square block onto the scale. She quickly grabs a few crumbs from the plastic and piles them on the scale. She pulls a sandwich bag from her bag and dumps the cocaine from the scale into the bag.

"We sat around starving while the whole city took turns eating around us. We were patient," she says as she breaks a square corner off the block of cocaine. She lays it on the scale and pinches away at it a few times putting the crumbs to the side. "We didn't cross each other."

She splits the last of the cocaine evenly and packs the equal amounts into plastic sandwich bags.

Knock, knock, knock!

The light tapping on the door startles them all. Skelter quickly shuffles the bags of cocaine and the scale in a pile. Their hearts are racing with nervousness.

Knock, knock, knock!

They all stand still, frozen stiff, not wanting to make any noise. The persistence of the person on the other side of the door worries them.

Knock, knock, knock!

Skelter looks to her Middle Child with a look of agitation, she mumbles. "What the fuck?"

He tiptoes to the door as Skelter is dumping the bags of cocaine into her bag. The man stands at the door nervously. "Who?"

"Miss Jenny," the voice says from the other side of the door.

"Not right now, Miss Jenny. Give me a minute. I will come down to your room in a little while."

"No, just give me a second. It's really important."

He looks to Skelter and with his eyes he signals that he will open the door. He slowly parts the door, just enough to see Miss Jenny's face. The old senior citizen granny stands at the door, old, ran down and shriveled up. "What's up Miss Jenny?" Even with the woman being a crackhead he still shows her the highest level of respect.

Miss Jenny leans in closer to the door. "I got my hands on four Oxycodones for you. Twenty milligrams," she adds. "Just give me twenty dollars." Miss Jenny has his full attention. He's forgotten that he's in the middle of business. Right now the only thing on his mind is the cure for his addiction.

"Yo!" Skelter shouts with rage.

The young man ignores Skelter as he fumbles in his pocket. He retrieves a few bills and quickly hands the woman a twenty-dollar bill. She drops the pills in his hand. Before she can walk away, he slams the door shut. She takes off in search of her drug of choice. Old addicts selling one drug to get the drug of their choice and young addicts doing the same.

Skelter looks to the young man with disgust. "That shit mean more to you than this huh?"

The young man shakes the pills in his hand like rolling dice. "Nah, not at all," he claims, not even believing himself.

Skelter pulls the sandwich bags of cocaine out of her bag and piles them on the table. "As I was saying before I was rudely interrupted." She looks to the young man and rolls her eyes. "We stayed loyal to each other. We didn't go out there begging motherfuckers. We just tightened our belts and stayed patient." She slides 336 grams in front of each of them. "But now our patience has paid off. That's three hundred and thirty-six grams for each one of y'all," she says proudly.

The young men can't believe their eyes or their ears right now. They have never seen this much cocaine in their life, let alone had this much of their own. Neither of them have ever had more than an ounce, so to have 12 ounces is like a dream come true to them. In their minds they feel like they have made it to the big league.

"How much we have to bring you back off this?" Skelter's First Born asks. He's the businessman of them all.

"Nothing," she replies. Do y'all. It's yours. Fuck it up if you want. One thing though. If you fuck it up, I ain't got nothing else for you. If you do the right thing and flip your money and stack it, it's plenty more where this came from. When it's time for you to re-up I will sell it to y'all for thirty-six dollars a gram."

Deep in her heart she believes they all will end up messing it all up. One or two of them have a little hustler in their blood but she feels it's only fair to treat them all equally. One thing she believes is that every man deserves a chance to prove his worth. She remembers times when she was flat on her back and couldn't find a helping hand anywhere. All she needed was a chance and she couldn't get that chance from anywhere. Today she's giving each of them their chance to prove their worth.

A smile spreads across Skelter's face. She's happy to finally be in a position to help those that she cares for. She looks into their faces one by one. "They all ate around us and didn't make a plate for us or even break off crumbs from their plate. It's our turn."

• • •

ACROSS TOWN

The Dominicans stand in the alley, surrounding a dumpster. They are enraged. The GPS led them right to the bags. Too bad the bags were empty. Apparently someone emptied the contents of the bags and threw the empty bags into this dumpster. So close but yet so far.

Quabo looks up at the raggedy building. He then looks to Tortura. "Let's get out of here before we draw attention to ourselves."

"I say we knock on every door until we find who we are looking for," Tortura suggests.

"Nah, not a smart idea," Quabo replies. He came here believing he could possibly retrieve some of the product. Now those hopes are shattered. This thing isn't about the money anymore. It's personal. "At least we now have a starting point. Even if the person isn't in this building, they have been to this building. We will sit on them and sooner than later they will fall onto our laps. I'm a patient man. I got all the time in the world."

24

AS PEBBLES'S (MANSON'S son's mother) phone rings she squints, straining her weak eyes to see the display. Her eyes squinted any tighter they will be closed shut. Blind as a bat yet she still refuses to wear eyeglasses, thinking they will taint her appeal. So overly confident, yet so insecure.

The words Unknown Caller causes her heart to race. She assumes this is a jail call from her son, Rahmid(Baby Manson). As happy as she always is to hear from him, she's always worried. Sometimes she feels jail is the safest place for him. The few months that he was home running the streets, every night she feared she would get the phone call that he was dead. She realizes jail isn't much safer but she feels it's less trouble for him to get in inside than on the outside.

She quickly accepts the collect call. "Hello, baby," she says happily and full of life.

"Hello," says the voice on the other end. "Hello?" he says again in a baffled state.

Pebbles recognizes the voice on the other end. She sighs while mumbling under her breath. Her attitude changes. "Yeah, what's up?"

"Hey baby," the man says with sarcasm. "Expecting somebody else huh? Shit, I thought you was happy to hear from me. Guess you got yourself a new baby, huh?"

"Shakir, please don't start with your shit. I thought you was Rah-Rah."

"It don't matter but dig this," he says with a burst of life in his voice. "You know I never like to be the one to get you all worked up and worried and shit but I got some real shit to tell you. Life or death shit, dig me?"

"Yeah, yeah, what's up?" Pebbles asks impatiently.

"When your son call you tell him to keep his eyes open. I think something in the midst of coming his way."

"Something like what?" Pebbles asks nervously.

"Listen, I don't know all the details and all the players involved. Sitting in the masjid, minding my business and some things came across my ears. I don't know all the details but spit these two names at him and he will probably be able to put the pieces of the puzzle together. Smith and Gunsmoke are the names. You know I'm not in their little dumb ass *gang banging* network and you know how I feel about *gangbangers* but those two names hold weight in here with the dummies in the dummy network and I'm almost sure they are about to bust a move real soon."

Pebbles ignores his sarcasm. She's used to this coming from him. They have a love and hate type relationship. Shakir loves her but has a great deal of resentment towards her. Shakir and Pebbles have had an on and off relationship dating back over 20 years ago.

When her and Manson have been on, her and Shakir have been off. The two of them always seem to miss each other and have rarely been home at the same time. When Manson has been home Shakir would be locked up and vice versa. Manson and Shakir hated each other and the only reason Shakir is still alive today is because they were never home, on the streets at the same time.

Shakir is the first man that Pebbles ever loved. Manson knew that and hated Shakir for it. Although Manson came into the picture and stole Pebbles' heart after she and Shakir had been together for 2 years, he hated Shakir as if Pebbles was taken from him. The fact that Manson found out that Pebbles had still been in contact with Shakir while they were together made Manson hate him even more. Manson found out about them being in contact but what he didn't know was they had still been in physical contact as well. Just knowing they were in contact almost started a war bigger than World War 2.

The only thing that stopped that war was when Manson got locked up for a gun beef and went to jail two days later after him finding out. As much as she hated him being locked up, she felt as if it happened for a reason. The last thing she wanted was for the two men she loved to go to war and one, specifically Shakir, end up dead. She felt relieved.

The war between Shakir and Manson may have ended but little did she know she had a battle of her own on its way. One month later she found out she was pregnant and she didn't know which of them was the father. With abortion not even being an option, she did what she thought was the right thing to do and tell Manson he was the father. Only thing though she wasn't sure if he really was. She felt bad about it but she knew any other way could end in Shakir and herself losing their lives.

She was always torn in between her decision. To make herself feel better about such an act she cut all ties with Shakir. Months after Rahmid was born Shakir found a way to get in touch with her and questioned her all about it. He demanded a blood test, believing the baby could possibly be his. Of course she avoided it. With years of Manson being a proud father she couldn't imagine what he would do if he found out otherwise.

She continued on as normal as possible even though she felt horrible about not knowing who her child's father really was. Finally the curiosity had gotten the best of her and she needed to know at least for herself. She agreed to let Shakir swab and alone she swabbed her son. What she found out was the biggest issue she had to face in her entire life. She found out that Shakir was indeed the father.

With Rahmid 8 years old, at this time, she couldn't muster the courage to tell Manson the truth, so she didn't. She also never told Shakir the truth either. She lied to him, telling him the results of the DNA test were negative. Until this day they both believe the lie. It hurts her whenever she thinks of it but now that she believes Manson is no longer alive, it makes it a little easier to deal with. Still she fights the battle of telling Shakir the truth but shame for her act makes her not do so.

"Fucking goofy ass gangbangers," Shakir mumbles. "Got his fucking son out here banging, trying to be like him. You know how to pick em, girl," he says sarcastically. "You sure know how to pick 'em."

"Oh, it would've been so much better if he was yours, huh? He wouldn't be a gangbanger but he still would be in and out of jail just like his father," she spits with venom.

"Yeah, alright," Shakir replies with very little words of retaliation. "Just be sure to tell him what I said. Remember those two names. Hopefully you can get to him before they do. I called you all last night," he says sliding in his normal jealous rage.

Pebbles ignores that as well. "Shakir, listen he may call tonight and he may not. I need you to call me back in a couple hours and if he hasn't called I will need you to warn him."

"Warn him? Nah. I'm not getting my name mixed up in no gang shit. I know how that shit ends. Young dummies talk too much. Be done told motherfuckers who told him and now I'm caught up in the middle of that dummy ass shit."

"Shakir, are you calling my son a dummy?"

Shakir ignores her question. "I will call you back in a couple hours. Hopefully by that time he be done called you back."

"Shakir, please keep an eye on my baby in there. I'm depending on you. Can you promise me you will watch out for him?"

Shakir intentionally ignores her request. "I will call you back in two hours."

The thought of breaking the news to Shakir that Rahmid is his son creeps into her mind. Maybe the time is right? She's not sure if she's just tired of living the lie or if maybe it's just her desperation of wanting her son protected. "Shakir...," Pebbles blurts out before she gets the dial tone. And the lie continues.

Pebbles screams out a sigh of frustration as she holds the phone to her ear. A million thoughts race through her mind and as much as she hates to think of her baby being hurt, she can't scratch the thoughts out of her head. She feels helpless. She asked Shakir for help but truthfully in her heart she knows Shakir isn't the war type. He's always been more about his money than violence. But she would hope that maybe his love for her would bring the gangster out of him. Or maybe if he knew that Rahmid was his son, he would have no choice but to look out for him.

Pebbles throws the phone onto the couch and starts pacing the floor. Her son is all she loves in the world and if something happens to him she feels she would have no reason to live. Pebbles stops at the mantlepiece where she stares at a picture of her, Manson, and Rahmid as a small baby. Her eyes start to water.

She starts to talk to the picture. "I can't believe you left me out here to raise him by myself. I told you how your absence affected him and I told you he needed you to guide him. And what you do?" Tears pour from her eyes like a rainstorm.

"You come out here and get your dumb ass killed. I will never be able to forgive you for this shit," she says as she backhands the picture off the mantlepiece. The frame shatters into pieces as it lands on the hardwood floor; the same way her world shattered when she got the news that Manson had been killed by the Feds.

25

CAMDEN/HOURS LATER

THE DOMINICAN WOMAN opens the door slowly, allowing her visitors to come inside. She's a nervous wreck and hasn't slept a wink since that living nightmare of being held hostage in her home for those days. Every time she doses off, she wakes up trembling and in a cold sweat. She may never be the same after living through that.

Quabo, Tortura and another man walk by her without saying a word. They all stop short, waiting for her to lead the way. She closes the door and walks past them. As she passes Quabo, she looks in his eyes for some type of warmth, comforting, consoling but she finds none. He stares back at her coldly, not even blinking.

She leads the way into her apartment. She says a few words in Spanish to her two children and they get up and run out of the room playfully. She then waves her hands in the direction of the couches, inviting them to a seat. No one accepts the invitation. Tortura and the other man stand at the door as Quabo paces around the coffee table.

She knows her brother to be a man of very little words. He always listens more than he talks and she knows this but right now she just wishes he would say something. He stares at the ceiling as he paces slowly. Finally, he looks to his sister. "Where is he?"

She points to the back of the apartment. "In the bathroom," she says.

No sooner than she says that, her husband comes walking into the room nervously.

"Sol, excuse us please." Since a kid he's been calling her Sol, which means sunshine. "I have to ask you and the children to go onto the porch. This is not for their ears."

The woman looks at her brother baffled. She doesn't like the sound of what he's saying. "We will stay in the bedroom," she whispers.

"Sol," he says with a stern look in his eyes. She recognizes that look and takes off immediately.

The man instantly starts pleading his case. "It's been a nightmare," he says with tears already in his eyes. "Those people, they mean business. It all happened so fast, there really was no time to react. All of our men were in position and did the best they could do. I thought my life was over. I know they would've killed all of us. We were laying face down on the dirt, just waiting to be killed. Old man Hector, he saved my life."

Quabo continues to pace circles as if the man isn't speaking to him. Not once has he looked into direction. The man continues to plead his defense as Sol and her children step into the room. They all run over to their uncle and give him a hug. He cracks a loving smile at them as he looks at his sister. He signals with his eyes for her to carry on and she does.

Before leaving the apartment she looks over her shoulder at her husband. The look in his eyes begs her not to leave but she's helpless. Quabo is her younger brother but at a young age he stepped up and took control of the family like an older brother would; so she respects him as such. What he says is what she does.

Once the door is closed Quabo speaks for the very first time. "You didn't see any of their faces?"

"No, they all wear masks. Black masks, no opening. Just their eyes."

Quabo nods his head up and down with a devious smirk on his face. He pulls out his phone and scrolls with deep concentration. He holds the phone close to the man's face. He presses the button and the man watches his movie play out. "Watch closely. You see how you keep looking over in this direction? What was it over there that you were looking at?"

The man shrugs his shoulders. "Nothing," he mumbles with a convincing face.

"Hold up one-second and I will show you what you were looking at. Hold, hold, let me slow this down. Look right…here. The robbers they come out from this direction. Seems like you knew they were there."

"No, no," the man cries. "I promise I didn't know."

"Ok, now look right here," Quabo instructs. They watch as Jeezy is dragging the man by the collar. "Look now," he says. "The robber, he pats down both men. He doesn't pat you down. You know why? Because he knew you didn't have a gun and he wasn't worried about you. He knew you were with them," Quabo says with a smile.

The man can't deny the truth. He feels it's now best to come clean if he wants his life to be spared. He looks up at Quabo and with his mouth open he attempts to speak but nothing comes out. "W, w, wait, I can explain," he says with tears already pouring from his eyes.

Quabo looks to his accomplices and doesn't have to say a word. They come storming over. "Please, let me explain," he cries as he drops to his knees in submission. "They made me. I can explain. Just give me a chance, please," the man begs as he's being dragged from the floor by his collar.

"No need to explain. At this time you can't save your life," he says with a smile. "You can only make it less painful or more painful for yourself." Tortura nods his head up and down in confirmation of Quabo's words. This is his favorite part.

"Sol gave me this," Quabo says as he holds the USB key that holds the footage from the camera they have installed for their security. "Take him."

"No, please," the man cries at the top of his lungs as he's being dragged out of the room.

The door opens and Sol stands there watching her husband being dragged away. She runs into the room and chases behind them screaming vulgar words. Quabo snatches her mid-air and carries out of the room. For the first time in life she shows no respect for him. She fights him, scratching and kicking him as he carries her away, barely bothered. He closes the door behind them.

In the bathroom the man is on bending knee, begging for his life with praying hands. One man leans against the door, watching quietly, with no sign of emotion on his face. Tortura stands over the pleading man. He holds a long nose revolver close to the man's face. Slowly he shoves the barrel of the gun up into the man's nostril.

"Please, don't kill me. I don't who they are or where they are from." He weeps loudly. "They come into my house and threaten to kill me and the family. Please, look at the video. You will see what I am saying is true. I beg you, plea…," the man says as he watches the trigger being squeezed in slow motion. Tortura would love to have some fun with the man but Quabo made him promise to get it over with quickly out of respect for his sister and the children.

It seems to take an eternity for the trigger to be mashed but finally the squeeze is complete. The man's mouth drops open in fear as he waits for the boom but there is no boom to be heard. The silencer on the revolver muffles the sound. The bullet spirals through his nostril and pierces his brain. His body flings backward. Tortura props one foot on top of the man's chest. He stares into the man's eyes as he dumps, not one but three more shots into his face. The man's eyes close instantly and all movement ceases.

MINUTES LATER

Sol is in the bedroom sobbing quietly as she packs all she can into the few bags and suitcases she has laying on the bed. Quabo stands at the doorway, emotionless and cold as steel. Once she's packed up all that can fit, she makes her way to the doorway, not once looking him in the eyes.

He wraps his arm around her shoulder and leads her through the corridor. As they pass the bathroom she can't help but to peek through the cracked door. Her heart sinks when she sees her husband's body from the waist down. The top portion of his body is obstructed by the door but his legs are as stiff as a board. She pictures his face as he lays there dead and she almost lets out a loud cry.

"Sister, I'm sorry. There was no other way. Don't worry, you will be ok. You can always find another husband," he says while looking her square in the eyes with no compassion. She rolls her eyes with disgust. He carries on casually as if none of this has happened. "You have the identification and passports, right?" She nods her head up and down causing her tears to fall more rapidly.

The Pacifica van sits curbside. Quabo guides his sister into the middle row seat and slides in right behind her. Her children talk and play loudly in the last seats, not having a clue of all that has happened. The door is closed shut and the driver pulls off casually. They have seen their father for the very last time and they don't know it.

Quabo stares straight ahead as he whispers to his sister, Sol. "Your flights to D.R. are booked already. We will drive you straight to the airport from here. Flight takes off in two hours." The woman looks at her brother pitifully. "It's for your own safety. You stay there for a few years and I will send for you. It's best for both of us."

For the first time tonight, Sol lets out an audible sigh. She plants her face in the palm of her hands and sobs harder. This breaks her brother's heart but one thing he knows for certain is all this comes with the game. Too bad she never signed up to be a part of this game. This game chose her.

Quabo opens his laptop and quickly plugs the USB key into it. He waits impatiently as it loads. His heart sinks as he watches the details of the event that morning. The look on his sister's face when they first grabbed her rips his heart.

Suddenly a smirk spreads across his face. Seeing the bare faces of the intruders lift his spirits. He zooms in and studies all of their faces. Using his phone he snaps pictures of their faces on the computer screen. It's something about the one with the hood on that indicates leadership. The way the individual instructs and commands is confirmation.

Quabo zooms in and right before his eyes clear as day is Skelter's face. He first believes it to be a man with a hood on his head until he sees the ends of her hair draped over her shoulders. He freezes the video and stares at her face long and hard. He hands Tortura the laptop. Tortura looks at the screen studying it just as hard. He looks back at Quabo who is smiling from ear to ear. "Another piece to the puzzle."

26

SHORT HILLS, NEW JERSEY

TONY PACES AROUND the office with an unlit stogie in his mouth. He chews on the cigar as the thoughts rip through his mind with lightning speed. This Jane Doe case occupies his mind day and night. He hasn't felt this motivated since the days of defending the Mayor.

The Mayor's cases were always complex because the Feds always had it out for him and they tried every tactic they could to finish him off. Tony had to always find loopholes that were not even there. In most of the cases he was like a magician, creating magic. The Mayor always made it interesting because he had no fear of them. As much as Tony preached to him about staying low and out of the way, he actually enjoyed the fact that he didn't. It's as if the more trouble the Mayor got into the harder Tony had to work. The Mayor kept Tony inspired. It wasn't about the money. It was about the adrenaline rush. He's faced some of the most vicious prosecutors and stood in front of the most wickedest of judges and has come out victorious. He feels like it's nothing left in the game to conquer.

He hasn't felt that adrenaline rush in almost a decade now. When the Mayor died, it seemed to him that the game died in the city of Newark. Also a part of him died. None of his cases have been as complex as the Mayor's. He's had no real challenges. Simple cases, no highs and no lows. They've been all business for him and he's been doing his job for the money, with no real passion for it. He's been so bored with his career that he's ventured out in to so many other businesses and partnerships, just chasing that high. That is until meeting Jane Doe.

This information she claims to possess has sparked his flame. Although he wouldn't admit it to her, she was right when she said he will make history with this case. To go against the Government and win will put him in the history books. As far as criminal law, defending drug dealers and murderers nationally, he's made history over and over again. Going up against Uncle Sam and taking him down will make him an International Living Legend.

He understands the repercussions that will come with this and he's willing to put it all on the line. But first before striking war he must be sure that he has a solid case and Jane Doe is not just some looney tune sending him on a wild goose chase. He has no problem putting his ass out there but he has to be sure that it's solid ground that they are standing on when he puts his ass out there. If what she says has any truth to it, he's willing to stand on front line against the Government and battle tooth and nail. In this case, it's not about the money or the notoriety. Well, maybe it is about the notoriety but it's also about the corruption the government has been getting away with.

Sitting a few feet away from him is one of his good friends, who happens to be an employee of the FDA (Food and Drug Administration). Tony couldn't think of anyone else he could call on to get the answers that he's in need of. If no one else can aid him in this matter, he's sure she can. An employee of the FDA for three decades so he's sure she knows all about drugs, side effects and all else they entail.

The woman reads over the list of drugs that Jane Doe has given Tony to research. Her eyes stretch open wider and wider as she goes down the list. She looks to Tony with a face of stone. She looks as if she's saw a ghost. "Where did you get this list from?"

Tony is taken aback by her question. He promised Jane Doe he would keep her safe. Throughout all of this he has handled this sensitively. Whether researching her, or even the information she has shared with him, he has done all the research himself. Normally he would let his interns do the research but he didn't want to take any chances. She explained to him that all this is Top Secret and he is handling it as such. Unless, right here right now this woman tells him it's all bullshit.

"Why you ask that?" Tony questions.

"Tell me where you got this from and I will tell you why I ask?"

"This is no bartering situation," Tony says with a smile. "Do you know what it is?"

"Yes," the woman replies. "It's all bullshit."

"Bullshit?" Tony asks as his hopes are crushed. He can't believe Jane Doe had him bobbling on a string like this. Desperation made him vulnerable. He feels like an idiot.

"Yes, all bullshit," the woman replies. "The items on the list are all code names. Secret code names. The drugs on this list don't even exist. But to those who know, they know exactly what they are code for."

"So, do you know?" Tony asks. The woman shakes her head from side to side. The look on her face concerns Tony. "What's the matter? Why are you looking like that? Do you know what they are code for or not?"

"I rather not get involved in this," she says as she gets up from her seat. "I know but I don't know. Back in college I was involved in an underground group of brainiac derelicts. This group had gotten their hands on some Top-Secret information and blasted it all over the internet. In days we were all tracked down and our doors were kicked down by the Feds. We were all taken into custody and interrogated. Luckily we knew very little about what we had discovered, or rather we pretended to know very little."

Tony listens with attentiveness. He feels hope again. "So, what do you know about it?"

"Very little but enough to know that these codes symbolize serious business. And whoever gave this to you knows much more than I do."

"Or maybe they don't," Tony says. "Maybe they just figure that I don't so they can tell me anything."

"Maybe so but I don't know what to tell you. Only certain symbols and codes I know a little about and the side effects. The others are foreign to me."

"Well, in that case how much will it cost me for you to familiarize with the ones that are foreign to you?"

"What do you mean?"

"I mean, how much will you charge me to get back in touch with your group and get to the bottom of this?" Tony asks. "Name your price."

"Tony, you know I love you but this right here is a mess that I don't want to step in. Trust me when I tell you, this is not what you want right here. And even if you think this is what you want, I'm telling you I want no parts of it."

"That's respected," Tony says respectfully. "I will never involve you in something you want no parts of. But as a friend I'm asking you to introduce me to someone who may have a different stance on the matter. Someone who can find me the answers I'm looking for and who can use a little financial inspiration," he says with a huge smile. "I really need you."

Hearing him say this touches her heart. She hates to tell him no. They've been friends for over 25 years. They entertained an on and off relationship for years. That relationship carried on for years until she got married. Both of them were married at the same time.

Coincidentally around the time of his divorce, she reached out to him. Apparently it was a trying time for her because she and her husband were going through marital difficulties as well as financial difficulties. She leaned on Tony. He was a listening ear, a shoulder to cry on and shamefully, a dick to ride on.

He wasn't proud to be having an affair with a married woman but at the time he was bitter about his own marriage and divorce so that was his self-justification. It wasn't all sexual. He was a friend to her and she could call on him for anything and she has. Thanks to him, her and her husband's financial problems were erased. Tony saved their house that was in foreclosure and he paid 2 years tuition for both of their daughters who were in college at that trying time. Because he's done so much for her she can never tell him no.

"Tony, as your friend, you know I will do anything you ever ask of me. I have a husband," she says as she looks away with embarrassment. She hates the fact that she had an affair on her husband. It still bothers her today. "I have four children, and two grandchildren. I have too much to lose."

"You won't lose a thing," Tony claims. "All I'm asking of you is to get the meanings of the codes and we will pretend this never happened. I just need to be reassured that I am not chasing a pot of fool's gold at the end of the rainbow. And for that I will give you anything you ask of me."

"Anything?" she asks.

"Anything!" Tony replies with certainty. "Any amount of money you ask for I will provide."

"If I do this for you I don't want money in return," she says.

"What is it that you want then?"

"If I find out all you need to know about these codes what I want from you is," she says before pausing for some seconds. She hates to say this. "Once I get them for you I will want you to lose all contact with me. Never ever reach out to me again. Act like you never knew me and if you ever get problems about this, I need you to promise me you will protect me and never bring my name up."

"Protect you?" Tony asks defensively. "I ain't no fucking rat! I will never roll for nothing in this world!" He feels disrespected.

"Never called you a rat. I just need to know that my name will never come up and once you get what you want you will forget me and never contact me again. I don't want to be dragged into this mess because this goes deeper than you can imagine." Her eyes display the fear that's in her heart. "I will give you what you ask of me but promise me you will give me what I ask of you. I will trade you the list of drugs plus any other codes and symbols I can come up with for our friendship. That's what I will need from you. Can you promise me you will lose contact with me?"

Tony stares into her eyes and senses the seriousness. He knows her well and right now he knows that she's dead serious.

"So, will you promise me that once I give you the information, our ties are cut forever?"

Tony is speechless, with no answer for her. Or maybe he has the answer just not ready to give it to her.

27

NORTHERN STATE PRISON/C-WING

THE PRISON YARD is filled with energy as the inmates carry on with their activities. Some of the best physiques ever seen on men can be found right here on this yard. Men with picture perfect model bodies that should be posted on Men's Fitness magazines but instead they are here caged up like animals. Some of them are satisfied with having the biggest muscles in the jail and they wear that as a huge badge of honor.

Scattered all over the yard are men in groups doing push-ups, burpees and any other body building exercises. Some jog and sprint around the track like track stars while others walk the track, conversing about business and future plans. More men are on the basketball court than any other part of the yard. What is not so transparent to the eyes are the men who are making their drug moves secretly. There are others who are not working out or doing anything constructive. They are just sitting around plotting on mischief they can get into, like bored and devilish kids.

Although this C-wing is also part of the Gang Unit, it is the least dangerous part of the Gang Unit. F-wing is where the most dangerous, most powerful and most impressionable gang members are housed. Here on C-Wing it's quite the opposite. It's filled with throwback, washed-up gangsters who once had power but their power has faded out over the years. Also the weaker, wanna-be gang members occupy this wing. On this wing you will also find inmates who have lost their minds to the medication.

This unit is filled with men who have been drugged up by the authorities. Some have been drugged up involuntarily, to calm them down and keep peace on the Unit. Others pretend to be crazy just so they can get the medication just to be able to cope with prison life. There are also those that will do anything to obtain the medication for the sole purpose of getting high. Years and years of them being medicated has taken control of their minds. Now they walk around like zombies, the walking dead. They are referred to as being on what is called 'goofy time.'

Baby Manson has isolated himself from the other inmates. He has not one man he can call a friend on the entire Unit. A handful of these men he knows from the street but none from a personal level. A few of the men in here have tried to get to know him but he's kept them at an arm's length, not trying to get too familiar with any of them. There is a group of men under the same Blood sect as he but even from them he keeps distance from. He's comfortable with moving like a solo act.

Surprisingly he's the only one at the pull-up bar. Usually the pull-up bar is packed with men waiting their turn. Baby Manson is a solid 245 pounds and built like an action figure but he keeps it all concealed under a big hoodie. As heavy as he is he pulls up on the bar like a monkey with picture perfect form. Men spread throughout the yard can't keep their eyes off him as he pulls up 50 repetitions in a clip.

ACROSS THE YARD

Gunsmoke scans the yard with a keen eye, identifying the position of every key person on the yard. He looks across the yard at a man who sits on the ground with his face buried in a magazine. The man looks over the magazine at Gunsmoke. He gives him a head-nod, letting him know that he's on point. Gunsmoke looks to his left where he sees two men standing together in the cut, sneak puffing a cigarette. Gunsmoke gives one of the men the eye signal and the man secretly passes a knife to the other one. Three men stand in the corner of the yard, all of their heads on a swivel, watching around the yard. Once Gunsmoke confirms that all of his men are in position, he makes his exit. He leaves the yard without looking back.

As Baby Manson is on the pull-up bar, on his thirty-sixth rep, he notices a man walking the track toward him. The man has his hat pulled snug over his eyes and his head tucked in the collar of his coat. Both hands are inside his coat pocket. Baby Manson jumps off of the bar before completing his set.

The man looks up at Baby Manson as he's descending in mid-air. He takes his hands out of his pocket and before he can make a move, Baby Manson eases behind him and throws him in a full-nelson wrestling move, one hand locked on the side of his head while the other is rested underneath his chin. He cuts off the man's breathing passage.

"Fuck you want motherfucker?" Baby Manson asks.

The man struggles to breathe yet he holds both hands high in the air, palms up. His hands waving in a begging position. "Candy, candy," the man manages to utter as the life is being choked out of him. "Give me candy, please?"

Baby Manson now realizes who the man is. This man, everyone calls Candyman is crazy off the medication. He walks around all day begging for candy. He doesn't talk and hasn't talked for the past 7 years.

Baby Manson loosens his grip and pushes the man with all of his might. As Candyman falls onto his back, the high pitch shrieking scream sounds off from across the yard. Baby Manson turns around where he sees a man rolling around in agony as he screams at the top of his lungs. He holds his abdomen, in a fetal position as the blood stain in his hoodie and the blood stain in his chest get bigger and bigger. The stains connect quickly and eventually blood covers his shirt. Everyone watches from a distance, not a soul going anywhere near him.

The man rolls around, leaking blood profusely. Minutes pass and his movements are now less aggressive. The alarm sounds off and in 2 minutes officers have entered the yard. They run around in riot gear ready for war.

"Lay down!" says the voice through the bullhorn.

Baby Manson puts his hands on his head as he gets onto his knees. His very first experience with this and it's quite eye opening. He thought this only happened on television and to see it in real life up close and personal is an altogether different experience. Today he now recognizes the difference from the County Jail and Prison. Another thing he recognizes is he may be on the least violent wing of the prison but that doesn't mean it's non-violent.

28

THE ALL BLACK-MATTE, darkly tinted Mercedes Coupe GLE SUV, with black AMG rims sits quietly parked at the curb, yet it still screams for attention. Tony sits comfortably in the passenger's seat of the Mercedes, while Dre sits slouched down in the driver's seat, head leaning against the window. He's crying the same blues as he's been crying for the past few years.

"Man, I'm tired of this shit. This ain't how it supposed to be bruh," he says as he shakes his head in pity.

Tony is fed up with Dre's complaints yet he continues to be a listening ear for him. He does realize how hard it's been for Dre with him trying to do the right thing. It's like all the chips are stacked against him. If it wasn't for Tony, Dre would've been fallen to the wayside. Tony always manages to find a way for Dre to eat. He treats Dre like a brother all because of the relationship he had with the Mayor.

"Just when I was getting a little groove, here come another monkey wrench," Dre says with agitation. "Fucking bail reform program. Who ever heard of some shit like that?"

Dre not long ago lost his only method of providing for himself. The Bail Bonding company he had was in no way getting him rich but it kept his lights on and food on his table. Tony bought the company from a friend 2 years ago and brought Dre in as a partner. The friend who sold the company, sold it for dirt cheap because he knew the business was coming to an end. Although Tony claimed partnership, not once did he ask for a dime of the profits. He merely bought the company for Dre to have a stream of income, until something better came along for him.

New Jersey's new bail reform law has put Dre and every other Bail Bondsmen in the State out of business. Criminal offenders are no longer able to post bail. It's up to the judge to either hold or release the offender. Based on the crime and the offender's past criminal history the offender can either be held to fight his case from behind bars or released only to return to fight his case at his prescribed court dates.

"Pressure on my ass bruh. I don't—" Dre manages to get out before Tony interrupts.

"You know, I'm really looking forward to this Honduras trip. Rocky Patel is a cool guy, I would love for you to meet him. I know you're not much of a cigar smoker but you should come along just to get away," Tony says, intentionally changing the subject. "You ever seen the women from Honduras?"

"Really bruh?" Dre asks with evident agitation. "I'm sitting here stressed the fuck out and you're not even paying attention. The only thing on your mind is cigars."

"Not true," Tony claims. "I am paying attention. Just as I have been paying attention the past few months. I just wish you would've paid attention when I told you four years ago that the law was passed. We all knew it was coming to an end."

"I paid attention, just didn't know what direction to go in next. Well, I knew what direction to go in, but I was trying not to go that way."

Tony chuckles. "In 2018, I can't believe you still even consider going that way. Bruh, it's nothing left out there. It's a different day. There is no money on them streets. There's nothing but a bunch of young junkies calling themselves hustlers. I remember the days I could charge a hundred racks to defend a murder case. Them days are long gone. These young boys fight murder beefs with public defenders. We are living in a different time period. The game isn't what it used to be."

"I ain't them though," Dre says defensively. "That ain't my story. The game is what you make it."

"I say this with all due respect," Tony says. "But you sound just like one of those old head washed-up ex-kingpins still living in the memories of yesterday. Those glory days are over, long gone. You got to step into the **right now** and get with the times."

Dre takes offense to Tony's words. "Washed up? Me? I could never be washed up."

"I didn't say you were washed up. I said you sound like the washed-up ex-kingpins."

"Same shit," Dre says with aggression.

"What part of this you don't understand?" Tony asks. He's getting fed up with Dre. "Ain't no money on them streets no more. Think about it, when the last time you found a dollar bill on the street? I remember you could walk the streets and find a twenty-dollar bill laying on the ground. The money was plentiful, like it was falling off the trees. Ain't not even a penny laying around on the ground no more. Shit tight out here, tighter than mosquito pussy."

Dre sits back non-receptive as usual. He isn't paying the least bit of attention to Tony. "You know, as much as I hate to admit this, my little brother had the right idea. Regardless of what, he always kept his foot on the gas pedal. When we met up down that Maryland House, he said some shit that rings in my head every day, all day. He said I was living like a coward, laying low, hiding and shit. And asked me how long I think I can live like that before I have to eventually come out to refuel my bank account. He was right and exact about that," Dre says as he stares in a trance.

He shakes his head slowly. "You know it breaks my heart every time I think of the fact that I didn't stand side by side my baby brother. If I was by his side like he asked me to be, niggas would've never been able to get up on him like that. I would've never allowed it. You see, he allowed money to blind him...I don't. I would've spotted a snake a mile away. All he wanted was me to be with him shoulder to shoulder," Dre says as the pity fills his eyes. Suddenly his eyes light up with a joyful spark.

Tony looks over to the direction that Dre is staring in. A young woman dressed in full Islamic garb stands at the entrance off the building. Her face glows like an angel. She's dressed in all black overgarment covering her from shoulders to toe but her petite but curvy frame can be viewed in form of silhouette. A black headpiece covers her head and drapes over her shoulders, but her fine baby hair edges peek from underneath the headpiece. She stands there with a bag of her belongings held tight in hand.

She takes a deep breath of freedom. She hasn't smelled Newark's air in over 10 years. She stands there looking around in awe. She's been locked up so long her freedom seems unreal. She stands there in fear as if it's a crime for her to step away from the building. She looks around nervously expecting corrections officers to pop out of nowhere on her.

Dre gets out of the car happily. He stares at the girl over the roof of the car. He watches her without saying a word. She sees him and her whole demeanor changes. She takes off running toward him. She crosses the street, not even looking both ways. She races to him like a daughter to her father. She jumps in his arms and he embraces her with a tight bear hug.

She backs away, blushing like a young schoolgirl. "Sorry, sorry," she apologizes sincerely. "I ain't supposed to be touching on you like that," she says very piously. "But I can't help it," she says with a smile before jumping in his arms once again. "Allah please forgive me."

They squeeze each other tightly as Tony makes his way over to them. The woman finally backs away. Her face is covered with tears. She holds her hand over her mouth to muffle the sound of her crying.

"Lil Mama," Tony says as he cracks a smile. "Welcome home."

"Halimah," she says, correcting Tony. "I left Lil Mama back on the streets ten years ago."

"My apologies," Tony says.

"No worries," she claims. She switches back to her original station. She's equally as happy to see Tony and she runs over to him and gripping him with a tight bear hug. She gathers herself and backs away from Tony. She flutters her eyelids to fight back the tears. Finally she gives in and leans her head back and allows the tears to flow. She holds her hands over her eyes with shame.

"I love y'all. Y'all just don't know how much," she says with her tears still crawling down her face.

Dre wraps his arm around her shoulder and brings her close to him. He walks her to the Mercedes and opens the passenger door for her to get in. He slams the door shut behind her and walks around to the driver's side. "Follow me!" Dre shouts to Tony who is getting into his own Mercedes that's parked a couple hundred feet away.

Lil Mama sobs hard in silence. Dre looks at her with a smile. She looks over at him and is finally able to speak. She wipes her tears. "Don't judge me," she says giggling like a schoolgirl. She grabs hold of his hand.

She grips his hand before catching herself and pulling away from him. Although her touch is totally innocent she knows it's not permissible for her to be touching a man that isn't her husband. She also does so to keep the lust away. It's not his lusting that she's worried about; it's her own.

Back when she was younger she had a thing for Dre that she never even expressed to him. Although they worked together every day she kept her feelings for him a secret. She respected how he treated her like a daughter or little sister and never once made a pass at her. She respected it but secretly she hated it and often dreamed about it being another way. Overall the level of respect she had for him was huge because she knew many men of his status would have taken advantage of such a young and naive girl.

"Judge you? Never. Go ahead and cry and get it all out."

Lil Mama shakes her head with the tears dropping at a rapid pace. "Wallahi, I didn't cry the whole bid. As much as I wanted to I didn't. I promised myself no matter how tough it got for me, I would not cry. But I would cry tears of joy once it was over. It's over finally." She looks up to the sky. "Alhamdullilah, it's over!" She looks to Dre while gripping his hand tightly. "I need you to know that I thank you."

"I need you to know that I thank you as well," Dre interrupts.

"Thank me for what?" Lil Mama asks.

"For standing up. In a day like this you don't find many like you."

"Oh, you don't have to thank for me for that. I didn't stand up for you...I stood up for me. There was no other way. Them feds were coming to see me three times a week. Each time they had a sweeter deal than the last time. And guess what? I never even considered it. I ain't built like that. Let me ask you though?" she says as she looks closer at him. "Did you ever think I was going to roll?"

Dre drives with his attention on the road, not once cutting his eye at her. He doesn't reply but his silence is an answer in itself. Finally he cuts his eye at her briefly. "Honestly, I didn't know what to think. But to be even more honest, if you had rolled I wouldn't even have been mad at you. I've seen brothers—same mother, same father—roll on each other. Nothing surprises me. In the real world ain't no honor in that shit. That no snitch, fake mob style shit we watch on television ain't real. That's movie shit for entertainment purposes only. I learned that shit while I was away. I mean, you got a very few motherfuckers who stand up but the rest of the world don't operate on that honor and moral system. I appreciate the fact that you did stand up, even though you did it for you and not for me."

Lil Mama watches him with the same googly eyes that she used to watch him with. She's so caught up in his eyes and his smile, totally forgetting that so many years have passed. She's not even in the moment right now. She's in the days of yesteryear.

Lil Mama had a secret crush on Dre back then but after doing all the time she's done and him being by her side it's now more than a crush. It's full blown love. When the rest of the world forgot about her, Dre was still there supporting her every day of her incarceration. Financially, she didn't want for a thing on the inside and she was able to help her family from her position.

"So, talk to me," Lil Mama says. "What's good? I know you got something going on?"

Dre looks at Lil Mama and his mind goes back to the days when she would be riding with him as he dropped game on her. She was a pretty, young, misguided 19-year-old. His plan for her wasn't to simply use her as a mule but to groom her. Foolishly he thought he was helping her, not thinking he really was ruining her life. "Damn, look at you. I look in your eyes and still see that pretty lil girl."

The look in Dre's eyes melts her away. She finds herself speechless, just staring at him with a starry look in her eyes. She thought she would be able to contain herself around him but it's now obvious to her that she can't. "Can I ask you a question?"

"Of course," he replies.

She pauses for a few seconds, not comfortable with the question she would like to present. "Whatever happened to that crazy chick you had? Y'all still together?"

Shame covers Dre's face. "Not at all. We weren't together then. But how could I ever be with a chick that I can't trust? What type of nigga would I be if I kept in contact with someone who tried to send us away forever?"

"So who?" She decides to stop while she's ahead. All these years she's managed to refrain from expressing her feelings for him. She doesn't know if that's a good thing or a bad thing but she would hate to take the risk and tarnish the relationship they have. She tears her eyes away from him. "That was a crazy one there." They share a chuckle. "It's a little easier to laugh at the matter now that it's finally over."

After a twenty-minute ride filled with the two of them catching up, Dre finally parks on Oraton Parkway in East Orange. She looks up at the huge warehouse building which has been converted into Lofts. "Damn, this new huh?"

Dre hands her a key ring with 4 keys on it and she hesitantly grasps it. "What's this?"

"The key to your apartment," Dre replies. "The rent has been paid for a year. Apartment 4B it is." Lil Mama places her hand over her mouth and the tears start to roll once again. Dre reaches underneath the seat and hands her a Hermes pocketbook. She looks inside and is surprised to see the purse filled with cash. "That's forty-thousand in there," says Dre. "Give me a few weeks and I will drop some more on you."

Lil Mama interrupts him by shoving the case back at him. "I can't."

"Yes, you can, and you will," he says as he drops it onto her lap. "Listen, nothing I can do will ever be enough to repay you for all the time you missed but I will make sure you are good. I need you to know that I appreciate you." It takes all her power to sit in this seat and not jump over the middle console into his lap and give him a kiss that is long overdue. She fumbles clumsily with the door and gets out while she still has a little self-control left.

Dre exits the vehicle as well. "Lil Mama," he says over the roof of the vehicle.

She turns around. "*Halimah*," she says.

My bad, Halimah," Dre apologizes. He tries to plant it in his head that she no longer wants to be called Lil Mama. He tosses the keys over the roof. She catches them in midair. "Go to the leasing office and tell them you're my sister and you need a garage key."

Being referred to as his sister crushes her heart yet she's still grateful for him. "Ok," she mumbles as she walks away semi-broken hearted.

"I will hit you in a couple hours to check on you. If you need me before then, call me. I'm leaving the car here with you in case you need to make a move."

"I ain't moving nowhere with no license," she says with a smile. "Call me a punk or whatever but I will not get sent back to that spot for driving. I will walk from here to West Bubblefuck first."

"Well, I will leave it anyway," Dre says with a dazzling smile. He walks toward Tony's car that is parked a few feet behind. He gets in and drops himself into the seat. Despair fills the car immediately.

Tony pulls out of the parking space and sits for seconds as Lil Mama walks into the building. He pulls off. "You don't seem like a happy camper," Tony teases.

"Hey man, I just gave that girl the few little pennies I had left. I don't know what I'm gone do or even how I'm gone do it."

"What you give her? If you don't mind me asking."

Dre sighs before speaking. "Forty," he mumbles."

"Forty dollars?" Tony asks.

"No, forty large," Dre replies.

Tony's eyes pop out of his head. "You crying broke and you give her forty-thousand?" He doesn't see the logic in this.

"Hey man, that girl just did damn near a dime for me. I couldn't let her come out here fucked up. Like, if that was the case I could've taken her place in the joint. Like, what would she think of me if she knew I been out on these streets all this time and I can't get it right? I been in that spot she just left and I know the fear that comes with coming home broke and trying to start over. After what she just done for me, if I can ease her mind that makes me feel good. As far as me, I'm a hustler. I will figure it out. One way or another," he says with confidence. "By hook or by crook."

29

ROGER GARDEN APARTMENTS-TRENTON

SKELTER SITS BACK on the loveseat listening closely to the man that is speaking. Right now she's trying to put a solid team together. She's never been in a position like she's in right now or even this or close to it. She always dreamt about herself in this type position but never imagined it possible.

For years she's sat on the bench and watched the mistakes the money dudes made. She always told herself if she ever got her turn she would do it all differently. One of the biggest mistakes she's watched 95% of the players make is being attention seekers. They all loved the spotlight. She's watched the rise and fall of all the biggest drug dealers of her era and those before her and its always been the spotlight that ended it all for them. And that's the reason she plans to move like a ghost, heard but rarely seen.

"But how shit looking out here?" Skelter questions with much concern.

"Aye man, shit is fucked up out here," Blue Blood says with defeat on his face. "I mean, I ain't gone lie to you, I'm doing my lil numbers, getting every dollar I can get my hands on." His eyes stretch wide open with emphasis. "Young boys done fucked these streets up, you hear me?"

"You know," Skelter interrupts. "I'm gone be honest with you. I hate when I hear old heads say that shit. The streets ain't no more fucked up now than they were back in the day. It's still plenty of money out there. Old heads just can't get out of that old mindset of yesterday and capitalize off of today. They can't accept the fact that the old way of thinking don't work no more."

Skelter continues on. "And they also don't realize their network has decreased. They have less motherfuckers for them to get money with. At twenty-five you probably had fifty people you could call on. Today at your age, you probably can't call on five people. Most of your friends, dead or in jail or fiends. So, really it ain't that the young boys fucked up the game. It's the fact that maybe you're too old for the game."

"Wow," Blue Blood says in awe. "I never fucking looked at it like that. But I beg to differ though," he says with a smile. "I ain't too old for this shit and the young boys have fucked the game up," he says with emphasis. "Just look," he says as he walks into the kitchen. He opens the door to the cabinet over his sink. He pulls out a plastic bag and carries it over to the table where Skelter is sitting. He dumps the contents slowly onto the coffee table.

"Look, pills," he says while holding the medicine bottle in the air. "Dope," he says while exposing a sleeve of 10 bricks. "Weed," he says as he holds a sandwich bag filled with a little less than a pound of weed. "I remember the days that you picked one thing to sell and you mastered that craft. Dope dealers only dealt with dope and weed dealers only dealt with weed. And the niggas who had their hands in everything never had no success with nothing.

Jack of all trades, master of none. Today you have to have your hands in everything just to make some money." He grabs a carton of Newport cigarettes from the coffee table. "Look, I even got bootleg cigarettes for sale," he says with a smile. "So, don't tell me about accepting the new way of thinking. I ain't complaining because I ain't no complainer, just making a note of what's going on out here in these streets. In the thirty years that I been in the game, I never saw it this damn bad." Overall though, I'm grateful to be here and to be getting my hands on a couple dollars.

He continues on. "All this shit I got my hands on and I still ain't getting no real money. If it wasn't for that little cushion I had, I would've been fucked up. I'm still living off that Block Party run we caught." His eyes light up brightly as he reminisces. During that Block Party run he managed to put together $170,000. When it all ended he owed Manson $200,000 for the dope that was fronted to him on consignment. Blue Blood, Skelter, and Helter split the money three ways.

At the end, he was a quarter million strong. Here it is not even four years later and he's ripped through all the money. He got it fast and he blew it fast. That's the game and how it goes.

"Damn, I was up like a motherfucker," he says. "But over the years that has slowly come to an end. Man, I can use another run like that right now!"

Skelter lifts a bag and lays it on the coffee table. "I got another run for you," she says as she reaches in the bag. She drops not one, not two, but three kilos onto the table. "What you know about this right here?" Skelter is well aware that Blue Blood originally made his bones selling cocaine. When she was a kid he was one of the biggest coke dealers in her projects. Right now she's just testing his chin to see if he still has the champion mindset. Hearing him talk, confuses her. He almost sounds like a man that has been defeated after taking so many losses.

"What I know about it? Cocaine is my motherfucking life!" Skelter watches as his body language changes. His eyes have a different look in them. "I been trying to get my hands on some blow for a minute now but it been a drought since forever and prices sky-high like a motherfucker."

"Well, it ain't no drought for us," Skelter says. "And I got a price for you that nobody will be able to beat."

"Word?" Blue Blood asks in a state of amazement. "What's the ticket on it?"

"Thirty-one a joint for you," she replies. "That's if I have to give it to you on the arm, straight consignment," she says with emphasis. "Money on the wood I can do it for you for twenty-nine."

This price she gives Blue Blood is indeed lower than she's given anyone else for she knows he's a different caliber of man than the others. She knows that the number dictates who they can supply. The higher the number the lower caliber of dealers they can supply. The people who pay $40 a gram buy 10 and 20 grams while the people who pay $32 a gram buy kilos. By giving Blue Blood a number like this she gives him free range to reach out to even the biggest of dealers in the city.

Blue Blood is astonished by the numbers. The lowest numbers he's heard in the hood is $34. He can slide in and make $3,000 profit off of every kilo. He immediately thinks of the longevity in this. He would hate to start something he can't finish. "I mean, I ain't getting in your business, but once I open up will you be able to keep the work coming?"

"I'm gone tell you like this," she says as she stands up and takes control of the conversation. "Right now you the second person I came to with this. I know you got the power to take us to the next level. This level I'm on right now, I ain't never played on this level. I ain't gone sit here and bullshit you. This shit just kind of fell in my lap. I ain't got no problem letting you control the point guard position. To answer your question, can I keep them coming," she says with hesitation. "Right now I have my hands on enough of these shits to lift the city up. And when we get through those we will have to play it by ear. Right now let's just get money and live for the moment."

"Say no more," Blue Blood says with confidence in his eyes. "You tell me how much inventory we got on deck and I will take it from here. Sit back and watch me work!"

30

SHORT HILLS MALL, NEW JERSEY

PEBBLES STRUTS THROUGH Neiman's quite braggart, without even saying a single word. Both of her arms are filled with shopping bags. Her huge oversized sunglasses has people staring extra hard at her believing that she could possibly be a celebrity figure trying to hide and conceal her identity. Her tight fitted motorcycle jacket with the pink exaggerated fox fur collar makes her look like something straight off the set of Love and Hip-Hop New York but her tiny waist and huge voluptuous booty makes her look like someone out of a Straight Stuntin' Magazine page.

The Black men in passing stare at her booty with lust as the white men stare at it in total disbelief, like she's a freak of nature. The White women and Black women in common stare at her with jealousy and hatred. Pebbles is addicted to the attention her booty gets her. Whether good attention or bad, she's just loves attention period.

"Excuse me."

Pebbles looks over her shoulder at the woman who is following steps behind her. She stops short. She looks down her nose over her sunglasses. "Yes?" Pebbles asks with sassiness.

The middle-aged Caucasian woman stands there with confusion on her face. "Basketball Wives?" she asks with innocence.

Pebbles presses her finger against her lips. "Shhh," she says as she looks around as if she's hiding. "No, Housewives of Atlanta," she whispers. She gets this so much that she's now used to it and has fun pretending with the people. It's not like she feels she's pretending because in her mind she's a celebrity, just not on a national level.

"I knew it," the woman says cheerfully. "I watch so much ratchet television that I get my shows mixed up." A weird look crosses her face. "I'm sorry. I don't mean that with any disrespect. I mean, I'm not calling you ratchet. I was saying the shows are ratchet. Well," she says while scratching her head at a loss of words. She realizes she's digging herself deeper and deeper. "Can I get a picture?"

"Sorry Dear, no pictures today. I don't have my security with me and it can get crazy. I can sign an autograph for you," she says with an apologetic smile.

"Good enough," the woman replies as she quickly hands Pebbles the napkin that she holds in her hand. She hands her a pen as well.

Pebbles quickly scribbles an illegible signature that no one could possibly ever figure out. She just hopes the woman doesn't ask her name. Pebbles' phone rings and interrupts the moment. She's saved by the bell. She looks at the display and is happy to see the call that she's been waiting for days. "I have to go now. Nice meeting you," she says as she grabs the woman's dangling hand. She walks away leaving the woman standing there star struck.

"Hello," Pebbles shouts into the phone as she's walking.

"Ma, what's up?"

"Boy where you been? I been waiting for you to call me for days."

"Ma, you know I don't be playing the phone like that. I jail. I check in every couple days to make sure you good and that's good enough for me. You good?"

"No, I'm not good."

His heart skips a beat. "What's up? What happened?"

"I got a call the other day and the person told me to warn you about something."

Baby Manson's heart pounds hard. He's worried about his mother's safety. His first thoughts are maybe something in his past has come to haunt him and whoever he done something to has come to his mother to take it out on her. The fact that he's inside and can't help her makes him feel totally helpless. "A call? From who? Warn me about what?" Rage is flowing through the phone line.

"He said he overheard some people talking and wanted me to warn you."

"He who, Ma?"

Pebbles pauses in deep thought. She can't give up her source. That could lead to many other problems. "That doesn't really matter. What matters is these two names. Smith and Gunsmoke. You know them?"

Fury takes over. He's so tired of hearing Smith's name and his threats. For the past couple years Smith's name has been stuck to him like glue. They've been missing each other but he's sure they will one day have to face each other. He can't wait for that day.

"You know them?" Pebbles asks.

"I know of them."

"You had problems with them?"

"Ma, I don't have problems with nobody," he says, trying to ease her mind. He hates her to be worried about him.

"Well, apparently they have a problem with you and they plan to do something about it."

"Ma, who told you this? People just be talking because they got a mouth. I ain't got no beef with nobody, Ma. I'm chilling. Somebody lying to you."

Pebbles isn't buying his story. She knows Shakir would never lie to her about anything, let alone something this serious. "I'm not telling you who told me. It doesn't matter. It's a girl I know brother and he into what you into and he heard that. That's all I can tell you."

"Well, tell them thanks but no thanks for the information. I'm good."

"Rah-Rah stop with the arrogant shit. Just like your fucking father. Somebody care enough about us to warn you and you too arrogant and stupid to take heed."

"I ain't being arrogant Ma," he says with attitude. "Whatever gone happen, gone happen. However they want to bring it, I will take it."

"Rah-Rah I don't want to hear that gangster shit. I ain't one of your little dumb ass friends in the street. I haven't been able to sleep in days since I heard the shit."

"Ma, get your rest because I'm sleeping well every night. Feet up, eyes closed tight. Sleeping like a baby. I ain't missing no z's and neither should you. I'm gone call you later though, alright? Love you Ma." He hangs up the call before she can reply.

"Rah," she says before hearing the dial tone. She holds the phone staring at it. She's a nervous wreck right now. She fears for her son's life.

He's always been headstrong. His gang banging reputation doesn't impress her the least bit. The streets may know him as Baby Manson but she knows him as little Rah-Rah. A kid who grew up a mama's boy, crybaby who was always scared of the dark. She will never see him as the villain the streets make him out to be. In her mind she believes that he's playing the role for the people and deep inside he's still the little boy that was afraid of his own shadow. She has to find a way to save her son's life and quick.

TEN MINUTES LATER

Pebbles's Range Rover 'Autobiography' floats along John F. Kennedy Parkway. The sound of singer Ella Mae's 'Boo'd Up' seeps through the speakers. She stops at the traffic light and vanity leads her to looking into the rearview mirror just as it does every other traffic stop. She allows her tongue to glide across her thick and soft, red matte colored lipstick. The honking of the horn interrupts her brief loving herself moment. She cracks the window and throws the bird at the driver behind her before pulling off.

Pebbles cruises into the huge parking lot and parks in the very first vacant spot. She looks into the mirror, applying a fresh coat of lipstick, nice and evenly. She mashes her lips together and puckers up before slamming the visor shut. She gets out and smooths her clothes out before slamming the door and prancing across the parking lot.

From the office window, Attorney Tony Austin watches Pebbles walk. He stands there blowing smoke rings into the air. Her confidence intrigues him. He laughs to himself as she struts through the parking lot like the world revolves around her.

As suave and debonair as Tony may be, he always finds appreciation in a nice hood-rat. The hood side of him makes him never forget where he came from. Pebbles reminds him so much of his ex-wife Mocha. Her game, her confidence and her rough around the edge demeanor. All of those ingredients is what got Tony caught up in Mocha's web.

To take a hood-rat to new levels and polish them up is like working on a science project to him. His biggest downfall in life has been falling in love with the underdog. He loves to see the look on a person's face who has been losing their entire life, when they finally win. All his life he's taken losers to the championships turning them into winners. The downfall comes in when the loser forgets who led them to the championships in the first place.

Tony sits behind his desk, in deep concentration of the smoke rings that he blows into the air, when his secretary steps into the office accompanied by Pebbles. "Mr. Austin, your next appointment is in fifteen minutes," the secretary says loud and clear. She wants Pebbles to get the hint that time isn't necessarily on her side. Pebbles pays the secretary no attention. Her eyes are locked on Tony. She's speechless for seconds just caught up in his presence.

Tony notices her glare and attempts to break her trance. "I apologize for the smoke. You caught me during my lunch hour."

"Oh, no problem," she says as she looks away from him. "I thank you for having me with such short notice, without an appointment. I apologize for practically bombarding my way in here but it's a life and death situation."

Tony stands up slowly. A look of concern covers his face. "Talk to me. Life and death?"

"Yes," Pebbles replies. "My son's life," she says sadly. "I received a call informing me that there is a threat on my son's life."

Tony is confused. "I mean, how can I help?"

"I don't know, maybe get him transferred to another jail?"

"Of course that is a possibility but I don't know about that. Does he want to do that?"

"I didn't even ask him what he want to do. I want to have him transferred."

"I'm afraid it doesn't work like that. He's not a juvenile anymore. His mommy can't just save him. He's a grown man. Plus, if he puts in for a transfer and the word gets out that he transferred for fear of his life, his jail stays can be hard from here on out."

"I ain't trying to hear none of that. He ain't built for prison. He's just a big overgrown kid. He thinks he's gangster but really he's not. He's my baby and I fear for his life in there. As we speak, he's probably in there scared to death. I know my child," she says with confidence.

MEANWHILE IN NORTHERN STATE PRISON/C-WING

Baby Manson inhales a deep breath as he steps into the crowded Day Room. Young men barely old enough to be in grown prison show their true age by roughhousing with each other, wrestling and slap-boxing. The more mature inmates pay them no mind as they sit quietly in the corner playing Dominoes. The more intelligent ones sit in silence completely focused as they challenge their minds with Chess matches.

A group of rowdy men go back and forth with aggressive name calling and shit talking as they engage in their card game. With all of this going on, a great deal of the men still have their eyes focused on the television screen as Love and Hip Hop holds their undivided attention. Explosive cleavage and exposed ass cheeks in tiny shorts is like soft porn to them. They lock the images of these reality television celebrities and save those memories for later when they're in their rooms. If those women of reality television land had a dollar from every inmate across the country who has masturbated to their visual those stars would be rich.

Baby Manson walks across the room. He puffs his chest up and holds his head high. All motion seems to cease and all eyes are on him. The group of men who were roughhousing stop their play and all stare at Baby Manson coldly. Some recognize him yet they don't speak. Before he makes it halfway across the room the word has spread about exactly who he is. It's evident that the most of these men are all from the opposite side.

Baby Manson peeps the whispering and cold looks yet he continues on, looking straight ahead and focused. His eyes are on his target, Gunsmoke, who is in a small huddle. He's holding court with a group of men surrounding him. They all watch Gunsmoke closely with their undivided attention.

Even the card games stop as Baby Manson walks throughout the room. It's as if everyone is ready to move on him as soon as the command is given. Baby Manson realizes that this can end badly for him in the drop of a dime but still he carries it without a sign of worry or fear. Gunsmoke stops talking and locks his eyes on Baby Manson as he approaches. His crew lock their eyes on Baby Manson as well. If looks could kill he would be a dead man right now.

Baby Manson steps into the huddle, staring dead at Gunsmoke, as if the rest of the men are not even here. He taps him on the chest, aggressively with his backhand. "Let me talk to you for a minute," he says as he steps away from the huddle.

All the young men look at Gunsmoke, awaiting the green light to go. Instead, Gunsmoke shakes his head negatively. He follows Baby Manson into the corner where they stand alone face to chest. Baby Manson towers over Gunsmoke like the Jolly Green Giant. Baby Manson's body language translates his aggression for all to see.

"What up?" Gunsmoke asks as he looks Baby Manson up and down with snarling lips.

"Yo, you looking for me?" Baby Manson asks.

"Looking for you for what?" Gunsmoke asks, displaying some aggression of his own.

"I don't know," Baby Manson says before giving Gunsmoke a look over from head to toe, back up to the head. "That's why I'm coming to you. Word came past my ears that you said when I touch here it's gone be this and it's gone be that." Baby Manson lies just trying to get a gauge on Gunsmoke and his true gangster. "I came here to tell you, if it's going down, let's get it over with, right here, right now. We don't have to wait around and let shit linger. We can get right to it."

Gunsmoke is amazed at the heart that Baby Manson is displaying. He figures he's either one courageous individual or he's one retarded individual who doesn't realize the danger he's putting himself into. Either way, Gunsmoke has no choice but to respect his gangster.

Baby Manson steps a little closer. "I'm gone ask you again, are you looking for me?"

Gunsmoke chuckles with a cheesy grin on his face. Baby Manson identifies that chuckle as a nervous reaction. "Man, niggas always trying to get some shit started. I ain't got no problem with you. I don't even know you. Niggas just want to see us beefing so we can go to war and finish each other off because they scared to move on us themselves."

Baby Manson can see the cowardliness in Gunsmoke's eyes despite the aggressive body language he may be displaying. Baby Manson is sure he is putting on a show for all his followers who are watching. Regardless of how animated his body language may be if they could hear what he just said they would agree with Baby Manson that he just copped a plea. His aggressive body language and the plea he just copped don't match up.

If his words were not enough to reveal that he's really a coward, the look in his eyes just confirmed it. Gunsmoke just said the words that a many of cowards have said in order to weasel out of a war. Even though he views him as cowardly, still he must keep his eyes on him. He knows cowards like this too well. They will try and rock you to sleep by telling you there's no beef but as soon as you close your eyes they will make their move.

"Well, dig this," Baby Manson says as he taps Gunsmoke's chest once again. This time the tap is even more aggressive, more impactful and more disrespectful. "Right now I'm gone take your word for it that we don't have an issue. Your man supposed to have an issue with me so that means me and him got an issue. Until you tell me that me and you got an issue or I hear again otherwise, then me and you ain't got no issue. As a man I'm telling you this though, the next time I hear chitter chatter about what you gone do to me, you gone have to do all of that that you say you gone do," he says as he zooms in face to face with Gunsmoke. "Because I'm gone do what I got to do with no hesitation, feel me?"

"I feel that," Gunsmoke whispers. He feels like he's been punked right now and it shows all over his face.

"I hope we clear," Baby Manson says as he takes two steps backwards. "Do know this…I ain't hard to find if niggas looking for me." Baby Manson stops abruptly. "Oh and tell your man to stop trying to put people up to do his dirty work. All that's gone happen is he gone put a bunch of you motherfuckers in a bad situation. Tell him save all that energy for when we finally see each other. Then he can do all that shit he act like he want to do." Baby Manson bops his head up and down before turning around and walking away.

All eyes are zoomed in on him. He stares into the eyes of a few men just to show them that he means business. He exits the room with his head held higher than when he walked in.

TONY'S OFFICE

Pebbles looks at her pink faced Presidential Rolex and realizes she has went many minutes over the time limit. There's one more thing she must say though because the words are burning a hole in her tongue. The last time she saw Tony she was embarrassed by Manson. Manson smacked her in the back of the head for staring at Tony. That slap in the head didn't stop the thoughts that were running through her mind though.

She always had thoughts of him. In her mind she believes that Tony was just as into her as she was into him. She hated that she never got the chance to find out and promised herself if she ever got another opportunity she would find out if the feelings were mutual. She knew it would be disrespectful to make a move on Tony before but now that Manson is out of the picture it doesn't seem as disrespectful. Or maybe her desires just makes it seem that way.

She looks at her watch once again and realizes it's now or never. She has to shoot her shot. "I know I have held up a lot of your time and I really appreciate you squeezing me into your busy schedule but I have something that I would like to get off my chest," she says as she puts her forefinger dead and center of her cleavage line. Tony watches her finger as it slips in between her breast and disappears.

He pulls his eyes out of the trap and looks her in the face. She stares back at him with squinted, confused but still seductive eyes. "Do you remember that very first time we were around each other," she says pausing and giving him time to reflect. "Well, I deal with energy and I trust my energy radar. My radar is hardly ever off. That time we saw each other, I felt something in between us. I could be wrong though," she says with uncertainty.

Tony is amazed at her cockiness. He's so much of a charmer that he could never crush her but for her to think she has a chance with him is mind boggling to him. He admires her confidence though. He asks himself what he did that could lead her to believe she has a shot with him. He's sure he never gave her any indication or door opening. What he doesn't realize is he didn't have to. Just like dogs can smell fear on a human, hood-rats can smell hood-rat lover on a man.

His silence throws her confidence off yet she continues her advances. "It's a simple yes or no answer. I ain't asking you to elaborate. Unless you want to," she says with a sexy smile.

For a few seconds Tony gets caught up in her smile, her pretty teeth and her luscious lips. "I don't really recall that day to be honest." He lies to her even though he's completely aware of that day. "You're a very beautiful woman," he says. Tony will never crush a woman's confidence for confidence means a lot to him. He has always made it a practice to build them up, not tear them down.

"Pardon me if I didn't sense the energy that day. I have tunnel vision," he says with a smile. "I'm engaged to be married."

"Awl," she sighs. "Congratulations," she says, not meaning it at all. "Let me be the light at the end of that tunnel though." She smiles seductively. "For you, I would be one of those co-wives." She smiles, allowing him to believe she's just kidding. "Shit, I did that for years anyway. See, one thing about me is I knew all about Manson and all his little sidekicks. Trust, ain't nothing slow about me. With all of his little chicks, nobody took care of him like me," she brags. "Them lil bitches he had didn't mean nothing to me…excuse my language. I'm a real ass chick and I play my position."

Tony is now all ears. She seems to be talking his language. He listens attentively as his mind wanders. He takes a tight pull of the cigar butt he holds in his fingertips. He leans his head back, allowing the smoke to marinate in his mouth.

"As a young girl, I learned to appreciate a man while you have him. Like, I ain't no emotional chick who gone lose her mind and try to expose a man. Especially if he kept it real with me from the start that he has a situation. What a chick like me gone do is try to be his peace away from home and when we together we just make each other happy. Just dealing with what we have and not worried about nobody else when we together."

Tony turns his head to the left, not to blow his smoke into her face. He looks back at her. "I can dig that totally," he admits. "But Manson wasn't just a client of mine…he was more like a friend. Even if I wasn't engaged to be married, I could never snake a friend."

"Snake a friend? Do you know that in Islam when a man dies, his friends—even his brother—can marry the wife of the deceased? To take care of her and the family that their friend of brother left behind?"

"Are you Muslim?"

"No," she replies bluntly. "But I dealt with enough of them and I'm just spitting the game to you that they spit to me over the years." She busts out laughing and so does Tony. "Hey, it's worth a shot, right? For you, I will wrap up like a ninja. Be running around here in all black, like a mummy, can't see nothing but my eyes." She amuses herself so much that she can't even keep a straight face.

Tony chuckles hard. He can't deny her persistence or her sense of humor. He hasn't seen this much game in a woman since his ex-wife Mocha. This is like mental tennis for him; Steel sharpening steel. He could easily shoot his shit back at her and they go back and forth but he knows the danger in that so he must end it right here. "You got more game than EA Sports," he says with a dazzling smile. "I'm flattered but we got two strikes against us. One, my fiancé ain't going with that and two I don't rock like that, going against my man back, deceased or alive."

"Well, I'm gone leave you with this," she says. "I said my say… laid it all on the table. I ain't no sweat hound bitch so I ain't gone keep pressing you. But anyway your mind wanders and your curiosity peaks, you know how to get at me. If ever you need some peace of mind, I can be all of that." She ends it right there and turns around and walks away. With each step her rear sways from side to side hypnotically. She stops at the door and turns around to look at Tony. "Oh, and you said we have two strikes against us. In my younger years of playing softball, it took three strikes to be out. Tell me if I'm wrong, but I think I get another swing."

31

TORTURA SITS IN the passenger's seat with his face damn near pressed against the windshield. "*Girar a la derecho* (make a right turn)." The driver bends the corner so hard with all gas that the vehicle almost tips over. Three of their vehicles have been patrolling the area for the past two hours. Finding that bag in that alley lets them know one thing and that is the culprits are somewhere close. They plan to patrol this area day and night until they find who they are looking for. The three vehicles have covered all of Trenton.

• • •

Behind the dark tinted windows of the Dodge Durango, Skelter sits on the edge of the back seat. She has her elbows pinned against the two front headrests, sitting dead and center so she has a clear view up ahead of her where the older model Jeep Cherokee is parked. The driver, her youngest Godson has his full attention on the Cherokee as well. Skelter lays the 9-millimeter on the vacant passenger's seat, never once taking her eyes off the Cherokee.

Inside the Jeep Cherokee, Bruh in Law nervously counts through stacks of money. He's so nervous he can barely keep count. He had Skelter come along for reassurance. Even with her a few hundred feet behind him he still isn't comfortable making a move of this magnitude. His eyes bounce from the money to the outside surroundings, over to the passenger. The passenger counts along with Bruh in Law, silently, just making sure he didn't give him a single dollar more than what he was supposed to.

Bruh in Law felt a weird energy coming from the man the moment he got into the car but he can't put his finger on what it could be. Whatever it is he doesn't like it. Usually the man has a lot to say, today he hasn't said five words. His cocky aura isn't present today either.

Bruh in Law drops the last stack of money into the plastic shopping bag. He inhales more nervousness as he peeks around once again. "That's nineteen thousand, eight, eighty, right?" the man asks, already knowing the answer to his question.

Bruh in Law reaches into the backseat and grabs hold of the handles of the shopping bag. He hands the man the bag and the man immediately pulls the sneaker box from the bag. Bruh in Law secretly tucks the bag of money under his left thigh as the man is opening the sneaker box. Under the wrinkly wrapping paper there lies 560 grams in a sandwich bag.

"Cool," the man says as he opens the door. "Like I said, if my people like this I will get like four or five birds the next time. I'm just getting this little bit to see how it goes," he lies with a straight face when truthfully, this is all his money can afford. "Later," he says as he gets out and slams the door.

Bruh in Law now figures out what the change in the man is. His change has everything to do with the roles being reversed. This same man Bruh in Law usually buys his work from. The man hated to be on the buying side and not the selling side but Bruh in Law gave him a price that was even better than the price he usually gets it for. Usually the man buys it for $37 a gram and sells it for $40-$41 a gram.

The extra couple thousand he will make in the long run was the incentive to lose Bruh in Law as a customer and become a buyer. His ego is tarnished by having to buy a little more than a half a kilo from a man who he's been lying to and pretending to be some real plug with kilos on deck. He's not the big deal he's made himself out to be. What Bruh in Law is about to soon find out is once a man sits in the plug's seat is when he finds out who is who and what is really what.

The man walks in front of the Jeep and crosses the street. A black, tinted out Ford Explorer is cruising up the block. Just as the man is approaching the yellow lines, the Explorer is a few feet away. The man spots the Explorer and his heart beats with fear. Police are known to ride in Ford's just as such. He doesn't want to make them think he's up to something so he puts on a fake confident demeanor. He stares at the windshield, which is tinted as well, and nonchalantly he waves the car on, to pass him. Instead of passing, the Explorer stops in the middle of the street.

For a quick second he thinks of taking off in flight but he doesn't want to overreact and give them a reason to jump out on him, when maybe they wouldn't have. He feels he's better off on feet than to get in his car. The last thing he wants to do is get in his car and get boxed in. Here he stands in the middle of the street, dead to the rear with over a half of a kilo in his bag. He's standing still and so are they. He's not sure of what he should do.

Just as he's about to cross the Explorer gasses up and slowly passes him. He looks straight ahead as nonchalant as he can. The vehicle gasses up, and so does he. So nervous, he passes gas as he takes his steps across the street. He peeks out of the corner of his eye and notices the brake lights on as if the driver is cruising with his feet on the gas. This tells him the driver is prepared to stop any second. The man quickly gets into his Jeep

The Explorer slow rolls pass Bruh in Law's Cherokee. Bruh in Law can feel eyes piercing through the tints. He's afraid to move. He looks straight ahead as if he doesn't see the car, but his foot is already on the brake, prepared to shift the car into drive and take them for the ride of their lives.

The Explorer slowly passes Bruh in Law's Cherokee and slow rolls up the block. Skelter and her Godson sit in the Durango a few cars away, watching the Explorer creep up the block. "Shit looking type weird," Skelter says as she studies the vehicle. She looks at the license plate. "Them ain't no local police. That might be State boys or even worse...the big boys. Sit still, sit still. Don't let them see us in here." The Explorer slowly approaches and rides right pass them without notice of them.

What or who is behind the tints of the Explorer is much more dangerous than the police. Tortura is turned around in the passenger's seat with anxiousness. He debates if he should back up or not. *"Eso fue movimiento justo alli* (That was a move right there)," Tortura says to Quabo who sits in the backseat. *"Yo digo que los sacudamos y descubramos lo que saben* (I say we shake them down, find out what they know.) *Y robarles por su trabajo* (And rob them for their work)."

Tortura has no clue the work they have is, in fact, their work. They just happen to be cruising and came across this move in progress. In their travels they have witnessed a many moves in progress. In the few days they have been traveling through Trenton they have not only learned their way around, but they know what areas have action and what areas have no action. In just a few days they have figured out how the whole city operates.

"Acabo de perder mas de dos millones dolares y quieres que explotemos nuestra portada robando a alguien por cacahuetes? (I just lost over three million dollars and you want us to blow our cover and get out and rob somebody for peanuts?) *Que es lo Maximo que puede tener sobre el un par de bolsas de heroina basura?* (What's the most he can have on him a couple of bricks of garbage dope?) *Eso tiene sentido para ti? (*Does that make sense to you?)"

Tortura becomes furious. *"Tiene sentido para usted que hayamos estado viajando por dias y no hayamos matado a nadie y usted haya perdido mas de tres millones de dolares?* (Does it make sense to you that we are riding around for days and haven't killed nothing and you just lost over three million dollars?) *Si nos movemos ahora, podemos obtener algunas respuestas y recupar su producto antes de que no quede mas!* (If we move now we can get answers to where your product is at before it's no more left!) *Tenemos que empezar a actuar y dejar de mentir!* (We have to start acting and stop talking!) *Es por eso que no necesito que Vayas conmigo!* (This is why I don't need you riding with me.) *Necesito moverme Como se moverme.*(I need to move how I know how to move.) *Lo he hecho a tu manera Durante Dias y no hemos obtenido ningun resultado.* (I have done it your way for days and we haven't got results.) *A partir de aqui en adelante, lo estoy haciendo a mi manera y no me importa lo que digas!* (Starting from here on out, I'm doing it my way and I don't care what you have to say!)"

In the midst of their little verbal spat, Skelter, Bruh in Law, and the buyer manage to flee the scene. Skelter and the others may never get to know who was behind those tints until it's too late, and Quabo and Tortura would hate to find out they were so close to their mark without even knowing it.

ONE HOUR LATER

SKELTER SITS AT the coffee table with stacks of money piled in front of her. She counts through a hefty roll in her hand like a bank-teller. She's in her glory right now. She's put out a total of 5 kilos so far and this is the first piece of big money she's gotten back in return. She feels like all her years of financial struggle are now behind her.

She places the money on the table and quickly grabs hold of another stack. She looks across the table at Helter's boyfriend. "See, Bruh in Law, I told you, you could do it. Look, in just a couple days you blew through over eight hundred and fifty grams."

The man blushes in acceptance of her approval. He's shocked that it was much easier than he expected. Almost makes him want to really advertise and market the product to see how much he really could move. But of course the scary side of him keeps him in his lane.

Skelter continues on with her pep talk to motivate him to work harder. "This shit sell itself. All you have to do is let the people know you have it. Before you know it you will be selling whole bricks to motherfuckers on some BMF shit," she says further gassing him up. She knows a little battery charge can go a long way.

She drops the last pile of money onto the table. "Twenty-eight thousand, nine hundred," she says with satisfaction. She can't believe that she's finally alive.

Skelter packs the bulk of the money into her Gucci fanny pack and straps it over her shoulders. She slides $2,000 over to Bruh in Law. She snatches the few remaining stacks from the table as she stands up. "So, you ready for another one?"

"Nah, not yet," Bruh in Law replies quickly. "Let me just finish up what I got left." He was hoping that moving through it so quickly would buy him some time but now he sees that isn't the case. He got through that first one safe and sound and is not ready to commit to another one just yet.

"You only got a hundred grams left. That will be gone in no time. I'm gone bring you another one in about an hour."

"Nah, hold up."

"Hold up nothing. We about to get to this money. See you in an hour. Get your people on the phone now and you probably can get through that one as soon as you get it. Time is money, don't waste a second of it," she says as she exits the room.

Skelter realizes once she drops work off in a person's hand and they owe her, it's accounted for. Kilos sitting in her possession have no value until she's put them into the hands of people that can move them. The second she drops it in their hands, the stopwatch starts ticking. Right now she's searching for the right people to drop the work on. She doesn't have many people she trusts so right now she plans to overload the few people she does have.

Skelter makes her way into the living-room where Helter sits rocking her baby to sleep. She walks over to the couch and drops 4 stacks next to Helter. "That's thirty-five hundred," Skelter says.

Helter looks at the money and quickly looks up to her sister with a look of gratitude covering her face. She doesn't feel worthy of the money for she hasn't moved a muscle to earn any of it. Skelter split the initial cash she got from the house down the middle all the way down to the last penny, $35,000 apiece. This makes close to 40 grand she's been given and she for feels guilty for taking every penny.

Skelter runs her fingers through the baby's hair as she admires her preciousness. Helter looks up to her. "Thanks."

"Thanks?" Skelter asks in a slightly agitated tone. "Since when we start thanking each other?"

"I know but you bringing all that money to me and I haven't done anything for it."

"That never mattered before. When we were kids if somebody gave one of us fifty cents, we gave the other one a quarter. Ain't nothing change. Only difference is instead of fifty cents, I got more than fifty bricks and I'm gone bust the profit down with you off every one of them. And you don't have to leave the house to get your money. I'm gone bring it to you and drop it on your lap."

Helter shakes her head from side to side, without the words to reply. She's the oldest of the twins but Skelter always carried it as if she was the eldest. Regardless of how the chips were stacked against them she could always depend on Skelter to make it happen for them. Skelter never really needed her physical backing. She more so needs her mentally.

Just having her sister by her side to bounce ideas off as the voice of reasoning was Helter's true purpose. Even though she rarely listened, just having her there was enough. She more needed her by her side for spiritual bonding more than anything else. Helter knows this and it bothers her that she can't be out there with her right now.

Truthfully she's found a way out. Her baby has given her a sense of purpose in life. Choosing a man that is a good boyfriend and father is also a game changer. She just wishes her sister could find a way out as well but she really doesn't see that in her sister's future. This new arrangement that she's just come across has her digging herself deeper in the game, on a level that is new to both of them. And that's what Helter fears the most.

She's afraid her sister may not be able to operate on this level and everything may go bad for her. She also knows the repercussions to this last ordeal are limitless. She's sure in no way will anyone take a loss like this without seeking revenge. She's left a trail of dirt that she may never be able to clean up.

A sad expression crosses Helter's face. She peeks into the bedroom to make sure her boyfriend is not coming in. She keeps her eyes on the bedroom as she prepares to whisper. "Hak told me everybody talking about Jeezy and them all being murdered and you the only one who didn't get murdered. Nobody really knows what actually happened but they feel like you behind it. People know y'all were moving around together right before they got murdered."

"Man, people always gone talk. Don't nobody know shit."

"Nah, they really don't but they think they know that. Talking about you grimy and it sound like something you would do. He says they just don't know why you would do it."

"I don't really give a fuck what they think."

"But you should give a fuck. Can't have everybody against you out here. I think you should just lay low and don't be out here doing too much. If they see you out here shining and showing out they will put it together. It won't look good that all y'all were in it together and you the only one who still around."

"I don't give a fuck how it look," Skelter shouts. "The only motherfucker that I care about is Jeezy and I had nothing to do with his murder. I did my best to hold him down but it went down the way it went down. Them other two motherfuckers were just pawns on the board. This shit is chess and in chess the Queen only protects the King. I don't have a King to protect so everybody else on that board is meaningless to me. Also, if you know anything about chess, the Queen moves in any direction she chooses to.

Meaning, I do what the fuck I want to do when the fuck I want to do it. My only mission right now is to prevent myself from being captured by my opponent, and be checkmated, whether it be the police or anybody else on the opposite side. And I'm gone do whatever the fuck it take to do that. With that being said, I'm gone need you to holler at him and find out who it is that's running their mouth about shit they know nothing about. Got me?"

Helter nods her head in agreeance. "Absolutely," Helter replies. "I'm on that as soon as you leave."

"Cool and once you find that out, I will make sure they never open their mouths about my business ever again."

• • •

A shabby man walks hunched over struggling with every step he takes. He squints his face with agony for every step he takes causes his bones to ache even more. He stops mid-stride and grabs hold of his abdomen. He leans against the wall to hold himself up as the pain rips through his body. He's in so much discomfort that he doesn't notice the Ford Explorer sitting parked in front of him, running idle.

Quabo watches the man from the backseat. "I know that look," Quabo says to Tortura. "He's dope-sick. Let me get out and help him."

"Help him?" Tortura asks with sarcasm.

Quabo ignores Tortura and gets out of the truck. Tortura and the other men watch Quabo with confusion as he walks over to the man. The man tries to stand up erect. He watches Quabo approach him and fears he could be the police or maybe even somebody that he may have stolen from. He wants to run but can't muster up the energy to do so.

"Yo, what's up?" Quabo asks. "You good?"

"Yes, I'm cool," the man replies. "I'm just not feeling good, today." Tears of pain trickle down the man's face. He wipes his eyes with pride.

"You need something?" Quabo asks. "Can I help you?" Quabo places his hand on the man's shoulder to comfort him. "Come on man. I know that look you have in your eyes. You need dope don't you?"

The man can't lie if he wanted to. "Yes, I'm sick. I been trying to get this monkey off my back but it ain't easy though," he says as he grabs hold of his abdomen. The pain that just dropped into the pit of his stomach is enough to knock him off his feet yet he manages to stand.

"I'm sure it ain't," Quabo says with a fake sense of compassion. "My heart goes out to you. I had that same monkey on my back for years," he lies in attempt to connect with the man and build his trust. "What you need to get off empty? Five bags? Would that do it?"

The man's teary eyes brighten up. "Yes, that will help me a lot." There is a God, he says in his mind. He feels like his morning conversation with God paid off. His prayers have been answered.

Quabo nods his head. "What if I can give you money for a bundle? That will hold you, right?" The man nods his head. This help would save his life right now. "Ok, check it out. I will help you but I'm gone need your help though. One hand washes the other."

"Anything," the man replies. "Just tell me what you need from me."

Quabo digs into his jacket pocket and pulls out a folded sheet of paper. He unfolds it and places it in front of the man's face. "You know her? How about him? Or him?"

The man studies the picture of Skelter closely. As a dope fiend who travels all over the city, chasing the best dope on the street at the time, he's familiar with almost every face in the city. He's come across so many people during his travels that it takes him a while to figure out if he's ever seen the face before. He looks at Quabo and tries to figure out if he's a cop. He wonders what he can be looking for her for.

He thinks back to a similar situation where he was dragged into somebody's case and was assigned a key witness to a murder. Buying dope from the wrong place at the absolute wrong time and the next thing he knew Homicide detectives were dragging him to the county jail where he sat for months because of an old warrant. It came out that he knew nothing of the homicide but the process of proving that was a long one.

The process of kicking his dope habit was an even longer one. Right now he thinks of being trapped off in jail, not able to get dope for days and the pain that comes with that. He would rather die than to be dope-sick for days. That vision of him in a jail cell, rolling around in pain, half dead plays in his mind like a nightmare. He quickly decides to stay out of this before he's dragged into another situation like the other one.

Quabo pulls a stack of bills from his pocket and gets to flicking through them. "You said a bundle will help you right?"

The man thinks harder. The money entices him and makes him lose sense of what trouble he can possibly get himself in. He also thinks of how he can easily get himself out of the pain he's in this very moment. "She looks familiar...real familiar," he says while staring closely at the picture. He squeezes his temples in deep thought.

Quabo pulls a crisp hundred-dollar bill from his knot of money. He holds it in between his fingertips enticingly. The man looks at the bill with saliva dripping from his mouth like a thirsty dog. He flips though his mental rolodex and faces and places all start to come together.

"I don't know her but I think I know where I've seen her. The Projects, I think that's where she be."

"You sure?" Quabo asks.

"Eighty-five percent positive," the man replies.

Quabo hands the man the bill. He fist bumps him. "What's your name?"

"They call me No Toes," he says as he points down to his oversized and beat up Beef and Broccoli colored Timberland boots. "Lost four of my toes to frostbite many years ago," he says sadly.

"Sorry to hear that, No Toes," Quabo says sympathetically. "But where can I find you if I need you or if you need me again? I mean I have no problem dropping a bundle off on you every morning so you can get off empty."

This sounds like music to his ears. He lowers his head in shame. "I'm homeless," the man says with embarrassment. "But I have a little spot where I sleep at night. It's right around the corner. I can show you where it's at."

"Perfect, that will work," Quabo says. "I want to be able to drop in on you and give you the help you need until you can get that monkey off your back." Quabo waves the man on as he starts walking to the van. "Come on." The man follows behind Quabo with his eyes fixed on the hundred-dollar bill.

Quabo opens the side door for the man to enter the van. He quickly realizes the van is packed. As he looks around and sees guns on the lap of every man in the van, big guns, he stops short with fear. Judging by the artillery and the looks in these men's eyes he counts out the possibility of them being police. He can smell a killer a mile away and in this van he smells at least four.

"Don't worry about them. Get in," Quabo says as he nudges the man.

The man is hesitant to get in until Tortura looks back at him. "Come!" Tortura shouts aggressively. "Fuck!"

The man gets in and sits down nervously watching all around him as Quabo gets in and sits in the middle row next to him. "Where do you need to go to get your medicine?" Quabo asks. "Just tell my driver which way to go."

"Right at the corner," the man says as he keeps his eyes on every gun in the vehicle. He's so scared that he could defecate on himself; well again that is. He already did it once about 15 minutes ago just as he does almost every day when he's dope-sick. His mind quickly erases the guns and danger around him as he thinks of the dope that he's about to get to ease all of his pain. He sits here eyes watering, mouth dry, bones aching, and stomach turning but he's happy to know that in a matter of a few minutes he will be cured.

MINUTES LATER

The stench coming from the man is a cross between garbage truck leakage, urine and defecation. Quabo and the crew are damn near dying from suffocation from holding their breath for so long. The man is also suffocating himself as well as he has his nose buried into a small bag of dope. With one sniff, he devours the entire bag. He uses the tip of a pocketknife to slit another bag and he devours that one faster than the first one.

He looks up from the bag briefly. "Coming up, right there on the right," the man says before taking a huge sniff.

"Pull over," Quabo instructs.

The driver pulls over and parks across from the buildings. "Right here is where I've seen her before. Right behind those buildings right there." Quabo and Tortura take surveillance of the area. This is the first time they've seen these buildings. "Looks quiet around here but trust me it's a lot going on around here. The murder rate is astronomical. This ain't no place to be fucking around." With just a few sniffs it's like the man has taken on another personality. He's now alive.

Quabo looks around at the foot traffic and immediately identifies the most of them as dope fiends. "What they selling back there, dope?" Quabo asks.

The man takes two back to back sniffs before replying. "They got everything a motherfucker want back there but mainly garbage dope. Five-dollar bags," he adds.

Quabo pulls his knot of money out once again. "Do me a favor," he says as he peels a twenty-dollar bill from the pile. "Go back there and get yourself four of those bags."

"Really?" The man feels like he's hit the lottery today. He started his journey this morning with no clue of where he would get money from to get his morning dosage. He now has enough dope to last him all day and part of the day tomorrow. Talk about being at the right place at the right time. "Won't God do it," he mumbles to himself.

Quabo extends the bill toward the man. The man snatches the money and Quabo slides the door open. The man excuses himself as he slides past Quabo. "Be right back."

Just as his feet touch the ground, Quabo speaks. "And while you're back there take a look around and see if you see her."

The man nods up and down without saying a word. He walks off, crossing the street with a burst of energy they didn't see in him a few minutes ago. He's like a whole new man. They watch him until he disappears.

"*Tirar hacia abajo al otro de la calle* (Pull down there on the other side of the street)," Tortura says to the driver. "*Por si acaso intenta algun negocio divertido* (Just in case he tries some funny business.)"

The driver quickly does as he's commanded to do. From down the block on the opposite side of the street they watch the area closely. Their heads on swivel, careful not to miss a beat. They know how dangerous this could be for them for they have no clue of who this man really is and how well he may really know her.

This all could very well be a trap. Any minute they can come out of nowhere and ambush them. With them having no knowledge of the area it leaves them at a huge disadvantage. The more they think of the possibilities the tighter they grip their weapons in their hands.

In minutes, the man reappears walking from the next alley that he used to enter. He looks around lost when he doesn't see the van. From where they are they can see him shrug his shoulders baffled. He walks off in the opposite direction, quickly burying his nose into a bag of dope. They watch without moving, just waiting to see if anything looks weird to them. Right before he gets to the corner, Quabo speaks. "Go," he says waving the driver on.

The man doesn't notice them cruising on the side of him because his nose is practically glued to the bag of dope. The driver hits the horn and the man looks up. His eyes stretch wide open as he spots the van. He sprints across the street at them with no sign of pain or aching bones. His missing toes having him running awkward and off-balanced, with a skip, hop, bounce, trot.

Quabo slides the door open and he climbs in. "I looked all over back there and not a sign of her. It was kind of empty back there though."

"It's ok," Quabo says. He doesn't want to come across super desperate even though he is. "We got time. We will find her and you will help us, right?"

"Hey man, you helped me, so I have to return the favor. Pure strangers pull up and offer me a hand while people I've known all my life won't give me a hand, or even a hot meal when I'm hungry."

"Speaking of hungry," Quabo interrupts. "Are you hungry? I got you on that, don't worry. Now tell me which way to go to get to where you stay. I need to know where I can find you if I need you or to see if you need me."

"Just go straight," the man advises.

Approximately six blocks later, the man finally tells them to pull over at an abandoned house that he calls home. Rubbish floods the front of the house and all over the porch. Not a window on the house; each window frame empty.

"This where I will be right here. I'm here most of the time unless I'm out on the prowl trying to find a way to get my medicine," the man says with a snaggle toothed smile. "Just pull to the alley right there and hit the horn. The Master bedroom is right there," he says while pointing to a side room. "I will hear you."

"Ok," Quabo says as he slides the door open for the man to exit. "I will be back, and of course, I won't come empty handed. I will always bring a gift for you," he says with a smile.

The man smiles back in return. "I thank you," he says as he gets out of the van.

Just as he's walking away Quabo gets out behind him without him even realizing it. "Hey!" Quabo calls out. The man stops in his tracks. "Yo, check it out," he says as he stares into the man's eyes. "I ain't even gone lie to you…my friends back there don't trust you. They want to kill you because they think you may run your mouth and tell her we looking for her." Quabo's mission is to instill the fear of death in the man.

"Kill me?" The man asks in a high pitched, scary voice. "Run my mouth? Word is bond on my Earth(Mother), I ain't gone run my mouth! Shit, I done told y'all where she be. Done brung y'all to her spot and everything. Do you know they would kill me for that? Them motherfucking kids over there don't play. They murder for fun. You ain't got to worry about me," he says in further attempt to save his life. "Look man, I done brought y'all to my home. It ain't much but it's where I rest my head. This is where I'm at most of the time. I ain't got shit to hide. I be right here."

"Nah, I believe you. Now I just got to go back in there and make them believe you, feel me? Don't worry about nothing. I got this. Me and you just have to be right here though," he says as he puts his fingers to his eyes and close to the man's eyes as if they're connected.

"Definitely," the man replies. "Any time of the day just come and hit the horn. I will be here. If not here, I be over at the Post Office during business hours, getting my hustle on, out front of there."

"Ok, I got you," Quabo says as he backpedals. "I may pop back on you in a few hours or so."

"Ok, I'm here. I got enough dope to last me the rest of the day so I don't have to move. I'm gone go in here and put my feet up and relax."

Quabo gives him the thumbs up before turning around and getting into the van. Before pulling off they watch the man walk up the alley. Tortura speaks to Quabo in English. "I don't trust him. You can never trust a dope fiend. The sneakiest people in the world. Dope brings the worse out of everybody. Dope dealers and dope addicts all the same… dirty and filthy. It's a filthy game. I don't trust the people who use it, just like I don't trust the people who sell it. They are all filthy. Once he gave us the information we should have killed him so he could never tell anybody we been around here questioning him."

"No need to kill him," Quabo replies. "We will use him to help us catch her. One thing I learned a long time ago is if you feed a stray dog they will always come back to you to eat again. He's a stray dog and dope is Dog Food. As long as we feed him he will keep coming back to us and he will lead us right to the girl. We finally have a solid location on her. Now we have to sit on her and wait for her to show her face. This won't be long now."

33

NEW JERSEY TURNPIKE/ALEXANDER HAMILTON REST STOP

THE REST STOP is busy with travelers as usual for this time of day. The beautiful RV Motorhome sits at the far end of the parking lot, blending in with all the other Motorhomes, but standing out luxuriously. The most beautiful and most expensive Motorhome most have ever seen in real life is parked right here before their very eyes. Groups of people are gathered around taking pictures of it and taking pictures standing by it.

Inside of the RV, Tony sits comfortably in the recliner in the living-room area. The blinds on the windows are closed airtight so no one can see inside. He can hear the oohs and the aahs coming from outside but he blocks them out. He fumbles through a stack of papers, reading every line of each document carefully.

Across from him sits Jane Doe. Tony's friend over at the FDA hasn't finished her search yet but she has given him enough information to confirm that Jane Doe is not just some crazy conspiracy theorist. His friend has confirmed that in order for her to know the things she knows she had to once be on the inside. Now that Tony is certain that they have legs to stand on, he's all the way in.

Jane Doe carries on with a conversation that Tony is paying very little attention to. He's so consumed with the reading of the documents. Doesn't matter that he's not listening because he has a small tape recorder on the table to catch anything that he's missed. Tony has learned that Jane Doe is a rambler and throughout her rambling she drops some heavy jewels. He plans to listen through her rambling to get to the key points that are necessary. He can't afford to miss the smallest detail because that detail may be just what he needs to build an airtight case.

"What people fail to realize," Jane Doe says as she adjusts the surgical mask over her mouth. "America is a business...a corporation. It's always at their best interest to make money. As a businessman I'm sure you can relate. It's never personal. Every man and woman has an obligation to this country and that obligation is to contribute some type of revenue to the system," she says as she shrugs her shoulders. "Simple as that," she adds.

"You will give Uncle Sam what you owe him, one way or another," she says. "If you are a student, your contribution will be through the student loan program. If you are an employee, your contribution will be the taxes that are taken out of your check every pay period. If you are an entrepreneur, your contribution will be the taxes you pay every few months through your LLC. And lastly, if nothing else but a criminal—which is considered the lowest on the totem pole—your contribution will be the amount of money that can be made off you through the prison system. Society considers the criminals the smut of the earth when in actuality the criminal is the most important part of American business. Crime fuels the economy!"

Jane Doe now has Tony's attention. She's talking his language. The other stuff she talks about goes way over his head so he just sits back and listens with hopes of learning. Now that she's speaking his language he can see what she really knows. Tony loves a great debate because to him it's like mental tennis. It keeps his mind sharp. He listens to her point of view, looking for an opening for debate.

"Let's take a man that hasn't contributed anything to society. He's charged with a crime that carries a twenty-year prison term. Prison owners receive forty-thousand dollars per inmate."

"Seventy-thousand," Tony says in correction.

"Ok," Jane Doe submits with no debate. "Seventy-thousand dollars times twenty years," she says quickly calculating in her mind. "That's one point four million. Now you have a man that was worth nothing on the streets, out in the world, but he's worth close to a million and a half in prison. It's more lucrative to keep him in prison."

Tony nods his head in agreeance. "Now, let's take it a step further," she says. With a twenty-year sentence, the average man will need medication to cope. They hook him on the medication and now he's worth even more to the system. Now let's say the others who are up in age develop diseases whether naturally or **unnaturally,**" she emphasizes. "Now they are worth even more to the system."

Tony's been on the side waiting like a girl about to jump Double Dutch. Finally, he chimes in. "Did you know that the groups that own privatized prisons are the same groups that own the Charter schools in the ghettos?"

"Now that I didn't know," Jane Doe admits.

"And both are funded by the same Wall Street groups," Tony further informs. "Also, did you know that third grade test scores of our children determine how many prisons that will be built in the future? Add in the fact that they will push our children through this pipeline because it makes great business sense to do so. So, they make money off our children in the Charter Schools and once they graduate, if they graduate, they will lock them into the prison system and continue to make money off them for the rest of their lives."

"And don't forget to add in the many drugs they will be hooked on along the way," Jane Doe interrupts. "Speaking of drugs, I have proof of clinical researching wherein young children have been swabbed and the results determine what their future will be. So that proves some truth in what you're saying about determining how many prisons should be built for the future."

"Exactly, Tony agrees. "Through these Charter Schools they program them and get them ready for prison. Walk the straight line, without turning your head. Sit in this cubicle without turning your head.

This area wears blue shirts and that area wears green shirts. That's color-coding no different from in the prison system," he says with a sad expression on his face.

"I've witnessed with my own eyes, classrooms where the white Principal sits two floors up on a highchair in the middle of the class, watching over her class like a warden in a prison," Tony claims. "Let me ask you, if Charter Schools are so great how come there are none in the suburbs?"

"Great question," Jane Doe replies. "But don't ask me. Why haven't you presented that question to the masses? You are a powerful man. They will listen to you. But your power is limited to this much of the world," she says as she holds her hands in a small circle. "After we are done with this case that will change," she says confidently.

Tony's eyes brisk across something that shocks him. He holds the document closer to his face and reads it over and over, allowing it to register. "Wow," he says as he lays the paper down. He points to the line for her to see.

Jane Doe looks emotionless. "Yes, and he's not the first that was done to," she says. "He was too valuable to this country. Word got out that he was working on a deal with a Japanese company. That meant the money would have been taken to Japan. He went for his six-month physical and was diagnosed with it. Researched the results of the last six month physical where there was no trace of it. In a six months' time period, he was full blown.

Takes years to reach that level. It was later proven that he contracted it through injection. That injection is believed to be the flu shot that was administered two months prior. The head of administration deemed it a requirement to have that shot. He died and a younger and more obedient scientist took his place. Needless to say, the contract is still here in the States."

"Wow," Tony says in awe. "And this right here is all the proof we need?"

"Yes," Jane Doe replies. "But I have more," she claims. "I have famous celebrities that the world loved, software programmers, politicians. I have more than enough proof to blow this case open."

"Well, let's go then," Tony says anxiously.

"I have proof that local pharmacies are spreading disease that flu shots in the ghettos."

"Wow, Tony says in no shock at all. "I always thought that."

"Well, you thought right," says Jane Doe.

Tony is fired up. "Let's get to it. I'm ready."

"Patience," she says as she grabs hold of his hand. "I want to reveal to you my entire arsenal before we strike. We can't play with them. We have to be fully prepared because as I told you, once we strike, your life will never be the same." Jane Doe's words sends chills through his body. It also sends his battery a charge.

"Well, I've held up enough of your time," she says as she digs into her purse. "Plus my oxygen tank is almost empty," she says as she plucks at her oxygen tank. "Got to get back to my safe-haven."

She pulls out a checkbook and a pen. She quickly rips a check from the book and slams it on the table. She looks Tony in the eyes with a soft and caring look. "You still have not given me a price for taking on this case. I need you to make this worth your while times ten," she says with a bright smile. She hands him the pen and slides the blank check closer to him. "Fill in the blank. Remember, money is no issue. And keep in mind, this case can change your life for the worse, so it would be in your best interest to charge me a price that is worth putting it all on the line."

For the first time, Tony thinks about the risk that he's taking and not focusing on the notoriety this can bring him. He ponders on the thought. Jane Doe can see his wheels turning. "Again, I say money is no issue," says Jane Doe as she taps the blank check. "Whatever amount you put in the blank, be sure to make it worth your while."

34

COLORADO ADX

TEN CORRECTION OFFICERS, all Blacks, all dressed in riot gear stand at the door, preparing themselves for the fight of their lives. None of them really want to enter but it's part of their job description. They hate the fight part but love the part where the inmate is in shackles at their mercy while they beat on him like a slave. It's always pleasurable for most of them to dominate a man and make him submit.

Inside the cell with his back against the wall, prepared to rumble is Manson. Manson stands tall with his chest puffed high. Today he hasn't been drugged up as of yet, so he isn't drowsy or in his normal trancelike state. Instead, he's vibrant, full of energy and feeling as strong as a bull.

"Bryant, step out of the cell," one of the officers yell.

Manson leans his head back as he takes a deep breath. He clenches his fists tightly at his thighs. "I ain't coming out. Y'all got to come in and get me."

"Bryant, you know how it will end if we have to come in and get you. Make it easy on yourself and just step out on your own and not make us drag you out."

"I'm gone warn y'all," Manson shouts. "I'm feeling strong today. Y'all gone have to murder me in here because I'm feeling like I can slaughter at least two of y'all right now."

"Last chance Bryant, step out!"

"No need for another chance," Manson shouts back. "I said what I said. I ain't coming out. Now come on in and get me."

The officer sighs with frustration. "Ok, Bryant, I tried," the officer says as he signals for his men to enter. They line up at the door, from biggest to the smallest. Just as they are ready to invade the cell a voice is heard from behind them.

"Hold up." Everyone looks to the back and spots the white officer, a frail, little man. He walks up to the door and looks to the head officer. "Wait, let me talk to him." Manson sees the man at the door that has earned his trust but right now he sees him for what he is; an officer.

"Go on and talk to him but seems he has his mind made up," says the head officer. "I tried to talk to him. He must like getting beat to a pulp. Maybe he's become addicted to the pain," he says accompanied by laughter.

Manson becomes enraged. "You think y'all cause me pain? Ten of you motherfuckers at a time and I still manage to walk away on my own two feet, every time. No pain," he shouts irately. "Ain't a pussy motherfucker alive that can cause me pain," he says with a sinister twinge in his eyes.

"Ok, well, today is your lucky day then," the officer shouts back. "Today, we are going to show you what pain feels like…since you've never felt it."

"I told y'all minutes ago to come on and get it," Manson says over a devilish smile. "One thing for certain, one or two of you motherfuckers gone rest in peace today. All of y'all should call your wives and children right now and tell them you love them because you never know which one of you not gone make it out of this cell."

These words infuriate some of the others while it terrifies a few others. The head officer smacks the wall. "That's it, let's go. This motherfucker talks too much! Only thing he gone respect is a boot on his head."

"Y'all got twenty-two boots out there," Manson says, including his friendly officer. "Come on inside and try and put them on my head. I ain't off the meds today. Trust me, today will be a different day for y'all. Best believe I will not be the only one leaking blood when it's over."

The head officer takes a step forward but is pulled back by the arm. The friendly officer looks to the head officer with pleading eyes. "No, please let me go in and talk to him."

"Go in with that looney toon motherfucker?" the head officer asks with surprise. "You don't even have on the proper gear."

"Don't worry, I got this," the man says. He steps past the officers and to the front of the doorway. "Bryant, I'm coming in to talk to you."

Manson stares the officer up and down without speaking. Although he has a certain level of trust for this officer he can't forget that he is an officer. All of them play for the same team. Right now it's them against him. Manson stares him up and down trying to read his body language.

"Bryant, I'm coming inside," the officer says in attempt to get some type of okay from him.

Manson looks in his eyes to see if he can see cross in them but he doesn't. He sees the same genuineness that the man always has in his eyes. But still they could be using him as the bait. "Whoever comes in here is taking the chance of losing their life," Manson threatens.

"Bryant, nobody is losing their life here today," the officer says in a calm tone. "I'm coming in here to talk to you and hopefully you will leave out with me with nobody having to get physical. And we all live to see another day. Now, I'm coming inside," the man says as he takes quick and confident steps toward Manson.

Manson clenches his fists tighter and holds them up by his chest, preparing for battle. The officer discreetly shakes his head from side to side, only for Manson to see. The officer places his hands high in submission as he gets within feet of Manson. "Listen," he whispers barely loud enough for Manson to hear. "It's almost over. Don't do this." He now stands face to face with Manson. "I told you I was retiring in a few weeks but I had so much vacation time they owe me that I can do it sooner," he says in his lowest whisper. "In less than two weeks I will be out of here. And my promise to you is still my promise to you."

The officers at the door all strain their ears to hear the man but they can't. They notice Manson's relaxing stature as if he's in full trust of the officer but can't understand it. For years they have had to enter the cell in riot gear just to stand within feet of Manson but this man stands before him man to man. They can't make sense of it.

Manson stands in peace. He slowly turns around and allows the officer to cuff his hands behind his back. The officer cuffs him and they walk out of the cell close together. The man takes the lead at the door.

The officer looks to the crew of officers who are all standing in disbelief. "At the end of the day, we all are men," the officer says. "Real men deal with respect. In order to get respect you must give it," he says as he guides Manson through the doorway. "And I trust no one will lay a hand on him because he stepped out voluntarily just as you requested."

The officer looks over his shoulder back at Manson. He winks at Manson slyly. "I got you," he mumbles before walking off. "I got you."

35

BRUH IN LAW sits in the driver's seat of his Jeep. He waits patiently as the passenger counts through his stack of money for the third time. Bruh in Law, as much as he didn't want to play this position, and was practically forced into it, is now becoming more comfortable with it. Dealing with his addict customers, it takes him an entire day to make the same amount of profit that he can make in just one move this way.

Bruh in Law looks around, watching out for police in the area. He digs into his left pocket and retrieves the plastic bag filled with a beautiful square, 50-gram chunk of cocaine. He stares at the chunk in admiration, spinning it around to view from every angle. So caught up in the beauty of the cocaine he doesn't see the long nose revolver which is inches away from his face. "You know what time it is," the man says calmly.

Bruh in Law looks up and the sight of the gun sends him into a fearful frenzy. Out of nervous reflex, he slaps the gun away from his face. Meanwhile with the other hand, he forces the door open. Like a flash of lightning, he dashes out of his own car and takes off across the street. He sprints up the block, never once looking back.

The passenger thinks of chasing him but the package of cocaine that he's left on the seat makes it senseless to run behind him. He opens the dashboard where he finds a few stacks of money. He tucks the money and the cocaine into his pocket before flipping the middle console open where he finds two smaller baggies of cocaine. The man gets out of the Jeep nonchalantly, gun tucked in his waistband, drugs and money in his pocket. One of the easiest scores he's ever made, just like taking candy from a baby.

ONE HOUR LATER

Bruh in Law paces on his porch, fists clenched tightly. He's furious but more than that he's embarrassed. He can't believe that he's allowed this to happen to him. He's sure by now the news has spread halfway around the town. He's never been disrespected like this in his life. Main reason being, he's never had himself in a situation to be disrespected like this. He hates the fact that he allowed Skelter to force him in this situation.

As he looks up he notices Skelter's rental speeding up the block. He races down the stairs and he meets the Durango in the middle of the street. The driver's window rolls down slowly. The back window rolls down slowly and there Skelter is, sitting in the middle of the back seat.

"What's up? You sound like it was a life or death emergency," she says as she lays two handguns onto her lap to let him know she came ready to play.

He's too embarrassed to even admit this but he refuses to let it go like this. He knows if he doesn't tell her what happened, she will eventually find out. He understands the streets have no secrets. He's afraid of how she will react to him if she finds out from the streets so he rather tell her himself. "Yo, nigga just worked it on me," he says before banging his fist into the palm of his hand. He stares at the sky. He's fighting the tears of rage from dripping from his eyes.

"Worked it?"

"Yeah, nigga just got me. I went to serve him fifty grams and I look up and the gun in my face." Regardless of what, he refuses to tell the truth about running and leaving his car. He will not be able to face her or Helter after that. "Nigga made me get out my shit," he lies. "Took everything and then said, now get out and run," he further lies.

"So, what you do?" Skelter questions curiously.

"I got out, and I didn't run, but I jogged off. Like, if I had my shit on me, I could've spinned on him and let him have it."

"So, why didn't you have your shit on you?" Skelter asks. "You making moves with niggas serving them and you don't have it on you?"

"I know, Sis," he says trying to find a soft spot in a heart that he knows has none. "I been kicking myself up the ass too. He hit me good. Altogether like two hundred grams and forty-five hundred in cash." He stomps the ground angrily. "Yo, I got to see this nigga, yo! Fuck that!" His embarrassment has turned into rage.

"Who is the nigga?" Skelter asks.

"He some lil nobody ass nigga. That's what makes it even worse. I've been serving him for years. A couple grams here and there," Bruh in Law adds. "I reached out to his man, not even him. Like the little shit he be buying, wasn't even worth my call. His man must have told him what I had going on. I got to see both of them though!"

"You know where to find them?" Skelter asks.

"Hell yeah!" Bruh in Law replies. "He from Locust."

Skelter leans over and forces the door open. She looks to Bruh in Law with war in her eyes. "Well, get in and let's go see them then."

MINUTES LATER

The Dodge Durango rental is parked in the back of an abandoned house. Skelter stands in front of the truck while Youngest Godson is kneeled down in front of her. He unscrews the Maryland license plates from the truck and quickly screws in a New Jersey plate. At the back of the truck Middle Godson is doing the same. They always keep spare license plates lying around for times like this.

Bruh in Law stands in the cut, searching for an escape. His rage has evaporated and has been replaced with fear. He wishes there was something he could say to get himself out of it but he knows that's unlikely. Both young men stand up at the same time. Their eyes are lit up excitedly. They live for the action. Youngest Godson snatches the driver's door open and hops in while Middle Godson makes his way to the passenger's seat.

"Come on," Skelter says to Bruh in Law as she passes him. She climbs into the backseat.

Bruh in Law walks toward the opposite side, taking baby steps. With each step he can think of another reason he shouldn't be doing this. He keeps all of the reasons to himself because he's sure Skelter will not accept not a one of them. Once Bruh in Law gets into the backseat, all of the doors are slammed shut simultaneously.

The Durango cruises down the narrow alley. Once they get to the end of the alley, the driver peeks around with caution and sees the coast is clear. He mashes his foot on the gas pedal causing the tires to burn rubber. The truck bounces off of the curb and speeds through the block. Bruh in Law's eyes are on the road and his heart pounding with fear. Ain't no stopping now, he thinks to himself. "God, please don't let them be out here," Bruh in Law prays silently to himself. "Please, God."

TEN MINUTES LATER

From a block away, a group of men can be seen huddled in front of the townhouses. Skelter is leaned over so she can see in between the front seats. She watches as she quickly thinks of a plan and an escape. She likes to picture the whole movie before actually moving, just to picture it all unfold mentally first.

Bruh in Law is petrified right now. He's so terrified that he's close to opening the door and jumping out. He looks around and is surprised as to how they can be this close to making a move and still remain calm. This is the most frightening moment of his life and they sit back calm like just an ordinary day.

Halfway through the block and now the faces of the men can be made out. The driver slows down as they peep the area. "You see him?" Skelter asks.

Bruh in Law's heart bangs through his chest as he lays eyes on the man. He's in clear view standing in a huddle entertaining the crowd. Seeing him smile like this infuriates Bruh in Law to no end. He's still terrified, just equally angry. "Yeah, right there with the black sweatsuit," he says as he points up ahead.

"Perfect," Skelter says as she nods her head like a mad scientist. "Right up on them," she says. "Open the roof once we get close. Bruh in Law, let's change seats."

"Huh?" Bruh in Law asks nervously.

"Change seats," she repeats as she climbs over his lap. Bruh in Law slides over close to the window, still not sure about what it is he's supposed to do. That is until she hands her gun over to him. He looks at her cluelessly before looking down at the gun. "Safety off, one in the head, eleven in the chamber," she says.

They creep up the block slowly. Bruh in Law is so scared he can barely contain himself. The very first movie he's ever been in and he's skipped over the co-star role and is the main actor. He would rather have a cameo role right now; just standing in the backdrop but instead he has been assigned an all action role.

As they get closer, he holds his finger up to the power window, ready to roll it down. He grips the gun tightly in his other hand. His heart is banging so hard and fast he can feel it in the palm of his hand. He takes a deep breath to try and slow down the rate of his heartbeat.

Skelter looks over at him shaking her head. "Fuck going out the window on him. We don't do drive-bys. We jump out and give 'em the whole clip."

Bruh in Law swallows his heart and it sinks into his boxers. Just as they get closer, the driver makes a sharp cut to the right and the truck bounces onto the sidewalk. Bruh in Law hesitates before getting out and that gives the men time enough to pay attention. A few back up nervously and one man takes off running.

Bruh in Law finally busts the door open and with a trembling hand he aims at his mark who is standing in the middle of the huddle. The man sees the gun and recognizes who is behind the gun and he backs away nervously. A quick cut of the heels and he takes off running. Bruh in Law feels a sense of power he's never felt in his life as he holds the gun tightly.

He feels defeated as his mark seems to be getting away. Bruh in Law steps onto the sidewalk to get a clear aim at the man. He looks down the barrel at his mark who is now cutting across the street diagonally. He squeezes the trigger. *BLOCKA!*

MEANWHILE

Quabo and his crew, doing their normal patrolling of the city, they turn onto a block. Coincidentally, it's the same block that the action is in pre-production. They hear a single shot ring and duck low as they grip their guns. The driver spots a man running in front of them. The driver slams on the brakes and his eyes quickly divert across the street where the gunman stands. The man has his gun aimed and he seems ready to fire again. The driver slams the gear into reverse to get out of harm's way.

With the van backed up out of the way, the mark is in clear sight. Bruh in Law squeezes. *BLOCKA!* In seconds, the man's leg buckles, indicating that he's been hit. He grabs the back of his leg and continues to run like a maimed deer who is being hunted. Bruh in Law fires one, two, three, four more shots with no success. *BLOCKA! BLOCKA! BLOCKA! BLOCKA!*

A man appears on the porch a few feet away from them. He fumbles with his pants until his gun is revealed. He aims at Bruh in Law and before he can shoot, Middle Godson pops out of the sunroof and fires a string of shots. *BOC! BOC! BOC! BOC! BOC!*

The man throws 3 shots of his own back before he backs away looking for cover. *POP! POP! POP!*

Skelter dashes out of the backseat and before she sets foot on the ground, she pulls the strings of her hood tight to cover her face. She runs toward the man squeezing non-stop. *BLOCKA! BLOCKA! BLOCKA!* She doesn't stop firing until the man is tumbling backwards. He lands on his back and his gun falls out of his hand. He rolls around, not able to get up. Skelter runs up to the porch and from the ground level, she dumps 3 more into him. *BLOCKA! BLOCKA! BLOCKA!*

She turns around where she finds Bruh in Law stuck in fear. He's watching all of this and none of it actually registering. It's like one big blur around him. "Come on, let's go!" Skelter says as she zips past him on her way to the driver's side.

In the midst of her running, she spots the black Explorer in the cut. "Oh, shit," she mumbles to herself. She thinks the police have witnessed it all. Her heart pounds with fear. She dives into the backseat. "Go, go!" With Bruh in Law, barely in his seat, the driver pulls off.

Another man runs out of an alley with his gun held high. He runs out onto the street and squeezes his trigger. *BOC! BOC! BOC!* Skelter turns around in her seat, expecting to see the Explorer coming behind them or at least grabbing the gunman but instead she sees it speeding the opposite way, away from the danger.

"Damn," Bruh in Law shouts. "Now, we done started a war!" he sighs with fear.

"No," Skelter says. "They started the war. We 're just going to finish it."

Bruh in Law looks at Skelter, and at this moment, he realizes this is just the beginning of his living nightmare.

36

NORTHERN STATE PRISON/C-WING

BABY MANSON WALKS the POD in search of a particular person. He quickly spots the only correction officer that he halfway has a liking for. Officer Tillis is the most liked in all of Northern State. The respect that inmates have for him is not out of fear. He's never been on super-cop time, just a man doing his job. All the inmates show him top of the line respect because he shows them the same.

Baby Manson makes his way across the room. All eyes are on him as he approaches the officer. He's careful not to look too cool and friendly with the officer because as an inmate that's never a good look. The other inmates all wonder what he could possibly be whispering to the officer.

"Aye, Tillis," Baby Manson says in greeting. "I need you to go check on my bunkie. He laying in the bed fucked up. Nigga been crying and the whole shit. He in a lot of pain."

"Who, Hall? What's wrong with him?"

"I don't know but he twisted. Check him out for me though. And do me a favor and don't tell him I sent you. You know I ain't on no snitch time. Just tired of seeing him in pain like that. It's been going on two weeks."

"No doubt," the officer says as he walks away.

Officer Tillis stands at the door. From where he stands he can see the man rolling around in pain on his bunk. He watches for seconds before speaking. "Hall? What's up? You alright?"

The man grunts. "Yeah, I'm good," he says as normal as he can. The pain he's in is evident in his voice.

"Look at me," the officer commands.

The inmate sucks up the pain as best he can as he uses all of his willpower to pick himself up. He sits on the edge of the cot as straight as he can. The pain and discomfort can be seen all over his face. "What's up?"

"Hall, you don't look good," Tillis says with compassion. "Let's go to medical."

As much as he hates to do it, he realizes he has no choice. He's been laying here for almost two weeks, foolishly hoping the pain would eventually go away but it's only gotten worse. Even if the pain goes away the problem causing the pain never will. In fact, he's sure some real damage has been done by waiting around for two weeks.

"What got you in pain like this?"

The inmate gets up from the bed slowly. He steps toward the officer, each step causing more pain than the last one. "I have no clue," he lies. The truth will soon reveal itself though.

MEANWHILE ON F-WING

Smith, dressed in full Islamic attire, stands in the cut having a private conversation with an officer as well. This caramel brown beauty with a booty is the only officer he has ever liked. Officer Jones, standing at about 5'2" inches tall and 150 pounds is the sexiest thing to ever put on a correction officers' uniform. Her uniform pants grip her ass like a glove. Tight and firm booty meat explodes into curvaceous hips and spills over onto her thighs. Heavy with no sag at all, her perfectly rounded bottom sits up tall at attention. It should be illegal for her to work around all these horny, sex-deprived men looking the way she does.

There is one that isn't deprived and that is Smith. Jones makes sure of that. Jones realizes how dangerous it is to be dealing with an inmate but she can't help herself. Ever since a little girl, she's' been in love with the bad guys. With Smith being the baddest of the bad guys in this prison, she had to have him. Even if it means losing her career behind it. What a price to pay?

Smith has managed to get into her head and control her mind, just as he does almost everybody else he comes in contact with. He's a master at mind manipulation. In the few months that he's been dealing with her she's made his stay an easy one. She makes sure he gets everything he wants and she always finds a way to sneak and give him what they both want; sexual contact. It's not just the rush of dealing with an inmate that turns her on. It's the sneaking around and having sex with an inmate all throughout the Wing that turns her on even more.

"So dig this, mama," Smith says while staring into her beautiful babydoll eyes. Cocoa brown skin, full luscious lips, and long, thick locs has her looking like a pretty African Goddess. For a moment Smith gets lost in her beauty and his mind wanders, picturing her covered up in full Islamic garb, with only her beautiful eyes showing.

Officer Jones notices the sparkle in his eyes as he looks at her and she blushes. She bites down on her bottom lip, exposing the huge but sexy gap in between her front two teeth. "Why you looking at me like that?"

Smith shakes away the vision. "Like I was saying," he says. "I got something that need to be handled over on C-Wing. I don't really know how you gone pull it off but I got a couple of my men that I need to be moved over there... like Asap," he says with great emphasis.

"That's gone be hard," she claims.

"It's only hard as you make it," Smith replies in rebuttal. "All things are possible," he says while staring into her eyes. "This shit killing me. I can't sleep until I get this shit done," he says while shaking his head from side to side. He knows how she hates to see him stressed and frustrated so he's pouring it on extra thick right now. "I'm saying, if you can make this happen for me, it will take a huge load off my mind. This shit has to happen like yesterday."

"Ok, I will try," she says with skepticism.

Smith shakes his head vehemently, "No," he denies her reply. "You won't try."

"I said, I will try," she says almost helplessly. "What you want me to say?"

"I want you to say you got me and you will get it done," Smith says sternly. "Don't, when I tell you I got you, no matter what it is, I make it happen?"

Officer Jones thinks of all that he's able to do for her even under these circumstances. She's come to him with rent issues, late car payments and other financial problems and all he's had to do is make a phone call or two and was able to get to her whatever money she's needed and some. Now that he's asking her for a favor she feels obligated to make it happen. "Yes, you do, every time," she replies.

"Ok, then," he says rather smoothly. "Now tell me you got me and you gone find a way to make it happen for me, the way I do for you."

She stares into his eyes in a trance like state. "I got you and I will find a way to make it happen for you the way you make it happen for me."

"Good enough," he says. "Now, go on away from me before these nosey motherfuckers have something to say."

Jones walks away at his command like a robot that has been programmed by him. "Yo," he whispers before she gets too far away from him. Jones turns around quickly. "You know I love you, right?"

Jones nods her head up and down with sparkling eyes. "I know you do."

"Good. Now get that done for me so I can finally sleep and get this shit off my mind."

"I got you," she whispers before walking away.

MEDICAL UNIT

The inmate is being escorted out of the medical unit by two officers. Hands shackled in front of him and his ankles shackled together, he takes baby steps. The pain he feels is unbearable now just as it's been for the past 2 weeks. Embarrassment is what has kept him from seeking help but now he's on his way to face the music. He's escorted to the transport van to be transported to the hospital where he is already set up for emergency surgery. And this is the point that he's been dreading.

37

QUABO SITS NEXT to No Toes, who has his nose buried deep into the crease of a bag of dope. He sniffs every particle from the bag not leaving a spec anywhere. They've been riding around for hours in search of a trace of Skelter or any one of the people in their pictures. They sat at a front row seat, watching the movie she just made not even an hour ago and they had no clue it was her. Quabo has heard all about the murder rate in Trenton but neither one of them were impressed with what they just saw. To them it was all a bunch of wasted ammunition. They don't have any plans of wasting a single bullet. Every round will count.

No Toes pulls out another bag of dope and gets right to sniffing. He hums a tune in between sniffs out of habit. *Sniff, hum, sniff, humm.*

Tortura gets irked to no end. He turns around and looks at Quabo. "*Eso es!* (That's it!) *¡Este drogadicto nos está utilizando!* (This junkie is using us!) *¡Este drogadicto nos está utilizando!* (He doesn't know the girl!) *¡Este drogadicto nos está utilizando!* (He's stringing us along just so you can keep him high.) *Este drogadicto nos está utilizando.* (No more wasting time!) *Este drogadicto nos está utilizando.* (It's time to go to work!)

No Toes is so entertained by the dope that he doesn't realize the conversation surrounding him. Tortura turns around and with an open palm uppercut, he slams the bag of dope onto the bridge of No Toes's nose. He holds onto the bag of dope for dear life. His nose is tingling and vision blurry, yet he can see Tortura kneeling before him with his gun aimed at his head. Tortura presses his forearm against his neck, cutting off his breathing passage. He shoves the barrel of the gun into one of his nostrils. No Toes looks to Quabo to save him.

"My man believes you are bullshitting us," Quabo says cool and calmly. "He thinks maybe you don't even know the girl and you've been lying to us all the while. We have been around there so many times and no sign of her. If you know anything, now is the time to speak because I can't hold him back any longer."

Tortura slides the hammer back and is ready to blow. "I swear to G.O.D., my word is my bond! That's where I remember seeing her at. I can't control when she comes around. Please, give me more time. I will do whatever y'all need me to do. I will stand out there day and night until I see her if y'all want me to."

Quabo looks to Tortura and shakes his head. Tortura snatches away angrily. He drops himself back into his seat. "*Eso es!* (That's it!) *No mas charla!* (No more talking!) *Tiempo para negocios.* (Time for business.)"

• • •

Bruh in Law went back to the original scene and got his Cherokee. He still hasn't admitted to Skelter that he ran out of his vehicle cowardly. Skelter and Bruh in Law were dropped off to the Jeep while the Durango was driven to a hideaway spot. They're sure the entire police force may be in search of the Durango right this very moment.

Bruh in Law drives his Cherokee, super cautiously. He looks around with fear of being ambushed. Skelter rides in the backseat with 2 guns on her lap just in case the enemy spots them and decides to make a move. She leans back calmly but her attention is on everything moving.

"So, you said that was a fifty-gram move that you got burnt for, right?" Skelter asks.

Bruh in Law pauses before replying. The 50 grams he lost is really nothing but $2,000. It's the $6,500 he had in the dashboard and the hundred grams of cocaine he had in the middle console that makes up for the biggest part of the loss. Altogether he got burnt for about $12,000. He hates to tell her this but he has no choice. He fears she may overreact on him for taking such a huge loss. He's never owed anyone this amount of money. This is the very reason why he always despised and stayed away from consignment. With his work practice of buying what he can afford, if he ever loses, it's his loss and no one else is affected by it.

"What's that, eighteen hundred?" she asks as if it's a mere drop in the bucket.

"Yeah, that was just for the shit I was bringing him though," Bruh in Law admits shamefully. "I had another hundred grams in the middle console and almost seven thousand in the dash."

Skelter calculates in her mind. Her silence is terrifying him. He peeks back and forth into the rearview mirror, expecting her to bust his head open any minute now. She stares out the back window not even looking at him. She speaks. "What's that, like twelve grand?"

"A little less," he replies, as if this will make it better for him.

"That ain't 'bout shit," she says. Bruh in Law looks into the mirror, not believing his ears. "How much of it can you give me right now?" She finally faces forward. They lock eyes in the rearview mirror.

Bruh in Law has a few dollars of his own laying around but most of his money is working capital. "I mean, I can drop a few grand on you right now but."

"A few like five?" Skelter asks anxiously. "I can take five now and the other six and some change you can pay me back off the next drop. I will bring you three joints and you should be able to pay me off those."

Bruh in Law's heart sinks. He was sitting here trying to figure out how he could ease himself out of their business arrangement, not realizing he has just dug himself deeper into it. By being indebted to her he will never be able to get out of it.

"Shit, you fuck around and be able to blow through those three in a week and get me right out your pocket."

Bruh in Law sits in silence. He realizes that he made a deal with the devil and there's no way he could ever breach their contract.

38

RUTGERS HOSPITAL NEWARK

THE INMATE LAYS stretched out in the hospital bed. His ankles are chained to the bed to prevent escape. He's just fresh out of surgery an hour ago and still under anesthesia. He lies there peacefully. Officer Tillis sits in the chair next to the bed, just skimming through a health magazine while the other officer stands near the window scrolling through his phone.

On the nightstand there's a tray with a plastic ziplock bag on it. Inside the plastic bag there's a 2-ounce, travel size bottle of Frank's Red Hot Sauce, covered in saran wrap, inside of it. The bottle of Hot Sauce was surgically removed from the inmate's rectum. The officers sit patiently waiting for him to awaken so they question him as to why he has a bottle of anything inside of him.

NORTHERN STATE PRISON/F-WING

Smith stands in a corner of the dayroom. Standing before him is one of his thoroughest soldiers, Slim Thug. Slim Thug stands here giving his full attention to Smith. He knows how serious Smith is about having his orders followed precisely.

"Dig," Smith says. "I basically pulled a rabbit out of the head by being able to get this done. We can't let this move be made in vain. I need this done immediately. Don't waste no time. I need both of them handled asap," he says as he pounds his fist into the palm of his hand. "You and Trills gone get moved over there together so both of these situations should be handled before the weekend, right?"

NORTHERN STATE PRISON/C-WING

Baby Manson stands at the pull-up bar awaiting his turn. He watches as the man pulls up gracefully. This man, known as Short Fuse, is an old head in his early 60's. Short Fuse is known as a few things in the jail and pull-up master is one of them. Certified killer is another. Standing at just barely five feet tall, he's more dangerous than any giant. He's respected in every penitentiary in the state of New Jersey. Both old heads and youngsters respect him the same. Having been imprisoned the past 30 years consecutively he's a prison legend.

Baby Manson and Short Fuse unofficially met here at the pull-up bar 3 days ago. They haven't spoken a single word to each other or even introduced themselves. The first day they took turns pulling up and they did the same on the second day. The third day Baby Manson came out late and found Short Fuse just stretching his muscles, waiting for him to come and join him.

Baby Manson completes his last set and jumps down off the bar. He exhales relief after a strenuous workout. He looks to Short Fuse and gives him a head-nod before walking off. He notices Short Fuse reciprocates the head-nod yet neither of them say a word. Baby Manson walks off and can feel the man's eyes melting on his back. He continues on walking until he gets to the entrance of the jail. He turns around to see if Short Fuse is still watching. He's not watching him but what he is doing, alarms Baby Manson. Short Fuse and Gunsmoke are standing face to face indulging in conversation. They commence to walking toward the entrance still in deep conversation.

Baby Manson slides to the side where he can't be seen. A smile spreads across his face. The smile isn't an ordinary smile. It's a smile of rage. The thought that Gunsmoke could be using Short Fuse to rock him to sleep has him ready to overreact right this moment but he knows better than to do that. He has an even better plan. He quickly walks off so they don't see him and realize that he's seen the two of them together. As he walks slowly, he puts together his plan.

39

SKELTER SITS IN the living room of Blue Blood's apartment. She hasn't called or even bothered him since their last meeting. She gave him all the freedom he needed to do what he has to do and get through the workload. Today she received a call from him. She feels like it's a good sign that he's called her instead of her having to call him. Blue Blood's long and saddened face has her thinking she may be wrong in this case.

Blue Blood looks at her as he sighs frustration. He never thought he would see this day. All his life he prided himself on being a hustler who could sell anything. He always joked saying he could sell ice to an Eskimo. For the most part it's true. In his heyday he could sell anything he put his hands on, from drugs to cars and even houses during his short-lived real estate career. But today he feels defeated.

It hurts his heart to even admit this. "Man," he sighs. "Streets fucked up," he says in preparation for what he has to say. "Niggas out here fronting like they getting to the money but it's all a game, a show for the people. Everybody want consignment and nobody got their own money. This shit taking way longer than I expected it to."

Skelter already knows where this is going. This is a sad song that she doesn't want to hear. She hoped it would be a lot more simple than this. She's familiar with the problem of having no work but she never knew you could have work and have a problem moving it. "How much you got left?"

Blue Blood frowns with pity. "I still got four and a half joints," he says sadly.

"Four and a half after all this time?" Skelter doesn't even see this as possible. "So, you only sold a half a key?"

"Not even," Blue Blood replies with shame. "Actually, I gave my man three hundred grams to help me move it. He should be getting with me by tomorrow on that. And I got money for like two hundred grams. Shit crazy out here. I remember the days when the average nigga was buying no less than a hundred grams at a time. That was the minimum. Ain't a motherfucker came to me yet for a hundred grams. These lil niggas want five and ten grams. The game is fucked up!"

"Here you go again with that, I-remember-when-blast-from-the-past shit," Skelter says. "I gave you five joints and you can't even get through them," she says rubbing it in. "Are you now ready to admit that it may not be the game? You just may be too old for the game?"

"Nah, never that!" Blue Blood shouts. "I ain't had no coke in years. I'm just getting my feet back wet. Plus, right now the boy, El-Chapo got shit on smash. You know he been holding the coke game down since forever. Anybody who getting any real money is hollering at him for it."

"What number he charging?" Skelter asks curiously.

"The same number I'm charging but you know how this shit goes. He the hot boy. Motherfucker got the Porsche, the Range and the 18 Beemer. He on every set, iced out with jewels and popping bottles. It ain't about the work he got because I got it for the same number and I heard ours is better. But," Blue Blood says, holding one finger in the air. "Only difference is, he's a brand. He that nigga that everybody want to deal with just so they can brag to other motherfuckers about dealing with him. Me, I ain't on them sets and my name ain't ringing like that so it ain't no big deal to be buying from me. They want to buy from the cool motherfucker. Clout chasing."

Skelter understands all he's saying to be true. "So, what happens if the cool motherfucker ain't around no more for them to buy from?" Skelter asks with eyes cold as ice.

"Then it's a bunch of motherfuckers who will be left plug-less, no connect," he says as it sinks in what it is that she's saying.

"There it is then," she says. "Say no more!"

"But on another note," says Blue Blood. "A lot of motherfuckers love the boy. He fed and still feed a lot of families. A lot of people will be fucked up if he ain't no longer around. And a lot of people will want answers. Some of those people I know personally and I know they won't stop until they get the answers they're looking for," he says in warning.

"Well, we will worry about that when that time comes," Skelter says nonchalantly. "For now, we need to get rid of anything standing in the way of us moving this work."

40

IN THE BACK of The Projects drug activity takes place everywhere. In the corners, in the alleys, on stoops and in the center of the playground, junkies and dealers make transactions. It's wide open business as if it's all legal. Out here everything from marijuana to heroin to opioids can be bought, retail and wholesale.

No Toes limps through the alley and looks for a familiar face. He doesn't recognize his dealer of choice and that bothers him. He's been buying from this man for weeks and has trust for him. The last thing he needs is to try a new dealer with a new stamp of dope and be disappointed in the end.

He limps toward a huddle of four young men. "Birdbox," he yells out, saying the dope stamp that he's in search of.

"That's me," a young kid says as he steps up. "I just sold out of Birdbox. I got Jurassic Park," he says. "Same shit, just a different name," he claims. "How many you want?" he asks as he flashes a couple bundles.

No Toes is skeptical. He doesn't trust it. "Nah, I'm looking for that Birdbox. I never had that Jurassic Park. I ain't heard nothing 'bout it either."

Suddenly the familiar face pops up. "There go my man right there," No Toes says pointing to a young man across the field.

The young man spots him and runs over to him. "What's up? That Birdbox right?"

"Yessir," No Toes sings cheerfully. "Give me three."

They make the transaction and No Toes walks away. He opens the bag as he's walking. Over the tune of his humming he hears, "Aye Unc!" No Toes turns around and waits as the young man runs to him. He holds a closed fist. "Yo, check this out for me," he says holding his fist in the air. No Toes holds his palm out, expecting dope but instead it's a couple tiny baggies of cocaine. "I don't know if you be smoking but if you do, check it out. I'm gone be having that now, too. If you run me some sales I will look out for you."

"Ok, thanks," No Toes says graciously.

Unbeknownst to No Toes, this coke is what Quabo and Tortura are in search of. Also unbeknownst to No Toes, this young man is the closest thing to Skelter. He's her Middle Godson.

No Toes walks off, nose deep in the bag of dope. He takes back to back sniffs of the dope as he limps through the alley. Once he steps out of the alley and onto the street he looks to his right where the Ford Explorer sits deep in the cut. He can't see that far in the distance but he knows they are watching him.

He shakes his head from side to side slowly, indicating to them that he didn't see her back there. He then crosses the street where he walks up the steps of an abandoned house. He sits on the top step of the raggedy porch and blends right on in. This here abandoned house is the post that he's been assigned to. Quabo has promised to feed him all the dope he needs just as long as he doesn't leave this post. Sounds like a wonderful deal to him.

"*Solo hay una mantra de hater sue las cucarachas salgan de su!* (There's only one way to make cockroaches come out of hiding!)" Tortura shouts with rage. He's fed up. "*Hay que exterminar!* (We must exterminate!) *No voy a tomar un no por respuesta* (I'm not taking no for an answer.) *Estamos entrando ahora mismo!* (We are going in right now!) *Y seguiremos atacando hasta que ella salga de su escondite!* (And we will keep attacking until they come out of hiding!)"

Although Tortura has his mind made up, he's still expecting Quabo to talk him out of moving just yet. Instead, Quabo stares straight ahead in silence. Tortura takes Quabo's lack of response as all the response he needs. Tortura gets on the phone and starts shouting commands and instructions in Spanish.

In minutes all their vehicles appear on the block, blending in with the regular area traffic. A raggedy work van, an older model Suburban and an older model Explorer all creep up the block bumper to bumper behind each other. A minivan parks right at the main exit of the Projects. Another minivan parks a few feet away on the opposite side of the street.

Tortura and Quabo sit back in the cut away from the action. From where they are parked they have a clear view of everything. Tortura reaches over and flashes the high beams. As soon as he does, the line of vehicles take off one by one, still bumper to bumper.

Back of the Projects is action packed. Wide open drug transactions take place like a Drug Walmart. Customers cop and go while others bust the bag open as soon as they make their purchase. It's as busy back here as New York City Penn Station.

All activity seems to stop abruptly like a freezing of time. Everyone's attention is diverted to the three unfamiliar vehicles that are creeping up the entrance. It's like a movie playing in slow motion. The movie doesn't speed up until the doors of the vehicles pop open and men equipped with handguns and rifles start firing randomly....but it's already too late.

Some people hit the ground for cover, out of natural response. Others use walls and garbage cans or anything else they can use as shields. People disperse in every direction. Some drop like flies from being struck. In less than two minutes, the whole area is cleared and the only sign of life back here are the few people that are laid out in the middle of the courts. And some of them have been left lifeless.

The very last handgun sounds off. *Pop! Pop! Pop!* The sound of a machine gun closes out the credits with rapid fire. The man holding the machine gun keeps ripping in the air, giving all of his men time to get into their vehicles. He hops into the van, standing on the ledge, still firing as the driver backs the van up. Finally he slams the door shut and the driver busts a wild U-turn. The vehicles come speeding out just as they crept in, bumper to bumper.

Quabo and Tortura watch with satisfaction as their vehicles speed up the block. Once all are of out of sight they start to focus on the entrances of the Projects. Tortura looks at his watch. "Ten, nine, eight," he counts. "The roaches should be coming out in, five, four, three, two, one," he says as he looks up. Just as he planned, young men start popping out from everywhere. They all run around in disarray. The sneak attack has them all discombobulated.

Quabo and Tortura study the faces of every person that comes out looking for the faces that they now have instilled in their minds. They are livid that not one face matches the faces they are looking for.

Sirens roar loudly. "Pull off," Quabo commands.

"*Seguiremos exterminando hasta que aparezcan las cucarachas*. (We will keep exterminating until the cockroaches show up.)" Tortura shouts with rage.

As they pass the abandoned porch, No Toes has his eyes locked onto the van. Quabo rolls the window down slowly in passing. Using his index finger he points at his eye, signaling for No Toes to keep his eyes open. No Toes nods his head up and down discreetly before looking away. With his head turned he flashes a 'thumbs up."

"*Seguiremos atacando, mañana, tarde y noche hasta que encontremos nuestra marca*. (We will attack morning, noon, and night until we find our mark.)" Tortura shouts angrily. "*Este es solo el comienzo*.(This is just the beginning.)"

41

BABY MANSON LAYS back on his cot with a million thoughts running through his mind. While most of the inmates are out on the Big Yard, he's here trying to gather his thoughts. He has a major plan brewing and he just hopes all goes well. He's already had one error and right now he can't stand another.

Loud voices and movement on the tier interrupts his thought process. The noise is an indication that recreation time has just ended. He sits up from his relaxing position and seats himself in a more upright and firm position. He's still thinking, just more on point while doing so.

An inmate shoots him a 30 to Life as he passes the cell. They lock eyes the entire time, neither one of them blinking. Baby Manson is used to this type behavior and is able to let most of it pass unless he feels like it's a real issue that needs to be addressed. He's learned that most of these men are harmless groupies who just want to be known and accepted and will do anything to get the attention of men. They will go all the way through with the tough looks just to be noticed and when addressed they have no problem bowing down. In all actuality, all they wanted was a conversation with a man they hold in high regard. Even if that conversation is based on them being caused bodily harm.

Baby Manson can't let this pass. One of the rules in prison is to keep your eyes out of another inmates' room for you may see something you were not meant to see. A man's room is the only little privacy he has. Baby Manson feels like he has to address this because it is a form of disrespect.

"Aye yo!" Baby Manson shouts. The man quickly turns around. "You got a problem with those eyes? You looking for something?"

"What?" the man asks.

"You all in here like you looking for something."

The man has nothing more to say. "Yeah, alright," he says as he walks away.

Baby Manson keeps his eyes on the man until he's out of sight. As he turns, he's greeted by a familiar face. Short Fuse stands at the doorway with a grimace on his face, lips snarled like a mad dog. Baby Manson can even hear him growling under his breath. Baby Manson's eyes slide down and fix on the man's right hand which is by his side.

Cool and calm, Baby Manson discreetly slides his hand underneath his thigh. He grips his knife tightly and stands up, preparing for battle. Baby Manson steps toward Short Fuse with his knife gripped behind his thigh and murder in his eyes.

"I should cut your motherfucking heart out," Short Fuse says through snarled lips.

Baby Manson creeps toward him with the thought of lunging at him and poking him in his heart once he gets within leaping distance. "What?" Baby Manson asks just trying to buy himself some time as he gets closer.

"You left me out there alone," Short Fuse says as he lifts his hands in the air, palm up. Baby Manson now realizes the man is without weapon. He still doesn't trust him though.

"We been out there getting money together all week in the Big Yard. Workout partners," he says. "I push you, and you push me. Motivation for each other," he says with his eyes squinted. "And today you leave me stranded. No courtesy or nothing?" Short Fuse asks. "I'm out there waiting for you and you just don't show. I would never leave you hanging like that. Maybe that's what you used to in them County Jails but here in prison it don't go like that. We pay every set we owe and we don't leave each other hanging."

Baby Manson eases up after realizing the man isn't coming from a place of malice. He's giving him a lesson on jailing. Although he doesn't need the lesson he will take it out of respect for his elders. "I can respect that drink," Baby Manson says humbly. His demeanor changes quickly. "But all that talk about cutting my heart out will take this somewhere totally different. I don't accept threats. I move on them."

Short Fuse smirks. "I like your style, Lil Bruh."

Baby Manson's face crumbles with agitation. "With all due respect, please don't ever *Lil Bruh* me. I'm always gone respect my elders, especially those who have put it down before me, but I can't be *Lil Bruh*."

"I say that will all due respect for you because I like how you move. No harm no foul. Once you get to know me you will know I ain't them. Mine never come from a bad place. I respect the youth just as I respect my elders. The youth that deserves respect and I consider you one of them. I don't know you but I like how you move and that is the only reason me and you are having this conversation in the first place."

"Well, since we having this conversation," Baby Manson says. "I'm a straight shooter, so I'm gone shoot from the hip. What's your angle? What's your stance? I seen you kicking it with one of my opps so before we go any further I need to know what he means to you."

"What who means to me?" Short Fuse asks curiously.

"Gunsmoke," Baby Manson replies. "I'm gone keep it all the way G with you because I sense your G. I was fading away from you because I felt you may have been getting close to me for him because he ain't got the heart to get with me. And if that's the case, it ain't no need in me and you playing this game. We can go on ahead and get right to it."

Short Fuse flashes a proud smile. "I like your style. Remind me of a young me. But let me tell you one thing about me. I ain't no washed up old head that no young motherfucker can put a battery in my back to do their dirty work. I'm a lone cowboy, like Lone Ranger.

Ain't many motherfuckers that can call on me to do nothing for them. I ain't doubting your gangster but let me tell you about mine. I ain't no sneak attack motherfucker. I ain't got the time nor the energy to be rocking nobody to sleep. If I got an issue with a motherfucker I go right at him, face up and he will know it's coming. I play fair. I like a challenge and I like my enemy to see me coming. I ain't never sucker punched a motherfucker or shot a motherfucker in the back."

"Respected," Baby Manson says. "So, with that being said. What side you stand on if by chance I come for him? I ain't looking for you to stand with me because you don't know me. But what I need to know, are you standing with him?"

"To answer your question to the best of my ability," he says before pausing. "I stand with those who stand with me and in the twenty-five years, six months and three days that I been in these spots, very few have stood with me because I never called on nobody to stand with me. So to answer your question, I stand alone."

Officer Tillis appears in the doorway, interrupting their conversation. They both divert their attention to him. Gentlemen," Tillis greets.

Baby Manson reciprocates the greeting with a head-nod. Short Fuse doesn't even acknowledge him. He's anti-police, correction officer, even security guard, and has no liking or use for any of them. He looks to Baby Manson. "We will pick up on this conversation at a later date," he says as he extends his hand for a handshake.

Baby Manson grabs his hand with respect. "No need to pick up on it. It's all been said, understood and respected."

"Good enough," Short Fuse says before making his exit.

Once Short Fuse is no longer present, the Tillis speaks. "Aye man, just a heads up. Three inmates came over from F-Wing this morning and two of them I know for sure are affiliated with ole boy."

"Oh yeah?" Baby Manson says as the wheels are turning in his mind.

"I don't know what the move is about but I just want you to know."

"I appreciate that but I ain't worried," Baby Manson says cockily.

"But on another note," the officer says. "What's up with your man, Hall? Frank's Red Hot Sauce," he says as he pretends he's holding a bottle of Hot Sauce, doing a commercial. "*I put that on everything*," he says before he busts out laughing. Baby Manson finds this humorous as well. "And you knew it the whole time."

"Man, I knew nothing, just knew the man been in pain," Baby Manson lies but his face tells the truth. He fights back the smirk that's creeping onto his face.

"You know I been on the job for 20 years," Tillis says. "I've seen it all and heard it all but that right there though, was the first and *I put that on everything*," he clowns once again. "He kept his mouth shut and wouldn't answer any questions. He can't be charged for nothing. I been around a long time and I know what's going on. All I'm saying is be careful because they gone have eyes on y'all now."

Baby Manson shrugs his shoulders as he attempts to lie once again. "I don't know what you talking about." In all actuality he knows exactly what the officer is speaking about.

"Just show me some respect is all I ask," Tillis says sternly. "Keep it away from me so I don't have to do my job."

Baby Manson nods his head respectfully. Tillis turns around and walks away from the cell. As he's walking who does he see coming toward him, but Baby Manson's cellmate. The man walks as upright as he can, trying hard not to show the pain that he's in from his surgery. He should be resting as the doctor prescribed but he refuses to do so.

The closer he gets the harder Tillis has to fight to keep a straight face. The inmate is well respected in this prison. He's known to be solid, upright and respectful. It's hard for the officer to imagine him and what he has indulged in yet he can show the man nothing other than respect.

The inmate stands in front of the Tillis who still fights to keep a straight face. "Uh, Tillis," the inmate says as he stares the officer square in the eyes. "I know you've heard about my unfortunate circumstances," he says eloquently.

That's it, the officer can no longer hold it in. He busts out laughing in the man's face. "Unfortunate circumstances?" Tillis asks over laughter. "Stop your shit, man. Out of respect for you I'm trying to keep a straight face and you gone hit me with that? What was that all about man?" The officer continues to laugh despite the fact that the inmate finds no humor at all.

The inmate retains his upright stature. "I got a ton of respect for you as a man so I feel I owe you an explanation but this present time is not the time. Despite what it may appear, whatever you may be thinking, it was not that. I am in no way, form, or fashion the freak booty type. Maybe one day in the future we will discuss this. Just not right now," he adds. "As a man that I have enormous respect for I would hope you would keep this matter between us."

"Don't worry, Hall," the officer says. "I respect you the same and this stays with us," he says as he walks off. "Keep yourself out of trouble," he shouts over his shoulder. "Walk light," he says with sarcasm. "And I do mean that literally," he says while letting out a low chuckle.

This matter is nothing new to the officer. While the other staff members looked at the man as maybe he was on some freaky type time Tillis knew better. He figured he had intentions of *boofing* dope (inserting dope into one's rectum in order to sneak it into the prison). He used the Hot Sauce bottle as practice to prepare for a smooth ride once he got the dope.

The inmate wasn't the mastermind behind the attempt to get the dope inside...Baby Manson was. The inmate is only the mule. His job was going to be to meet his wife in the visit hall as he does every other Sunday. Only difference this time is she would pass him a bag of dope that he would *boof.* After this turn of events, Baby Manson had to come up with another plan quickly and he did.

In the palm of Baby Manson's hand, he holds the key to a brighter future. He holds a plastic bag filled with raw dope. One hundred grams of raw dope to be exact. May not sound like a big deal on the outside but on the inside, this is enough dope to supply the whole prison.

With him owing his connect $70 for every gram, he's able to score 280 bucks profit off each gram, minimum. At lowest, he has the possible profit margin of $28,000. He can be greedy and monopolize by selling directly to the dope fiends who pay up to $1,000 a gram but that would take too long. So he figures by selling to the dealers at a price that they have room to make money for themselves he will be able to move the product faster and he will give everybody the opportunity to eat.

He nods his head up and down with a sparkle in his eyes. The hardest part was getting the dope into the prison. Now taking over the prison will be easy. Sure there are other players in the mix and already established, but he plans to do whatever it takes to rise to the top. His goal is to control the heroin market inside this prison and he refuses to let anyone get in the way of his goal.

SKELTER SITS LOW in the backseat staring out of the window as Middle Godson gives her all the details of the shooting that has just taken place. Youngest Godson drives barely awake. The perk he popped 20 minutes ago has him barely alive. He falls back and forth into his nod. No one is even worried that he's high because he does his best driving when he's high.

"That shit was crazy. Niggas jumped out with big shit, barking. Motherfuckers could shoot too! Motherfuckers screaming and dropping like flies. Shit was crazy! Seven niggas left on the stretcher and four left in a body bag."

Skelter takes a long pull of the blunt. She exhales the smoke and watches the smoke seep into the air. She's perplexed. She never even imagined those guys to be anywhere near as serious as what she's hearing. She figures somebody from that block had to have spotted one of her Godsons because she was hooded up.

"So, all you niggas back there and not one of you had a strap?"

"On some real shit, it didn't matter if a motherfucker was real right or not. That shit was coming too fast. Niggas didn't even have time to think."

"Something about this shit don't sound right," Skelter says. "I can't even see them coming like that. Based on what you saying them niggas had way too much big shit. Maybe that came from somewhere else. Somebody out there ain't telling the truth. Somebody did something."

If she didn't get rid of everybody linked to that robbery she would think that *somebody* could possibly be her. She's almost sure there's no way this could be for her. "Well, we really don't have much to go on, so we got to move on this shit. We got to hit them hard too. They up right now. We have to take the lead. I have to admit though…I'm impressed with their work ethics. But ain't no way them little niggas gone ever outwork me," Skelter says with certainty and determination.

MINUTES LATER

BRUH IN LAW opens the door slowly. He peeks his head out nervously before stepping out onto the porch. Once he sees the truck awaiting him he steps with more spunk. He wears a false sense of confidence but inside he's trembling with fear. He has no idea what Skelter is here to tell him, but he's sure whatever it is he truly doesn't want to hear it.

He steps to the curb as the back window rolls down slowly. "Get in," Skelter says before she slides over. Bruh in Law opens the door slowly and drops himself in the seat. As he closes the door, he looks over to her ready to hear whatever bad news she has for him.

"Shit just got super crazy," Skelter says. "Niggas came through and scored."

"What niggas?"

"Them niggas from the other side," Skelter replies. "Came through with all types of shit. Knocked like four motherfuckers down and twisted another four. We got to get over there and even the score."

Right now Bruh in Law feels like disappearing. The fact that all of this started over him bothers him the most. He understands with all of this revolving around him he's probably a main target right now. This scares him to death but it also puts a battery in his back.

"So, now what?" Bruh in Law questions.

Skelter looks at him with fiery eyes. "Time to go to work."

TWENTY MINUTES LATER

Skelter and the crew sit at the far end of the block, parked and bringing no attention to themselves. Up ahead on their right side is a group of men, doing what they do, smoking, sipping and shit talking. The young man who robbed Bruh in Law stands on crutches, leaning against the wall. The cast on his leg they're sure is because of Bruh in Law. Bruh in Law feels a sense of pride seeing this.

Skelter becomes furious immediately. She expected the block to be a ghost town with what just happened. For them to be out here as if nothing has happened is like a slap in the face. This baffles her. After such a big score they would have to be retarded to be out here so care-free like this. It's just not adding up to her.

Skelter speaks while keeping her focus on the 4 men standing huddled up. "I don't want nobody left standing at the end of this." Skelter looks around at her men. "Y'all ready?" The sound of bullets being slid in the chamber answers her question. "Go," she commands.

Youngest Godson creeps out of the parking space and drives down the block at a moderate speed that doesn't cause anyone alarm. The entire time down the block and not one of them looks up. Skelter can't believe they're making it so easy. Or maybe they're not. Maybe they're setting a trap to reel them in. She grips both of her guns, resting them on her lap, just in case she has to jump out for reinforcement.

The driver cuts a hard right and the truck bounces onto the side-walk. All three doors fly open at the same time. Middle Godson sends the first shots into the crowd. The crowd opens and two men flee. Skelter chases one man down, ripping shots at him until he falls.

Middle Godson takes off behind the other one. The man on crutches drops one crutch, and while holding the other one, he tries to hop away on one leg. Bruh in Law corners him and backs him against the building. He aims at the man's chest and fires. *Pop!* The man raises his arm high as to use his crutch as a shield. The bullet pierces through his forearm causing the crutch to fall out of his hands. The man slides down the wall and crouches himself into a tight ball to try and protect himself. He closes his eyes tight and prepares his body for the shots.

Bruh in Law scans the man's body looking for an opening and finally he finds one. He places an imaginary X right on the hook of the back of the man's head. He squeezes. *Pop! Pop! Pop!* The man's body tilts over stiffly. He rolls onto the ground, balled up in the fetal position. He's his very last breath two gunshots ago.

It's all one big blur to Bruh in Law. He can hear Skelter in the background but he can't make out the words behind him. He turns around to find her sitting in the backseat waving him on. Her mouth is moving but the words he can't make out. He feels like he's in the Matrix. He takes off toward the car and dives in.

The driver speeds off and Bruh in Law looks around still in a blur. He looks down at his hand and stares at the gun in total shock. Skelter plants her hand on Bruh in Law's shoulder and smiles proudly. He sees the pride on her face but the words that are coming out of her mouth are not registering. He looks back down at the gun, still in shock at what he's just done.

"Congrats nigga!" Skelter says. "You caught your first one. They all get easier from here on."

THE NEXT DAY

BABY MANSON IS late making his way into the Big Yard, for he had business to handle. In just 2 days he's distributed dope across 3 of the 6 wings that make up this prison. He's gotten rid of only 15 of the 100 grams but hasn't made back a single dime in return as of yet. Right now, he's just building his foundation. He has no doubt in his mind that the money is going to come because he's already heard reviews that he has the best dope in all of Northern State.

Baby Manson walks the track slowly, just as he does every time he hits the yard. He likes to walk the track first to get his mind right and prepare for his workout. He also likes to walk the track just to take surveillance of everything. He likes to know what's going on around him at all times.

Three quarters around the track and Baby Manson immediately spots a new face. He watches the man standing in a huddle of men who all seem to be talking and joking. Baby Manson doesn't know the man personally but he does know the man to be up under Smith. He's sure this man is 1 of the 3 men who were shipped over here the other day. Baby Manson keeps his head straight while watching the man through his peripheral. The man continues on, not once giving indication that his eyes are on Baby Manson.

Baby Manson has spun the whole track and has not noticed another new face. He's looked low and high and no sight of the other 2 men that were shipped over. The suspense of not knowing is killing him. He was hoping to have identified them so he can carry on with the next phase of his plan but he now feels like he's stuck in limbo until he finds out who they are.

Baby Manson approaches Short Fuse who is on the bar pulling up. They lock eyes as Short Fuse continues on. While Baby Manson is stretching his muscles, waiting for his turn he hears vulgar language to the right of him. To the right of them is a group of inmates leaning against the wall. Baby Manson is familiar with all of their faces but only 2 of the men he actually knows. One man, who is a young and wild man, just got to the prison not even 2 weeks ago. The young man is pacing around with rage on his face.

Short Fuse drops himself from the bar and they stand face to face. They greet each other with a fist bump. "Pardon my tardiness," Baby Manson apologizes humbly. "I had some business to handle."

Short Fuse acknowledges Baby Manson's apology by head-nod. Baby Manson jumps on the bar with his eyes still locked onto Short Fuse. A weird look is on his face. The look causes Baby Manson concern. By the fifth rep Baby Manson notices the vulgar language getting louder.

He can now make out clearly what the young man is saying. "I don't give a fuck about that back in the day shit. I'm from the show-me era. You got to show me what you made of today. Fuck what you was made of yesterday," the man says loud and clear.

Baby Manson finishes his set and drops himself from the bar. He looks over to the huddle of men and is surprised to see them all looking in the direction of him and Short Fuse. "Fuck all them old ass war stories. Old motherfuckers be fucking punks with those fake ass intimidation tactics." Baby Manson looks over again and he notices the man looking up at Short Fuse who is on the pull-up bar. "Wish the fuck he would say something! I will slap fire outta his old ass."

Short Fuse drops from the bar and his eyes scan across Baby Manson's. The look on his face is shocking to Baby Manson. Short Fuse is carrying on as if the man isn't talking to him. It's obvious that the man is feeling himself because he's talking louder and louder. Clearly he's taking the battery charge that his acquaintances are giving him. He's walking around, talking loud with his chest puffed high. The battery must be fully charged now because the young man is now making his way over to them.

Baby Manson jumps off the bar and stands strong in his spot. He looks the young man up and down as he approaches. The man's demeanor changes once he gets close to Baby Manson. "Pardon me," he says with respect as he steps around Baby Manson. He stands before Short Fuse face to face. "Say something," he barks in Short Fuse's face. "All these years you had all these niggas fooled and you a bitch. Say something and I will slap fire out your old ass."

Short Fuse doesn't say a word but he stares at the young man without twitching an eye. The man continues on with his disrespect and it's ripping Baby Manson apart. He almost feels obligated to step in and do something. Even though they are only workout partners and not friends, the mere fact that they work out together seems like a disrespect to him as well. Baby Manson has to quickly remind himself that Short Fuse made clear mention that he stands with no one.

"I'm here to expose your hoe ass. This ain't the 80's no more, you old washed up throwback motherfucker." Short Fuse smirks and shakes his head. Baby Manson isn't sure but he believes it to be a nervous reaction of some sort. "What," the young man says as he steps closer. "You think it's funny? You think I won't slap you?"

Seeing Short Fuse being disrespected like this bothers Baby Manson's. To say the least, he's shocked. The way Short Fuse's name rings bells and to see him be violated like this is unbelievable. Baby Manson knows all about old heads who made a reputation for themselves off of bullshit and intimidation only to later be exposed. It's obvious that Short Fuse must be one of those old heads.

Even still, he hates to see this because regardless of what, he respects his elders. Short Fuse is almost 60 years old and even at his strongest for an old man he's no match for such a young man. Baby Manson believes old heads should be respected until their last day and no young man should ever want to destroy their legacy. He would never be the one to destroy an old head's legacy and put a strike on their gangster report. He's seen old heads put it down their entire life and once they are old and frail a young man disrespects them and just like that all their gangster shit is no longer void. They always will be remembered by the day they took the L. Baby Manson shakes his head sadly. Today, Short Fuse has taken that L.

"I thought not," the man says as he looks Short Fuse up and down. He then walks away back over to his group. Baby Manson looks at Short Fuse and the blank look on his face bothers him. It's as if he isn't ashamed that he took an L. Baby Manson then looks over to the group who are cheering the young man on and he becomes enraged.

He feels like this is an attack against him as well. He looks to Short Fuse for some type of signal that he wants to roll. Regardless of the fact that Short Fuse distinctly told him he stands alone, he still wants to come to his aid; for the sake of his own pride. "What's up?" Baby Manson whispers. "What you want to do?"

Short Fuse looks away from Baby Manson without replying. He walks away with his head swinging low. Baby Manson wants to help him but how can he help him when he isn't even helping himself? Baby Manson watches as the Short Fuse's legacy ends. His whole G report is being wiped clean as he makes his way into the building. From this day on, he will only be remembered by the L he just took and all his juice goes to the young man that destroyed his legacy. This one booboo will cancel out all the gangster shit he has done his entire life.

44

LATER THAT NIGHT
ANN'S PLACE-TRENTON

IT'S THE LOCAL bar where the biggest drug dealers in the city are mixed in with working class folk. On any given night you may find a couple off-duty cops sprinkled in the mix as well. This place is just one big melting pot. The drinks are cheap and the women are plentiful. The game can be played on any level the player decides to play on.

In the far corner a man in a janitor's uniform sits with a beautiful older woman as they sip on Long Island Iced Teas. Across from them there sits a crew of young girls all sipping on bottom shelf liquor. The clothing they barely have on is so enticing that they are sure they will not be drinking bottom shelf all night. To the left of them, there sits Blue Blood who is sitting here, just him and his good friend, Captain Morgan. He sips on Captain Morgan moderately as he keeps a close eye on the group of bottle popping ballers in the back.

The back of the bar looks like a New York City or Miami nightclub instead of a local hole in the wall bar. Everything about the back is different, the people, their clothing, their jewelry, and even their drinks. Nothing less than bottle service going on back there. Huge diamond-studded watches and necklaces illuminate the dark and dreary bar. The women back there are Trenton's finest mixed with women from other places as well. Back there is the creme de la creme.

The main attraction back there is a handsome, suave and debonair man in his mid 30's, who sits laid back in the cut. He's always in the cut, a man who doesn't necessarily care for the spotlight. As much as he despises the spotlight, it's always shined on him because there's no bigger name in all of Trenton. Love it or hate it, he is the town's poster boy.

This man is the El-Chapo of the city. They call him Chapo for short. He's been flooding the city with cocaine for the past decade. While most kingpins rule with violent force, he rules with love. He's loved by many because of the love he shows. He's known for giving any and everybody the opportunity to make money.

Of course love isn't enough to keep the wolves from preying though. Usually love is what brings the wolves. With Chapo, the love he shows is his defense. Because he's been so genuine and loving with the people, there are men who will put their lives on the line for him and want nothing from him in return. To cross Chapo is to lose your life and he won't have to lift a finger, press the button, or put his hand in his pocket to pay for the service. So many people will come to his defense purely out of love.

The light flicks on and off as it does every night at 1:30 A.M. "Last call for alcohol!" shouts the deejay through his microphone. Patrons rush to get their last drinks before the bar shuts down. Blue Blood has his last conversation with Captain Morgan as he gulps down the last drops that are in his glass. Through his glass he notices Chapo standing up. Through his peripheral he watches as Chapo peaces everybody up. The most beautiful and most classy dressed young woman in the bar stands behind him waiting as he says his farewells.

Blue Blood holds his phone underneath the bar while he shoots a quick text. The reply comes back immediately. Blue Blood looks up just as Chapo is approaching. Blue Blood tries hard to keep his eyes locked in Chapo's eyes out of respect but the beautiful woman is hard to turn away from. Chapo, a slight bit tipsy trips over his feet but his woman catches him. He diddy bops over to Blue Blood flashing a wink with his hand held high. Blue Blood grabs his hand but Chapo leans in for the gangster hug. He has Blue Blood in a tight bear hug. "Be safe out here, my nigga," says Chapo.

"No doubt," Blue Blood replies. "You do the same."

"Always," Chapo says as he pulls away from Blue Blood and wraps his arm around his woman. He uses her as a crutch to lean and walk on. She wraps her arm around his waist and leads him out of the door.

The woman hits the power locks from the key ring and the stainless-steel Bentley GT that's parked across the streetlights up the block. Chapo and the woman make their way across the street toward the Bentley. Traffic seems to get busy just as they attempt to cross the street. The woman pulls Chapo back as cars are coming from both sides. He pulls away from her. "Fuck that, they can wait," Chapo slurs. The pedestrian always has the right of way," he says as he drags her in front of the cars. Traffic halts as they cross.

The woman leads him behind the car on her way to the passenger's seat. She grabs hold of the door and just as she opens it for him to get inside, a shadow appears in front of them. The woman looks to her right where she sees a masked bandit standing with his gun held high. Chapo looks too but it's already too late. The bandit reaches over the woman's shoulder and fires two rounds at Chapo's head. Already in a seated position, Chapo falls on the curb, landing on his butt. The woman backs up screaming with fear as the gunman stands over Chapo and fires three more rounds. After the first round, Chapo falls flat on his back. His hand drops as his last breath escapes him.

A dark SUV appears out of thin air and the gunman races toward it. He hops into the front seat and the SUV pulls off. By the time the SUV hits the corner, the entire bar has been emptied. Everyone runs over to the Bentley, praying this isn't what they think it to be. "Yo, somebody call the ambulance!" one man shouts. "Hurry, hurry!"

"Oh, no!" a young woman shouts.

The people start to swarm the woman who is standing there in total shock. "Yo, who the fuck did this? Did you see their faces?"

The people run around frantically like chickens with their heads cut off. It's a sad night as Chapo lays stiff as a board in cold blood. They can't believe this is true. Tonight they lost a legend. Drunken tears flood all of their faces.

Blue Blood stands close enough to hear everything but still out of the way. He looks at Chapo spilled on the concrete. He shakes his head with a drop of sadness. He hates that it has to go like this but in order for one man to come up, another man has to fall. It's the way of the game. Blue Blood lights his cigarette and walks off into the night.

45

THE NEXT DAY

WHILE ALL THE normal activities of the Dayroom are taking place, something out of the ordinary is also going on. In the far end of the room, a group of 20 inmates are gathered around in the chairs formed in a tight circle. While the rest of the smaller groups of men are loud and rowdy, this group, the biggest group of them all, is amazingly quiet.

Smith sits in a chair against the wall as the circle of men are formed around him. He reads from the Quran eloquently, with precise enunciation of the Arabic language. All the men are attentive as he speaks. He holds one finger in the air as he translates the English of that in which he just said in Arabic.

Smith has been holding these classes 3 times a week right here in the Dayroom ever since he got banned from the Jumu'ah Service. He even holds a small Friday service of his own. He refuses to allow them to stop him. He has not only these men standing with him on this but at least another 2 dozen more are riding with him.

Together, him and the other gang members are taking a stand to get their point across. Every week, Jumu'ah service has less brothers in attendance. Smith plans to use his gang-banging leadership role to get all the fellow gangbanger Muslims with him on this. He knows there's strength in numbers and he believes once the Imaam understands the influence he has, he will accept him back into the congregation.

C-WING

Music plays faintly from a MP3 player. Loud snoring overrides the harmony in between beats. Gunsmoke lays back on his cot, resting beyond peacefully. Not being here for long, he's still on the County Jail schedule, wherein the inmates stayed woke all night and slept during the day.

His snoring loops with the beat and creates a harmonious tune. His mouth wide open, he sleeps in a comatose state. In fact in so much of a comatose state that the man entering his cell doesn't even have to tiptoe inside. Hoodie drawn tight over his face, hands stuffed in his pocket, he takes two long steps and there he stands over Gunsmoke. The man removes his latex glove covered hands and immediately places one hand over Gunsmoke's mouth.

Gunsmoke awakens. His eyes open abruptly and at the sight of the hooded man, his eyes bulge with fear. He attempts to scream but the man clasps his hand tighter over his mouth, muffling the sound. Gunsmoke's eyes land on the knife right before it comes downward. Three quick pokes into Gunsmoke's jugular vein leaves Gunsmoke weak and almost motionless. The man doesn't stop there. He pokes him non-stop until Gunsmoke stops moving.

The man looks down at Gunsmoke who lays there, eyes wide open, mouth wide open, not breathing at all and he finds great satisfaction. He grabs a sheet that lays at the foot of the bed and covers Gunsmoke from head to toe. He tiptoes to the entrance of the cell, where he stands, peeking out. Once he finds the coast to be clear, he steps out of the cell and make his way down the tier casually.

. . .

Meanwhile at the other end of the tier, Baby Manson sits on his bed, crouched over busy at work while his cellmate plays the lookout position. Laid in front of Baby Manson is grams of raw heroin. He separates each gram into what is called a box piece. A box piece has the thickness of 2 single strands of hair and the length of a half an inch.

One box piece can be sold to another dealer at the price of $10 while it can be sold to a white boy or an addict for $15. Overall a gram can be broken down into about 70 box pieces. Seven hundred dollars can be made off of the $70 that it costs him per gram. Baby Manson looks at the 79 grams of dope he has in his bag and calculates $700 per gram, he calculates at over $55,000.

He hates the fact that he's sitting here in prison but the truth to the matter is he has a better situation here in prison than he's ever had on the streets. He has to thank his best childhood friend for putting him in this position. His best friend has the streets on lock right now. He lucked up on a life changing plug where he has his access to unlimited kilos of raw dope. Baby Manson wishes he was out on the streets with his best friend, living it up, but unfortunately that is not how the ball is bouncing right now. So, as usual he plays the hand that he's dealt, and while his best friend is controlling the streets and living like a king, he plans to control this prison the same way and also live like a king, here on the inside.

. . .

A young man enters the Dayroom and walks quietly over to the group of men. Smith continues on speaking from his notes as the man approaches. The man steps to the young man who sits right next to Smith. This man is head of security for Smith. No one has access to Smith directly and everyone must go through his security first.

The man whispers to Smith's security. Smith's security then leans over and whispers into Smith's ear, interrupting him. Smith gives the man the signal that it's permissible for the man to approach. The man leans in close to Smith's ear. "Gunsmoke, just been handled."

Smith's face shows no emotion whatsoever. "Handled, handled, or just handled?" he whispers.

"All the way handled," the man whispers.

"Cool," Smith replies. "Half the battle," he says. He then turns back to his group and gets right back to teaching as if nothing has ever happened. He doesn't think twice about it. Gunsmoke had a job to do and he couldn't do it. The repercussions for not following orders can be severe. Smith will handle his own just as he will handle an enemy when they don't follow his orders.

46

ROGER GARDEN APARTMENTS

PITCH BLACK DARKNESS, so the four men scaling the wall can only see each other's silhouette. They all are uniformed, dressed in all black with shiny chrome handguns in their hands. The first man hits the edge of the alley and stops. He scans the area to see what lies before them. It's quiet back here with very little action. All the dealers seem to be in one huddle which is perfect for the gunmen.

"Now," the man says to his team. He leads them onto the other side. All four of the men go in separate ways. The sound of open gunfire rips through the air, causing the men to flee in different directions. The gunmen fire at their targets relentlessly. The sound of an assault rifle barks loudly.

A young man standing in the cut hardly able to be seen, fires not once but twice. The intruders in no way expected this. They continue firing but only to get away. The assault rifle yielding man sees them backing off and gets a burst of confidence. He comes out of hiding and lets the rifle rip. The men go from backpedaling, shooting with each step to turning around and running away at full speed.

A young man creeps through the darkness and catches the very last man just as he's stepping into the alley. The young man aims at the back of his head with less than 2 feet in between them. He fires. *BLOCKA! BLOCKA! BLOCKA!*

The man collapses lifelessly. His gun falls beside him. The young man jumps over the man like a hurdle and runs through the alley firing at the other men as they attempt to get away. Two of the men stop and fire just to get the young man off their heels. *BOC! BOC! BOC! BOC!* The young man ducks low for cover and in those 2 seconds that it takes for him to duck, the men disappear. He races through the alley and once he's on the other side he sees a vehicle speeding away.

The young men surround the man with caution. So, dark they can't tell if he's still moving. One of the men rush in and snatches the gun off the ground. He aims at the center of the ski-mask and fires, *BOC! BOC! BOC!* The bullets are absorbed with very little movement, confirming he's dead.

"Pull his mask off, quick," Middle Godson instructs. One man leans over and quickly snatches the mask off his face. They all watch with curiosity, waiting for it to be revealed who the man is. None of them recognize the face but what they do know is that its not a young man. Middle Godson quickly fumbles around for the man's wallet and locates it in his back pocket. He snatches the wallet out of the man's pocket. "Grab him," he commands.

The group of men zoom in and all grabbing a part of the man, they lift him up. The dead weight makes the man feel as if he weighs a ton. Together they lug him with all of their might. Not much a burden though for they have gotten quite used to carrying dead bodies. A many of dead men have been dragged over what they call the threshold. The threshold is where they take the bodies away from here. Skelter has taught her Godsons that bodies bring heat so in order to keep the heat off them they must keep the bodies way from set.

Just as they cross the threshold, the sirens roar. No soon as the young men are out of sight what is now in clear sight is an entire police force, running in from every direction with their guns in hand. Police scour the area. What they are looking for they will never find. Gunshots, with no bodies leads to no investigation. Skelter's Godson can't wait to find out who this man really is.

ONE HOUR LATER

Skelter sits in the backseat as her Godsons are all around her. She stares at the New York license in quite disbelief. She reads the name 'Alejandro Ruiz' over and over again. She inhales a deep breath before speaking. "This right here just changed the dynamics of the whole game. This has nothing to do with that Locust retaliation. I swear I knew that was too heavy to come from them. This beef is bigger than them. We got a real war on our hands."

Skelter wonders how this has come back to her. How did they know to find her here? She thought she covered her tracks. Knowing that they are this close to her makes her uncomfortable. She's sure this isn't the last that she's heard from them.

"When you ran out front did you see the car they left in?"

"Yeah, like a black tinted out Explorer."

Suddenly it hits them and they think of the few times they have seen the Explorer floating around. Skelter's heart skips a beat. The fact that they were that close up on her without her knowing is too close for her comfort. This only incites her to move faster for she doesn't know what else they may know and what else they may have in store. She realizes she must act fast and dramatic if she wants to make an impactful statement.

"I need y'all to get that body from the spot and bring it to me. Meet me back here as soon as you're done. We have to move fast. We have to make a move before they make their next move."

• • •

NORTH CAMDEN

The air in the room is tense as Tortura paces around angrily. Quabo sits back in the cut in silence. He hasn't said a word in the past 20 minutes. He has given Tortura full permission to handle this as he may. They have an agreement that once blood is shed it's out of his hands and he takes the leash off of Tortura.

Members of the crew are all around the room with their eyes on the middle of the room where three men are lined up in a single file. The driver of the Explorer faces the first man. All of them stand petrified, not knowing what is next. Tortura paces circles around the line of men. Their assholes tighten up with fear every time he comes near one of them.

"*Hicimos un pacto. Antes de dejar morir a uno de los nuestros, morimos todos juntos.* (We made a pact. Before we leave one of our own to die, we all die together.)" Tortura shouts. "*Pero esta noche rompiste ese pacto.* (But tonight you broke that pact.)" His voice crackles with rage.

"*Violó la hermandad cuando dejó a su hermano morir solo.* (You violated the brotherhood when you left your brother to die alone.)" He stops directly in front of the driver. Beads of nervous sweat drip down his face. "*Cuando se viola la hermandad hay que morir.* (When one violates the brotherhood he must die.)"

Tortura reaches down his waistband and grabs hold of his gun. He extends his gun over to the driver. "*Estos hombres dejaron morir a nuestro hermano, así que ahora deben morir. Y los matarás.* (These men left our brother to die so now they must die. And you will kill them.)"

The man grabs the gun with no hesitation. He knows hesitating can only cost him his own life. He stands there holding the gun, awaiting the command to go. He grips the gun tightly.

Tortura looks to the line of men. "*Dará un paso adelante y recibirá su castigo o solo lo empeorará para usted.* (You will step up and receive your punishment or you will only make it worse for yourself.)" He looks to the first man in line and waves him forward. The man steps up with his feet as heavy as cinderblocks. Tortura looks to the driver and gives him a signal to go. The man lifts the gun, aims at the man's head and with no hesitation he fires a single shot. *BOC!* The man drops dead before them.

"*Siguiente!* (Next!)" Tortura shouts.

"*Por favor, no.* (Please, no)," the man pleads with tears in his eyes. Tortura looks away from him with no compassion. He signals for the driver to shoot and he does. *BOC!* The bullet crashes through the side of his head with enough impact to lift him off his feet. He tumbles backwards, feet flying in the air, landing on his neck.

"*Siguiente!* (Next!)" Tortura shouts.

The last man walks up showing no sign of emotion. "*Pido discul-pas a la hermandad. Les permití que se llevaran su vida y para eso doy mi propia vida.* (I apologize to the brotherhood. I allowed them to take his life and for that I give my own life.)" the man says with his head held high and his chest puffed up courageously. He stares the driver in the eyes without blinking. They lock eyes before the driver pulls the trigger. *BOC!* The man stumbles backwards, blood dripping down his face abundantly. He staggers before hitting the wall, where he stands using the wall to hold him up.

"*Acabar con él.* (Finish him)," Tortura commands.

The driver steps over the other two men and walks over. The wounded man peeks at the gunman through bloody eyes. He nods his head at the man as to say go on and take me out of misery. And the driver does. He plants the barrel of the gun, top center of the man's dome, and squeezes the trigger. Like a nail being drilled into wood, the man is drilled into the floor.

The driver turns to Tortura looking for his approval for finishing the task. Tortura holds his hand out for the gun. "*Ahora es tu turno.* (Now it's your turn)," Tortura says.

"*Pero yo era sólo el conductor. Yo no estaba allí para ayudar.* (But I was only the driver. I wasn't there with them.)" the man says with tears welling up in his eyes.

"Lo sé. Como el conductor, toda la responsabilidad recae sobre ti. (I know. As the driver. All the responsibility falls on you.)" Tortura says. With no further delay he aims the gun in between the man's eyes and squeezes. *BOC!*

He turns and walks away before the man hits the floor. He carries on normally. "*Han tomado uno de los nuestros. Ahora atacaremos mañana, tarde y noche. Nadie podrá respirar y mucho menos hacer un dólar por ahí. Los mataremos de hambre y luego los mataremos uno por uno.* (They've taken one of ours. Now we will attack morning, noon and night. No one will be able to breathe let alone make a dollar out there. We will starve them then kill them one by one.)" Tortura stops short in the middle of the room. He stares in a deep trance, thinking of a master plan.

47

THE NEXT DAY-CAMDEN

A **GORGEOUS, DOMINICAN** woman steps out of a red 5 series BMW. She strides elegantly, bopping from side to side so her long hair can sway in the wind. She balances the coffee in her hand so she doesn't spill a drop. She stops short in front of the storefront where she sticks a key into the lock. She uses her shoulder to force her way inside.

A strong force behind her catches her by surprise. She's pushed to the floor where she looks up finding a masked bandit standing over her. The bandit locks the door and aims a gun at the woman. The woman is in so much of a shock that she wants to scream but nothing is coming out.

"Get up, bitch," Skelter says from underneath the mask. The woman is slow in doing so, which makes Skelter snatch her by her collar. The buttons of her beautiful blouse pop and beautiful firm C cups, are fully exposed. "Turn the camera off right now, bitch. Where the camera?" Skelter asks as she places the gun against the woman's temple.

The woman leads Skelter over to the workstation and she quickly fumbles behind her salon tools where the camera is hidden. She hands the camera over to Skelter who slams it on the floor and stomps it into pieces. "Anymore?" Skelter asks. "If you lie to me and I find another one, I will blow your whole face off," she mumbles underneath the ski-mask.

"Yes," the woman says with tears dripping down her face, turning her make-up into a muddy mess. "One more in the back," she cries.

"Let's go, bitch. Lead the way." Skelter holds the gun to the woman's head as she leads the way. She fumbles over the door ledge until she finds the camera. She hands it to Skelter and she slams and stomps this one as well.

Skelter grabs her phone and dials quickly. The receiver picks up on the first ring. "Back Clear." Skelter cracks the door open. She stands there peeking outside. As she stands here, she repeats the words of Law number 17 of her favorite book. "Keep others into a suspended terror," she mumbles to herself. "Create an air of unpredictability. Being predictable gives power to others. If you behave unpredictably and inconsistently, people stop trying to predict your movements. The more unpredictable you are the people will become intimidated and terrified about what your next step will be," Skelter says as her eyes pierce through the woman's eyes.

"Please, don't hurt me," the woman pleads. "I have money in my wallet. Here, take my jewelry," she says. She snatches her necklaces from her own neck and hand them over to Skelter. The woman holds her hand up in the air to take off her ring.

"Shut up, stupid bitch," Skelter says. "This ain't no fucking robbery," she says as she shoves the jewelry out of her face.

"Please, take it all," she says as she twists the gleaming 10 carat engagement ring from her finger. The diamond gleams brightly, blinding Skelter. She'd be a fool to pass up on this. She snatches the ring from the woman and shoves it into her pocket.

A white van pulls up and Middle Godson and Oldest Godson jump out with hoods over their heads. They walk unsuspectedly to the back of the van. They open the doors and pull from the back of the van a roll of what seems to be carpet. Together they carry the roll of carpet into the back door of the salon.

"To the front," Skelter commands. The Godsons drag the carpet to the front of the salon while Skelter locks the back door securely. She drags the woman to the front.

"What's going on here? Please, just take it all."

Skelter ignores her and continues dragging her. Once she gets to the front room the Godsons are standing there awaiting further instructions. "Which chair is yours?" Skelter asks the woman. The woman points to the first chair. Skelter then looks to her Godsons. "Sit him in that chair."

The woman watches with suspense as the carpet is unrolled. When she realizes a dead body is in the carpet she loses her composure. She attempts to scream but Skelter places her hand over her mouth. The Godsons struggle to sit the man in the chair as the woman watches, not believing her eyes. Although his face is covered with blood she still recognizes him. She doesn't know him personally but she does know him as one of Quabo's men.

"Now, what we gone do is call Quabo," Skelter says as she places the gun on her chin. "Get your phone." The woman grabs her phone out of her purse. "Listen to what I want you to say. Listen carefully because you must say it exactly like I tell you, word for word, or I will blow your brains out and sit your dead body in the chair next to him. Understood?"

"Yes," the woman whispers as she cries in silence.

Skelter repeats the words she wants the woman to say five times and makes her repeat it back to her just to be sure that she has it right. By the sixth time she has it down to perfection. She then instructs the woman to call Quabo.

"Yo," Quabo answers cheerfully. He can be heard loud and clear because he's on speaker.

"Baby," the woman says, just as she's been instructed to. "If one more shot gets fired in Trenton, I'm a dead bitch."

"Huh?" Quabo asks.

Skelter nudges the woman with the gun, signaling her to continue on. The woman speaks. "Take this as a warning. My life is being spared today. Also, the man that was left behind, he's sitting here in my chair waiting for you."

Quabo goes hysterical. "What? What are you talking about? Who is there with you? I'm on my way."

Skelter snatches the phone. "You sent your man for me and I'm sending him back to you," she says. "Now, listen, I'm sparing your bitch right now. If one more shot gets fired I will not be sparing anyone else. You've been warned. Take the loss and stay the fuck out of Trenton." She ends the call.

Skelter shoves the woman into the middle chair. "Now, sit the fuck there and don't move until he gets here. I will be outside watching and if you move I will shoot you on sight."

The woman nods her head up and down nervously as she sits down. She can't keep her eyes off the dead man sitting not even three feet away from her. Skelter goes into the woman's purse in search of any type of identification and point of address. She quickly locates her driver's license and dashes toward the back door. Her Godsons follow at her heels. They hop into the van and pull away from the scene of the crime cool and calm, careful not to draw any attention.

48

NORTHERN STATE

BABY MANSON HAS spun the track already and now he's at the pull-up bar stretching his body and preparing for his workout. He's finally identified the 2 other men that were recently shipped over to this wing. Although he pretends to be in his own world, right now he knows the exact whereabouts of all three of the new faces. He's a master at watching people without actually watching them.

One of the men, the first one to be shipped over, is across the yard just kicking with a group of gangbangers from his sect. The second man, another obvious gangbanger is a few hundred feet away from Manson blending in with a group of men who are doing push-ups based on Playing Cards. The third man, who seems like a total square is sitting with a group of die-hard Christians. The men he's with are Christians who don't mix with others. They stay in their group and rarely even speak to anyone outside of them. Baby Manson charges that man off as harmless. He knows better than to underestimate anyone and he will keep his eye on the man but his full attention is on the other two.

Baby Manson is no dummy and he knows it's no coincidence that once these men have been shipped over from the other side, Gunsmoke is now dead. Baby Manson is almost sure that hit was behind him. He's seen instances like this so many times where dudes have been whacked for not following orders of whacking someone else. He's also sure if Gunsmoke was killed for not doing what he was supposed to do, then these men were also sent here to do what Gunsmoke didn't do.

It's been airtight around here the last couple days. Whole jail has been on lock ever since the guards found Gunsmoke dead in his bed. It's been chitter chatter and gossip surrounding it but for the most part a bunch of lies being told by dudes who really know nothing. One thing for certain though, everybody is walking on eggshells because no one knows if they may be next.

Baby Manson spots Short Fuse walking into the Big Yard. This is his first time seeing him since the day he took the L. As Short Fuse is walking toward the pull-up bar, he passes the young man who chumped him off that day. The young man and his group are all taking turns in their workout circuit. Once they see him all action stops. The young man whispers something to his group and they all break out in laughter, secretly ridiculing Short Fuse. Short Fuse continues on pass them as if he doesn't even see them. Baby Manson watches all of this and gets even more angry now than he was the day it happened.

Short Fuse walks up to Baby Manson and greets him with a fist bump. With just a pointing of the finger he asks Baby Manson if it's ok for him to jump in. Baby Manson gives the ok and watches Short Fuse with confusion as he pulls up ever so gracefully as if he has no care in the world. It's taking everything inside him not to bring this conversation up. He can't understand how any man with pride could ever step foot back out here and pretend that he hasn't been humiliated. He really expected Short Fuse to never show his face in the Big Yard but here he is standing here with no shame.

Short Fuse hang jumps from the bar and Baby Manson jumps up, hanging onto the bar. Just as Baby Manson gets to his twelfth repetition, he watches Short Fuse step away from the bar. With his back arched like a sneaky cat, he creeps, light on his feet. He makes a strong cut toward the group where the man who humiliated him is. That man is laying on his back, knees up, doing abdomen curls. Right in between head to knee motion, Short Fuse picks up a jog. As he's jogging, he reaches into his sweatpants.

The young man looks upward and is surprised to see Short Fuse standing over him. His mouth opens with shock. They lock eyes, upside down. "You see me clearly, right?" Short Fuse asks before flashing a smile. The next thing the young man sees is an object coming downward. He tries to scramble to his feet but it's too late. The lock-in-the-sock crashes into his forehead with heavy impact. His forehead splits open upon contact, bursting open like a watermelon.

The men all gather around as if they are about to make a move on Short Fuse until they see Baby Manson walking over. Baby Manson stands on his G-square, eyes on all of them, letting them clearly know he's involved. "Don't nobody touch him," Baby Manson says with aggression.

Short Fuse bangs the lock-in-the-sock onto the young man's forehead, in the exact same spot over and over again. "Learn...to...keep... your...mouth...shut...young...boy," he says banging his head with every syllable. The blood squirts from his head like a water fountain.

He stops banging him long enough to chastise him. "That's the problem with you young motherfuckers," he says with spit jumping out of his mouth and landing on the man's bloody face. "You talk too much. You fucking with a nigga that got graveyards of bodies on his jacket. Respect my gangster!" Short Fuse says before standing up for leverage.

He uses all of his strength to wind up before dropping the lock on the man's head one final time. The sound thumps loudly but not louder than the kick to the young man's head. To add insult to injury Short Fuse hog spits on the man's face . "I'm sparing you today. Next time I will take your life!" He looks to the crowd of men. "And any fucking body else that want to test my gangster, speak now!"

The alarm sounds off and Short Fuse is positive that the guards are on their way coming for him. He slowly drops to his knees, as he drops the lock-in-the-sock in front of him. He's both knees on the ground, with his hands on the back of his head in submission. With eyes still on the crowd, he continues to speak. "When I come out the hole, anybody who want it can get it. I don't pick and choose. This shit is for everybody," he says with an evil grin.

"On the ground, everybody on the ground!" The Officers come swarming in prepared for riot. All the inmates dive onto the ground in compliance in fear of mace being sprayed. Once everyone is on the ground the officers rush in and gather around Short Fuse who isn't putting up any resistance.

As Short Fuse is being dragged away, he looks over to Baby Manson. "When I get back, I owe you a set," Short Fuse says with all seriousness on his face. "I hate owing people and I never leave a debt open. I make sure every man gets what he deserves from me. No debt ever left unreturned," he says with emphasis.

Baby Manson smiles admirably. He's never been more impressed in his life. Short Fuse may not know it but he's just earned himself a spot in Baby Manson's heart. It's at this very moment that he realizes that he wants Short Fuse on his team. He's sure together they will make one hell of a force.

49

TONY STANDS OVER his desk. Across from him there sits a casually dressed, middle aged man Caucasian man that Tony has no clue of who he is or why he's here. He came into Tony's firm and demanded to be seen by Tony and wouldn't take no for an answer. He claims he has important information that Tony needs to hear.

"My reason for being here is pertaining to one of your former clients," the man claims.

"And who might that be?" Tony asks with his normal casual attitude.

The man hesitates before speaking. "Damien Bryant also known as The Black Charles Manson," says the man slowly.

"Okay, and what about?" Tony asks with somewhat of an edge. Tony is always paranoid and believes everybody to be a FED until they prove otherwise.

"Well, I'm here because you're the only person that I could get in touch with," he admits. "With all the coverage of his case your name was mentioned more in the articles than his was. Seems with the level of the crimes that were committed, the articles and write-ups were more centered about you than the nature of their crimes. That says a lot about who you are and must be."

Tony shrugs his shoulders with a false sense of modesty. He still can't figure out where all this is going. He stands in silence because he knows silence will make the man talk more. "Let me ask you, have you heard anything from him?"

"Heard anything from him?" Tony asks with signs of irritation. "How can I hear anything from a dead man? Is this some type of joke? Is this supposed to be funny?"

"No joke whatsoever," the man replies. "And my very reason for being here. I come all the way from Colorado. I did my time of twenty-five years in Colorado Supermax."

"Welcome home," Tony interrupts.

"No, not twenty-five years as an inmate," he says. "I did twenty-five years as an officer there. Well, it's just like being a prisoner. Being locked up all day," he says with disgust spreading over his face. "I just retired last week."

"Congratulations," Tony says respectfully.

"Thank you. I'm here to inform you that Bryant has been there the past three years."

"Huh?"

"Yes, he's been in the hole, away from population, no contact with other inmates whatsoever. The only people that knows he's there are jail staff."

"This must be some type of misunderstanding. You have to have the wrong guy. I've seen the newspaper article stating his death. I've seen the death certificate and even went to the funeral."

"Was the funeral open or closed casket?"

"Closed," Tony says slowly as his mind entertains the fact. "But what about the morgue? His wife had to identify the body. Or did she?" Tony asks aloud as he really asks himself.

"Listen, I don't know all the underlying details. But what I do know is Bryant is very much alive and I am the only officer that could step within feet of him. We developed a rapport over the years and I promised him once I retired I would reach out to someone about the matter."

Tony listens attentively. He can't believe his ears. "But why?" Tony asks.

"The FEDS have been pressing him every week for the past three years. They want him to roll. They've offered to let him free if he will just work with them. They offer to send him to a different part of the country with false documents and identification to work as an informant."

"Motherfuckers," Tony says with hatred rolling off his lips.

"He won't roll. He's solid as a rock. After all they put him through, he still remains solid. They starve him. They urinate on his food and even defecate in it. They abuse him like a slave and most of the time they keep him medicated with enough thorazine and Ativan to calm down a stampede of elephants."

"So, is he sane?" Tony asks. "Like, is he himself?"

"Barely sane," the man replies sympathetically. "Some days he's himself and others he's a madman, lunatic."

"Damn," Tony replies. Hearing this hurts his heart.

"He's not the only one there though with this same issue. There are maybe twenty or thirty others who have been lost in that prison. Most of them eventually roll. The others end up dying from the physical abuse or the medical abuse of heavy dosage of medication. Some are even used as guinea pigs once the Feds realize they won't roll over or they are no longer mentally competent enough to be used."

Tony takes a seat as he allows all of this to digest. He understands and respects the craftiness of the Feds and knows they are capable of almost anything but this right here tops anything that he's ever heard them do. "What do you mean guinea pigs? For what?"

"For their new drugs. Some of these dudes are walking zombies from being used as experiments and no one knows it. They are just charged off as crazy."

Tony's mind races. All he can hear is Jane Doe's voice. How ironic is it that her and this man are speaking along the same lines? The pot just got sweeter. He figures if he can tie this case with Jane Doe's case here, it will be a major explosion. Tony stares out of the window in deep thought.

"My heart goes out to those guys," the man says with sincerity. "I mean, I understand they are criminals who deserve to pay for their crimes but some of the stuff I've seen with my own eyes I can never forget. I would like to expose this shit so this doesn't happen to anyone else. And I know you are the man to do it. Only one thing though," he says as holds his finger in the air. "My identity can't be disclosed. I need my pension to stay in place."

"Listen to me, the information you just revealed to me can change your life drastically. What's your pension five or six grand a month, seventy-two grand a year? You have no idea the value of the information you have just given me. It's like the missing link of a gigantic puzzle, and once I put it together I can't even explain to you how I will be able to change your life financially. You have just hit the mega-millions and you don't even dig it. And most importantly your identity will not be disclosed so your little five grand a month will still be in place. You can use that to pay your landscapers for the month," Tony says with a smile.

"But for right now, I need any and all proof that you have that these men are being held captive there. Also, the medicine that you spoke of that's used to tranquilize these men, I will need a list of every one you can remember."

"Oh, that's easy," the man says as he reaches in his pocket for his phone. "I came prepared," he says with a smile. "Give me a phone number and I can send everything I have to your phone."

Tony flashes a smile. "My man!"

He loves it when a plan comes together. This ties in so well with the Jane Doe case. These two cases together will make him iconic. This case will make him a bigger name than the only attorney that he feels is bigger than him and that is Johnny Cochran. In no way does he feel that Johnny Cochran has put in more work than him. He feels the OJ case just made him a household name. This case he's putting together now will make him more than a household name. He will be Rockstar status. His name will ring bells in Russia, Germany, and Japan like Michael Jackson and the Beatles.

50

LATER THAT NIGHT

ITS PITCH BLACK out with a heavy downpour of rain. The yard of a tiny house with a wide-open field in the back has twenty men gathered around a muddy hole in the ground. The men stand in the field with shovels, hard at work. Quabo and Tortura stand under a lonely tree for cover. They watch as the men give their brother an improper burial. With no family here in the States and very little family back in Dominican Republic, the only people that will truly miss him are all standing here in this field. They have buried a many of men to protect themselves from being charged with murder but it hurts them to have to bury one of their own.

"My lady will never be the same," Quabo says sadly. "The shit she saw she will never be able to forget."

"She will be fine. Just needs a little time," Tortura says.

"She threatened to leave me," Quabo says. "And I don't think it's a threat."

"Leave you and do what? Be with who? She will never find another like you. She's not going anywhere."

"I think we should let things cool off for a second. I don't want this to fall back on her. They know who she is. They have her address. If we make another move, I'm sure they will come for her."

"So, that's your answer? Just stop now?" Tortura asks.

"Just for a second until I figure out how to get her out of here. She has her business that she has to tend to. I can't be worried about her."

"So, don't worry then," Tortura says coldly. "We are not stopping now. We can't. This isn't about the money anymore. It's principle. They took one of ours. Stopping is not even an option. They would rather be dead than to live the life I have in store for them."

Tortura pauses briefly. "And about your girlfriend, I will tell you just like you told your beautiful sister about her husband; you will find another one," he says as he walks away. He leaves Quabo standing there sulking in those words.

MEANWHILE IN TRENTON

Skelter sits back quietly as her sister, Helter lays her out. "That's my daughter father. If he gets murdered, my daughter—your niece—will grow up without a father like we did. Is that what you want for her?" Helter asks with tears pouring from her eyes. "He was fine until you dragged him into all of this mess. It's all your fault!"

Skelter is pissed off that Bruh in Law pillow talked and told Helter everything. Really, she expected nothing less from him but to sit here and hear all that he's told her infuriates her. "My fault? You the one who brought the fuckboy into our world. You had the baby with him. It's your fault," she says taking no blame at all. "I should do him dirty for running his fucking mouth."

"I swear if you do anything to him I will never speak to you again."

"Wow," Skelter says with a hurtful smile. "Over a fucking nigga? I can't believe my ears."

"It ain't just no fucking regular nigga," she says in total defense. "This my daughter's father!"

Skelter stands up with very little words left to say. "I'm gone need you to start looking for another apartment. I'm sure shit is about to get crazy around here and I can't be worried about you and niece. That shit will only get in the way and slow me down. Fuck him. I ain't worried about him. I will let you do all the worrying about him."

Secretly Skelter is jealous that Helter, on many occasions, has taken Bruh in Law's side over hers. That makes her hate him even more.

Helter cries pathetically. Skelter has never seen her like this and although it hurts her to see her sister like this she doesn't show it. "Don't worry about the money. Find you a spot anywhere, no matter how much the rent is. Make sure it's a building with a gate and security," Skelter says. "The faster you do that, the faster I can put my foot on the gas and really bring the heat to these motherfuckers.

"And as far as that fuck nigga of yours, you better tell him to keep my name out of his mouth. I'm already five minutes off his ass and that clock is ticking fast."

51

DAYS LATER

BABY MANSON PACES small circles in his cell. The anticipation has his heart pounding and his blood boiling. In the palm of his hand he holds his weapon tightly. The pawn may be the weakest piece on the chessboard but Baby Manson has fixed it where it has more value off the chessboard. The piece has been melted down and sharpened with a tip that's sharp enough to cut through leather.

It's almost Recreation time and his anxiousness has everything to do with that. He's not excited about Rec in itself though. His anxiety comes from the fact that Rec is the only time that he will be able to get to his enemy. Every second counts and if he uses every one of his seconds properly his enemy won't make it to the yard.

His goal is to be the first one out of the cell so he can meet his enemy at the door. That will be the best way to catch the man by the element of surprise. He has to have perfect timing in order to do so. If he's slow, he blows.

Baby Manson stops pacing and stands at his cell with adrenaline bubbling.

"Rec!" the officer shouts just as the doors are buzzed open.

Baby Manson slides through the barely opened door and busts the quick right down the tier. He's the first one out of his room and has the next man behind him beat by a second. In seconds, inmates appear all over the tier. His heart sinks with defeat as he sees his enemy stepping out of his cell and walking hurriedly along the tier. "Damnit," he mumbles to himself as he walks behind the man, gripping his knife tightly.

He may have missed his calling but he refuses to let this opportunity pass him by. He realizes if he misses this opportunity, the next time they may have the jump on him and he can't afford to have that happen. He picks up his pace to catch up with the man. He's sure to blend in with the flow of walking traffic with hopes of the man not seeing him. He keeps his eyes fixed on his prey. In his mind he envisions the scene playing out from start to finish.

The flow of traffic bends around the corridor on their way outside. As soon as the man disappears, Baby Manson does a light jog just to catch up. He bends the corner and there the man is a few people up ahead of him. He positions himself perfectly to be to the right of the man. He allows some foot traffic to catch up with him so he can blend in.

Just before they step into the gym, Baby Manson takes one giant leap and there he is shoulder to shoulder with his enemy. His enemy looks to his right quickly where he finds Baby Manson shoulder to shoulder with him. Baby Manson links arms with the man and pulls him close. With his other hand he sticks his knife into the man's side. The man tries to pull away but Baby Manson overpowers him. He holds him close as he pokes the knife in him repeatedly. He feels the man get weak but he continues to poke.

The man stumbles and the foot traffic gathers around them. Baby Manson lets the man's arms loose and the man trips over his feet. He falls to the floor, rolling around in pain as the people stop and look in awe. Baby Manson continues in stride, concealing his knife. He blends along with the foot traffic long enough for him to disappear. He can hear the chaos behind him but he continues walking, never once looking back.

"One down," he mumbles to himself. "One more to go."

52

TEANECK, NEW JERSEY

THE BLUE MAYBACH G-Class G 650 Landaulet with the tan gut looks like a gourmet peanut butter and jelly sandwich floating along Route 46. The front two-thirds of the truck is fully tinted out. The last third of the truck is the convertible top, which is peeled back, allowing the peanut butter gut to ooze. The G wagon on steroids is what Tony calls it. The most expensive SUV in the world right now is priced at $650,000. Only 100 made and Tony has one out of those hundred.

The sound of rapper, Post Malone's voice can be heard over the wind. "Hundred bands in my pocket, it's on me...Get more bottles, these bottles are lonely." Tony drives with a super laid-back demeanor despite the fact that he's driving fast enough to be in a NASCAR race. Tony raps along with the song. "Cut the roof off like a niptuck." Tony frowns his face and goes into character as he sings. "G-wagen, G-wagen, G-wagen, G-wagen." He peeks back and forth in between the road and Dre who sits in the passenger's seat. "If you can just practice a little more patience, I promise you all your money problems will be over."

"Patience?" Dre asks. "How much more patient you want me to be? On some real shit bruh, I rather be dead than to be broke. I don't know how a broke motherfucker goes through his whole life like that. Shit mind boggles the fuck out of me."

Tony shakes his head with agitation. "You did a whole sixteen years…I'm sure the hardest time of your life. In jail everybody broke. How did you do it for sixteen years?"

"Well, actually I wasn't broke. My little brother made sure I had everything. But even if he didn't that's different. You're supposed to be broke in jail. No excuse for no man to be broke while out here with his freedom. And that's the part that fucks me up. I'm out here free and can't seem to get it right. Like I'm a waste of air," he says feeling like a true failure. "My lil brother always said if a dude out here ain't getting to the money and just in the way, he should go to the nearest jail and knock on the door and trade places with a motherfucker that will come out here and do what he supposed to be doing. I totally get it now."

"No disrespect to lil bruh," Tony says as he hits the blinker to switch lanes. "But his mindset was all the way twisted. That's what we both loved about him but we can't deny his thought process was all wrong." Tony makes the strong right, making his exit off the highway and in his entrance into the Teterboro airport. Upon entrance of the airport Tony is happy to see his private jet.

"Like I was saying, I just need you to be a little more patient and what I have in store for you will be life-changing. Can you do that for me?"

"What choice do I have?"

"You have a lot of choices, just don't make a bad one or you will hate yourself forever." Tony looks to Dre who sits sulking in depression. "You sure you don't want go with me? I can just park in the lot. You need to get away to clear your mind. Oh and speaking of," Tony says as he pulls a few hundred feet away from the jet. He has to close the roof just so he can hear himself over the sound of the loud propellers. "I need to know what you are going to do about the Honduras trip. You in?"

Dre sighs. "Yeah, I'm in."

Tony's eyes light up with cheer. He's been begging Dre to come with him and it was looking like it wasn't going to happen. "Don't bullshit me man."

"I would never bullshit you," Dre replies.

"Good," Tony says as he grabs his briefcase and his overnight bag from the back. He gets out and grabs his suit bag from the hanging rod. "I will be back tomorrow night," he says as he slams the door shut.

Tony is greeted by his pilot at the staircase. He boards his plane and the doors are closed behind him. "How long is this flight to Colorado?"

"Four hours and four minutes," the stewardess says.

"Perfect," Tony replies. "Just enough time for a power nap and I will get there in more than enough time before the business day is over. I need to be in and out of here like a robbery.

ONE HOUR LATER

A quiet and residential block in the suburbs of New Jersey. Each house on the block is more beautiful than the next. Not a house on the block is worth less than a half of a million dollars. For a middle-class family, this block is *the* block to be on.

Dre sits parked across the street from a beautiful yellow house that he has been watching for the past 20 minutes. This house belongs to his family that really doesn't consider him family. He hasn't been near this house in over ten years now and he sees there has been a lot of changes made since then.

The house looks to have been renovated with a new porch, new paint job, all new windows and even a new roof. At one time this house was one of the most basic ones on the block. Today it stands out as one of the nicest. Dre is almost sure the renovation was all funded by the million dollars in cash he gave to his uncle to hold for him before his fall.

He's sure his uncle got the news of his death and probably then looked at the million dollars as free money. He doesn't blame him the least bit but being that he isn't dead, he needs to get his hands on that money. The desperate part of him wants to believe that the million dollars in cash is still there behind the wall his uncle built. The realistic thinking part of him understands that 10 years is a long time and that million dollars could have been spent a long time ago.

There's only one way to find out and that is ring the bell and talk to his uncle. The only problem with that is his uncle thinks he's dead, just as any other family member. To reveal the truth to them and make them aware that he really is very well alive can open up another can of worms. At this point, on his last legs financially, he's willing to reveal the truth if that is what it takes to get his hands on whatever money his uncle has left of his. He's been debating for months about coming here but fear of being exposed has kept him away.

Desperation has led him here today. Today he must talk to his uncle. One thing he knows about his uncle is that he loves money and he can be bought. So he has already decided to let his uncle keep a portion of whatever money he has left just to remain silent. He just prays there's some money left. He also prays his uncle is willing to part with the money that he has considered his all these years, believing Dre was dead.

Dre psyches himself up before getting out of the truck. He slams the door shut and just as he's walking away the uncertainty kicks in. His heart pounds in his chest for he knows what this can lead to. Only two things can happen at this point. One, Dre can talk to his uncle and get hold to a couple hundred grand, hopefully. Or, two, he can talk to his uncle and his uncle can turn him in and keep any money he has left. Dre only likes one of those options and hopes the other doesn't come into play.

Dre stands on the porch with fear of pressing the doorbell. He sighs deeply before pressing it. His heart thumps as he hears the sound of creaking stairs behind the door. He considers taking off while he still has a chance.

Just as he turns to walk away the door opens behind him. He turns around and what he sees baffles him. "Yes," the middle-aged Caucasian woman says. She has the same perplexed look on her face that Dre has on his.

"Hello," Dre says nervously. "I'm sorry to bother you but I'm looking for the Blackhead family."

The woman's expression calms. "Oh, sorry Dear, but they no longer live here. We bought the house from them over ten years ago."

"Oh, wow," Dre says. Just around the time of his death, he thinks to himself. He needs whereabouts but doesn't know the approach he should use. "I'm a close relative and I been away in Japan with the armed services and they are the only relatives I have left. Was just trying to get in contact with them."

"Oh, I'm sorry. I thank you for your service though," she says sincerely. "But I don't have any contact information on them, sorry. They divorced and sold us the house. You haven't heard this from me, though, but from what I hear it was a messy divorce. The husband left the wife for a young woman a third of his age."

"Tragic," Dre replies and meaning every sense of the word. Not for the sake of their marriage but for his own sake. "Ok, thank you," he says with a fake smile. "Have a great day," he says as he turns away. He walks down the stairs with despair.

"Wait," the woman shouts. Dre turns around with hope that she has some information of their whereabouts although he believes it doesn't matter. He's sure wherever his uncle is the money has already been spent. He's sure the young girl has drained him for every dime. He always knew his uncle was money hungry but didn't think his uncle would allow money to tear up his family. "Leave me a name and a phone number just in case I come in contact with one of them."

"Nah," Dre says sadly. He continues on down the stairs. "It's not even that important,"

Dre feels defeated all over again. At least one good thing came out of this and that is he can now count this money out as an option. The dreams and the thoughts and the debating can now stop. The bad part about it is some days this was the only hope he had to hold onto. Now he has very little hope left.

53

FRIDAY 1:17 P.M.

IN THE GYMNASIUM the Friday Jumu'ah Service is taking place. The Imaam stands at the podium giving one of his best sermons ever. Sadly not many are present to hear it. Over the past weeks the congregation has gotten smaller and smaller. This week the presence is less than a third of what he's used to. He's gotten wind of what's been going on. In the beginning he didn't think it was possible but now he realizes the graveness of this situation.

F-WING

In the dayroom it's a totally different vibe than ordinary. All the televisions are off and there is no game playing whatsoever, no cards, no checkers, no chess nor dominoes. The room is filled with Bloods as well as Crips. Most of the time the Bloods and Crips can't get along but for this hour they can stomach each other. They stand on different squares but they have one thing in common, and that is Islam.

Smith a.k.a. Lil Mumit a.k.a. Mujahid has brought all the gang members here together on one accord. They put any differences they may have to the side for this hour. They have been told this hour is sacred and they all will come in peace or they will leave in pieces. All these men stand behind Smith in the banning of the official Jumu'ah. It all started from small Arabic classes to small Taraweeh Prayers and now they stand here with their own Jumu'ah service. Smith calls it the 'La Hukm' Movement which means No Judgement.

He has a point to prove that he can rally up more men to follow his movement than they have at the traditional service in the gymnasium. Some of these men are standing with him voluntarily while others are standing with him by force. He's done research and found out no one has taken a stand like this since 1978 when Royall Jenkins branched off from the Nation of Islam (N.O.I.) and founded his own movement, the United Nation of Islam (U.N.O.I.).

Royall Jenkins was a member of the NOI, but after the death of Elijah Muhammad, he left the organization and started his own. He styles himself as 'Royall Allah in Person'. His movement is based on most of the same philosophy of The Nation of Islam with his own modifications. Smith plans to follow the Sunnah strictly with no rule bending or modifications of his own. He just has appointed himself as the religious leader of this prison.

As Smith speaks low but clear enough for the crowd to hear, his eyes cut to the doorway where an officer stands. The officer realizes what's going on and he quickly goes into a rage. He storms toward the group of inmates angrily.

"Y'all gone have to break this up, right now," he demands. Smith looks at the officer as if he hasn't said a word. He continues on with his speaking. "Yo, did you just hear me? I said break this up!" Smith continues on, not even looking in the officer's direction. The officer quickly gets on his walkie talkie and calls in for back-up. In no time at all, three officers come to his aid. As the officer's approach, Smith's followers all stand to their feet. They form a half circle around Smith as if to protect him from the officers.

"Y'all gone break this up or do we have to break it up?" an officer asks as he keeps his eyes on the men. The officers are outnumbered but they can't show sign of weakness.

The inmates all on edge, look to Smith waiting for whatever he decides. For his approval these men will do anything and Smith knows it. A part of him wants to display his power but he has a bigger goal in mind. He doesn't want the problems so early in the game so he chooses to digress.

Smith looks to his men and swipes his hands across his throat as to say, cut. He walks off, looking deep into the eyes of each officer one by one. The group of inmates follow closely behind.

C-WING

Baby Manson tries not to look suspicious. He peeks around to make sure the coast is clear before stepping into the bathroom. As he steps inside what lies before his eyes is too good to be true. One of Smith's hitmen that he sent over is facing the wall, in the shower as he washes his face.

Baby Manson tiptoes behind him with his knife gripped tightly in his hand. Just as he gets close enough behind him to strike, the man turns around. His eyes stretch open with fear as he backs against the wall. Just as Baby Manson is ready to attack the sound of a familiar voice catches his attention and snaps him out of his zone. "You crazy, Sanders," says the officer as he bends the corridor on his way into the shower area.

Baby Manson quickly tucks his knife as he steps away. He keeps his eyes on the man who is standing in uncertainty. The look on his face confuses Baby Manson. It's as if he has no clue of who Baby Manson is and why he was about to be attacked.

Baby Manson quickly walks around the officer who watches him with skepticism. Standing in the stall is the Christian inmate. He just witnessed Baby Manson in his pre-attack. Baby Manson has no clue of him being here.

He ducks back in the stall as Baby Manson passes. He watches him with a close eye. After Baby Manson exits the bathroom, the man diverts his attention over to the other inmate who still wears a look of confusion. He's quite shook up that his life was that close to being over. For what reason he has no idea. The Good Christian chuckles to himself for all of this has been quite entertaining to watch. It's also been informative and eye-opening.

As Baby Manson is walking the tier his name is called. He turns around and there is Officer Tillis. "Watch your movements," he warns. Baby Manson assumes he's speaking of what almost took place in the shower.

"What movements?" he asks with a false sense of innocence.

"Luckily, a good friend of mine was watching the camera that day or you would be assed out."

Baby Manson now realizes Tillis is talking about the other day when he poked the man up near the gymnasium. He has nothing to say in reply. "I got him to make the tape disappear for the time being. I don't know if I will be able to make the tape disappear forever though."

"Talk to him for me and whatever I need to do to have it destroyed, just let me know," says Baby Manson.

"I will try," Tillis replies. "I can't make no promises though. He can be a real dick-head when he wants to be. Hopefully this won't come back to haunt you."

"You said he's your friend, so maybe you can talk to him like a friend and let him know if this haunts me, it will eventually haunt him.

54

FREMONT COUNTY COLORADO-COLORADO ADX

THE WARDEN, A middle-aged white man dressed in a cheap suit, stands over his desk. Ku Klux Klan is the best way to describe him. The prejudice and hatred for black men shows on his face as he stands across from Tony. Initially, he refused to meet with Tony but Tony had to use his connections to get in here. He called three powerful people who explained to the warden how powerful of a man, Tony is.

"Have a seat," the warden says in form of more of a command than a suggestion or offer.

"No, I rather stand," Tony says. He understands by sitting and allowing the man to stand over him, he's giving all power to him. The both of them stand butting heads like two Rams.

"Who do you think you are to come making demands? You may be a hot shot attorney in New Jersey but I have never heard of you. Your name holds no value here."

"Yeah, yeah, yeah," Tony says, brushing the man off. "I ain't one for small talk. My reason here is a client of mine, Damien Bryant. The name probably doesn't ring a bell but he's one of the many inmates you have buried here underground." The man can't hide his uneasiness. He swallows hard. "He's also known as the Black Charles Manson," Tony further adds.

"I have one thousand inmates here and you expect me to remember one by name?"

"The fifty to one hundred men you have hidden from the world are they counted in that one thousand inmates that you speak of?" Tony asks.

"I have no clue of what you're talking about," the warden replies with a straight face.

"Yes, sure you do," Tony says sarcastically. "I have proof that my client and close to one hundred other inmates have been hidden here in your prison with your permission. Those inmates are starved and tortured daily."

"I have no knowledge of any of this going on in my prison. This is so false."

"I have proof," Tony says.

"Yeah, well, provide it then," the warden says hastily.

"You may want to sit for this," Tony says as he pulls out his phone. He scrolls for a second or two before placing the phone in the warden's face. He presses play and a video of Manson sitting crouched in the corner of his cell plays clearly. "That right there is my client." Tony scrolls again and presses play. "Watch this video here. This one shows my client being beat on. Look at the way his eyes roll in his head. You see how heavily medicated he is?"

"Well, when an inmate refuses to comply we have to do what we have to do."

"Well, you're right and I have no problem with that. The problem I have is that my client is nowhere on your roster of inmates. And I have a problem with this right here," Tony says as he hands the warden the newspaper article stating that Manson died in the raid in Brooklyn.

The warden's cocky attitude is replaced with nervousness, yet he tries to play it off. "Listen, all this is new to me. I'm asking that you leave my office and if you would like to discuss any of this any further, I will direct you to my attorney."

"Fine," Tony says as he gathers his belongings. "I was hoping we could get through this informally. But if I have to contact your attorney

I will be going all the way through with procedure. I will come back with a search warrant to search the entire facility. I will contact the local and international press. Through my key witness, I have enough footage to bury you," Tony says with confidence.

"Furthermore, I have thoroughly researched you, and you are quite a businessman to say the least. I know that you are working hand in hand with the Feds allowing them to use your facility as a torture base to get the men to roll over as informants. I'm sure you get some type of financial kickback for that. I also know that you and your investment group have eight prisons being built from the ground up right now as we speak. I also know that you and that same investment group have a total of twelve Charter Schools spread out in different ghettos in the country. I know all about the school to prison pipeline. Once I shine the light on you hiding federal inmates that are assumed to be dead and getting a kick back from the feds for doing so, I'm sure your prison development projects will self-destruct. And last but not least, the Dishonorable Judge Suzanne Damello," Tony says with a smile.

"Name doesn't ring a bell," the warden says.

"Sure it does. She was part of the cash for kids scandal wherein judges were giving minority young men astronomical prison terms for almost misdemeanor crimes so prisons could make more money off of them. In return those judges were given kickbacks of cash. Judge Suzanne Damello being one of those judges," Tony says with a dazzling smile. "She also just happened to be your girlfriend at the time. Have you heard from her by chance?"

The Warden is no longer cocky. He sits there in full submission mode. "What is it that you want from me?"

"For starters, I'm not leaving here without seeing my client. Secondly, I will need you to ship my client out of your facility to the facility of my choice. Somewhere closer to home."

"That may be hard to do," the warden claims.

"Not as hard as it will be to undo all the drama that I am prepared to bring to you if you don't. Now, as I have requested, I wish to see my client, now."

55

ROGER GARDEN APARTMENTS

A MAN IN his late 20's pedals a bike slowly along the sidewalk. He slows down even more and lifts his front wheel. He pops a wheelie for about 10 feet. He zips around the people that are walking toward him, never once allowing his front tire to touch the ground.

A woman walking in front of the bike with determination causes him to stop. He allows his front tire to touch the ground and he swerves in front of the shabby looking woman. "What's up, Auntie?"

"You still got that Empire," she asks as she straightens the wrinkled bills in her hand.

"Yeah," he replies. "How many you want?" he asks as he sticks his hands down inside the front of his pants. He spreads his legs wide so he can dig in between the crevice of his ass cheeks. He digs as if he's digging for gold. Finally he pulls his hand out and in the palm he holds a folded napkin.

He opens the napkin where 30 something small bags of dope lie. He quickly pulls 2 bags from the bundle and drops them in the woman's hand. She holds a bag in the air and plucks it hard for the dope to settle in the bag, making sure the bag is filled with dope and not skimpy. She does the same with the second bag before she walks off.

The man sticks his hands back into his pants and tucks the napkin in between his ass cheeks. He then takes 3 strong pedals before popping a wheelie. He wheelies the block for 20 solid pedals before his body jolts like he's just run underneath an invisible wire or clothesline. He crashes onto the ground with the back of his head splattering onto the concrete. The bike continues rolling without a cycler.

Blood gushes from the man's head. Another young man runs to his aid, amazed at what has just happened. He stares in disbelief as the man lays on the ground with blood pouring from his forehead. The man runs closer and just as he kneels onto the ground, his neck snaps backwards and his head slings forward before he tumbles over. He lies on top of the other man, both covered in blood and not breathing.

People come running from every direction, trying to understand what has happened. They see holes in both of the men's head and blood everywhere but they can't figure it out. "Somebody call 911! Hurry!"

Directly across the street, an old and raggedy work van sits parked, undetected. Inside the van are three men, a driver, Tortura, and one of Tortura's snipers. The sniper, an older man, is on his knees with an HK416 Assault Rifle resting on a shooting stand in front of him. The van has a specially designed hole in place fit for this rifle. The nose of the rifle extends a quarter of an inch outside the van, just barely visible. From here he was able to tag both of the men without being noticed. The silencer on the rifle kept the noise down.

Right here right now, he's prepared to wipe *out* everybody present. He looks to Tortura waiting for the command to do so. "*No, eso es demasiado fácil.* (No, that is too easy.)" Tortura says. "*Lo fácil me aburre.* (Easy bores me.) *Me gusta divertirme.* (I like to have fun.) *Pongámonos de dos en dos cada vez y mantengámoslo entretenido.* (Let's knock off two at a time, every time and keep it entertaining.) *Hemos terminado aquí por ahora.* (We are done here for now.)"

The man slowly pulls the nose of the rifle inside. He slides a metal clasp down to close the hole. Tortura looks at his watch to make note the exact time of shooting. He plans to attack every couple hours to keep the pressure on them.

He looks across the street where it is now packed with people surrounding the 2 victims. What he enjoys most about all of this is the look of confusion on their faces. They have no idea what has just taken place. He plans to torture them by playing tricks with their minds. He's sure once he gets into their heads his prey will fall right into his hands.

"Vamonos. (Let's go.)" Tortura says. *"Regresaremos en dos horas una vez que las cosas se hayan calmado.* (We will come back in two hours once everything has settled down.)"

The driver manages to ease out of the parking space and pull off without notice. Tortura smiles a demonic laugh. *"Que empiecen los juegos mentales.* (Let the mind games begin.)"

56

COLORADO ADX

TONY'S HEART BEATS with a weird type of nervousness as he sees a shadow appear though the glass on the door. The man peeks over the officer's shoulder as he opens the door. Tony has to double take as the man bound by ankle and wrist shackles is escorted into the room. This isn't the Manson he remembers. He has to squint his eyes and tilt his head on an angle just to be sure it's him.

It's hard to see his face underneath all the facial hair and the hair on his head. His hair stands up on his head in an out of shape afro, sort of like Don King's hair. His overgrown beard covers his face up to his cheekbones and covers his Adams apple. His mouth is barely visible due to the overlapping mustache that apparently hasn't been cut in years.

All in all he looks like one of the characters from the Planet of the Apes. His cheekbones protrude and eyes show signs of weakness, like a man who has been starved. He's skinny and frail looking. He looks nothing like the energetic, full of life, upright and strong man Tony remembers him to be. It hurts Tony to see him like this but he flashes a half of a smile trying to play it off. He looks into Manson's eyes and they are not only dark, cold and empty, he also sees lack of awareness in them. Tony wonders if Manson even knows who he is.

Manson sits down slowly. His blank and emotionless expression slowly transitions into a smile. Manson says not a word. His smile just gets bigger and bigger. Tony places both fists against Manson's shackled hands.

"I'm sorry, man," Tony apologizes. "I had no clue."

Manson shrugs his shoulders. "No problem," he mumbles.

"How you feeling?" Tony asks with genuine concern.

"You see how I look?" Manson asks in a low hoarse whisper. Tony's eyes lower with sadness. "Well, I feel a hundred times worse, but hey," Manson says. Manson smacks his lips as his mouth begins to dry up on him. In seconds his tongue is dry and heavy as cement. He licks his lips and he has not enough saliva to moisturize his lips. All this is side effects of his medicine. His body has gotten dependent on the medication and when it's time to take a dosage, this happens. He rather be dry mouth than to be in zombie land and that is why he has to be beaten and restrained to give it to him.

"But it's over now," Tony says with confidence. "You weathered the storm. I got you from here." Manson smiles a bigger smile. Tony notices him twitching like a man who has Parkinson's disease. Manson notices Tony looking down at his trembling hands and he becomes self-conscious about it and tries to stop the trembling but he can't.

Manson struggles to open his mouth. He swallows the last drop of saliva he has in his mouth before he speaks. "Thanks for coming back for me, Big Homie."

Tony clasps his hands over Manson's hands. "No need to thank me," he says. "I haven't done anything yet. Trust me, I'm about to put on, though."

57

QUABO AND TORTURA sit double-parked in front of the abandoned house that No Toes calls home. They honk the horn as they have been doing for the past 20 minutes. They have been popping up here for the past two days. They haven't seen him in about four days now and they are starting to think the worse. Tortura believes he is intentionally hiding from them. Normally, Quabo would say Tortura is overreacting but this is one of the few times Quabo doesn't believe he is.

Tortura has gotten tired of hitting the horn with no reply so he decides to go inside. He and Quabo walk through the abandoned apartment in search of No Toes. Not to their surprise, there's no sign of him. They comb the second-floor apartment where he pointed out that he stays. They hit the attic, the first floor, and the basement, and there's no trace of him. Not a shoe, not a blanket on the floor, nothing that indicates him being here.

Tortura stops short and looks at Quabo. "I told you we should have gotten rid of him. Told you he couldn't be trusted but you didn't listen. Now he's one more man on the menu."

CAMDEN

Skelter sits quietly in the backseat with thoughts ripping through her mind so fast that she can't keep track of them. She really thought the stunt she pulled with Quabo's wife would make them think twice about attacking again but it seems they've been attacking harder ever since. She will never admit it to another but this is the biggest war she's ever had to fight. She's fought many big wars beside Manson, but never has she fought a war of this magnitude with her being the leader.

She always was in the lieutenant spot, pretty much just moving on command. This war here will truly determine who she is as a leader. For the past three days they have been attacked, sometimes three times a day, but never less than twice. Skelter has been staying away but keeping her ears to the street.

No one has a clue what all the shooting is about. It's been chitter chatter but none of the rumors are anywhere close to the truth. Skelter is worried that if the word gets out that the shootings are for her, that will be an altogether different war. Some may join forces with her but she's sure her enemies would rather join forces with anyone against her; especially if a price is put on her head.

Skelter made the threat that if another shot got fired she would come for Quabo's wife. Several shots have been fired so they leave her no choice. She must react or they will not take her serious. She created her best spectacle the other day but she didn't get the results she expected. Now she's kind of unsure of what she can do to catch their attention. But she's sure she must do something and quick.

As they cruise through the block the first thing they notice is the gates of the beauty salon are pulled down. A stack of mail piled up in the mailbox is an indication that it's been closed for a few days. They look to all the signs that has Quabo's trademark on them. They pass the laundromat, the liquor store, the phone store, the barbershop, the restaurant, the travel agency and they finally get to the corner where the bodega is. "Fuck it," Skelter says. "We have to go with plan B."

TRENTON

It's like a ghost town around the outside of the projects. The random shootings has everyone fearful. Quabo and Tortura's men sit across the street from the projects scoping the area. They have no prescribed target in mind. Their plan is to blast the very first person to show their face. Tortura has explained to them that constant pressure will eventually cause a fear that will cause the enemy to become sloppy due to desperation to survive.

An Audi A8 pulls in front of the projects and parks directly in front. A dealership license plate sits in the front window. The driver's door opens and a man with salt and pepper hair and beard gets out of the car. He's well dressed with suit and tie, looking quite refined and fashionable. No one would ever think this man to be a dopefiend. After a long hard day of selling cars, the man is in need of his fix.

A young man appears in the alley. He stands close to the wall, out of the way. "Yo, Unc," he says to the man. "Get in your car and pull around the back," the young man instructs. "It ain't safe out there."

"Huh?" the man asks with a dumbfounded expression.

"Hurry, Unc, just do what I say. Pull around the back."

The man steps away with no understanding of what this is about. He picks up his pace. He gets to his car and snatches the door open. Just as he steps one foot inside, a vehicle comes flying out of nowhere at full speed. A gun is extended out of the window. *BOC! BOC! BOC!* The gun sounds off before the Audi door is knocked off the hinges. The door flies high in the air at the same time the man's body is thrown into the passenger's seat of the Audi. The driver of the van speeds down the block, not once pressing the brakes.

The man lays face first on the passenger's seat with his feet dangling over the driver's seat. The shots have been heard from many miles away, yet no one runs out nosily. They all have seen what nosiness can get them and they want no parts of that.

CAMDEN

Middle Godson and Oldest Godson step into the bodega, almost shoulder to shoulder. Middle Godson pulls his skullcap low over his eyes while Oldest Godson adjusts the strings on his hoodie. They both lower their heads, assuming the doorway has a camera on it. Middle Godson, floats around by the potato chip rack as if he's indecisive.

Oldest Godson makes his way to the back. On his way to the back, he sees two young men coming from a back door which is partly opened. He knows exactly what this is about. He makes his way to the back door and just as he figured, illegal betting is taking place. A Dominican stands at the laptop taking bets from the two young men who stand before him.

Oldest Godson wastes no time at all. Just as he enters, he draws his gun. "Y'all lay down," he shouts. The two black dudes dive onto the floor. Oldest Godson aims at the Dominican and fires. *BLOCKA! BLOCKA! BLOCKA!*

The man behind the front counter ducks for safety after hearing the shots. Middle Godson runs over and climbs onto the counter. He looks over where he finds the man reaching. With quickness Middle Godson aims at the back of the man's head and squeezes. *POP! POP! POP! POP!*

A man standing at the grill looks around in shock. As Oldest Godson passes him on his way out, he sends 4 shots at the man. *BLOCKA! BLOCKA! BLOCKA! BLOCKA!* The second shot hits the man and sends his body crashing into the wall before ricocheting and falling onto the burning grill.

Middle Godson and Oldest Godson run toward the door where Skelter stands, holding it wide open for them. Just as they exit, another man appears coming from the back. He's yielding a gun and he isn't afraid to use it. He aims and squeezes. *POP! POP! POP!*

Skelter pushes the door closed, holding it open with only enough space to stick her hand inside. She fires to back the man up. *BLOCKA! BLOCKA! BLOCKA!* The man ducks for cover and that gives Skelter time to get to the getaway car. She dives into the backseat and Youngest Godson speeds off.

Skelter feels good, as she believes she just has evened the score. What she doesn't know is another one was just killed around her way minutes before this. The Dominicans are still many deaths ahead of her. When she does find it out, it will either kill her spirits or motivate her to go that much harder. Only time will tell.

58

NORTHERN STATE/C-WING

BABY MANSON STANDS alone in front of his cell. He watches as inmates come from getting their commissary. In prison, a man can be whoever he wants to be. So many tell lies of who they were on the street and the lives they lived and for the most part no proof otherwise is presented.

Regardless of what a man says, commissary tells the real story. The clear bags hold no lies in them. Dudes who claim to have had it all on the street come back from commissary with just two cans of soup in the plastic bag because that's all they can afford. Some of these so-called Made Men never even go to commissary. Men tell you who they want you to believe they are. Commissary tells you who they really are.

In here, it's easy to see who is who because there are no rented cars, or leased cars, or gleaming jewelry to blur your vision. Most of their pride and ego has been left on the streets. Starving in jail brings out a level of desperation unknown to the outside world. So, on the inside if a man finds a way to survive, he has no problem getting in where he fits in and playing his position.

Baby Manson knows this which is why he has his eyes on the men with very little commissary bags. He's sure when he propositions them with an offer to bring them out of poverty they will have no problem playing whatever position he appoints them to. This dope will not only bring him money but it will also bring him power.

Right now, more than ever, he realizes he needs the power. Although he feels like a force all by himself he realizes he can't be a one-man army for long. After the stabbing of Smith's soldier the other day, things have been quiet. He's sure their silence isn't due to submission. He's certain they are just planning their next move, just as he is his.

This dope he has in his possession has opened so many doors for him. In just the short time he's had it, the carpet has been rolled out for him and he's treated like royalty. Everyone wants to get close to him to be a part of what he has going on. He plans to use this dope to control the prison. In order to do that he has to remove one man, his top competitor.

Baby Manson watches as his competitor walks casually along the tier. A smooth, older brother in his early 40's but doesn't look a day older than 28. Jail has preserved his youth. That and the fact that he's never indulged in drugs nor alcohol usage. Not a single grey strand in his thick, creamy wavy hair, and not a single facial hair present. The baby faced, old head is something like a big deal and it shows. His commissary bag is overflowing with the most expensive items.

The dope game is paying off for him. Right now, 75 percent of the dope that is sold in Northern State Prison comes from him or a member of his team. Baby Manson plans to stop that. In Baby Manson's travels he's heard the name, Shakir, more than he would like to. Hearing how the man is praised makes Baby Manson hate him, but to see him only intensifies the hate. If he was an emotional man he would allow his jealousy to make him react but he isn't. He's a thinking man, and as a thinker, he has a better plan.

59

TRENTON

THE AREA IS filled with warehouse factory buildings, dumpsters scattered around, and tractor trailers being loaded and unloaded. This area is isolated from the rest of the city. The only business one would have here is actually the business that is taking place here; shipping or receiving. The only sign of casual life is a new model Jeep Cherokee, which is cruising the area, dipping around the many trailers and dumpsters.

The Cherokee stops directly in front of one of the biggest but oldest looking warehouse buildings. Inside the Cherokee, Skelter shakes the hands of Youngest Godson and Middle Godson. Oldest Godson gets out before Skelter and waits for her to catch up with him. She gets out, slams the door shut, and makes her way to the barely noticeable door of the warehouse.

With so much graffiti covering the building, the door is barely visible. Skelter sticks a key in the door and using all of her might she pushes open the heavy steel door. She steps inside and her Godson follows at her heels. He slams and locks the door behind them.

They get into the elevator and hit the button for the 5th floor. The old and raggedy elevator jolts before lifting. A long and shaky elevator ride ends with a huge bump as it stops. The 5th floor is occupied by print shops, toy companies, and even sweatshops. Skelter and her Godson walk the long empty corridor side by side until they reach the very last door.

The tag on the door says, 'Brazilian Barbie Hair Weave.' Skelter sticks a key into the door and leads the way inside. What is supposed to be an office or workplace is really Skelter's apartment. In the corner she has unopened packs of Brazilian Weave that are doing nothing but collecting dust. Sometime ago she came up with the idea to start her own hair company, and she did, but once it didn't take off like she hoped, she tossed it to the side and never looked back.

She's turned this spacious, high-ceiling workplace into a spacious, one-bedroom loft style apartment. Her furniture is quite basic, all from Ikea. She's not much of an interior designer but the set-up and the color schemes make it the perfect bachelor's pad, even though she's no bachelor. It's not a lap of luxury but it is a safe haven away from her chaotic world.

Skelter takes a quick tour around the apartment, peeking in closets and so forth just to make sure all is well. It's a habit of hers whenever she comes home. After finding all to be well, her Godson extends his hand for a fist-bump. "Next day," he says as he makes his way toward the door. They have a rule of not leaving until they know she's inside safe and sound. Although they are the only ones outside of Helter who knows she lives here, they still practice safety precautions.

Skelter closes and locks the door behind her Godson. She snatches the remote from the kitchen countertop and quickly powers on the huge 90-inch screen that's plastered on the wall. She tosses the remote onto a leather bean bag as she passes it. She stands in front of what she calls the windows of the city. Fifteen square feet of window surrounded by old and chipped window paned squares. Through the worn and streaky glass bears the most beautiful view of the city.

She always gets a kick out of knowing that from this view, she can see the entire city, famous landmarks, even the projects that she's from and no one knows she's here. With all the dirt that she's done in life, her safety is primary. She could never live just anywhere and have peace. For the past three years she's been living here and she has never felt this safe anywhere else.

Skelter kicks off her Timberland boots, and immediately loses two inches of her height. She loves wearing them because normally standing at 5 feet 3 inches makes her feel like a midget amongst giants. May seem like a mere two inches but to her, height evens the playing field and she thinks it makes them see her as an equal.

She extends her arms, allowing her motorcycle jacket to escape her. She unbuttons her jeans and slides right out of them. She pulls the hoodie over her head and allows it to fall onto the mound of clothes. She walks over to the full-length mirror in the bedroom area.

She stares at herself through the mirror and the picture that lies before her eyes is the closest depiction of who she is. What would be a surprise to most is her toes are beautifully manicured and neatly painted, as they always are. Her long, slender but toned legs have a sexiness to them that no one would ever know because she keeps them covered in men's jeans most of the time. Her thighs are what they call, slim thick. Her small but perfectly rounded booty explodes from the sexy purple satin and lace panties. Washboard abs look to be carved or sculpted into her torso. Her firm but full boobs sit restrained in the sports bra, as they always are, just to keep the attention off of them.

Her fingernails are the very opposite of her toenails. They are unpolished, unkept and bitten down to nubs due to worry and stress of her everyday life. The skull cap tilted on her head represents the gangster in her. She may be hard on the exterior, but on the inside she's all woman, just a cold and scorned woman. It's this contrast that makes it hard for any man to deal with her. This is the very reason she's been single for so long.

Skelter makes her way over to her nightstand where she picks up a half a blunt from the ashtray. She lights it and takes a long pull. She exhales the stress of life. She never gets high or drinks during the day because she realizes how vicious the streets are and she needs to be on point while in them. At night, once it's all over, she smokes in the comfort of her own home so she can decompress.

After a few pulls, she feels as light as a feather. She floats back in front of the same mirror freeing herself from any article of clothing she has on, except her hat. She stands in front of the mirror, puffing from the blunt and appreciating her body. She's so hard and manly acting sometimes that even she forgets she's a woman. It's times like this where she has to stand before the mirror to remind herself.

Her eyes scan her perky breast with the budding butterscotch nipples. Her breast have always been her favorite part of her body. She holds her breath and poses, admiring them from every angle. Her ab muscles ripple. She looks so sexy to herself that she makes herself horny. Her nipples swell before her eyes.

She turns around with her butt facing the mirror. She stands on her tippy toes, to watch her ass lift and her calves flex. She slowly turns around as she takes another pull of the blunt. The skullcap on her head is killing her picture right now. She snatches it off and tosses it on the dresser. She takes the pins out of her hair one by one, until her long hair drapes over her shoulders. There she stands all woman, beautiful, and soft.

"In other news, earlier today at Roger Garden Apartments," the news anchorman says. Hearing this snatches Skelter's attention. She turns around fast enough to catch whiplash. Her heart sinks as she sees her projects filmed on the screen. The camera shows police tape and detectives swarming the scene.

"Shooting leaves one dead and three injured," the anchorman says. "Detectives are on the scene right now. This is the second shooting today," the anchorman says. The camera flashes on the car salesman laying dead in his car. "Still not certain if these shootings are linked," says the anchorman.

An older woman with a bonnet on her head stands next to the anchorman. "It's like a battlefield out here," the woman says fearfully. "We are afraid to come out of her homes. They're shooting out here two, three, and even four times a day. We are prisoners in our own homes!"

Skelter grabs her phone from her pants pocket and sees ten missed calls on the screen. She wonders who that one casualty could be. She dials and the receiver picks up on the very first ring. "Yo," she says.

"You saw the news?" Oldest Godson asks.

"Yeah," she replies sadly. "Who was it?"

"The lil nigga, Boom," he says with no compassion whatsoever. "What's up though? Want us to come back through and scoop you?"

He has fire in his voice that says he's ready to get to it. "What we doing?" he asks for the second time.

Skelter holds the phone for seconds, not even knowing how to reply. She has no plan. This beef is the very first beef that she will ever say is clearly over her head. She's never had an enemy come at her back to back like this and to this degree. The attacks have her off balanced. She will never tell her team this because she would hate for them to lose faith in her. Even though she has no plan she has to pretend that she does just to keep their spirits alive. "Yeah, come scoop me."

She ends the call and makes her way back over to the mirror. Piece by piece she puts on her clothes, covering her nude softness. Once she's fully dressed, she pins her hair up neatly. She places her hat on her head and tilts it at the perfect angle, like a King who is adjusting his crown but underneath he's really a Queen. Heavy is the head that wears the crown.

60

SHORT HILLS

TONY, FRESH OFF his flight from Colorado, steps into the lobby of his firm. "Good afternoon," he says cheerfully to his secretary. The look on her face causes him concern. With her eyes she signals him to look in the direction of the waiting area. The two men, one black and one white, sit skimming through magazines. Dressed down casually, with no sight of a gun or a badge, Tony still identifies them as police. Their polished but quirky demeanors tells him they are not regular cops. He can smell a Fed a mile away.

Tony looks to his secretary, wondering what this could be about. She shrugs her shoulders. "They've been waiting for you for two hours," she whispers.

Tony walks over to them and greets them respectfully. "Afternoon, gentleman," he says with a fake smile.

Both men look up and neither of them hide their hatred for him. "Afternoon," one man replies. The other man looks back to the magazine he was reading from. "I hope you enjoyed your flight."

"As a matter of fact, I did." Tony looks over to his secretary assuming she's told his whereabouts. She shakes her head nervously. She knows how he feels about her sharing information about his whereabouts. "My secretary has told me that you've been awaiting me for over two hours. I would apologize for having you waiting but I had no knowledge of you coming here," he says sarcastically. "Do we have an appointment that I have forgotten about?"

The Black man stands up. "Can we speak in your office?"

"Absolutely," Tony replies. "I charge for that, you know." Tony cracks a smile but neither of the men find humor in him. "This way, gentleman," he says as he leads the way into his office.

Once inside Tony offers them both a seat at his desk. The more friendly man accepts the invitation as the other just stands at the door. Tony drops his briefcase on the desk and quickly removes his blazer. He opens the humidor and grabs a cigar. "Cigar?" he offers.

"We don't smoke and we both hate the smell."

"Sorry to hear that," Tony says with evident sarcasm as he lights his cigar and rudely blows cigar smoke across the desk. He sits down and opens a bottle of Elijah Craig. He pours himself a three-finger shot and offers it to them with hospitality. "Let me guess, y'all don't drink either?"

The man ignores Tony's question. "Mr. Austin do you know who we are?"

"Uh, not personally," he says in reply. "But I'm sure I know who you are with. Why you are here, I have no idea," he says as he sits down. He takes a sip of the Bourbon. "But I'm sure you are about to tell me."

"I'm Special Agent Martin and he's Special Agent Lewis. Our reason for being here has to do with your Colorado meeting."

"Y'all didn't waste any time huh?"

"Mr. Austin, you're walking on a tight rope."

"Doesn't help that I have baby oil on my feet either, does it?"

The agent's face turns cold as stone. He hates the fact that Tony seems so unbothered by their presence. "We've been sent here to warn you. We are aware of the demands you made pertaining to your client. And we will do our best to accommodate your needs."

"Do your best? You will do better than that. Listen, I know you guys are used to making deals and controlling the deals but in this case there will be no negotiating nor bartering. My client is to be shipped to a closer facility with no further harm done to him. And this must happen immediately."

"Just as you've stated, we are used to making deals. So, with that being said, what will you give us in return?"

"What will I give you?" Tony chuckles disrespectfully. "Go back to your bureau and ask them, in all the years of y'all paying me visits, have I ever given you anything? Not a got damn thing. And I'm not gone start today. And on top of that, I've never even represented a client that was willing to give you something."

"What we want is not too much to ask for from you. We just want your word that you will not shine light onto this matter. No press, no exposure, no lawsuits from your client. Your client gets shipped to the prison of his choice and we all walk away from this without ever looking back."

"And leave y'all to continue on with destroying the lives of those inmates who have been forgotten about?"

"So, what is the end game for you? Is it money? Do you plan to represent all those inmates that you speak of, in attempt for your selfish gain?"

"Money? Selfish gain?" Tony laughs arrogantly. "Money, I have enough of. Money isn't my motivation. Maybe fifteen years ago, but today I'm so far past that."

"Good to know that but can we count on you to walk away from this as if it never happened? We are hoping we can and for the sake of all of us. This can only turn out to be one big mess if you choose to go further with this. And I believe it's only fair to warn you that we will make your life a living hell if you open up this can of worms."

"Warn me? I don't take kindly to warnings. In all my run-ins with you guys I have yet to submit to your threats or warnings. Please keep your threats and your warnings to yourself." The agent's face transforms into the devil himself. "You ok?" Tony asks. "You seem flushed."

The agent laughs off his rage. "Well, I guess this concludes our meeting."

"Yes, I guess so," Tony replies. "So, what day should I be expecting my client to be transported?"

"Within a couple of days your client will be flown to his new location. He will have a new inmate number and social security number just to cover our tracks. Our end of the deal will have been handled. Then we will expect you to handle your end and keep the lights off of this matter. It will be better for us and for you. I know you have heard the saying, no destruction comes without warning. Well, you have already received your warning. Save yourself from your own destruction."

61

BABY MANSON WALKS the tier with determination in his eyes. As he steps along he scans his surroundings thoroughly. He allows himself to drop down the stairs, exerting very little energy. As he lands on the first floor, the few inmates on the tier keep their attention on him. Some watch him outright and others watch him on the sly. As he passes one man, the man gives him a head-nod of nervousness. Baby Manson ignores him and keeps on moving.

Baby Manson stops short at a cell near the middle of the tier. He knocks on the wall politely. "Pardon my intrusion," he says respectfully.

Shakir is laid out on his cot, staring up at his flat screen television. His cell looks like that of a boss. He has enough food stacked in the corner to feed both tiers. Stacks of books are piled up in the corner from the floor to the ceiling. Every electronic device permitted; he has. Sneakers, underwear, and extra uniforms all show that he is not in need of anything.

Shakir sits up slowly with a face that shows he's not happy about being interrupted. He looks Baby Manson up and down quickly, reading his body language. He has no clue of why he's here. "What's happening?"

"Is it alright if I come in?" Baby Manson asks.

Shakir rejects the invite by meeting him at the entrance. "What's up?"

Baby Manson extends his hand for a handshake. "Baby Manson," he says. Shakir shakes his hand limply. Baby Manson automatically reads that as a sign of his character. "Pleasure to meet you," Baby Manson says. "I've heard so much about you. We run in the same circles so everywhere I turn your name keep popping up."

"Is that so?" Shakir asks. "And what circle is that?"

"The money circle."

Shakir snickers. He finds it quite funny that Baby Manson could believe their names should be mentioned in the same sentence. Baby Manson has no clue that Shakir knows he's no money getter. Shakir knows firsthand from Pebbles that he has never earned a dollar for himself in the world. Every case he has caught she has had to put the money up to help him out of it.

Shakir decides to humor Baby Manson, just to see what else he has to say. "Oh that circle?"

"Yeah, basically it's only two names they mentioning right now in that circle. That's yours and mine."

"Oh, that's strange because I never heard mention of your name in that circle you speak of, until right now. And I'm hearing that from your mouth."

Baby Manson senses the sarcasm but overlooks it. "Well, honestly my name ring bells on a bunch of other tips. I just really stepped over into this new lane. My real reason for coming here is to introduce myself and kind of tell you who I am so hopefully we don't bump heads along the way."

Shakir catches the self-proclaiming that Manson is throwing his way and finds it entertaining. The fact that he's known this kid since he was a baby without his knowledge of so is even more humorous to him. "Bump heads, how?" he asks for further entertainment.

"Bump heads like me in your way or you in mine," Baby Manson replies.

"How could you ever be in my way?" Shakir says cockily. His arrogance has finally peeked its ugly head out. "I been doing this since you was a baby," he says with a cocky smile. "This shit is like second nature to me. I been flooding this prison the past seven years and even though there's a lot of competition, I really have no competition. My money too long for you to ever be in my way."

"I can respect that," Baby Manson replies. The cockiness agitates him. "But I'm trying to get where you are and in order for me to do that, I need you to not get in my way." He puffs his chest high. "As you just said yourself, your money long and you been flooding the jail for seven years. You should have more than enough now. Don't be greedy. Let somebody else eat."

Shakir notices a change in Baby Manson's body language. I know this kid don't think he running me out the game, Shakir thinks to himself. The nerve of this young motherfucker, Shakir thinks. He's livid right now. "I don't think I really dig where you're coming from," Shakir says. He wants to hear it come out of Baby Manson's mouth. "Break it down for me."

"You ever heard the saying, greedy people starve?" Baby Manson asks.

"Yeah, and?" Shakir replies with an edge of aggression.

"Yeah and don't end up one of those greedy people that end up starving. We can avoid head-butting in the future if you just take heed to what I'm saying now. I don't expect you to make such a big decision on spot like this. Take a couple days to absorb it all. I will come back to further chop it up with you."

Shakir chuckles disrespectfully. "No need to," he says.

"Ok, you said it," Baby Manson says as he turns around to walk away. "I guess we just had our one and only conversation then, huh?"

Shakir has no verbal reply. He doesn't know what he just committed to but as a man he feels he had no choice. In no way is he about to let a young dude force him out of the game. Especially not this young dude who he has no clue of their affiliation and common interest; Pebbles that is.

He has no connection whatsoever to Baby Manson regardless of what may or may not be. He blocked that out long ago back in the very beginning. His connection and love is to and for Pebbles. He would hate to have Pebbles in mourning over her only child but if her only child thinks he is going to press him, then Pebbles may as well get ready to mourn. He's sure she will never forgive him for it but if he lets Baby Manson push him out of the game, he will never forgive himself.

Baby Manson walks away, knowing in his heart that he just declared war. He tries to always stay ten steps ahead of the game, so in his mind he's already at war. His mindset is always, 'him striking first.' He never waits for his enemy to strike for their first strike may be the only strike they need to win the war.

As Baby Manson passes, the Good Christian's cell, Good Christian jumps off his cot and runs to the entrance. He watches Baby Manson for as far as he can see him and when he can no longer see him from there, he steps out of his cell and watches him some more.

Baby Manson can sense the heat of someone's eyes burning through his back. He turns around quickly and just as he does, Good Christian pops back into his cell, unseen. Baby Manson looks around in search of those eyes he feels but to no avail. It seems as if no one is paying attention to him at all but his gangster senses tells him differently.

62

TONY HAS A burning fire inside him that he can't control. He feels like he has more than enough ammunition to go to war with the government. The way he plans to tie these cases in together will be magical. He dreams about the day and in his dreams the trial is theatrical, a spectacle that all should see.

He plans to make this case memorable, making history. Just a few little codes that he's missing and he will be able to tie it all together. He picks up his phone and dials his lady friend from the FDA. He's been calling her for the past week but no reply.

He stops short in the middle of the room and waits for the phone to start ringing. To his surprise an automated service picks up instead. "The number you have reached is no longer in service." Tony looks at the display thinking he must have dialed the wrong number but her contact information is there boldly. He quickly dials again hoping for different results but they are the same.

He ends the call with confusion plastered on his face. There must be some type of mistake, he thinks to himself. This woman has had the same phone number since their college days. He can't imagine her changing her number without giving him her new one.

He quickly thinks back to their conversation when she told him once she gives him the information he should forget all about her. He didn't really believe she would go through with it. Plus, she never gave him all the information he was in need of. It's hard for him to believe that she would end such a long and strong friendship like this. He stands baffled until a knocking on his door breaks his thought process.

The secretary pushes the door open. "Mr. Austin," she says in a low sweet whisper. "You have a guest," she says as she looks at what she believes to be a crazy war veteran. Tony has kept Jane Doe's business and identity a secret even from those inside his firm. The secretary looks Jane Doe up and down with disgust and hatred.

"Okay, thanks," Tony says.

Jane Doe locks the door behind her and makes her way over to the desk quickly. "We have to make this quick," she says. "I'm operating off a half tank of oxygen. Talk fast. Well," she says before pausing. "You're already a fast talker, just talk faster."

Tony laughs along with her. "Okay, listen I just got back from Colorado and you will never know what I went there for."

"Get to it fast," she says. "Save the climax building preliminaries."

"A client of mine got arrested years ago by the Feds and it was in the newspaper that he died in the raid. Come to find out he's not dead at all and he's in a Supermax prison being beaten and tortured. The Feds have been trying to get him to roll for years and since he hasn't they have been drugging him up until the point that he's like a vegetable." Tony looks to Jane Doe expecting some dramatic response but instead she stands there looking unimpressed.

"Happens every day," she says. "In fact, it happens all over the country. And for the record they're not drugging him up because he's not telling. As I told you before, these inmates are used as guinea pigs, lab rats. Drug companies create these drugs and put them on the market. They have no real clue of what the long-term side effects of these drugs will be. By using the inmates as the testers, the medical staff can monitor the inmate's progress as well as decline as well as any side effects the drugs may have caused them. By having them in the prison for, let's say… ten years, they can analyze their studies in-house for ten years straight.

The whole system working together and it's big money for the drug companies because the prison market is huge for drugs. They spend billions a year on medicine for inmates. It works out for the prison itself because they get a kickback for their studies. The only one it doesn't work for is the inmates they are drugging up. Sad but true."

Tony listens in awe and the more she speaks, the more pieces to the puzzle he adds in his mind. "Quick question," he blurts out. "My client, in which I would say is more than a client. He's almost like a friend. I demanded a report of the medication that they have him on and I'm wondering what exactly it is," he says as he grabs a document from his desk.

He hands it over and she reads it over quickly. She shakes her head from side to side. "This is not good," she says. "Not good at all," she says as she hands the paper back to him. "Every drug on that list, I can show you proof of what it has done to people. And I will," she adds. "The next time we get together. My time here has run out," she says as she lifts her tank from her bag. "Gots to go," she says as she turns to walk away.

"One more question," Tony claims. "Is there any coming back for him? Like, will he ever be normal?"

She turns around to looks at Tony. "Honestly? No! Most of these drugs are addictive so I'm sure he has grown an addiction for them by now. It will be difficult getting him off the drugs in the first place. But," she says as she holds one finger in the air. "If you get him off the drugs, he will never be the same. I'm sure his brains are already scrambled eggs by now. He may be able to cope with life but as far as being the same… never."

This news breaks Tony's heart. He's really fired up now. This has become more personal for him now. He's ready to get on with it.

"Oh, before you go," he says just as Jane Doe reaches the door. She turns around slowly. He holds the blank check that she gave him during their last meeting. "I been thinking long and hard and I really don't how much to charge you for this case. I now more than ever realize how this could end it all for me."

"Are you starting to second guess it?'"

"No, not at all," he replies. "I'm just wondering how many zeros you are comfortable with? Five zeros?" Tony is just trying to get a gauge of her financial status.

"Listen, I already told you money is no issue for me. I'm very comfortable all the way up to seven zeros." Tony plays it cool but truthfully the sound of that has him in astounded. "Whatever number you come up with, I am in position to wire it to you today," she says with the very first sign of arrogance that he's ever seen from her.

"As a matter of fact let's get this over with right now," she says as she peeks at her oxygen tank one more time. "Let me make it easy for you," she says as she walks back over to him. "Give me a bank account and I will make the transfer right this moment just so you know I'm not playing and wasting your time. I mean business. I will wire you an amount and if by chance along the way you feel this case warrants more, don't hesitate to come back and renegotiate. Now, what's your bank information?"

Tony scribbles his information onto a blank sheet of paper. Jane Doe looks at it as she pulls her phone from her bag. She reads from the paper and types the digits into her phone. She holds the phone for Tony to see. "Is this the correct info?"

"Correct," he replies.

"Good enough," she says. She presses the button stiffly. "Done! Check your account and you should see a credit to your account from International Humanist Group. That's an account that doesn't trace back to me any type of way."

Tony pulls his phone out and hits his online banking. The numbers he sees she just deposited has intensified the flame inside of him. He counts the zeros out three times. The $10,000,000 deposit blows his mind yet he plays it cool. "It's here but the real test is, will it clear?"

"Trust me, my dear," she says with more cockiness. "It will clear. It was transferred from Bitcoin for further privacy. Give it three to seven days and you will be able to deduct it all if you choose."

"Nah, no need," says Tony. "I will deduct it once the case is done. I'm figuring 30-45 days and I will be fully prepared for this battle."

"Take your time," she says as she walks away. "We can't play with this. Anyway we blow this, life will be hell. So, in the meantime go on and treat yourself. I know how much you love those little fancy hotrod cars and rare watches. Get yourself a couple of them and enjoy them because once we cross this line there's no telling if we will ever enjoy life again."

Tony shrugs his shoulders. "A chance we have to take. I'm built for it."

63

CAMPBELL FUNERAL CHAPEL/TRENTON

SKELTER'S FACE IS pinned to the window behind the dark tints. Traffic is backed up bumper to bumper on both sides of the street. The sidewalks are packed on both sides as well. Today is Chapo's funeral and it seems that the entire population of Trenton is here today to pay their respects to him.

"Here it goes. I just found the video," Oldest Godson says from the passenger's seat as he scrolls through his phone. He hands the phone over his shoulder to Skelter in the backseat. Her heart thumps as she's about to press play. She does and right before her eyes she sees her Godsons' back as they are walking into the corner Bodega in Camden. Seconds later, she watches herself get out of the truck and walk to the door. There she stands holding the door wide open. She pays close attention to see if her face can be seen but it's a good thing it's barely visible.

Seconds pass and both of her Godsons come running out of the store. She watches herself in action, banging at the man inside the store. As she watches the scene it plays differently, watching it. In the heat of the moment she had no time to think. She had to adapt. Watching this away from the action, she sees how it looks from the sideline. The crazy part is she's impressed with how gangster it really appears. She plays the video over and over, analyzing and admiring it.

Apparently someone was recording without them knowing it. The person then posted it yesterday, on Instagram and it went viral. Skelter looks at the bottom and it states the video has been viewed by over 100,000 people. The young man doing the recording whispers 'World-Star' every few seconds. She gets angrier every time. This video worries her. She can only imagine how many of those 100,000 views are police.

"Here," she says as she shoves the phone at her Godson. "Stupid motherfucker so worried about likes and followers, he don't even know he just fucked up his life," she says with rage. "Go through his page and find out who the fuck he is. Let's see how many of those viewers and followers will go to his fucking funeral. Goofy ass."

Youngest Godson parks the truck deep in the cut, away from the action. Skelter hates for people to know what she's riding in. Her motto is if they know what you came in, they know what you have to leave in. She will never give anyone the opportunity to meet her at her car, beating her to the punch.

All three of her Godsons get out of the truck with their guns tucked in their waistbands. Skelter immediately pulls her hood over her head and tucks her hair inside the hood as she's walking. Youngest Godson and Middle Godson walk in front of her and the Oldest Godson walks behind her. They guard her every step like she's the First Lady because to them she is.

As they hit the block the funeral parlor is on, all eyes are on them. Skelter and her Godson's are infamous in the city of Trenton. Some people love them, some people fear them but all the people respect their gangster. Skelter has the reputation of being somewhat of a slimeball so many don't trust her. Because of that everyone has their eyes fixed on them.

Skelter hates to hear herself referred to as a slimeball because in her mind she has never crossed anyone who didn't deserve it. If she rocks with a person, she will go to war for them. She's proven herself to be one of the most loyal people to walk the earth but if you get on her bad side, loyalty and honor all goes out the window and she will go harder against you than she went for you.

As Skelter and her Godsons approach the funeral parlor the air is tense. One can actually see some of the people inhaling deeply with fear. Others watch from the backdrop with hatred covering their faces. Huddles of people whisper secretly. With all this happening there are still some who seem happy to see Skelter. They're smiling and saluting her like the G she is.

Skelter and her Godsons waste no time on the outside they go right on inside and march up the path to the front. She keeps her hood on like a Rockstar in hiding. The elderly people see her hood as a sign of disrespect but this isn't by far the most disrespectful thing they've seen here so far. Young men with jeans sagging to the back of their knees, showing shit-stained boxers and women with exposed body parts, crying over the casket has the place looking more like a strip-bar than a funeral. It's as packed as a strip-bar as well.

Chapo was loved by the young and old and everyone in between. It's a major event for the city and a great deal of the people that are here don't even know him. They are only there because it's the place to be. Everyone shopped for their best outfits just to be seen.

Skelter's Godsons lead her to the casket. They all stand shoulder to shoulder looking into the casket. Chapo lays there looking like nothing less than the millionaire he is said to be. In an all-white tuxedo with a ruffled shirt and all his diamond jewelry he lays there looking like the black Liberachi. His head shows no signs of the bullets that split his head open. Clean shaven with designer sunglasses on, he's music video ready.

Skelter shakes her head with sadness as if she isn't the one responsible for him laying here. This isn't her first time standing over a body that she laid to rest so each time it gets easier. She hates to come here and stand over her work, but she realizes if she doesn't her name may come up as a suspect. She always wonders if the dead is able to see her standing here. In this case she was masked up but in other cases her face was the last face the person saw before their death. She just imagines them looking down on her wishing they could tell the people she's the one who did it. It's a good thing for her that they can't.

After a brief moment of silence of pretending to care, she and her men exit in the same order they entered. They exit the funeral parlor and find a place to stand away from the people. Right in front of them at the curb is an all glass hearse with real gold trimming. The Harley Davidson Motorcyle that the hearse is hitched to is Chapo's pride and joy. The custom built Big Boy Chopper is picture perfect. It's glazed with candy coated platinum paint with glistening specs shimmering. The chrome pipes and chrome spoked tires is almost blinding when the sun hits it right.

Parked in front and behind the Motorcycle is an even more amazing sight. There are enough Rolls Royces out here to do a Rolls Royce commercial. Three Phantoms, four Ghosts, a Wraith and a Dawn all in platinum color matching the motorcycle. Skelter and her Godsons look around at the luxury car show in somewhat of amazement.

Skelter can feel the people's discomfort with her presence. She also feels the secret stares and whispering. She's sure her name has come up as a suspect many times. It always does.

Blue Blood appears almost out of thin air. As he approaches, Skelter's Godsons form a tight circle around her. They stand like a wall in between her and Blue Blood, even though they know him. Skelter has to give the signal for them to stand at ease and let him get next to her.

He stands right next to her. "Boy brought them out, didn't he?" Blue Blood whispers.

"Word," Skelter agrees.

"Lot of sad faces. Boy gone be missed. I'm sure a lot of these sad faces ain't as sad as they are pretending to be. I'm sure a lot of these motherfuckers got a bag of money they owe him. Good thing about that is they got to spend that bag of money with somebody. Who better than us?" Blue Blood says jokingly.

Blue Blood may be joking but a part of him does feel sad about the situation. He and Chapo have history together. He's called on Chapo a many of times for help and not one time has Chapo ever told him no. Because of that reason alone he feels like a creep. But, life goes on for the living."

Their attention is diverted to the doorway of the funeral parlor where a group of Chapo's best men are carrying his coffin out of the building. All of their faces covered with tears and no shame. Today they are putting a great man to rest.

Blue Blood nudges Skelter as a woman passes and stands to the side of them. It's the woman that was with Chapo the night he was murdered. Tears stream down her face. Chapo's family now step out of the funeral parlor.

He has a huge family from babies to senior citizens and everything in between. All of them walking in sadness and mourning while Chapo's team guards them, looking around at everything moving as they make their way to the Rolls Royces. Finally Chapo's wife steps out. She has the tightest security around her. She's dressed in an all black from head to toe; beautiful dress and black stilettos, dark oversized sunglasses, with long jet black hair draping over her waistline.

As the family is getting into the cars, one man walks over to the woman who stands next to Skelter and the gang. He latches onto her arm and leads her to one of the Phantoms. Just as he holds the door open for her to get in, Chapo's wife steps over to her. "Bitch, I wish you would get in the family car. You will be the next one laying up in that building," she threatens with rage in her eyes.

Chapo's wife has always had to put up with his many women. She got tired of fighting with him about it because it was obvious that he wasn't going to stop cheating. It was also obvious that she wasn't going to leave him for cheating. Eventually she got used to it and lived with it. She justified it to herself by knowing that despite how many women he had, none of them a deed in their names or his bank accounts in their names. They may have had him for a few minutes or hours but really they had nothing. She on the other hand has it all.

She knows that so many of his women are out here in mourning. Even if they are holding up and not crying loudly, she can pinpoint every one of his women because she knows his type, his mold. If she had to count right now at least ten women are here that he has close dealings with and more than two dozen women that he has had some type of dealing with in the past or present. Chapo's wife can look in the crowd and pick them all out one by one. She may have put up with his cheating while he was alive but she refuses to let a single one of them ride in the family cars.

One of Chapo's men steps in between Chapo's wife and his main mistress. "Come on now, Maribel," he pleads.

"Come on now, my ass," she says as she kicks off her stiletto. "Oh, you gone disrespect me too? Okay, put that bitch in the car if you want to. I will drag her ass up and down the block. He ain't here to stop this ass whipping now."

Chapo's wife has lost all of her class and is now ready to get out-right ghetto. It takes a group of Chapo's men to hold her back. She's trying to get to the woman who hides behind men for her safety. Maribel's sisters set up behind the mistress ready to destroy her.

In just the nick of time, Chapo's mother steps up. She steps in front of the wife. Standing next to her are Chapo and the woman's four little children. All are looking at their mom in shock. Chapo's mother shouts a few words and everyone falls in line. She looks to the mistress. "You go," she commands as she points. The woman walks away like a sad dog with its tail up the ass. The show ends and everyone gets into the cars.

Chapo's wife walks toward the Harley and has the attention of everyone on her back. To everyone's surprise she lifts her dress up to her knees and straddles herself over the seat of the motorcycle. She kicks her shoes off and hands them to her sister who hands her a pair of running sneakers in return. She quickly puts the sneakers on before starting up the motorcycle. She places the half-helmet on her head and straps it up.

She revs it up a few times as she looks over and gives the signal. In seconds she's cruising off. The string of Rolls Royce take off right behind her. All the spectators watch as she takes her husband for his very last ride.

Skelter and Blue Blood both share a semi-sentimental moment. "Ay yo, where you parked at?" Blue Blood asks. He looks away to hide the few tears that have piled up in the corner of his eyes. "I got something for you. Shit picked up crazy since this shit. I got like forty-eight thousand for you in my truck and I got another fifteen coming at you in like an hour."

This is music to Skelter's ears. "That's the best news I heard all week."

"Well, get used to hearing good news. It's our turn. I just hope you can handle the workload."

"Oh, don't worry about that. I got work," Skelter says.

"I also hope nobody gets wind that we behind this because if they do, we gone have a major war on our hands."

"Well, if that happens they will have to get in line. Won't be the first war we had to fight and it definitely won't be the last."

MEANWHILE

The surrounding area of The Projects is quiet due to almost everyone being at Chapo's funeral. A 7 series Alpina BMW pulls up and stops. The driver looks to his passenger who holds the door open ready to exit. "Grab me two Roxy's and a Zanny," the driver says as he digs into his pocket. As he hands the money over a crash with the impact of a Mac truck bangs into the back of his car.

The driver and his two passengers are dizzy from the impact. The Bronco with the ram bar, pushes them into the brick wall. As the BMW is smashed into the brick wall, the doors of the Bronco pop open and two men hop out, yielding automatic handguns. The men are dizzy and discombobulated yet they can see the men standing on both sides of them.

POP! POP! POP! BOC! BOC! POP! BOC! POP! POP! POP! BOC! BOC! BOC!

The shooting doesn't stop until all the men in the BMW are sitting lifelessly. The gunmen then run back to the Bronco, dive in and the driver speeds off. Three more points for Quabo and Tortura.

64

PEBBLES WALKS OUT of the CVS with the money bop. She's just cashed in over $10,000 in Western Union money orders. Her son, Baby Manson has appointed her as his Treasurer for his dope enterprise in the making. She hates the fact that he's doing something that could get him into more trouble than he's already in but she will never admit that she's proud of the hustler that he is. She figures it's bad but at least he's making money for himself.

Pebbles sits in her truck in the parking lot as a beat-up, old-body Jaguar pulls in the lot and parks right next to her. A raunchy, ghetto princess gets out with rows of fat oozing from underneath her 3 sizes too small t-shirt. She walks up to the driver's side of Pebbles's truck like she's on Rip the Runway. Her weave is so stale it doesn't blow in the wind. It's just flat and pasted on her head.

Pebbles rolls the window down and looks at the girl with a cold and fake smile. "Hey," Pebbles says.

The young woman puckers her lips, barely responding. "Uhm hmm," she says as she hands Pebbles an envelope. "That's fifteen hundred. He says the other half will be in my account in two days."

Pebbles counts through the stack of twenties quickly like a bank teller. "It's all here, just hit me."

"Okay," the young woman says before walking off.

Pebbles can't help but to be amazed how the young woman has managed to squeeze an ass the size of an Elephant's ass into such small jeans. Half of her ass is oozing over the top of the waistband and the other half is strangled in the jeans. "She's gone have to cut those jeans off," Pebbles says to herself. "Makes no sense. A hot damn mess."

Pebbles pulls off, and ironically, just as she does, her phone rings. The number flashing across the display she knows has to be Baby Manson. She presses the number to receive the call.

"Yo, what up, Ma," Baby Manson says.

"Hey, babe," she says happily.

"Everything good?"

"Just about," she replies. "I have three more stores to hit to collect for the lipgloss I put on their shelves and I'm done for the day," she says, using code language. Pebbles has been around the game for a long time and knows better than talking on the phones, so she makes sure to keep her conversation coded and limited.

"Alright bet," Baby Manson says cheerfully. He's so proud to be generating money and he feels like a big man doing so. "I just called to check on you. I'm gone let my lil bruh use the phone real quick and I will hit you later on."

"Ok, you be safe."

"Always," he replies confidently. "You good though? You need something?"

"No, babe, I'm good," she replies.

"You need a shoe or something? Go to the mall and grab something for yourself."

Pebbles blushes. This touches her heart that her son is trying to do something for her. She doesn't need his money because she makes her own but it's the thought that counts. She had him so young that they practically grew up together. She knows she didn't do the best job of parenting but she did the best job she could do.

No one taught her how to be a mother. She had to learn as she went along. She wishes she could have done a better job of raising him but she charges it to the game because she knows she did her absolute best. What she doesn't know is he doesn't see it as her not doing a good job. In his eyes she's the best mother one could have.

She quickly thinks of all the hard times they shared and how they overcame it. She remembers the times she had to do things that she didn't want to just to feed him. Some of those times she only had enough money to feed him and not herself. She thinks of the nights they slept cuddled up to stay warm in her dark and cold apartment because her lights had been shut off. With Big Manson in and out of prison, for the most part it was always just them. She always refers to him as her first love and she means that.

She becomes teary eyed thinking of all they've been through and for him to be here trying to reciprocate with just a small act of kindness means the world to her. "Nah, I'm ok. I don't need nothing but your love."

"That goes unsaid," he says strongly. "You sure though? You always been there for me through all my bullshit. Let me do something for you for a change."

"You want to do something for me? Stay out of trouble. That's what you can do for me."

"Alright Ma," he says with agitation. "Talk to you later."

"Ok, love you," she says.

"Love you too," he says before ending the call.

As soon as she hangs up, the phone rings again with the same number on the display. Pebbles answers quickly, assuming it's Baby Manson and maybe he's forgotten something that he wanted to say.

She presses the button and waits for the call to be linked. "Yo," Shakir says in his normal laid back tone.

"What's up, Sha?"

"Aye, yo, check this out," he says with his tone changing. "Your son…he need to stay in a child's place. He stepping in some grown man shit."

"Huh?" Pebbles asks, not understanding what he's saying nor his tone.

"I'm gone tell you like this." He pauses for seconds. "He come talking to me on some crazy type time. Like, in so many words, the job I got in here, he want that job," he says in code. "It's his turn to take over the job, whoopty whoop, this that and the third. But I'm gone tell you like this, you better talk to him. I don't know what he thinking but it ain't that deal. You know me…I ain't into none of that but I'm with all of that!"

"Sha, calm down," she says. She's trying to make sense of it all.

"I am calm," he says. "But this is a warning. You better talk to him."

"Sha, are you threatening my son?"

"I don't make threats."

"Wow," she says in disbelief. "I can't believe you're really on the phone telling me that you would do something to my son."

"I'm on the phone telling you I'm not gone let your son do something to me."

"Why didn't you tell him, Sha?"

"Tell him, what?"

"You know, tell him."

"Fuck no! I ain't telling him shit. He walking around this motherfucker on some stupid shit thinking he doing something. All he doing is making a bunch of enemies for his self and he don't even dig it. I been in and out of these spots all my life, you know it. And I seen how that shit ends. He better slow his roll."

"Well, I will tell him as soon as he call me back."

"Nah, don't tell him that. You ain't been tell him. No need to tell him now."

"Well, how else am I gone tell him how I know what's going on?" Right now she's in need of an answer.

"Aye, you'll figure it out. I'm out though."

"Wait, Sha!" she shouts but it's already too late. He's ended the call.

Pebbles pulls over so she can get herself together. She can't believe what she just heard. To hear Sha talk like that about her son, she feels betrayed. She thinks of the mess she's made by hiding the truth all these years. Now she feels like it's all her fault. If Baby Manson knew the truth this would have never happened. She thinks hard and figures there's only one way to fix this and she plans to. She senses a tragedy in the making and the only way she can think to stop it is by telling her son the truth.

65

TRENTON

NO TOES, LIMPS hunched over in pain. He calls himself in hiding with the big hood over his head but he could never hide because his walk gives him away. He peeks around like a nervous wreck in fear of being spotted by Quabo and Tortura. If not for his dope addiction he wouldn't be walking the streets period.

He's switched his place of residence from one abandoned apartment to another one, in an entirely different area. He had it made for the few days that they were linked...he had dope all day and food. Once the shooting spree started up, he realized the magnitude of the crazy people he was dealing with and wanted a way out. He's never in his life been that close to that many murders.

Quabo and Tortura are like terrorists in his eyes and he wants to stay as far away from them as he can. He feels like they are holding him responsible until they find her. He's witnessed firsthand their wickedness and fears the day they turn on him. If he had a way to disappear, like somewhere else that he could go to, he would already be there. He doesn't though, so he's forced to stay here and duck and dodge and pray they never run into him.

He's only popped out to hustle up enough money for his dope and he will get back to hiding. Right now, he steps slowly with his eyes scoping the ground, in search of a dollar bill or a twenty, or prayerfully a hundred-dollar bill that someone may have dropped. He's like a K9 with his nose sniffing the ground. No envelope or bag in his path goes unopened. He kicks leaves along the way, hoping something may be under them.

Three pennies lay side by side on the ground calling his name. He bends over and picks them up. He's now $6.97 away from his seven-dollar goal. He's even had to switch up where he buys his dope from. Roger Gardens has the best dope and he hates that he can't go there anymore but it's for his own safety. The new spot he goes to sells garbage dope for seven dollars. Sometimes he debates with himself if he should go for the better dope and take the chance of losing his life or get the garbage dope and live to see another day and another bag.

No Toes blows the dirt off the pennies as he walks, eyes in his hand. He's obstructed by a gate opening. A man steps from behind the gate, lugging two laundry bags. The hustler in No Toes sees this as a way to make the rest of the money he needs for a bag. He quickly looks onto the porch where three more laundry bags are sitting.

"You need some help, Sir," No Toes asks.

"Nah, I'm good," the man says. He makes his way to a tinted-out Charger that sits parked at the curb. The man peeks around nervously before dropping the bags into the trunk.

"Nice car," says No Toes. "I bet that thing fast ain't it?" He's now shooting his shot. He knows giving a compliment most times helps you get a few coins out of the egotistical. The man ignores him and his whole existence.

No Toes' attention is snatched by a woman stepping out of the house. She's carrying a baby in a carseat in one hand, laundry detergent in the other, and a baby bag on her shoulder. As she gets to the bottom of the steps, No Toes opens the gate for her. "Let me get that for you."

The woman flashes a cold smile. No Toes double-takes. His heartbeat speeds up. It's like he's seen a ghost. He can't believe his eyes.

Here he is up close and personal with the woman that has the city a battlefield. "Thanks," Helter says.

His guilt sinks in and then is replaced with fear. He walks off with no further attempt at hustling them. He can't get away from them fast enough. He peeks back and forth at them as he limps away.

Helter places the baby in the backseat as Bruh in Law packs the bags into the trunk. As No Toes gets halfway down the block, he backs up against an abandoned house, where he can't be seen. From where he stands, he has clear view of the man carrying on, loading the laundry bags into the trunk of the car. He pulls out his phone and dials, eyes bouncing from his phone to the Dodge Charger.

What lies ahead of him not even 1000 feet away is the end to his obligation to Quabo and Tortura. This valuable information will release him from bondage with them. This will not only give him his freedom back, it will allow him to save his own life. To save his own life means to sacrifice the life of a stranger and that to him is a no brainer.

Continued in Block Party 666 Volume 2

BOOK ORDER FORM

Purchase Information

Name: _____

Address: _____ City: _____

State: _____ Zip Code: _____

Books are listed in the order they were written and published

$14.95-No Exit _____
$14.95-Block Party _____
$14.95-Sincerely Yours _____
$14.95-Caught em Slippin _____
$14.95-Block Party 2 _____
$14.95-Block Party 3 _____
$14.95-Strapped _____
$14.95-Back 2 Bizness (Block Party 4) _____
$14.95-Young Gunz _____
$14.95-Outlaw Chick _____
$14.95-Block Party 5k1 Volume 1 _____
$14.95-Block Party 5k1 Volume 2 _____
$14.95-Heartless _____
$14.95-Block Party 666 Volume 1 _____
$14.95-Block Party 666 Volume 2 _____

Book Total: _____

Add $7.00 for shipping of 1-3 books
Free shipping for order of 4 or more books

Mailing Address:
True 2 Life Publications
PO Box 8722
Newark, NJ 07108
Make Checks/Money Orders payable to: True 2 Life Publications

Made in the USA
Monee, IL
13 May 2024

58383607R00180